Previous selections of the
Universal Book Club

CAPER SAUCE
by **S. P. B. MAIS**

THINE ENEMY
by **SIR PHILIP GIBBS**

MARY OF DELIGHT
by **NAOMI JACOB**

WEB OF DAYS
by **EDNA LEE**

A FLOWER FOR CATHERINE
by **FRANK SWINNERTON**

THE BEND OF THE RIVER
by **GODFREY WINN**

AT SUNDOWN, THE TIGER
by **ETHEL MANNIN**

HONEY FOR THE GHOST
by **LOUIS GOLDING**

MART OF NATIONS
by **WINIFRED DUKE**

DEATH WITHOUT QUESTION
by **THOMAS MUIR**

FRANCIS GRIERSON'S
MANY BOOKS INCLUDE

BOOMERANG MURDER

by

FRANCIS GRIERSON

5 & 6 ST. ANDREW'S HILL, CARTER LANE
LONDON, E.C.4

First published . . *1951*
Universal Book Club Edition . *October, 1952*

Printed in Great Britain
by The Anchor Press, Ltd.,
Tiptree, Essex

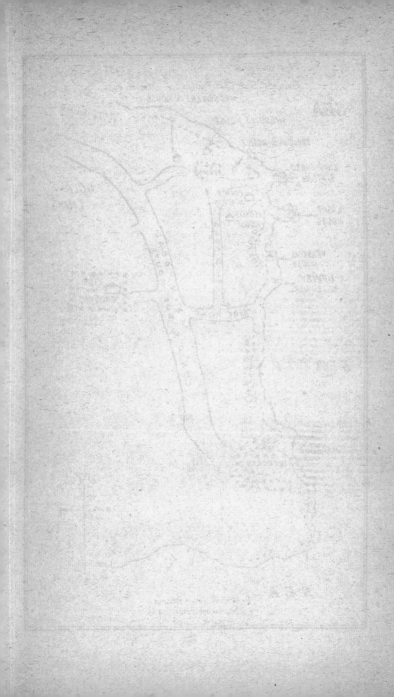

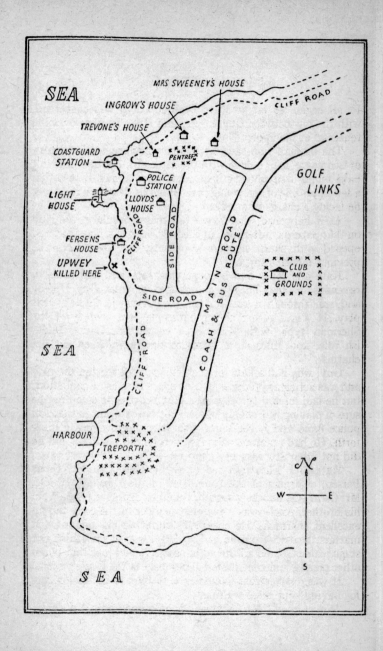

CHAPTER I

IT all began, so far as Kate Dermot Lloyd was concerned, with the row between Guy Upwey and Miles Trevone over the rehearsal at the Sports Club.

The barman who saw the incident grinned at the rivalry of two young men in love with the same girl, but he would not have found it so amusing if he could have known that within a few hours one of the young men would be dead and the other be facing a charge of murder.

As it happened, there were not many people in the club on that Saturday afternoon in the first week of a May that had opened with sharp showers apparently left over from the previous month's stock.

Kate and Miles had been playing golf, and had come in ravenous for tea. They had arranged to meet Guy Upwey and run through a scene from the Dramatic Circle's next play. It was a rather clever burlesque of a comedy of the Sheridan type, with Kate in a coquettish, Lady Teazle-ish rôle, and Miles as a dissolute dandy inflamed by her charms.

Guy, who had a flair for such things, had written the play and was acting as producer in such spare time as he could find; but he had refused the offer of a part because he could not be sure of playing it. For Guy was a detective-sergeant in the local police force and never knew what the morrow might bring forth. He had ambitions about which he did not talk, and he did not intend to miss any chances.

Kate and Miles had tea in the lounge with Mr. Oscar Fersen, chairman of the committee of the Dramatic Circle. Mr. Oscar—as he was generally called to distinguish him from his brother, Axel—was a popular member of the club and an excellent chairman. He cheerfully admitted his ignorance of matters theatrical, but he had a tactful way of smoothing out stage jealousies, did all the administrative odd jobs that bored other people, and contributed generously to the Circle's funds.

It was quarter past five when Guy hurried in, apologizing for having kept them waiting.

"Never mind," Mr. Oscar said good-humouredly. "We can't

7

expect the criminal classes to arrange their affairs to suit our rehearsals. Have some tea?"

"No, thanks. I've delayed you enough as it is," Guy answered. "If you've all finished, shall we get on with the good work?"

"Yes, let's," Kate agreed, getting up.

Guy put a comradely hand on her arm and steered her towards a side door at the end of the lounge, talking eagerly about the play.

Miles knocked the ashes from his pipe and lounged glumly behind the pair.

Mr. Oscar hesitated, a frown on his usually cheerful face; then he picked up his rubber-tipped stick and limped after them.

Dai Davies, arranging bottles and glasses behind the bar in readiness for opening time, relieved his boredom by watching the four as they passed into the long hall behind the lounge— Mr. Oscar having forgotten to close the door—and mounted to the small stage to begin the rehearsal.

Mr. Oscar drew a chair to one side, out of the way, and sat down, and Dai grinned as he saw him take out a silk handkerchief and polish the top of his stick. Mr. Oscar was very proud of that thick Malacca cane, with its ivory crook, beautifully carved into the likeness of an elephant's head and tusk. He liked to explain to new acquaintances that it had been presented to his grandfather by the Maharajah of an Indian State after some mildly vague but tremendously heroic exploit in which wild beasts and terrified mahouts were concerned. It was a club joke that when Mr. Oscar had to decide an administrative difficulty, or was preparing to floor an opponent in argument, he would stare at the age-yellowed effigy as though communing with and receiving secret counsel from it.

"Places, please," Guy said briskly. "Over here, Kate. Now, Miles, don't forget that the lovely lady isn't supposed to realize what a dirty dog you are. She enjoys a flirtation but she thinks she can stop it before you go too far. You've heard that one before, and you've generally got your own way in the end, so you start putting on the heat. Ready?"

Miles nodded, gave a quick look at his typewritten part, and put it back in his pocket. Striding across the stage he took Kate's hand and said:

"Odds fish, Madam, your beauty drives me to distraction! I can wait no longer to declare my love. Come, sweeting, end this dalliance and confess that you are not indifferent to my passion. Let me sip the honey from those ruby lips."

Kate (simpering): "La, sir! Unhand me, I beg. I vow I had not thought you so daring."

Miles (seizing her in his arms): "Daring? I will dare all to win so fair a prize! (He gives her a very gentlemanly kiss on the cheek.)

Guy raised despairing hands.

"No, no!" he interrupted. "You're always word-perfect in your lines, Miles, but you don't put any life into them. You're not a pageboy playing kiss-in-the-ring with a royal princess; you're a rake, determined to seduce an attractive wench who's been leading you on. Do try and remember you're in a theatre, not a Sunday-school. Here, let me show you what I mean."

Miles flushed but moved aside without protest.

Guy dropped his script, took the girl's hand, and played the scene; then held her close as he pressed passionate kisses on her lips.

Kate struggled to free herself.

Miles sprang forward, tore Guy away, and sent him sprawling on the dusty boards.

Guy got up, his face livid and his fists clenched; but before the two young men could meet Mr. Oscar had crossed from his corner and got between them.

"Very realistic, Guy," he declared pleasantly, "but your ardour was perhaps a little unexpected."

"I'll knock his damned head off if he tries it again," Miles said evenly.

"You will?" Guy sneered. "I've handled pretties like you two at a time before now, and you're welcome to a few painful lessons any time you like."

"Now, now," Mr. Oscar put in. "I'd hate to see Miles languishing in a dungeon for assaulting a police-officer, and I'm sure Guy's too sensible to risk his chance of promotion over a little misunderstanding."

His smile took the sting out of his words, but his hints were not wasted.

Miles thrust his hands into his pockets and turned away.

Guy mastered his anger with an obvious effort and said:

"Sorry, and all that. I was just trying to show how I thought the scene ought to go. Anyhow, a wretched copper isn't allowed to lose his temper, whatever civilians may do. How about it, Kate? Want to try it over again with Miles as a more gentlemanly ruffian?"

"No, thanks," the girl answered frigidly. "I've had quite enough for today."

"I think we all have," Mr. Oscar said quickly. "The bar must be open by now, so come on, Kate, and let your aged chairman and hopeless admirer buy you a drink. Lead the way, Officer of the Law. Miles, will you collect the scripts and see that the door is locked?"

Thus neatly separating the rivals, he allowed Kate to help him down the steps from the stage—quite unnecessarily, for despite the limp left by an attack of infantile paralysis in his early youth, he was surprisingly nimble and could out-walk, at his own steady pace, many younger men.

When they reached the middle of the long bar they found that Guy had tactfully chosen a stool at one end and had begun to consume a pint of beer.

Miles came in presently, went to the other end, and ordered a double whisky.

Mr. Oscar chatted of this and that while Kate silently drank her gin-and-orange.

When she had finished she slipped down from her high stool and said she must be going.

"Got your car," he asked, "or can I give you a lift home? The clouds look rather dark."

"No, thanks," she answered. "I rather want to walk, and I've got a mac if it rains." She paused, and added in a lower tone: "Thanks for everything. You're rather a dear, you know."

He watched her thoughtfully as she walked out, nodding here and there to people who had come into the lounge; then he caught the barman's eye and beckoned.

Dai Davies came promptly, for the committee winked at discreet tipping and Mr. Oscar was free with his money.

"How do you like your job here, Dai?" Mr. Oscar inquired.

"I do like it fine, thanking you, sir," the weasel-like little man assured him. "I hopes you and the rest of the committee is satisfied with me?" he added in sudden anxiety, for he, as steward, barman and general factotum under the honorary secretary, and his wife as housekeeper, had snug quarters, good wages and certain pickings they did not want to lose.

"No complaints, so far," said Mr. Oscar. "One thing I like about you is that you mind your own business and don't talk too much. I dare say you hear—and see—a good many funny things here?"

"Sometimes I do, sir," the little man admitted cautiously, "but I don't go repeating of 'em to other people."

"That's what I thought. Very sensible of you, Dai. Many a man has lost a good job because he couldn't keep his mouth shut. I'm sure you won't make that mistake. Now I must pay you for these drinks. I think this will just cover them."

A folded Treasury note passed across the counter.

"That's right, sir, exactly," Dai grinned, "and thanking you very much."

Mr. Oscar nodded, climbed down from his stool, and consulted his elephant. Then he strolled along to where Guy was half-way through his pint.

"How about a game of bridge tonight?" the older man asked. "I'll drag my brother away from his work and we can beat up a fourth somewhere." He glanced casually at the other end of the bar, where Miles had just ordered another double.

"Sorry, not tonight," the policeman replied. "I've got things to do at the station and I must be off soon. Thanks all the same."

"The slave of duty," Mr. Oscar remarked lightly. "Another time, then."

He wandered off to Miles and gave him a similar invitation, but that young man said he must spend the evening reading about torts and other legal horrors. Miles was articled to Kate's father and was working for the examinations necessary to qualify him as a solicitor.

Mr. Oscar remarked mildly that he was glad he had not to tackle such problems, which must need a clear head and cool judgment.

Miles muttered sulkily that he was just having a quick one and would be going home in a few minutes.

Mr. Oscar nodded and departed to the cloakroom. From there he went out to the garage, where the club had allowed a mechanic to set up a small business of his own as well as doing minor repairs for the members.

This man had put petrol and water in Mr. Oscar's car and examined the tyres, and it was ready for him.

Once more he consulted his elephant; then he shook his head, got into his car, and drove away.

Sunday dawned with the promise of a perfect spring day. Heavy rain had fallen during the night, but by six o'clock there was not a cloud to be seen in the sky.

Coastguard Samuel Briggs, wheeling his bicycle up a steep bit of the cliff road, stopped to take breath and to enjoy what to him was always the most beautiful sight in the world—a vastness of untroubled sea shimmering blue-green under the morning sun.

Briggs, an ex-petty officer of the Royal Navy, had paid a week-end visit to his parents in the busy seaport of Treporth, and had got up early to return for duty at the coastguard station on the cliffs near the lighthouse a few miles from the town. He was not due there until eight, but he had allowed himself time enough to call at his cottage, breakfast with his wife, and change into uniform.

At the point where he had stopped to rest a gang from the Corporation roads department had been at work for some days. The cliff road, just wide enough for a couple of cars or carts to pass each other with caution, was protected on the sea side by a low stone wall. Part of this wall had been crumbling under the buffeting of gales and rain, and the repairers had demolished a section which was to be replaced by new material.

Resting his bicycle against a wheeled wooden hut in which the men's tools had been stored, Briggs passed through the gap in the wall and stood near the edge of the cliff.

For a few moments he gazed seawards, then he glanced down at the water lapping lazily at the shore a hundred feet below him.

Suddenly he stiffened. Stunted but stout bushes were dotted about the top and face of the cliff. Choosing one that grew nearest the edge, he threw himself down beside it, gripped a tough branch, and worked himself forward as far as he dared.

What he saw was enough to make him scramble back to safety, white-faced and shaken.

Naval training teaches a man to act promptly. Briggs thought for a few seconds. There were houses not very far away, but nearer still was an Automobile Association box. Taking a tyre-lever from the tool-bag on his bicycle, he ran to the box. It was locked, as he had expected, but he forced open the door with his lever and took down the receiver of the telephone inside.

The operator, startled by the urgency in his voice, put him through to Sergeant Jack Jones, who lived at and was in charge of the police-station at the neighbouring village of Pentref.

"That you, Jack?" he asked. "This is Sam Briggs. I'm on the cliff road, Treporth side of the lighthouse. Listen, man: there's a chap fallen over the edge. Caught on a bit of rock he is, just above the shingle. Looks dead to me, but I can't be sure."

"Dammo, that's bad," said the sergeant. "Sounds like we'd want some tackle to get at him. All right, boy. Stop you with him, and I'll be there now, soon's I've 'phoned the inspector. You don't know who he is, I don't suppose?"

"I'm not certain, Jack," Briggs answered slowly, "but from his build and the coat he's wearing, I think it's the detective chap that lodges with you, Sergeant Upwey."

"Diawl!" muttered Sergeant Jones.

CHAPTER II

EARLY on Monday morning Chief Detective-Superintendent George Muir emerged from the Assistant Commissioner's room in New Scotland Yard and returned to his own more austere apartment. His talk with Sir Justin Soames had not been a long one, but it had given him a good deal to think about.

Placing a cardboard folder on his desk, he sent for Superintendent Ash.

In the reorganisation, some time before, of the Metropolitan Police Force, Muir had been advanced to the new rank of chief superintendent and Chief Inspector Andrew Ash had become a superintendent.

Bob York, who had been Ash's assistant in many of the latter's cases, had not been affected by these changes, but he had received special promotion from sergeant to inspector, largely because of Ash's recommendation and Muir's support.

When Ash came in Muir said:

"Sit down, Andrew. Pretty clear just now, aren't you?"

The burly man with the squarish face and steady blue eyes agreed that he was pretty clear; a few strings to be tied round one or two small jobs, but nothing to speak of.

"Right," said Muir. "Marshall or somebody can tie the bows and put the frills on. The A.C. wants you to take on a job that's come in from Treporth. Know Wales at all?"

"I've been in the north once or twice on holidays, but I don't know the south part."

"It doesn't matter. You'll have a sort of watching brief."

"What's the trouble, sir?"

"A detective-sergeant fell down a cliff—or, rather, the local people say he was pushed. He's dead, anyhow. He was found early yesterday morning and they made an arrest the same night."

"Then where do I come in?"

"The Chief Constable, Colonel Bassenthwaite Lake, tele-phoned to Sir Justin and asked him to send a man down. He takes a poor view of having his people croaked. I gather they've got a good case against the man they've pulled in, but he's pretty well known in those parts and Lake wants to make sure that the case is copper-bottomed before they go into court. Here's a file on it; Lake had it sent up by car last night, and telephoned a further message later on, which has been typed and included in the file. It's all yours."

He handed over the cardboard case.

Ash, as usual, thought for a moment before he replied.

"There's just one point," he said. "You mentioned a watching brief; am I to be in charge of the inquiry, or hang about and annoy the local men with suggestions?"

Muir laughed. "You don't generally annoy people very much," he answered. "That's why the A.C. picked you, but he told me to say that you've full discretion to do what you think best. You won't have any difficulty with Bassenthwaite Lake. I've met him two or three times, and I think you'll find he'll be glad to take any advice you give him. It sounds like an open-and-shut case, but you'll have plenty of time to go through the file on your way down. There's a good train about midday, I think. Anything else?"

"Shall I take anyone with me?"

"No. You can send for York if you find you need him."

Ash went to his room, arranged for a reserved seat in the express train to Treporth, and handed over to Chief Inspector Joe Marshall the odds and ends he had mentioned to Muir. After sending a message to the Treporth police giving the time of his arrival, he picked up the specially fitted case supplied to senior investigating officers, ordered a police car, and drove to his flat in Petty France. There he had a word with the caretaker's wife, who looked after his modest domestic affairs, and collected the packed suit-case he kept ready for emergencies. The car took him to Paddington in good time for his train, and he chose the first luncheon service so that he could spend the rest of the journey in uninterrupted study of the case.

As he ate his meal, which was served soon after they left the station, Ash recalled the conversation he had had with Muir.

They were old colleagues, and the fact that Muir had outdistanced the older man in the race for promotion had not affected their friendship. Though in public their relations were correctly formal, in private they were on the easy terms of men who had complete confidence in each other.

It seemed to Ash that Muir had that morning been a shade less communicative than usual. On the other hand, there really had not been much to say, and he had said what appeared to be necessary.

There was nothing particularly surprising in the fact that the Chief Constable of Treporth had asked for a Yard man. It was quite usual in murder cases and did not necessarily imply any lack of faith in his own police. The Yard man was, as it were, a specialist called in by the general practitioner. But, naturally enough, if the local doctor was sure of his ground, he preferred to have the credit for the cure.

The fact that the Treporth police had made an arrest so promptly suggested that they felt pretty sure of their ground, but it might turn out that there were difficulties that had not appeared so far.

Ash made his way back to his compartment, took out the dossier, and set himself to study its contents.

When at last he closed the file his trained mind had absorbed and arranged the salient points of the case.

A detective-sergeant named Upwey had quarrelled with a young man named Trevone. Upwey had been found dead, having fallen or been thrown over a cliff. Trevone had been arrested, and was that morning being charged in the magistrates' court with the murder of Upwey. The full reasons for the charge against Trevone were not made clear, owing to the brevity of the telephoned message, but enough was said to indicate that it was sufficient to justify a request for his remand on the capital charge. Such a request is not made unless the police are satisfied that the evidence they hold is, if not conclusive, at least strong enough to warrant their action.

Ash never allowed himself to form opinions in the opening stages of a case. As Dr. Hans Gross, the 'father' of criminal investigation, said, "a preconceived theory is the most deadly enemy of all inquiries". Ash preferred to collect and consider his facts before he tried to construct any theories—and even then his theories often collapsed like a house of cards.

Putting away the file, he lit his pipe and devoted the remainder of the journey to a combat with the author of *The Times* crossword puzzle.

When the train reached Treporth station Ash allowed most of the passengers to alight before he took his cases from the rack and stepped on to the platform. He declined the services of a porter and waited until a tall, thin, dark man came up and said:

"Excuse me, but were you expecting someone to meet you? The name is Hughes—Haydn Hughes."

"Good afternoon," Ash replied, taking out the leather case which contained the warrant card carried by all police officers.

Detective-Inspector Haydn Hughes glanced at it and smiled.

"Pleased to meet you, sir, I am sure," he said. "There is a car outside and my man will bring your bags."

He nodded to a plain-clothes man who stood near, and led the way to a car in the station yard. They got in and drove to the central police-station, which was part of a large building that housed the courts and the Corporation offices.

Hughes evidently had his orders, for he took Ash down a long corridor to a door on which was inscribed:

CHIEF CONSTABLE
COLONEL E. BASSENTHWAITE LAKE, D.S.O., M.C.

Throwing open the door, Hughes announced:

"Superintendent Ash, sir," and two men who had been examining some documents at a table stood up.

The Chief Constable, a lean man with sandy hair and moustache, came forward and shook Ash's hand.

"Very glad to see you," he said. "This is Superintendent Morris, my second-in-command."

Ash shook hands with a stout, rosy man who grinned cheerfully.

"I was afraid I'd miss you," the colonel went on, "but fortunately your train seems to have been punctual. I've got to dash off to a Watch Committee meeting, and you know what Watch Committees are! I forgot, though; you're not bothered with such things in London." He laughed. "I'm going to leave you with Morris and Hughes. They'll give you some tea and tell you what's been happening. We've got a room for you at an hotel, but I thought you might like to come and have dinner with me at my house and talk things over."

"Thanks very much, sir," Ash agreed.

"Right. A car will pick you up at the hotel at quarter past seven. Don't bother to change. Till this evening, then."

He hurried out, and Superintendent Morris proposed that they should go along to his room, which they did.

"You're snug here," Ash remarked, looking round the small but comfortably furnished office.

"It's not so bad," Morris responded with modest pride. "The colonel's a great one for looking after us. He's had his ups-and-downers with the Watch Committee, but he's got 'em to see that a contented police force is better than burglary insurance."

Ash nodded. This was one of the things he had wanted to know. If the local force was working smoothly, his own task was likely to be easier.

A policewoman brought in a tray with tea, bread and butter and cakes, and when she had gone Morris said:

"You'll have seen the stuff we sent to the Yard, but I expect there's a lot more you want to know. Haydn Hughes has handled this job, so I'll leave him to do most of the talking."

"And glad to be of service, indeed," the detective-inspector agreed in his deliberate and slightly mournful manner, and Ash noticed that his accent was much more marked than that of his superintendent.

"I'd like to begin with this chap Trevone that you've pulled in," Ash decided. "You got your remand this morning, I suppose?"

"Yes, sir. Seven days, in custody, of course. His solicitor pleaded Not Guilty and reserved his defence."

"What's the evidence against him, apart from his quarrel with Upwey?"

Hughes went to a cupboard and came back with two objects. One was a thin, curved piece of wood about thirty inches long, flat on one side and rounded on the other. He handed it to Ash, remarking that it had already been tested for finger-prints and other indications.

"A boomerang, isn't it?" Ash asked, a good deal astonished.

"It is indeed," Hughes replied. "And look at those initials cut into it, M.T. Miles Trevone doesn't deny that it's his property, given to him by an Australian airman he knew in the war. Take a look at it through this glass, Mr. Ash. See that mark on the edge? That mark corresponds as near as you like to the wound on the back of Guy Upwey's head."

Ash took the lens and examined the indentation—a slight one, presumably owing to the hardness of the wood, but visible even without the magnifying glass.

"Any prints, or blood or hair?" he asked.

"No, sir. We found it in some bushes on the cliff. There'd been heavy rain in the night, enough to wash marks away. Not but what the thing could have been wiped by the man that used it," Hughes added.

Ash nodded, and Hughes produced the second object. It was a stout buff envelope, endorsed with a date and initials, and from it he took a lead bullet of .22 calibre.

"Where did you find that?" Ash inquired.

"In Upwey's head," Hughes answered. "The police-surgeon

did the post mortem. This bullet had entered through Upwey's ear and lodged in his brain. There was no burning of the skin. It was the bullet that killed him, not the blow." He paused, then added heavily, "Trevone admits he owned a Webley air pistol that could fire a .22 bullet, but he says he missed it some time ago and thinks it must have been one of the things stolen when his house was robbed."

"Was there such a robbery?"

"Yes. It wasn't a real burglar's job—some sneak-thief who got in and pinched a few things while there was no one at home. He must have seen or heard the housekeeper coming back and got away without being seen."

Ash took the lens and examined the bullet before returning it to the inspector.

"What's the picture, as you see it?" he asked.

"It is like this, sir. I am thinking that—but wait you a minute and I will show you a map to make things clear to you."

He unrolled a large-scale map (*see sketch-map facing page 7*) on which the Sports Club, the village of Pentref, the place where the body was found, and other special points had been indicated.

"I am thinking," he resumed, "that after the quarrel at the rehearsal Trevone brooded over it while he was drinking whisky at the bar. He knew that Upwey was lodging with Sergeant Jones at Pentref——"

"Why? Isn't that rather far away from headquarters?" Ash put in.

"Yes," Superintendent Morris explained, "but it was only a temporary arrangement. Treporth was badly bombed, as you'll see when you get about a bit, and housing's as big a problem here as anywhere else. We've arranged to get our married men accommodated, but the new hostel we're to have for the bachelors isn't ready yet, and the men lodge where they can. Upwey asked if he could go to Pentref, and as he had a motor-bike, and there's a good bus service besides, the chief didn't object."

"Thanks. Go on, please, Inspector."

"The quickest way from the Sports Club to Pentref would be across this side road you see here, and then up the cliff road. That would be the way Upwey would take, especially as he hadn't got his bike with him, as it happened. I am thinking that Trevone went out first and laid in wait for Upwey on the cliff road. When Upwey came by, Trevone stopped him, perhaps offering to make things up between them. When Upwey was off his guard—maybe just turning away—Trevone hit him with the boomerang. That knocked him out. Then Trevone put the pistol close to his ear and fired the bullet into his brain. Then he threw him over the cliff, expecting that his head injury would be accounted for by the fall, and not thinking the bullet would be looked for, let alone found. After that he threw the pistol into the bushes and went home."

Hughes sat back with the air of a man who had said his say and would be glad to hear what, if any, flaws the London expert could discover in his thesis.

Ash recognised the attitude and decided (as the Sailing Directions say) to Proceed with Caution.

"That's a very interesting build-up, Inspector," he said with a note of respect. He thought he saw a twinkle in the eyes of Superintendent Morris, who was sitting a little behind Hughes, but he ignored it and went on:

"There are just one or two points I'd like to be more clear about. You see, you've been over the ground and talked to the people most likely to be able to help, and you can put me right if I'm getting off the road and into the ditch."

The inspector was understood to convey that it would be a pleasure to extricate the superintendent from any such mental morass.

"About this boomerang, for instance," Ash went on. "Trevone could hardly have foreseen the row at the rehearsal, so why should he have brought the boomerang with him?"

"He didn't," Hughes responded promptly. "It was there all the time. Trevone took it to the club one day and he and some friends tried their hands at throwing it, but they couldn't get the knack. Trevone says he put the thing in his locker and forgot to take it home. He says he forgot it was there. Most of the members have lockers in which they keep golf clubs and spare mackintoshes and things, and Trevone says he was a bit careless, and can't remember exactly what he had in his locker. He doesn't deny that the boomerang *may* have been there."

"I see. He seems to have made a good many admissions."

"As soon as I'd decided to arrest him, I duly cautioned him in the proper formula," Hughes rejoined stiffly, "and Mr. Morris will tell you that he was cautioned again when he was brought here in custody."

"Of course," Ash said hastily. "I'm sure you took the proper steps. What I meant was that he seemed very ready to talk."

"Aye, indeed," Hughes agreed, mollified. "He went on talking until his solicitor, who'd been telephoned for, told him to stop."

"I suppose he said he hadn't killed Upwey?"

"He kept on saying it. He said he was damned angry—those were his words—with Upwey at the rehearsal and he intended to make him apologise or take a hiding later on, but he didn't want to have any more fuss in front of people at the club, on account of Miss Dermot Lloyd. He said he knew Upwey would probably go home by the cliff road and he didn't want to meet him until they'd both cooled down a bit, so he himself went home by way of the main road and through Pentref village. It took longer, but he didn't mind."

"Any proof of that?"

"No, sir. We can't find anyone who saw him. We've tried all the drivers on that route, but there's not many buses and coaches running on Saturday afternoons. The company cuts down the services a good bit until the late evening, when people are going home from visiting Pentref or coming back from an outing in the country. Trevone says he went home. The man and wife—name of Edwards—who keep house for him were at the pictures in the little cinema at Pentref. They say he was at home when they got back and he didn't go out that evening."

"You've checked all the times you can, I suppose?"

"Yes, sir. He'd have had plenty of time to catch Upwey on the cliff road, do him in, and get home before the Edwards got back. I'll take you over the ground tomorrow, so you can see for yourself."

"Well," Ash said, "you've put it all very clearly, Inspector, and you've certainly cleared up some points that puzzled me."

"And now," Morris put in tactfully, "I expect you'd like to get along to the hotel and have a wash before dinner. Have Mr. Ash's bags put in the car, will you, Haydn?"

When the detective-inspector had left the room Morris added: "Thanks for handling him so well. He's a good chap and he knows his job, but he's touchy, like most of us Welsh blokes."

"If none of the Welsh blokes are more touchy than you seem to be," Ash replied, "I'm going to have a pleasant visit. When can we have a drink together?"

"Sooner than you expect. The colonel's asked me to drop in after dinner for a chat."

"Good," Ash returned heartily. "I'd like to hear what you think about the business."

"You're not going to get away with that," Morris retorted, laughing. "You'll do the talking, I hope, and I'll sit and listen. That's how I keep my job."

Ash, going out to the car, decided that he was going to like Superintendent Morris.

CHAPTER III

WHEN Ash arrived at the Chief Constable's house on the outskirts of the town he was shown into a pleasantly informal apartment compounded of library, smoking-room and repository for interesting things collected in many lands. Ash, in whose affections the printed word came second only to his profession, promised himself a nearer look at the crowded shelves when he knew their owner better.

The colonel gave him some dry sherry, and apologised for the absence of Mrs. Bassenthwaite Lake, who was staying with friends.

Throughout an excellent dinner Bassenthwaite Lake made no mention of the affair that had brought the Yard man to Treporth. A chance remark about a new novel disclosed their common interest in books, and they fell into a have-you-read and what-did-you-think-of discussion that lasted throughout the meal and over the port.

At last the colonel, with a reluctance he did not conceal, suggested a move to the library for coffee.

"Morris will be coming in later on," he said. "Sound chap, very sound." He produced a box of cigars, but when Ash begged to be allowed to smoke his pipe he agreed and said he would do the same. They settled down and a servant brought in the coffee and a tray with decanter, syphon, beer and glasses.

"We run this force on the principle of division of labour," he went on as he filled his pipe. "Morris takes care of the administrative work, Haydn Hughes heads the sleuth gang, and I attend to discipline and so forth and smooth the feathers of the Watch Committee when they get ruffled. I did some police work abroad, of course, but I'm not what you'd call a real policeman and I know my limits."

"Whenever a senior officer tells me that," said Ash, who had acquainted himself with Bassenthwaite Lake's record when he was seconded to the Indian Police, and later in the Security service at home and overseas, "I get ready to receive some useful hints."

"You won't get them from me," his host answered, grinning. "In any case, this affair of poor Upwey looks like being a *petite enquête*—a small affair from your point of view, though we don't often have to deal with murders."

"*Il n'y a pas de petites enquêtes*," Ash replied, quoting the dictum of a formerly world-famed police chief.

If the colonel was surprised he was too well bred to show it.

"Ah, you've read Guichard, then," he commented. "He was a shrewd old bird. It's quite true, of course. There *are* no little inquiries; one can never tell when what looks like a small thing will turn out to be a damned big one. But getting back to Upwey, has Hughes given you all the information you want?"

"He's given me a lot, sir, and he's going to give me some more tomorrow."

"Good. Between ourselves, Hughes is no fool. He looks rather like an undertaker who's called for the body, but he's got a lot of horse sense and he's pulled off several smart jobs that surprised me. And there's nothing wrong with his guts; we get a tough lot round the docks, but Hughes'll tackle anything on two legs. And yet, oddly enough, he lives for music. He's conductor of the police choral society and quite a minor swell in musical circles, which is saying something in this part of the world."

Ash recognised the gambit, and nodded.

"Please don't think that we Yard men regard ourselves as superior beings, sir," he said. "I've worked with a lot of provincial officers, and I've often wished we had some of them with us in London."

"We do what we can, but of course we don't get your wide experience," the colonel replied gruffly, but Ash saw that he was pleased. "I dare say you're wondering," Bassenthwaite Lake went on with a hint of embarrassment that mildly surprised the superintendent, "why I asked Sir Justin Soames to spare me one of you fellows when our case against Miles Trevone is so strong."

"Chief Superintendent Muir said something about Trevone being well known locally," Ash hinted.

"Yes, exactly," the colonel answered quickly. "Have to think of these things, you know—so long as they don't interfere with justice, of course."

"I'd like to get a bit of background from you, sir."

"Certainly. Miles Trevone——"

"Excuse me, sir, but may we begin with Upwey?" Ash suggested. "Hughes might not like saying anything that seemed disloyal to one of his own men," he explained, as the colonel looked up in surprise.

"Oh, I see. Yes, that would be natural enough. Well, Guy Upwey was an unusual type. Had rather a stiff time. His father was a Londoner, a stockbroker in a not very big way. Then he inherited a lot of money from a distant relative. He'd married the daughter of a Welsh friend and at her wish he bought a place near Treporth and they settled down here. After a time Upwey *père* got tired of pottering about so he opened an office in the town and began dealing in stocks and shares and things. He was a clever chap and he had almost the Midas touch—everything he touched turned metaphorically to gold. He made a lot of money in his private speculations, and his clients made a lot of money on the advice he gave them. This was before my time, you know, but I've heard the story a dozen times. Upwey kept up a big establishment and lived in lavish style. He was very generous and gave away a lot in public and private charities. He was very popular, and by all accounts he was as straight as a line.

"He was very proud of his boy Guy; sent him to a public school and gave him as much pocket money as he wanted.

When Guy finished school he came home and hung about for a bit before deciding what to do next. He wasn't keen on a university, and he was having a good time dashing about and generally raising a harmless sort of hell.

"Then the crash came. Mrs. Upwey died suddenly from heart trouble. It broke the father up. He'd always liked his drink and now he started boozing. He lost his flair for business, speculated wildly, and muddled up his clients' money with his own. I say 'muddled' because it was proved that he'd done nothing dishonest. He blew his brains out one night while the boy was at a party.

"A solicitor called Ivor Dermot Lloyd, who'd been Upwey's friend and legal man, went into his affairs and found there was enough money and property to pay all Upwey's debts in full and leave nearly a thousand pounds for the son.

"Dermot Lloyd—he's now defending Miles Trevone, by the way—and other friends offered Guy various jobs, but he refused them all. He took his money and cleared out. I don't know exactly what he did next, but after a time he turned up as a constable in a Midlands police force. The boy had brains and guts and passed his exams without difficulty. He got on the C.I.D. side and was marked for promotion when the war started. He tried to join the army but couldn't get released from the police, though he was lent to the Security people for a spell. During that time he visited Treporth a few times, on duty. He was promoted a sergeant.

"After the war Guy surprised his old friends by asking to be transferred to the force here. As you know, that's not always easy, but his case was unusual. I happened to be up in his neighbourhood on business and I interviewed him. I must admit he rather impressed me and I had a word with his Chief Constable and other officers. They were quite frank about him. They said that in some ways he was one of their best men, but he had a bit of a temper—not so much quarrelsome as impatient, and resentful of what he considered interference, even by his superiors. The worst mark against him was his tendency to do things on his own. He was ambitious and he wanted the whole credit for whatever job he was on. That naturally made him disliked, and it was rather serious in a force that's a good deal bigger than this. Once he was reprimanded and nearly lost his rank because he kept a bit of information up his sleeve instead of putting it in his report. The result was that the man they were after got away. Only Upwey's clean sheet saved him.

"I ought to say that when I talked to Upwey he was as frank as his chiefs had been, and he said he'd learned his lesson. He'd taken it into his head to come back to Treporth and make good, as he called it. I pointed out that he'd have to expect a good deal of gossip, but he said he was prepared for that.

"To cut short a story that has been rather long—but you asked for it—we were short of men at the time and I thought Upwey's local knowledge would be useful. Haydn Hughes had been at me for more help for some time, and when I told him and Morris about Upwey they thought it would be a good idea to take him on. So the transfer was arranged and Upwey came to us as a detective-constable. I made him a sergeant after a few months, partly on his record and partly because two other candidates on Hughes' list were hopeless when they tried the examination they had to pass. Since then Upwey had been doing very good work. And that," the colonel concluded, relighting his pipe, "is how Upwey came to join our force."

"Thank you," Ash replied. "Did he get on well with the people here—the civilians, I mean?"

"Oh yes. He was an amusing chap, and I believe he was very popular at the Sports Club."

"Exactly what is this club, sir?"

"It's a place off the main road about half-way between Treporth and a village called Pentref. Hughes will take you there tomorrow. There used to be a big army camp there and when the war finished some of the local people got permission to take over several large hutments that hadn't been pulled down. Money was raised and some of the local firms presented furniture and so on. The club's for men and women interested in all forms of sport—a wide term that includes bowls, billiards, cards, golf, fishing and goodness knows what. They've even got a small gymnasium for boxing and so on. It's a very democratic sort of show, no class distinctions, and all sorts of people belong to it. The only rule on that point is that the members must behave themselves; anyone who gets rowdy is chucked out. I'm an honorary member and our people keep a fatherly eye on the place."

He broke off as the door opened and Superintendent Morris was shown in.

The colonel made hospitable suggestions. Morris took a whisky-and-soda; Ash chose beer and the colonel followed his example.

"I've been telling Ash about Upwey," he explained to Morris. "Who's next, Ash?"

"I'd like to hear something about Trevone, sir."

Bassenthwaite Lake frowned.

"It's a damnable business," he said. "Policemen aren't supposed to have any feelings in such matters, but one can't help being human. There's a lot of rot talked about the *crime passionnel* in France, but it really means that their juries take into account the emotions they feel themselves. However, that's not our business. You've got all the dope on Trevone, I think, Morris, so check me if I go wrong. Trevone's father was a Cornish sea captain who used to call at this port. He, like the elder Upwey, married a Welsh girl and they made their home here. He did well and his wife also had money. They died during the war, leaving Miles a house on the cliffs near Pentref and enough money to live pretty comfortably. Miles did a good job in the R.A.F. and got the Distinguished Flying Cross. Towards the end of the war he was shot down and was in hospital for a long time. I believe he's physically fit again but he's still a bit nervy. He'd thought of reading for the Bar, but he once told me—I know him fairly well—that he was afraid he'd be too nervous to make a good pleader. He's interested in law, so he's taken articles with Dermot Lloyd, who was a friend of his father and did any legal business there was to be done for him."

"This Mr. Lloyd has a good practice?"

"One of the best for miles round. It was founded by his grandfather, William Lloyd, who added his wife's name, Dermot. He was succeeded by his son, John Dermot Lloyd, and *his* son is the present Ivor Dermot Lloyd. By the way, Ash, you'll have to get used to this name business. In a country where almost every other man—excuse me, Morris—is a Jones or a Thomas or a Davies or a Lloyd——"

"Or a Morris," the superintendent put in, grinning.

The colonel laughed. "Well, they have to do something about it, so you get Llewellyn Davies and Morgan Thomas, and

Morris Jones, and so on, to avoid confusion. There are several solicitors and barristers named Lloyd, so our one is always referred to (now that his father's dead) as Mr. Dermot Lloyd. Sometimes, too, people get nicknames from the place they live in, or their occupation or some other reason, like Jones the Bridge, or Morgan One-arm, and so on. It's a bit confusing."

"Thanks, sir," Ash smiled. "I'll try to keep my head clear. Getting back to Dermot Lloyd, it was his daughter Upwey and Trevone quarrelled about, I believe. What's she like?"

"Nothing wrong there. Nice girl, good-looking and good at sports. Served in the A.T.S. and got her commission. She's kept house for her father since the mother died, and I believe she's helped in his office at times when he's been shorthanded. I've played bridge at Dermot Lloyd's house a few times and met her there." The colonel took a pull at his tankard and leaned back. "Now, Morris," he said, "let's have your views."

"About what, sir?"

"About the whole show. Morris prefers to do the nodding mandarin stuff, Ash, but he can generally produce an idea if you squeeze him hard enough."

Superintendent Morris smiled faintly, as at a jest hallowed by age, but his tone was grim enough as he answered slowly:

"I've only two views that matter. The first is that one of our men has been murdered, and someone's going to swing for it. The second is that if Trevone did the job—and there doesn't seem to be any reason to doubt it—I find it hard to believe that there wasn't more between them than one row over a girl."

"Jealousy's one of the commonest motives for murder," Ash observed.

"It is," the other agreed, "and if Trevone had set about Upwey there and then it would have been natural enough. Hughes and I had a talk with Mr. Oscar Fersen, who was there when Trevone knocked Upwey down. Fersen's a sensible sort of man and he carries a lot of weight in the club. He seems to have done his best to patch up the quarrel. He says he was more worried about Trevone than about Upwey, though he admits that Upwey was to blame. But it seemed to him that Upwey had got his temper back and would probably have apologised if Trevone had met him half-way. After all, as

Fersen remarked, Upwey couldn't afford to get reported to the Chief Constable for making a disturbance in a public place, and annoying a respectable girl into the bargain. On the other hand, Trevone sat at the bar, swilling whisky, and Fersen couldn't get much out of him. As the colonel said just now, Trevone's a nervy chap at times, although he's pleasant enough as a rule."

"Do you think he might have got back at Upwey by reporting him to the chief?" Ash inquired.

"No. I think he'd have been more likely to try to knock Upwey's block off. But I can't get over the *way* Upwey was killed. I can see Trevone brooding over the row, and I can even see him taking the boomerang and hitting Upwey with it, though I'd have thought he'd use his fists; but it's the pistol business that gets me. Even if he'd decided to shoot Upwey, would he have thought of doing it so neatly in the ear, so it wouldn't be noticed?"

Ash nodded.

"You've met the man, and I haven't," he answered. "I quite see your point, but if Trevone didn't do it, who did? Do you know of anyone who had a grudge against Upwey?"

"Plenty, but they're men he caught and got sent down. Upwey was hard, very hard, and the longer the sentence a man got the better, in his opinion. He never went out of his way to say a good word for the chap in the dock. I know coincidences happen more often than most people think, but it'd be a pretty big one if some crook laid in wait for Upwey and did him in just after he'd had the row with Trevone. No, it won't wash. Trevone had the Rule of Three all right—Motive, Means and Opportunity. As I see it, there's evidence enough to hang him a dozen times—and *yet* I don't feel comfortable about it."

The rosy genial man had spoken with an unwonted energy that impressed the other two, and for some minutes they sat silently considering what he had said.

"I wish," Ash said thoughtfully, "you could find that Webley air-pistol Trevone admits he owned."

"So do we, naturally," the colonel agreed, "but I don't see that it's vital to the prosecutor's case. He admits he used to have one and he can't, or won't, explain how he lost it. He may have chucked it into the sea."

Morris, however, eyed Ash shrewdly and asked: "What's your point? Have we missed something?"

"Did you notice anything unusual about that .22 bullet Hughes showed me?"

"No. Hughes may have, but he didn't say so. What was it?"

"I'd suggest," Ash answered delicately, "that it would be worth while getting a ballistics expert to examine the bullet. We can get it done at the Yard, if it will save you any trouble."

"But what for?" the colonel asked.

"It's just an idea of mine," Ash explained. "You know, of course, that an air-pistol has a smooth bore."

"Of course," Bassenthwaite Lake agreed with the testiness of a man who had used most kinds of firearms against big and small game.

"Well, sir, I'm not an expert, but I thought I saw marks on the bullet that looked uncommonly like rifling."

The colonel and Morris exclaimed simultaneously, and with reason. The interior of the barrel of a rifle, instead of being smooth, has a spiral groove which gives the bullet a rotation, or spin, that makes its trajectory straighter, and as the bullet passes through it receives "rifling" marks which can be positively identified with the weapon from which it was fired.

"How the hell could Hughes have missed that?" the colonel muttered. "He and I are going to have words about it."

"The marks are very faint," said Ash, who had no wish to make trouble. "In fact, I may be wrong, and that's why I suggest an expert examination. But if they *are* rifling marks, it's a point in Trevone's favour—unless, of course, you can show that he also owns a .22 calibre weapon with a rifled barrel."

"Well, we're much obliged to you, Ash," the colonel said handsomely, "and we'll certainly get the bullet examined."

"All the same," Ash pointed out, "that doesn't put Trevone in the clear. The boomerang seems to be the big card in your hand, added to his quarrel with Upwey. Which reminds me of another thing I wanted to ask: what terms were Upwey and Trevone on, apart from the question of the girl?"

"Very good," Morris answered. "They'd known each other when they were little boys."

Ash nodded, and after some further conversation the party broke up.

Morris dropped Ash at the hotel, where he was received by an awed night porter, and said that Hughes would be there early next morning with a car ready to begin their tour.

Ash thanked him and went thoughtfully to his room.

"Now I wonder," he said to himself as he got into bed, "what it was that the colonel was so careful *not* to tell me."

CHAPTER IV

ASH had just finished an early breakfast the next morning when Inspector Haydn Hughes arrived in a car driven by a plain-clothes man. The inspector produced his map and indicated the route he proposed to follow.

Ash agreed, and they got into the car.

Beyond an occasional reference to places and people they were to visit Hughes said nothing as the car left the town and turned into the cliff road that bordered the sea.

Ash did not attempt to force conversation. Hughes, he felt, would talk when he was ready, and there was no point in trying to hurry him.

They had not gone far when the driver slowed to allow an approaching car to pass. Hughes hailed the bearded man at the wheel of the other car and both vehicles stopped.

"Morning, Mr. Oscar," he said. "Going far, sir?"

"As far as the railway station," the other replied. "I'm taking Mr. Ingrow to catch the London train. He's been down for his bit of fishing, but his cottage is being repaired so we put him up for the week-end. Why? Did you want to see me?"

"I'd be glad of a word with you when it's convenient."

"Of course. I've a few things to do in the town and then I'm going to the Sports Club. Would that suit you?"

"It'll do fine, sir. About two o'clock?"

"All right. I'll meet you there," Fersen agreed. He waved his hand and drove on.

"What about the other man?" Ash inquired. "I know him, but I didn't expect to see him here."

"Mr. Alfred Ingrow. Something high up in the Civil Service.

Got a little cottage near Pentref and comes down when he can spare the time. Very keen fisherman, he is. Not what you might call a good mixer; a bit too pompous for my liking; but he certainly can *fish*," Hughes conceded. "The man I spoke to is Mr. Fersen—or Mr. Oscar, as most people call him, not to confuse him with his brother, Mr. Axel."

"Not a local name," Ash commented.

"No. They're Swedes. They came to this country before the war and took a house called the Crow's Nest. We'll be passing it later. Mr. Axel's a big pot in the scientific line. Being a neutral, he wouldn't have anything to do with actual munitions of war, so to speak, but he gave the Government some inventions of his own that had to do with life-saving, and he didn't take a penny for them. Now he's working on something to do with lighting—some sort of invisible ray, I think. Anyhow, your Special Branch know all about him, and they gave us the O.K. on them both."

"Is Mr. Oscar an inventor too?"

"No. He runs the house and reminds Mr. Axel to eat his dinner," Hughes grinned. "Mr. Axel's pleasant enough, but when you're talking to him you feel as if he'd just landed on the earth from Mars, or somewhere, and was wondering when he'd be able to go back and get on with his job."

Ash smiled; he had met the type more than once.

Hughes said a word to the driver, who pulled the car close in to the side of the road and stopped.

"The place where Upwey was found is just ahead," Hughes explained. "After we'd made our search and got our pictures we told the borough surveyor he could let his men carry on repairing the wall."

They got out of the car and walked up the gentle slope to where a small gang was at work. Hughes said something in Welsh to the foreman, who nodded; the men, with the natural good manners of their race, refrained from more than an interested glance at Ash as they went on with their work.

Hughes drew the superintendent aside and briefly explained the lie of the land, after which the two men lay down and peered over the edge of the cliff.

Then Ash got up and prowled about by himself for a few minutes. He devoted some attention to the bushes where, Hughes told him, the boomerang had been found.

Hughes readily answered his few questions, but offered no suggestion or comment.

"I think I've got the hang of it now," Ash said. "Shall we get on?"

They returned to the car and drove slowly along the cliff road, which soon became broader and more level.

"That's the Fersens' house," Hughes said presently, pointing to a solid building of dark stone perched on the cliff's edge. It had a square tower with windows on every side, and broad stone steps led down to a private boat-house and a little jetty. "Built by a retired shipmaster, it was," the inspector explained. "He wanted a good view of the sea, but he didn't live long to enjoy it; drowned he was, in a squall, while he was fishing, and him having sailed the Seven Seas and got the best of them, as you might say, pretty well all his life. That's the lighthouse just beyond," he went on, pointing somewhat unnecessarily to the white-painted building on a spur of cliff that jutted out into the sea.

A few hundred yards farther on they stopped at a trim little house on the landward side of the road. This was at once the local police-station and the residence of Sergeant Jack Jones, in charge of the district which included the village of Pentref.

Hughes led the way into the office. The stout and cheerful sergeant had evidently been expecting them, for he was wearing his helmet as he sat at his desk, which fact enabled him to rise and salute smartly as Hughes declaimed Ash's name and rank.

Ash, to the sergeant's evident surprise and gratification, shook hands and produced the case of cigarettes he carried for social purposes.

"You can take off the old helmet, Jack *bach*," Hughes said drily. "Mr. Ash wants to talk with you off parade."

The sergeant grinned as he removed his headgear and they all sat down.

"Mr. Hughes tells me the coastguard called you when he found Sergeant Upwey's body," Ash began, filling his pipe.

"That's right, sir, and the nastiest shock it was I've ever had in my life."

"You knew him pretty well, of course?"

"He lodged with me and my missus while he was waiting

B

for quarters in town," Jones replied with a shade of hesitation. "No trouble at all, he was, and of course my missus is used to me going in and out at all hours, like Upwey did." He paused, but Ash's gaze still questioned him, and he went on: "As to knowing him well, sir, that's a bit difficult to answer. Of course, he was C.I.D. and I'm in the uniform branch, so——" He left it at that.

"You mean he didn't discuss his work with you?"

"No, sir, not unless it was something that concerned us both."

"I see. Now, Sergeant, I know it's not pleasant to have to talk about a man after he's dead, especially when you've been on friendly terms with him, but Upwey's been murdered, and I'm sure you'll understand that I'm only asking questions because Mr. Hughes and I want to get any information that may be useful."

"I understand, sir. What was it you wanted to know?"

"In the first place, was he what you'd call a quarrelsome chap?"

"No, I wouldn't say that. A bit hot-tempered-like, now and then, but pleasant enough most times."

"Did he drink much?"

"He liked his drop of beer, same as I do myself when not on duty," Jones answered frankly, "but I never saw him the worse for it. A strong head, he had, and he knew when he'd had enough."

"I was just wondering," Ash explained, "whether he and Trevone might both have been a bit tight——"

"When they met on the cliff road, you mean? Trevone might have been, but Upwey had a job to do—so he'd told me —and he wouldn't have been likely to overstep the mark."

"Do you know what the job was?"

"No, sir, he didn't say."

"About this fellow Trevone: you know him too, I suppose?"

"Yes, sir. He lives not far from here. I've been out fishing with him time and again."

"What's your opinion of him?"

"A real good sort, sir," the sergeant declared. "Couldn't hardly believe my ears when I heard what had happened."

"You mean you wouldn't have expected him to commit a murder?"

The sergeant frowned.

"As to that, Mr. Ash," he said slowly, "you know better than me that murder's a queer sort of game. What I mean is, I could understand Mr. Trevone getting excited and setting about Upwey with his fists, or even hitting him with whatever he had in his hand, but I can't see him planning all that beforehand."

"You've heard about the bullet that was found in Upwey's head?"

"Yes, sir; Mr. Hughes told me on the 'phone. I've kept it to myself, of course, but that's what was in my mind when I was speaking of Trevone planning it all out, like. Of course," Jones added, with an apologetic glance at Inspector Hughes, "I'm not saying he *didn't* do it, things being as they are. It only goes to show that you can't ever tell what a man will do, however well you think you know him. Excuse me for passing the remark, it not being properly my business, but you asked me what I thought."

"I did, and I'm much obliged to you," Ash responded. "I've made too many mistakes in my time to be surprised now by almost anything that can happen. But can you think of anyone else who'd be likely to have killed Upwey?"

"No, I can't," the sergeant admitted. "There was plenty that didn't like him a lot, same as they don't like me if I get them fined for being drunk or some other bit of bother, but that's all in the day's work and no bad blood about it."

Ash nodded.

"This girl Upwey and Trevone quarrelled about," he said, "do you know her?"

"Yes, sir. Known her for years, and so's my missus. There's been a lot of young men after her, and I don't wonder. But she's not what I might call a flighty piece. I'd bet a week's pay that whatever mischief there was between Upwey and Trevone wasn't of her making. Have you seen her, sir?"

"No. I hope to meet her later on."

"Then you'll be able to judge for yourself," the sergeant said with the air of a man who feels he has made a safe bet.

"Always one for a pretty face, weren't you?" Hughes put in, and Jones grinned. "Not but what I think he's right, sir," the inspector added.

The visitors left soon afterwards, declining the sergeant's

hospitable suggestion that they should allow his missus to steep the tea and give them a nice cup to sustain them on their journey.

They resumed their drive and presently passed the coast-guard station, but Ash decided that he didn't want at the moment to talk to the man who had found Upwey's body.

Miles Trevone's house, on the cliff road a little farther on, was their next port of call. Hughes had arranged for Dick Edwards and his wife, who kept house for Miles, to be there to receive them. Edwards, he explained to Ash, had been a sergeant rear-gunner in the Royal Air Force and had served with Trevone until he had been badly wounded and invalided out of the Service on pension.

Ash liked the look of the couple. They did not try to hide their anxiety for the young man who was their employer, but they indulged in no histrionics. They were quite definite that he had been in the house when they returned from the cinema and that he had not gone out again that evening. Mrs. Edwards was able to fix the time of their own arrival because, she explained, they had been just in time to hear a favourite item in the Welsh programme on the radio set in their sitting-room before she got the evening meal. She mentioned the item, and Hughes caught Ash's eye and nodded to intimate that he had checked it with the programme.

Ash did not discuss the point. He asked Edwards whether he knew that Trevone had owned a Webley air pistol.

Edwards said he did know it, and that it had been one of several articles stolen from the house. He had himself reported the robbery to Sergeant Jones.

Ash did not prolong the interview and Edwards went with them to the car. There, standing stiffly to attention, he asked:

"May I take the liberty of saying a word, sir?"

"Of course," Ash responded. "What is it?"

The ex-sergeant swallowed, but his voice was steady as he said:

"It's just this, sir. Mr. Trevone didn't kill Sergeant Upwey. You may be thinking I am saying so because he gave me and the wife this job, but it isn't that. I know things look bad against him, especially to one like yourself who doesn't know him. But I do. I was rear-gunner with him, and you get to know an officer on a job like that. I'm not saying Mr. Trevone wouldn't have knocked Upwey's block off in a fair fight, and enjoyed it, but he could no more have *murdered* him than I could—and that's God's truth, sir, so help me!"

"Let's hope you're right, Edwards," the superintendent answered gently. He wondered, as he got into the car, how often he had heard people say things like that. It was natural, after all. When one had reason to love, or even respect, a person it was almost impossible to imagine that person committing a crime. Human nature, Ash thought; and probably the best side of human nature. Unfortunately, people *did* commit crimes, and if police officers allowed themselves to be swayed by sentiment the criminals would escape scot free.

Ash, in common with other practical criminologists, had long ceased to be surprised by the attitude of the general public towards crime. People who read of a murder would denounce the police and metaphorically demand the head of the Commissioner on a charger if no arrest were made within twenty-four hours. Yet as soon as the culprit had been found guilty and sentenced to death the same people would sign petitions for his reprieve and would mourn outside the prison on the day of his execution. Ash wondered how those sentimentalists would have felt if the murderer's victim had been their own relative, or if they had had to see the suffering caused to innocent people by the criminal's act.

Hughes roused him from his reflections by remarking that they were about to pass through the village of Pentref.

The driver had been instructed to slow down so that Ash might look about him. It was a small place, but it boasted a church, three chapels and the same number of public-houses, a cinema and a number of shops. The Lloyds' house was pointed out, and another belonging, Hughes said, to a Mrs. Sweeney.

When Ash remarked that Sweeney was not a typically Welsh name the inspector explained that the lady in question was of Welsh birth but had married an American soldier during the First World War and had lived for many years in the United States. He had mentioned her because she and Kate Dermot Lloyd were friends and the girl acted as a sort of secretary to the older woman.

The car pulled into the yard of a small but cosy-looking

inn, where Superintendent Morris had ordered lunch to be ready for them.

The meal was plain but well cooked, and the beer was good.

By tacit consent they did not talk shop. Hughes had apparently decided that the Yard toff was also a fellow creature; he told in his dry way some amusing stories of the musical affairs which play so large a part in Welsh life, with special reference to the male voice choir of which he was the conductor. They were on excellent terms when the car came to take them to the Sports Club.

They went by way of the main road, the route which Miles Trevone declared he had taken on his way home on the day of Upwey's murder.

At the club they found Mr. Oscar Fersen waiting to receive them. Dai Davies, the steward, hovered in the background like an anxious acolyte.

At Hughes's suggestion they began with an inspection of the premises, including the cloakroom, the lounge and the stage.

Then Mr. Oscar took them to the office of the secretary, who was away on holiday, and suggested drinks.

Ash said he would prefer coffee, and Hughes approved.

Mr. Oscar rang for Davies and gave the order.

"And now, gentlemen," he said, "what can I do for you? I needn't say I'll be only too glad to help you, and poor Trevone as well, if I can."

Ash, observing him unobtrusively, saw a heavily built but not fat man with a big body, short legs and long arms. His sandy hair was cropped short, and his prominent chin and part of his ruddy face were covered by a thick moustache and a square-cut beard. His keen black eyes returned Ash's gaze with frank interest.

"Superintendent Ash has read the statements made by you and other witnesses," Hughes said primly, "but I was thinking that as he was coming to see the club it would be nice for him to have a talk with you about what happened on Saturday."

"Of course," Mr. Oscar agreed politely, hiding a smile at the inspector's phrasing. "What do you want to know, Mr. Ash?"

"Anything you care to tell me," the superintendent replied.

Mr. Oscar shrugged. "What I'd *like* to tell you, he answered, "would be that Miles Trevone didn't kill Upwey."

"But you don't feel you could go that far?"

Davies came in with the coffee and Mr. Oscar stared moodily at his elephant until the man had gone.

"I've been in most parts of the world in my time," he said slowly. "I've seen a good many queer things happen and I hope I've learned a few lessons. One thing I learned was that you can generally predict what a mob will do, but you never can tell what one man will do, however well you may think you know him. If you'd asked me a week ago whether young Trevone would ever stand in the dock on a charge of murder I'd have risked a heavy bet that he wouldn't; but only a fool refuses to face facts, and the facts—so far as I know them— are damnably against him. I liked those lads, Upwey and Trevone, and I was always afraid there'd be trouble between them, but I wasn't expecting this sort of trouble. It's hard, very hard, to believe that Trevone could have done it, but you police people know your business too well to bring a charge like this without good evidence. If I'd only had the sense to insist on Trevone coming with me that evening," he added bitterly, "all this would never have happened."

"I don't think you need blame yourself," Ash said. "From what I've heard, you did your best to keep the peace between them."

"I did try," the other admitted. "I wasn't so much worried about Upwey as I was about Trevone, but he assured me that he'd go home when he'd finished his drink, and I took his word for it."

"Was he drunk?"

"No. If he had been I wouldn't have left him. He'd had enough, and he was in a sullen sort of mood, but not quarrelsome. I thought it best to leave him to himself."

"Quite so. You didn't see him or Upwey again on Saturday, I believe?"

"No. I went to the cloakroom to get my hat and a parcel I'd left there. Then I went out to my car. The garage man had washed it down and attended to the tyres, which were a bit down. I drove home, stopping at a call-box to make a telephone call I'd forgotten while I was here."

If Mr. Oscar suspected that he was being tactfully asked to

account for his own time, he showed no sign of it as he sipped his coffee.

"I know it's unpleasant to be asked questions about your friends——" Ash began, but Mr. Oscar interrupted him.

"It'd be a damned sight more unpleasant to hear one of them sentenced to death," he said bluntly. "Ask me anything you like, Mr. Ash, and I'll answer you as well as I can, however unpleasant it may be."

"Thank you. Upwey and Trevone quarrelled about Miss Dermot Lloyd. They were in love with her, I take it?"

"Of course they were. So were half a dozen other young fellows, and I don't wonder. I'd be in love with her myself if I were twenty years younger. Don't get any wrong ideas about her, Mr. Ash. She's a fine girl, high-spirited, a good sportswoman and very attractive, but she's not a flirt."

"Do you think she favoured either Upwey or Trevone more than the other?"

Mr. Oscar shrugged. "Your guess is as good as mine," he replied. "I'm a sort of unofficial uncle to the young people here, and I do what I can to smooth out the little disagreements that you always find in a club of this kind, but I hope I've too much sense to interfere with their love affairs. And don't forget that I'm a foreigner, though I had an English mother. My father was a Swede. In this country—and especially in Wales—a foreigner is expected to mind his own business."

"That's right, by damn!" Hughes put in. "In South Wales a North Walian is nearly as much a foreigner as an Englishman is, to say nothing of people from over the seas. Meaning no offence to you or your brother, Mr. Oscar, but there it is."

"Natural enough," Ash smiled. "I've met the same sort of thing in English villages. It's like the old Cockney motto, 'Heave 'arf a brick at 'im, 'e's only a stranger!' I suppose there was a good deal of gossip about the girl and her young men?"

"There's always gossip, but I don't encourage it myself. I've no doubt people gossip as much about my brother and me as about anyone else. But I think you'll find that most people like and respect Kate."

They chatted a little longer and then Ash thanked Mr. Oscar for his patience. They must, he said, be on their way, but he would like to talk to Davies before he left.

He got up, but Mr. Oscar insisted that the two should stay where they were while he found Davies and sent him in.

"A beautiful stick, that is," Hughes remarked as the lame man got to his feet.

"I've been admiring it too," Ash said. "I don't think I've ever seen another like it."

"I don't think you have and I don't think you ever will," Mr. Oscar replied complacently, and he proceeded to relate the history of the stick with a pride he did not conceal. Then he handed it to the superintendent, who examined it with interest.

"A beautiful piece of work," Ash said, as he returned it. "A real museum piece."

"More than one museum would like to have it," Mr. Oscar agreed. "Perhaps I'll leave it to one of them in my will. I've had plenty of offers from dealers too, but I'd rather starve than sell it." He hesitated, then added: "It's got a little secret of its own, too, that very few people know about. Just watch me——"

Holding the barrel of the stick in his left hand, he pressed his right thumb and forefinger into the shallow cavities of the elephant's eyes. Then he gave the handle a half turn and it came away from the barrel. From the handle protruded a steel blade, fluted and intricately chased, and tapering to a needle-sharp point.

"Handy bit of protection for a cripple, isn't it?" Mr. Oscar chuckled as he restored the blade to its sheath. "By the way, I hope you gentlemen won't throw me into a dungeon for carrying a concealed weapon."

"I don't think we could if we wanted to," Ash smiled. "Sword-sticks can be bought anywhere, though not pieces of craftsmanship like this. But I don't think you're likely to push it into people for fun."

"I've only used it once," Mr. Oscar answered soberly, "and that time it saved my life. It was years ago, at Mozambique. I'd taken one of my father's ships out—I hold a master mariner's ticket—and we'd put in to pick up some cargo. I'd just left the agents' office and was strolling down a narrow street when a great brute of a dog came along with its muzzle slavering. It was mad, of course. The few people about, including a native policeman, bolted, but I hadn't time. The only weapon I had was my stick. I pulled the handle out and as the dog came at me I somehow managed to ram the blade down its throat until the point came out behind its head. I've never been so scared in my life. The policeman plucked up enough courage to come back and finish the animal with his pistol. He pretended he'd been saving some children, but I got him sacked, and I believe they did other things to him as well in their pleasant way. And now, Mr. Ash, I should think you've had enough of the old sailor's stories, so I'll go and find Davies for you."

The two police officers sat in meditative silence until a weasel-faced little man presented himself, divided between nervousness and pride at figuring in the local drama.

"This is David Davies, the barman, sir," Hughes said formally.

"Excuse me, Mr. Hughes," the weasel corrected him; "steward I am, of this club. Me or my missus do serve the members when the barman has his time off; but steward I was appointed by the committee, and my missus is cook-housekeeper——"

"All right, Dai," the inspector cut him short. "Steward you are, and we'll ask the judge to call you that if you have to give evidence. Now listen, boy. Mr. Ash has seen what you said in your statement, so all you have to do is to keep quiet and answer his questions."

"Sit down, Davies," said Ash. "As Mr. Hughes said, I've read your statement, and I shan't keep you long. After the rehearsal you served drinks to several people, including Sergeant Upwey and Mr. Trevone. Did you have any conversation with those two?"

"Not with Mr. Trevone, sir, not what you'd call conversation. He ordered his drinks and he paid for them, but he was very short with me. I could see he was in one of his moods, so I didn't pass no remarks."

"In one of his moods, was he? Do you mean he was rude to you?"

"No, sir. Mr. Trevone isn't like that. He's always the gentleman, but there's times when he's a bit quick in his temper. On account of the time he had in the war, no doubt," Davies added with a glance at Hughes.

"I've heard about that," Ash said. "From where you were

standing at the bar while the rehearsal was on you saw him knock Upwey down?"

"It was more of a push than a punch," Davies declared. "I am thinking that he didn't really mean——"

"Never mind what you are thinking," Hughes put in mildly. "It is the facts Mr. Ash wants to have, man. We know how you are feeling, but it will be the jury that will have to do the thinking."

Davies nodded.

"Other people besides yourself saw what happened," Ash reminded him. "When you were serving Mr. Trevone with drinks did he say anything about what had happened on the stage?"

"No, sir, I didn't mention it, either. I didn't feel it was my place."

"Did you hear him speak of it to anyone else?"

"No, sir. He didn't speak to anybody but Mr. Oscar Fersen, and I didn't hear what they were saying."

"I see. Did you have any talk with Sergeant Upwey?"

"A bit, sir, in between attending to the other members."

"What were you talking about?"

"Football, mostly. About the Treporth team's chances next season."

"He didn't say anything about Mr. Trevone?"

"Not a word."

"You've often seen them together here, I suppose?"

"Aye indeed, many times."

"Were they on friendly terms?"

"Certainly they were. They called each other by their first names and they were always chaffing, as you might say." Davies paused, then added reluctantly, "At least, they used to be."

"You mean they hadn't been so friendly lately?"

Davies hesitated. "I don't want to give you no wrong ideas, sir," he said. "It was just that they seemed a bit more acid, like, in their chaffing. Like as if each of them wanted to make the other look a bit silly, especially if Miss Kate—Miss Dermot Lloyd was there. That was natural enough, of course, seeing how things were."

"What things?"

"Well, it was common talk that they were both after the young lady."

"Did you ever hear them talk about her, or quarrel about her?"

"No, sir."

"I think you said in your statement that Mr. Trevone left the club before Sergeant Upwey?"

"That's right."

"Could you fix the time?"

"Not exactly. The bar got pretty busy and I had to go down to the cellar. I don't rightly remember when I noticed that Mr. Trevone had gone."

"The sergeant was still there?"

"Yes, for about another quarter of an hour."

"Did you at any time after the rehearsal see either Trevone or Upwey talking to Miss Dermot Lloyd?"

"I did not. They were at opposite ends of the bar and she was about in the middle. Mr. Oscar talked to her, and so did some others later on, but not Mr. Trevone or the sergeant. She didn't even look at them. I took particular notice," Davies admitted, "having seen what I did on the stage. I was a bit afraid there might be trouble."

"Did she seem much upset by what had happened?"

Again the weasel hesitated. "I think she *was* upset, sir, but she was too much of a lady to show it. Always the lady, Miss Kate is. All the same, there was something about the way she looked, and the way she kept tapping her fingers on the bar, that made me think Mr. Trevone and the sergeant hadn't heard the last of it, not by a long chalk."

"Is there anything else you'd like to tell me?"

"No, sir. I've told you all I know."

Ash thought that was probably true, although he did not much care for the man. Davies, he thought, would be likely to trim his sails to the fairest wind, but in this case he seemed to have no motive for telling anything but the truth.

It was, Ash decided, just another of those wearisome but necessary interrogations in which many questions had to be asked on the offchance of eliciting one new fact.

They went out to the lounge, where Ash again thanked Mr. Oscar for his help.

"I'm afraid I wasn't really very helpful," the latter replied, "but I'm always at your service if there's anything I can do. Hughes will tell you where I live, Mr. Ash; my brother and I will be glad to see you any time you care to drop in for a drink and a smoke. Hughes knows he's always welcome."

When they were in the car on their way back to the town Ash said: "You did that business about the stick rather neatly. What made you suspect him?"

"I didn't," the inspector answered promptly. "In the first place, there's no reason why Mr. Oscar should have done it. He was friendly with both the men—he's friendly with most people, for that matter."

"Well, then——"

"It was what you said about air-rifles set me thinking," Hughes explained. "Mr. Oscar has a stick that *could* be a gun like that, so it was worth making sure. I hadn't any excuse for talking about it in the ordinary way, but I tried to make it sound natural when he stood up."

Ash smiled.

"You're quite right," he said. "We're always telling our recruits never to take anything for granted. In this case it's obvious that Oscar couldn't have fired a bullet from a stick with a dagger inside it, but you were right to make sure. Where are we going now?"

"You said you'd like to meet Mr. Dermot Lloyd. Well, it seems he'd like to meet you too. You remember I was called to the 'phone while you were washing your hands before lunch? It was Mr. Morris, saying Mr. Dermot Lloyd had 'phoned him asking if you'd call at his office. He left it to you to decide."

"I'd certainly like to see him. Let's go there at once."

"Right, sir. I'll drop you at his office."

"Aren't you coming too?"

"I didn't know if you'd want me."

"Of course I do, if you can spare the time."

Obviously pleased, Hughes tapped on the sliding window and gave the driver his instructions.

CHAPTER V

MR. IVOR DERMOT LLOYD was a tall, grey-haired man.
When Ash and Hughes were shown into his private room he
rose, removed the horn-rimmed glasses he used for reading, and
greeted them with a pleasant courtesy quite free from effusive-
ness.

"I am very much obliged to you, Mr. Ash," he said, "for
agreeing to come here. You must have been surprised by my
invitation."

"I was," Ash replied, "but I was very glad to have the
chance of meeting you."

"Why?"

"Because I believe you were a friend of Guy Upwey."

Mr. Dermot Lloyd nodded.

"I was," he agreed. "Let me be quite frank with you, Mr.
Ash. I took a great interest in Upwey and Trevone. It's not
too much to say that they both looked on me as a sort of
unofficial uncle. Now I'm placed in the distressing position of
defending one of them against a charge of murdering the other.
I've been in practice for a good many years, but this is something new in my experience."

"I feel sure of one thing," Ash remarked.

"What's that?"

"That you wouldn't be acting for Trevone if you didn't
think he was innocent."

Dermot Lloyd flushed.

"Thank you," he answered quietly. "I won't pretend to
misunderstand you. As an Officer of the Court—as a solicitor
is formally described—I have a certain duty to my client. As
a private individual, I assure you I'm certain that Miles
Trevone didn't kill Guy Upwey. Whether that can be proved
or not, I don't know. You have a terribly strong case, but I'm
going to fight it in every proper way I can." He paused and
smiled. "This is a strange sort of conversation between the
solicitor for the accused man and the police officer in charge of
the case, isn't it? But my excuse—if excuse be needed—is that
it's a damned strange case, how ever you look at it. However, I
mustn't waste your time. You're wondering why I asked you
to come, and I'll tell you. It's because Trevone insisted on it."

"Trevone?"

"Yes. He wants to see you."

"I've no objection," Ash said thoughtfully, "but to put it bluntly, any interview I may have with him will be purely official, and anything he may say will——"

"Will be at his own risk. That's perfectly fair. It's a most unusual proceeding, but he said that if I wouldn't agree he'd apply to the police direct."

"The interview must take place in the presence of witnesses," Ash stipulated. "I shall ask Inspector Hughes to come with me, and I suggest that you should be present as well."

"Certainly. I was going to suggest that myself. Then I may take it that you agree?"

"Yes, though I still can't understand why Trevone wants to see me."

"I can't either, to be honest with you. One thing I'm sure of: he has no intention of making a confession. I put that to him squarely, and he assured me that the idea had never entered his mind. He could have made such a confession to Inspector Hughes or Superintendent Morris any time since his arrest if he had wanted to. No, it's nothing like that, I'm sure. I happened to mention that you had come down from London, and he insisted at once that I must ask you to see him. There's one thing I ought to make clear," the lawyer went on. "Trevone isn't suggesting that there's been anything improper in the handling of the case by Mr. Morris or Mr. Hughes. I'm not suggesting it, either. I've been associated with them both long enough to have complete confidence in their fairness—and, I'd like to add, their personal courtesy."

He made a slight bow to Hughes, and the inspector nodded his acknowledgment.

"When do you want us to see him?" Ash inquired.

"The sooner the better."

"I'm ready now, if you are."

"Good. I'll ring up the prison governor and say we're coming. But I was forgetting something: didn't you say you wanted to speak to me about Upwey?"

"I did, but that will keep. I'm told you know all there is to know about Upwey's family history, quite apart from this case, and I hoped you wouldn't mind my asking you a few things about him. Colonel Bassenthwaite Lake said he thought it might be arranged."

If Dermot Lloyd was astonished, he did not show it.

"Glad to help in any way that does not affect my duty to my client," he said with a smile that took the formality out of his words.

"As I said, that will keep for another time," Ash reminded him. "I'd like to see Trevone first."

A few minutes later the three men got into the police car and drove to the gloomy prison buildings that frowned at the sea from a hill on the outskirts of the town. The deputy governor took them to a small room used for interviews, and Trevone was brought from his cell.

Ash regarded the prisoner with interest. He saw a fair man of middle height, blue-eyed and clean-shaven. The jaw was firm and the mouth mobile. A likable face, but with a hint of obstinacy about it.

"This is Superintendent Ash," Dermot Lloyd said.

Trevone put out his hand, then dropped it in embarrassment.

"How do you do?" he said. "Thank you very much for coming."

"Before we go any further," Ash put in, "I think Mr. Dermot Lloyd ought to explain the legal position."

The solicitor repeated the substance of his conversation with the superintendent.

Trevone waited impatiently for him to finish.

"That's all right with me," he declared. "And I'm glad you said what you did about Superintendent Morris and Inspector Hughes. I didn't ask to see you, Mr. Ash, because I wanted to beef about having been arrested. There are two things I want to tell you. The first is that I did *not* kill Guy Upwey."

"You declared that in the statement you made after you had been charged and cautioned," Ash reminded him.

"I know I did. I'm not asking whether you believe me; I wanted you to hear me say it because you must have had plenty of practice in judging whether a man's lying or telling the truth."

"What is the second thing you wanted to tell me?"

Trevone reddened. "It's about Miss Dermot Lloyd," he answered. "I want you to understand that she had nothing to do with this thing. Guy and I had been a bit acid with each other lately——"

"Wait a minute, Miles," Dermot Lloyd interrupted. "You must remember this is an official conversation, and you've put your defence in my hands."

"Sorry, sir. But you don't mind my talking about what happened at the rehearsal, do you?"

"Go on. I'll stop you if it's necessary."

"I only want to make it clear that——" he paused, choosing his words. "What I mean is: I thought Guy was overdoing things, and I got annoyed and sent him flying. He got up and no doubt he'd have given me all I wanted if old Fersen hadn't had the sense to make us both shut up. It was rotten for Ka—— for Miss Dermot Lloyd, and I'm terribly sorry it happened. But surely you can see there's no need for her to be dragged into it? I mean, giving evidence in court and all that? It'd be simply horrible for her. Can't you keep her out of it, Mr. Ash? If it's any help, I'm quite prepared to admit——"

Dermot Lloyd cut in again. "You've made enough admissions already," he said, "and so far you haven't told Mr. Ash anything that wasn't in your original statement. I'm sure the police will take note of what you say, but you can't expect Mr. Ash to make any promises."

"Most certainly not," Ash agreed, but he said it mildly, a good deal impressed by Trevone's apparent sincerity. "Our business is to find out the facts, if we can. The lawyers decide what's to be said in court. But," he added, "we'll certainly pass on your request to the proper authorities. You agree, Inspector?"

Hughes nodded.

Trevone looked at each of them in turn.

"Thanks," he said. "I suppose that's all I can expect."

Ash waited a moment. Then he said:

"Is there anything else you want to say?"

Trevone shook his head.

"I was hoping you might want to ask me some questions," he answered.

"What for?"

"Well, only that it might help, somehow. I mean, I may not have put things very well."

"Your statement was quite clear."

"I suppose it was," the younger man admitted miserably. "I—oh, I know I'm making a ruddy fool of myself, but I'd hoped you might have found out something. . . . Damn it, Mr. Ash! If I *had* murdered Guy I'd take my medicine without whining, but it's pretty tough to know I stand a good chance of being hanged for something I haven't done."

There was an uncomfortable silence. Trevone rose, thrust his shaking hands into his pockets, and paced the little room until he had got a grip on himself. Then he sat down.

"Sorry," he said quietly. "Nerves still let me down sometimes. Forget it."

Ash said: "That's all right. It's part of the price you have to pay for winning D.F.C.s and things like that."

"Aye, indeed, man," Hughes muttered.

Trevone flushed and unconsciously straightened his back.

Ash reminded himself—not for the first time—that he was supposed to be a police officer dispassionately doing his duty, not a fashionable psychiatrist soothing a wealthy patient. He pushed back his chair and looked inquiringly at Dermot Lloyd; but the solicitor, instead of taking the hint, said unexpectedly:

"If there's anything you'd like to ask my client, I don't think I'm likely to object. Our case is that he's telling the truth and he's nothing to hide."

"Very well," Ash responded, rather surprised by the invitation. "We're just as anxious to establish the truth as you are." He turned to Trevone and went on: "I will ask you one or two things, then, and Mr. Dermot Lloyd can stop you if he doesn't want you to answer. On your way out of the club on Saturday evening did you go to your locker in the cloakroom?"

"I went to the cloakroom," Trevone answered promptly, "but I didn't go to the locker. There was nothing there I wanted."

"It's been stated that the locker was unlocked. Can you remember?"

"It probably was. I'm a bit careless about it. There wasn't anything of value in it."

"Do you agree that the boomerang was in it?"

"Of course. I was always meaning to take it home, but I

just forgot about it. It had been at the bottom of the locker for weeks."

"When did you last notice it there?"

"I honestly couldn't tell you."

"Very well. You said in your statement that you used to own an air pistol."

"Yes; it was pinched from my house some time ago."

"Was there anything unusual about the pistol?"

"Unusual? No. It was the ordinary Webley type. I don't quite see what you mean."

"Let me put it another way. It was an ordinary pistol when you first had it; did you alter it in any way?"

"Alter it?" Trevone repeated. "No, of course not. Why should I? It worked all right. If there'd been anything wrong with it I'd have taken it to a gunsmith."

"You've had a good deal of experience with firearms of different kinds?"

"Naturally. I used them in the war, and I do a bit of rough shooting now and then. If anything went wrong with a gun or pistol of mine I wouldn't mess about with it. It takes an expert to do a job like that properly."

"And nothing did go wrong with it?"

"No."

"Did you ever lend the pistol to anyone?"

"Never. I'm rather fussy about that. Too many people play the fool with weapons, and then someone gets hurt. I wouldn't mind lending a twelve-bore to a farmer, or someone else who knew how to handle it, for a day's shooting, but even then I'd want to be sure of my man. I've seen too many accidents happen to take silly risks. Don't you agree?"

"I do. It's a pity everybody isn't so careful. Going back to Saturday; you said that when you left the club you went home by the main road?"

"Yes. I didn't want to meet Guy Upwey."

"But you left before him, didn't you?"

"Yes. What I meant was that I didn't want to risk meeting him. I knew he'd go home by the cliff road and I didn't want him to catch me up. I knew damn well that if we met just then there'd be trouble, and old Fersen had made me see that it would be unpleasant for both of us afterwards."

"I see. On your way home did you meet anyone you knew?"

"No. I only wish I had! It would have been very useful now. As a matter of fact, I was so steamed up about that wretched row at the rehearsal that I pounded along without noticing anyone, but I'm not really sure. I said all that in my statement, you know."

"You did, but it's at your own request that I'm putting these questions——"

"Oh, rather! Don't think I'm objecting. I only wish I could remember more about it. I'd had a few drinks, you know."

"Frankly—and don't answer if you'd rather not—were you drunk?"

"Good heavens, no! I may be an ass in some ways, but I do know what I can carry. It's just that, what with the drinks and being worked up about the row with Guy, I wasn't in the mood to bother about anything else. By the time I got home I'd worked it off, so to speak, and got a grip on myself."

Ash nodded. He had not expected to extract any valuable information from the young man; his object had been to size up Trevone. He had watched the man's hands and feet—always so ready to betray their owner by spasmodic movements—and had listened for those overtones and undertones which could be so revealing. There were only two alternatives, he decided: either Trevone was a consummate actor or he was telling the plain truth.

His face was expressionless as he asked whether Trevone had anything more to say.

Miles shook his head. "Only that it was very decent of you to come," he said.

Outside the prison Hughes inquired what Ash proposed to do next.

Ash said: "We seem to have covered most of the ground. The only person I haven't met, I think, is Miss Dermot Lloyd."

"You can see her whenever you like," the girl's father answered quickly.

"Thank you. I dare say she won't be able to do more than confirm what other people have told us, but perhaps I'd better have a word with her, just for the record."

"Kate's been spending the day with Mrs. Sweeney at

Pentref," Dermot Lloyd explained. "She said she might stay the night, but I can ring her up and tell her to come to the office——"

"Please don't," Ash interposed. "There's no reason to upset her arrangements. I can run out and see her there. But perhaps you'd like to let her know I'm coming and explain that it's a routine job."

Dermot Lloyd agreed.

Hughes said he wanted to see Superintendent Morris and to attend to a few things at headquarters, so it was decided that the car should take him there, drop Dermot Lloyd at the latter's office, and then run Ash out to Pentref and bring him back to his hotel in time for dinner.

Alone in the car, except for the driver, on the way to the village, Ash reviewed the day's proceedings. Nothing that he had seen or heard appeared to diminish the strength of the police case against Miles Trevone. It was natural enough that the young man's friends should assert, and probably believe in, his innocence. It was interesting, too, that Jones, the police sergeant, should range himself on their side. Facts, however, were facts, and the prosecution was marshalling a grim array of them.

And yet Ash did not feel entirely comfortable, and his discomfort had been increased by his talk with Trevone. He was too old a hand to allow personal impressions to influence him against weight of evidence, but he would have felt happier if that evidence had been more definite than suggestive. He reminded himself that a witness may lie, but circumstantial evidence cannot; it was an excellent maxim, provided that the *inference* drawn from such evidence was the correct one. . . .

He turned his thoughts to the visit he was about to make. As he had told her father, he did not expect to learn anything important from Kate Dermot Lloyd; but she had been, after all, the bone of contention between the two young men, and there was no reason why he should not include her in his inquiries.

Dermot Lloyd, on the way from the prison, had talked freely about Kate and her friend, Mrs. Sweeney, apparently from a desire to keep a conversation going without discussing their visit to Trevone. Ash had encouraged him, realising the delicacy of his position as Trevone's lawyer and friend.

Kate, it appeared, had been helping in her father's office during a temporary shortage of staff, when Mrs. Jake Sweeney had appeared on the scene, bringing an introduction from her London lawyers. She was looking for a house, and it happened that Dermot Lloyd, who was winding up the estate of a former client, was able to suggest a suitable property on the fringe of Pentref.

Kate had run Mrs. Sweeney out in her car to see the place. Mrs. Sweeney had taken a great liking to Kate and had confided what she called a garrulous old woman's life story to the girl.

Mrs. Sweeney had fallen in love with the house, and had decided to buy it if Kate would help her, as she said, to make it into a home. Kate, nothing loath, plunged into the delightful task of buying furniture and what-not without having to worry about the price. Mrs. Sweeney, greatly impressed by the girl's efficiency and taste, had invited her to join the new household as companion, or secretary, or whatever she liked to call herself, with a comfortable salary as compensation for putting up with an old woman's whims.

Kate had explained that she could not leave her widowed father for whom she kept house, but had promised to spend as much time with Mrs. Sweeney as she could—an arrangement, her father remarked with a chuckle, which was made easier by the fact that his establishment was rigidly administered by one Mrs. Gwyneth Parry, who had been Kate's nurse and had returned to the family fold when her husband was killed in a colliery explosion.

"She thinks there's no one like Mrs. Sweeney," said Dermot Lloyd, "and indeed I must say I like the old lady myself—not that she's exactly aged, you know, but she's got a sedate sort of manner that is rather pleasant."

Deborah Sweeney, so Kate had explained to her father, had been born Deborah Fellditch about fifty years before the present date, in a village in North Wales. Her father, like his father and grandfather, was the local blacksmith, and his religious convictions were as strong as the arms with which he could lift two lusty men at the same time. He was a prominent figure in a particularly grim sect of dissenters who abhorred ritual, eschewed alcohol and tobacco, and sternly denounced the immorality of young people who went to dances, raced about the countryside in horseless vehicles (a sore point with the blacksmith), and patronised theatres and cinemas.

"It was pretty hard on Mrs. Sweeney—or Deborah Fellditch, as she was then," Kate had said. "She told me all about it one day. Not that she was unkind about her father, you know; she was rather sweet about him and her mother. She just said he was a good man, but he couldn't move with the times. She was about eighteen when she met Jake Sweeney, the man she married. She was a teacher in an elementary school. It was in 1917, and he'd come over with the American Army. He was a private in an infantry regiment. His father was a saloon-keeper in New York, but he'd given Jake quite a bit of education. Jake and his people were Roman Catholics.

"Mrs. Sweeney said she and Jake fell in love as soon as they saw each other. He wanted to marry her at once, before he went to France. You can imagine what old Fellditch thought of it. The idea of his daughter marrying a Papist publican's son nearly gave him a stroke. Jake seems to have behaved rather decently. He gave Deborah an engagement ring, asked her to try and bring the old people round, and went off to France. He got badly wounded and was in hospital for a long time. Then he came back and went to see Deborah's father. The old man literally threw him out. So Deborah and Jake got married and went to America——"

"And lived happily ever afterwards, of course," her father had suggested.

"They seem to have," Kate retorted, "judging by what she's told me. Jake seems to have been good to her. He didn't even ask her to become a Catholic. He took over the saloon when his father died and I gathered that he was up to the neck in the Prohibition racket. He was mixed up in politics, too; I don't understand all that, but apparently he was quite a noise in his party. Mrs. Sweeney said she wasn't interested in that side of his life; all she cared was that they were very happy together, though having no children was a great disappointment.

"Anyhow, when Jake died in 1939 she found herself a rich woman. They'd always lived well, but she hadn't realised that her husband was positively wealthy.

"She decided to come back to England. For some time

after her marriage she'd sent letters and cheques to her parents and her married sister, but they'd all been returned without even a word of acknowledgment, so at last she stopped writing. She wrote again when Jake died, but the letter was returned, so she knew the old people must still be alive.

"As soon as she got her husband's affairs settled she came to London and bought a big house in the Swiss Cottage district and furnished it. Her idea was that as her husband was dead her people would forgive her, and she'd be able to persuade them all to come and live with her.

"When everything was ready she went down to the village. She found her father and mother had died a month before, within a few days of each other. Her married sister wouldn't have anything to do with her, and the people she used to know had either moved away or forgotten her. So she came back to her house, not knowing what to do.

"She thought of going back to New York, where she had plenty of friends, but then the war happened.

"She did jobs of sorts for the Women's Voluntary Service, but it was when the air raids started that she really got busy. She had the cellars of her house enlarged and made as bomb-proof and comfortable as she could, and from what I could drag out of her she was rather wonderful. Anyone who had no other shelter was welcome, but she specialised in the children, especially children of poor people. Her house became something between a club and a kindergarten, and what she didn't do for them was nobody's business. Rather stout of her, I think, when she could have afforded to close the place and go and live somewhere safe.

"That gave her the idea for what she calls the Teeners. She decided that kids got into trouble of various kinds simply because they'd run wild during the war, and when it was over they couldn't find anything more amusing to do, so she started the Teeners. It's for girls and boys from thirteen to nineteen. It's not exactly a club. It hasn't got a lot of rules and regulations, and the members don't pay regular subscriptions. It doesn't matter what a Teener's parents are, or what the old people's opinions may be. The one hard and fast rule is that no Teener's may talk either religion or politics at any of the meetings. Mrs. Sweeney says those two subjects cause more quarrelling than anything else in the world."

"She's not far wrong," Ash admitted. "How do the Teeners spend their time, then?"

"They do anything they like as far as I can make out," Dermot Lloyd replied. "Kate says that Mrs. Sweeney gave up a lot of the rooms and cellars in her house and let the Teeners have them. There's table-tennis and darts and draughts and chess and so on; then there are talks on art, crafts, acting, music—all sorts of things. And there's a place where the boys can box and wrestle. All sorts of people give their services, of course, free. But the Teeners are encouraged to run their own shows themselves, as far as they can."

"It sounds very nice," Ash commented, "but who pays for it?"

"Mrs. Sweeney started it, but now there are quite a lot of branches. Suppose they want to open a club-room in White-chapel, or Paddington, or somewhere else: they scout round and find some tradesman or someone else who's got a spare basement or an empty room in a shop or a house. Mrs. Sweeney refuses to have anything to do with money, except what she gives herself. A bank manager is the honorary treasurer, there's an honorary auditor who keeps the accounts, and a committee decides how money is to be spent. When the thing was in full swing Mrs. Sweeney decided to take a rest. She wanted to be among her own people, but not in North Wales. That's why she came down here. Upon my word," the solicitor added, laughing, as the car stopped at his door, "I've been talking about her almost as much as Kate does. But we're great gossips in this part of the world, Mr. Ash!"

Ash had been mildly interested, but his object in going to Pentref was to see Kate Dermot Lloyd, not Mrs. Sweeney, so he was not too pleased when, having arrived at the house, he was shown into the drawing-room and found them both there.

Kate Dermot Lloyd was what he had once overheard his susceptible assistant, Detective-Inspector Bob York, describe as definitely decorative. She was below middle height, but her figure was good and she moved with the easy grace acquired from athletics and perfected by drill in her army service in the A.T.S., as it then was. Her hair was red gold and her eyes were brown with green flecks, and Ash decided that Upwey, Trevone and other suitors had good cause for their rivalry.

As to Mrs. Sweeney, he had drawn his own mental picture of that lady and it was not a flattering one.

He had imagined an imperious person with a loud voice, wearing too smart clothes and too many jewels. To his surprise, he found himself being received by a pleasant woman in a plain black dress, who welcomed him with a simple courtesy that was not without dignity. She was still apple-cheeked, though there were grey threads in her dark hair; her mouth was firm but humorous; her grey eyes were shrewd behind gold-rimmed spectacles; her wedding-ring and wrist-watch were of gold, but her only other ornament was a diamond clip at her throat. She had never, he found presently, quite lost the carefully acquired precision of pupil-teacher days, but had added a hint of American accent and phraseology; the mixturè might have been revolting, but was in fact oddly attractive.

Ash made a conventional apology for his intrusion, but said pointedly that he had come to see Miss Dermot Lloyd.

"I know," that young lady replied curtly. "Daddy 'phoned me. But I've nothing to say that Mrs. Sweeney can't hear."

"All the same, my dear," Mrs. Sweeney remarked, "it's not my affair, and I guess Mr. Ash'd rather talk to you alone."

She began to gather up her knitting, but Ash interposed:

"Please don't let me disturb you. Miss Dermot Lloyd can please herself."

Mrs. Sweeney nodded and began to knit with a speed that astonished the superintendent.

Kate pointed to a chair, waited until Ash had seated himself and said:

"Daddy told me you'd probably ask me a lot of questions. I suppose it's what you call the third degree, isn't it?"

Mrs. Sweeney looked at her and then at Ash; she did not speak, but the rhythm of her clicking needles seemed to accelerate a little.

"We don't use that expression or that method at Scotland Yard," Ash replied mildly. "Perhaps I'd better explain. I've been sent here to assist the Treporth police in their inquiries about the murder of Detective-Sergeant Upwey. The people I've seen so far have been very willing to help. Your father seemed to think you'd be equally willing, but there's no reason why you should discuss the matter if you'd rather not."

He half rose, but Mrs. Sweeney waved him back into his chair.

"Stay right here, Mr. Ash," she said. "What's gotten into you, Kate? If you must be rude to this gentleman you can take him outside, but you're not going to do it in my house."

Kate took it well.

"I'm sorry," she said. "It was a rotten thing to say, and I apologise. Only——"

"I know," Ash put in as she stopped abruptly. "It's very unpleasant for you, and you feel you've been badgered enough already. Isn't that it?"

"Not quite," she answered with the ghost of a smile. "Inspector Hughes didn't badger me; he was really very kind. Forget it, please. What do you want to know?"

"Anything you can tell me. I'd like to have your own account of what happened at the Sports Club on Saturday."

The girl thought for a moment. Then she began what was obviously a carefully colourless recital of the events which had preceded the murder of Guy Upwey.

Ash, listening automatically checking her statement point by point, found himself watching with a sort of fascination Mrs. Sweeney's nimble fingers, and the man's sock that seemed to grow rather than be knitted by her long needles. The foot and ankle were of a plain dark brown wool, but the top was being finished in a pattern of gay colours. A completed sock which lay beside her had a similarly variegated top, but although the pattern was similar it was not quite the same.

When Kate had finished what she had to say there was a short silence. Ash reflected that she was the first of Miles Trevone's friends who had not assured him of the young man's innocence.

"Thank you," he said. "Trevone and Upwey were old friends of yours, I believe?"

"Yes. I'd known them since we were all children."

"Coming to the present time, were they friendly with each other, as well as with you?" The girl did not reply at once and he went on, "I'm sorry if it sounds impertinent, but I must ask you plainly—were they jealous of each other about you?"

She answered steadily: "They both wanted to marry me, if that's what you mean. I hadn't given either of them any promise. I—well, I hadn't made up my mind. There was plenty of time," she added defensively.

"After you left the stage and were back in the bar, did either of them speak to you?"

"No—and it was just as well!"

"Why?"

"Well, I was very angry and I'd probably have told them so."

"Both of them?"

"Of course," she declared. "Guy was very—very silly, but there was no need for Miles to make a scene about it. If it hadn't been for Mr. Fersen things might have been much worse."

Ash, considering his next question, absently put a hand in his pocket, but remembered where he was and withdrew it.

Mrs. Sweeney, apparently engrossed in her work, remarked casually:

"If you'd like to smoke your pipe, we don't mind. My husband was a great smoker; he always said it helped him to think."

Ash smiled to cover his annoyance. In his lectures to C.I.D. classes he always impressed on his hearers the importance of watching other people's hands and feet, but keeping their own still, and now he had given himself away like a novice. He took out his case and offered Mrs. Sweeney a cigarette. She said she did not smoke, but Kate did.

Kate, after a moment's hesitation, accepted a cigarette.

Ash gave her a light and then made rather a business of producing his pipe and filling and lighting it. Somewhere in the back of his mind he was wondering of what Mrs. Sweeney's flying needles reminded him. It was often like that: some word or incident would nag at him until he could get back to the peace of his little bachelor flat and browse among the hundreds of books, mostly second-hand, on his shelves until he found what he wanted. He told himself sharply that Mrs. Sweeney had nothing to do with the matter in hand, and cursed himself for letting his thoughts wander. Sometimes he wondered why he had ever become a policeman when there were jobs to be had in bookshops. . . .

He turned to Kate and said abruptly:

"I believe you've been told that you may be required to give evidence at the trial?"

"Yes, they did tell me—but I was hoping I wouldn't have to."

"So does Mr. Trevone."

She caught her breath. "Did he tell you that?"

"Yes. I was talking to him half an hour ago. He asked me to go and see him, and your father was present."

"Was he——?" she began. She stopped, but her tone told Ash all he wanted to know. She loved Miles Trevone.

"He was quite cheerful," he lied, knowing that her father would not contradict that when he told her about the interview, "but he said it would be horrible for you to have to appear in court, and he wanted the police to promise not to call you as a witness. We wouldn't give him any promise, but we'll pass on his request to the people who decide such things. He also assured me he was innocent. Nearly all his friends have told me the same thing—*nearly* all," he added deliberately.

The girl flushed. "There's no need for me to tell you that," she said proudly. "When I said that about going to court I only meant that I can't see how I can help. Daddy said I'd be called for the prosecution, and I know enough about the law to know what a Crown Counsel can do with a witness."

Ash privately agreed, but he could not admit it officially.

"You can rely on the judge to see that Mr. Trevone gets a fair trial," he said formally, but something in his manner made the girl flash him a look of grateful surprise.

"I suppose I mustn't ask you——?" she began.

"No, I'm afraid not," he interrupted gently, as he stood up. "Thank you for being so patient——"

"Does that mean," Mrs. Sweeney put in, "that the third degree is finished?"

"Yes," Ash smiled. "I forgot to bring my rubber truncheon, so I can't use it."

"Then it's time we relaxed. I don't smoke, but I do drink, and I'm parched right now. Ring the bell, Kate."

"Thank you very much," the superintendent demurred, "but I'm afraid I——"

"Now, don't give me that stuff about being on duty," she broke in, laughing. "Where I came from, the Homicide Squad would have been counting the bottles in the cellar by this time. But you've admitted you're through with Kate, and I'll certainly be real hurt if you won't be my personal guest for five minute ."

"If you put it that way——" Ash said, amused by her manner.

A maid, apparently instructed beforehand, came in with a tray of bottles and glasses.

Ash chose sherry; Mrs. Sweeney followed suit; Kate, who officiated, had a gin and lime.

"I've never seen anyone knit so fast," Ash remarked, partly to make conversation and partly because he meant it.

Mrs. Sweeney looked pleased, and Kate said:

"Mrs. Sweeney knits socks and sweaters and things and sends them to people who need them. She's always doing kind things, you know."

"I've heard," Ash remarked, "that she did some very brave and kind things before she came here."

Mrs. Sweeney emptied her glass and held it out to Kate to be refilled.

"Listen, Mr. Ash," she said, "I don't want you to get the idea that I was a great and noble woman leading a great and noble crusade. I'm not like that. I just thought it'd be a good idea to get hold of some of the tough youngsters before they got so tough they'd have to be pounded. If it hadn't been for other people who turned my idea into a practical scheme, there wouldn't be any Teeners today.

"I wish I could have stayed with the crowd, but I'm not as young as I used to be, so I left the job to people who could handle it properly. I take a look at them now and then, but I'm going to end my days here. I'm as snug as a bug in a rug, thanks to Kate and her father. Must you really go?" for Ash had risen again. "I'll be glad to have my driver take you back to Treporth if it's any help."

"Thank you very much, but I've got a police car waiting outside."

"Kate, will you tell Mr. Ash's man he's just coming?" When the girl had left the room she said: "I'm certainly grateful to you for the way you handled this. Kate's crazy about Miles Trevone, though she wouldn't tell you so. Personally, I don't like to think he did it, but that's your worry, and I've lived long enough to learn to mind my own business. I just want to say you'll certainly be welcome here any time you come. And if you're not married, let me know when you want a pair of socks. I'll think out a special pattern for you!"

CHAPTER VI

Ash drove back to Treporth in the comfortable anticipation of a good dinner followed by a quiet evening with a book he had brought with him.

His day had not been wasted for he had conscientiously verified the statements in the *dossier* of the case, and had met the people principally concerned in it. He had not made any sensational discovery, but he had not expected to do so. It seemed to him that Hughes had prepared his case very well. It was true that the inspector had failed to observe the rifling marks on the bullet, but no doubt it would have been given a more expert examination before the trial. Such a point would hardly have been overlooked by the prosecution in preparing the case against Trevone.

On the face of it, the prosecution's case seemed to be as perfect as a case founded on circumstantial evidence could be, and circumstantial evidence was often the best.

And yet he was not satisfied.

Like most people concerned with the administration of justice, he was always a little afraid of the easy case. The more flawless it appeared, the more likely it was to contain some horrid little flaw which the eagle eyes of the police and the staff of the Director of Public Prosecutions had unaccountably missed. He was thankful that it was his business to deal with facts, but not to draw the brief for Crown Counsel.

Apart from that, now that he had spoken to Miles Trevone he understood why that young man's friends so vehemently declared that he was incapable of committing such a crime. To say that Trevone was not the murderer type would be absurd. Ash knew well enough that the killer could not be classified. The forger, the burglar, the pickpocket, the confidence man —they could generally be relied on to stick to their own line of business. The murderer was unpredictable. He remembered one young soldier who had murdered and mutilated four women with appalling savagery; yet his previous record had been admirable, he had been marked for promotion as intelligent and well-behaved, and Ash himself had been struck by the youth's quiet and polite bearing when he was arrested. The defence could find no reason to plead insanity, and the young man died on the gallows.

Trevone was certainly excitable, and he was still suffering from war strain, but while that might suggest the killing of a rival in a fit of jealous anger, it did not fit into the picture of a crime which was at least cleverly planned, if not so perfectly carried out as to avert all suspicion from the criminal.

But not one of Trevone's friends, not even Kate Dermot Lloyd, could do more than affirm belief in his innocence; not one of them could produce a single fact that the cleverest defending counsel could use to establish it.

Ash felt rather sorry for Kate. He had a great capacity for putting himself in the other fellow's place—too great, he sometimes thought—and he could imagine that she was torturing herself with the idea that she was already indirectly responsible for one death, and might soon be equally responsible for another. It was irrational, of course; but then, people often became irrational under the stress of emotion. He was glad for the motherless girl's sake that she had the support of Mrs. Jake Sweeney. That lady struck him, even on so short an acquaintance, as possessing the uncommon attribute of common sense. An amusing woman, too, with her knitting and her Yankee-Welsh phraseology. She seemed to have done a good job in London during the air raids; he decided, as a matter of interest, to inquire about that when he got back to London. . . .

Arrived at the hotel, he ate his dinner at a small table the waiter had tactfully reserved for him. He had his book beside him, for he delighted in the evil practice of reading at meals.

After dinner he found a corner in the half-empty lounge, ordered coffee, and settled down with his pipe.

When the superintendent went to his own bed of a night he never knew in what part of the country his next night would be spent. He kept a suit-case packed in readiness for an unexpected journey, and years of experience had taught him to reduce its contents to the most useful minimum, but whatever else it might lack, it was never without at least a couple of books. One of these might be new to him, and therefore possibly disappointing; the other would be an old friend with which he could have the delicious sensation of savouring in advance a favourite passage on the next page. Most of his library he had acquired by patient prowling among dusty shops, and he proposed, before he left Treporth, to manage an hour or so in those back streets likely to contain hidden treasures within his modest means.

The book he was re-reading this evening was the Erckmann-Chatrian collaboration in *The Story of a Peasant*. He was deep in that enthralling prose picture of France's revolutionary agonies when he suddenly put down the book and gave one of his rare, quiet, laughs.

He had captured the thought which had evaded him while he watched Mrs. Jake Sweeney at work on her sock: it was the thought of the Parisian hags knitting while they watched with savage satisfaction aristocratic heads falling under the knife of the guillotine. It was indeed ridiculous to compare such bloodthirsty females with the grey-haired woman in her simple black dress, but the association in his subconscious mind was obvious. It was just one more example, he thought, of how strangely the mind could work, and how amazingly one portion of it seemed able to detach itself and follow a side path while another portion plodded steadily along the main road of investigation.

He relit his pipe and returned to the affairs of Michel and Marguerite, Maître Jean and the Deputy Chauvel.

It was nearly ten o'clock when the night porter, approaching reverently, announced that Colonel Bassenthwaite wished to speak to him on the telephone.

Ash sighed, thinking wistfully of the bed to which he would soon have retired. The Chief Constable, he knew, would not have called him up unless there had been some important development.

He took the call in a soundproof box near the reception office.

"Sorry to bother you at this hour," the colonel said. "Hope you hadn't gone to bed? . . . Good. Look here, Ash, an extraordinary thing's happened. A man's offered to make a voluntary statement about Trevone. If what I'm told he says is true, it puts Trevone in the clear and we'll have to drop the case against him."

"That's interesting, sir. I'll come round at once. The man's at the station, I suppose?"

C

"No, he's in jail."

"In jail? But——"

"I think it'll save time if I keep the explanations until I see you. I'm sending a car for you."

"Does Dermot Lloyd know about this?"

"Oh yes, we've told him. He'll be there, and Morris and Hughes and Uncle Tom Cobley and all!" the colonel said, chuckling. "It'll be quite a gathering. See you presently, then."

By the time Ash had put away his book and put on his hat and coat the police car had arrived. He got in and was soon at the massive gates of the prison.

He was taken to the deputy-governor's room (the governor was away on leave) where he found an imposing assemblage and an atmosphere of suppressed excitement. In addition to the deputy governor there were the Chief Constable, Superintendent Morris, Inspector Hughes, Mr. Dermot Lloyd, and Mr. Bryn Jenkins, the solicitor who had appeared for the police when Miles Trevone was brought before the magistrates and remanded. There was also a young constable, armed with fountain-pen and note-book and panting to take a shorthand note of the proceedings.

The deputy governor opened the proceedings with a dispassionate air compounded of a judge charging a jury and a spectator watching a football match between teams in which he has no personal interest.

"I dined out this evening," he said, "and on my return, about an hour ago, I was informed by the principal prison officer that a remand prisoner named James Higgins had asked to see me about what he said was a matter of life and death. Such requests are not uncommon," he went on drily. "I asked whether the man was ill, but was told that he was not."

"Excuse me, sir," Ash said. "May I ask you to repeat the man's name?"

"Higgins—James Higgins."

"A smalltime crook, sneak thief and that," Superintendent Morris put in. "Been hanging about the town for some time. Cockney, by his talk. We pulled him in on Saturday night on suspicion of loitering near enclosed premises with intent to commit a felony, and he was remanded on Monday morning for inquiries."

Ash nodded, and the deputy governor resumed:

"I sent for Higgins. He told me he was prepared to swear that he was in the company of Miles Trevone during the time when, as I understand, Trevone is alleged to have murdered Detective-Sergeant Upwey. Higgins said he was willing to make a full statement even if it should affect his own case. As Trevone was not in custody when Higgins was arrested, I asked Higgins how he knew what happened to Trevone. He declined," said the deputy governor with a faint smile, "to tell me."

There was a general laugh, for everyone present knew of the 'grapevine' by which news passes in prisons almost as freely as outside, though the recipient usually knows better than to disclose the identity of his informant; if he does not, he runs the risk of having his face pushed in at the first convenient opportunity.

"I told Higgins that I would inform the police, and sent him back to his cell. I then telephoned to the Chief Constable, and he decided to ask you other gentlemen to meet him and hear whatever statement Higgins may wish to make."

The deputy governor leaned back and gazed at the ceiling, as one who had correctly adjusted the scales of justice and now left it to others to disturb their balance.

Colonel Bassenthwaite tipped the merest suspicion of a wink to Ash, and said formally:

"Thank you. If no one has any other suggestion to make, I think we may ask the deputy governor to have Higgins brought in?"

No one had any other suggestion to make so they all nodded solemnly. Ash caught himself thinking that it was rather like the moment when the conjurer is about to open the box through which he has apparently sawn the beautiful lady in halves.

The deputy governor lifted his telephone and gave an order.

Presently the door opened and a prison officer ushered in a short, slim individual with unusually small hands and feet, whose appearance suggested a ferret dressed in a man's clothes.

"James Higgins, sir," announced the prison officer.

The deputy governor nodded to the officer, who left the room.

"Sit down, Higgins," he said, pointing to a chair which had been placed in readiness.

Mr. Higgins jerked him something between a bow and a nod, and looked round the half circle of faces. When he saw Ash he started.

"So this is where you've got to, Snake," the superintendent said affably. "We wondered what had become of you. Thought you'd have a little country air for a change, eh?"

Jimmy Higgins, known professionally as 'Snake' because of the ease with which he could introduce his supple body through astonishingly small openings, grinned.

"Evening, Mr. Ash," he replied. "Hope you're keeping well, sir."

The colonel whispered to the deputy governor, then nodded to Superintendent Morris.

"Higgins," said the superintendent, "we've been told that you wish to make a statement about a certain matter. I am now going to caution you. You have been remanded on a charge of loitering near enclosed premises with intent to commit a felony. I now warn you that you are not obliged to make any statement; if you do so, what you say will be taken down in writing, and may be used in evidence. Do you clearly understand?"

"That's all right with me, Guv'nor," Snake replied cheerfully, as one to whom all this was *vieux jeu*. "That's what I've come 'ere for. I knows my rights, but when it comes to seein' a bloke swing for a murder what he didn't do, then to hell with my rights, if you'll excuse me usin' the expression."

"The deputy governor has told me what you said to him," Colonel Bassenthwaite Lake interposed, "but we've got to get it down on paper for the record. You heard what Superintendent Morris said and you understand that what you say may or may not affect your own case. Now it's up to you, so go ahead, if you want to."

"It's like this 'ere, Guv," Snake explained. "When I 'appened to find out"—he cocked a sly eye at the deputy governor—"that Mr. Trevone 'ad been pinched for doin' in the cop, I began a-thinking. Now, I knows Mr. Trevone—at least, I knows of him. A real gent, he is, and didn't he get the D.F.C. in the war? That's something, that is. Me, I did my bit o' service, too, but all I got was a month in the glasshouse

for pastin' a bleedin' corporal who tried to get orf with a broad
I was stuck on at the time. Fat lot o' good that did me, too;
she took up with a R.E. bloke while I was doin' my time. But
that was all this side of the drink and it don't signify. It was
when I was in France and Germany that I knew what we
blokes down below owed to the R.A.F. upstairs—blokes like
Mr. Trevone. And beside that, I 'ad what you might call a
personal reason for feeling I owed him a good turn."

He paused.

"What's all this got to do with the charge against
Trevone?" Morris asked sharply.

"That's what I'm a-comin' to, Guv," the little man replied.
"Can I take the liberty of arstin' a question?"

"What is it?"

"I've got an idea," Snake said cautiously, "that Mr.
Trevone says he went home from the Sports Club by way of
the main road, but there's them that says he went by the cliff
road. Is that right?"

"Yes. Why?"

"Well, I *knows* he's speaking the truth, Guv."

"How do you know?"

"Because I seen him, that's how I knows, and I'll swear it
on the Book, if you've got one handy."

The colonel, Morris and Ash were sitting together; after
whispered consultation the colonel said:

"That is a very important statement, Higgins. You're too
old a hand to need reminding that perjury is a grave offence,
even if it's—er—meant well. These officers agree with me that
you'd better say what you want to say without any questions
from us, unless they're necessary to make things clear."

"Right, sir. I'm a-goin' to tell you the truth, the whole
truth, and nothing but the truth, as the sayin' is. Blimey, I've
heard that one often enough," Mr. Higgins remarked, feelingly.

"It was like this 'ere," he went on. "Late Saturday afternoon I started out to go to Pentref. I didn't go by bus because
I didn't want any Nosy-Parker conductor remembering
having seen me. All right. So I'm nearly at the Sports Club
when I sees Mr. Trevone come out. I 'angs back a bit, not
wishing to be noticed, but he don't seem like he's noticing
anybody. He turns up the main road and pelts along like he's
training for a walking race. I'm following about fifty yards

behind, thinking it's a regular coincidence that we're both
going the same way at that particular time. A few cars pass
us, but we don't meet no one on foot. Mr. Trevone don't take
no notice of the cars, though one of 'em runs him pretty
close. So on we goes, like we was on a route march and expectin'
a ruddy general to pop out of the hedge at any time. Mr.
Trevone turns off at the side road leading to Pentref and I
does likewise.

"We skirts the village and comes out on the cliff road up
by his house. He opens the door, goes in, and bangs the door
shut. I 'angs about a bit, thinking he may have gone in to
fetch something, and be coming out again, but he doesn't.
Then the bloke and his wife what keeps house for Mr. Trevone
turns up from the village and goes into the house. I waits a
bit, sees there's nothin' doing, and goes and has a pint in a
boozer in the village. I stays there a bit, chewin' the fat with
one or two in the bar. Then I starts to go 'ome. On my way,
I stops to look at a house what an old lady has took. It's a
nice house and I'm admiring it, like, when a rozzer comes up
and pinches me. That's all, gents, but you can arst me any
questions you like. I ain't keepin' nothing back when Mr.
Trevone's life may 'ang on it."

There was a short silence. Then Ash said:

"You say you were on your way to Pentref when you first
saw Trevone. Are you willing to tell us why you were going
there?"

"I was going to do a job there, Mr. Ash," Snake answered
shortly.

"To put it plainly for the record, do you mean you were
going——?"

"I was going to get into a house," Higgins broke in with a
hint of impatience, "and it was Mr. Trevone's house, if you
want to know. I knew the servants would be at the flicks, and
I didn't think Mr. Trevone'd leave the club quite so early."

"You seem to know the place pretty well."

"'Course I do! Didn't I do a job there once before? Only I
had to do a bunk before I got anything much. Mr. Trevone's
got some nice stuff there, too," Snake added wistfully.

"It *was* you, was it?" Inspector Hughes put in.

"Yes, but I didn't leave no dabs for you to find, Mr.
Hughes," the little man grinned.

"What did you do with the air pistol, boy?" Hughes asked casually, but Snake sensed the keen interest with which the others waited for his reply.

"I didn't 'arm no one with it," he answered uneasily. "I thought it'd come in 'andy for a bit of rabbiting some day."

"Listen, Snake," said Ash gravely. "This is more serious than you know. No one suggests that you shot anybody, but that pistol may be very important to Trevone, and we want it. Have you still got it?"

"Yes, Guv. It's in my room in a house not five minutes' walk from 'ere. You can 'ave it if you go there. The key of the room's with the other stuff they took off of me when I came 'ere. The house——"

"I know where you live," Hughes interrupted.

It was arranged that Hughes should obtain the key from the officer who had charge of prisoners' property, and go to the house where Snake rented a room.

When the inspector had gone the deputy governor remarked:

"I think this is where the chairman might say, 'Gentlemen, you may smoke.'"

Unexpectedly he took a cigarette from his case and tossed it to Mr. Higgins, who caught it neatly. The deputy governor, Snake told himself in amazement, was a 'uman being after all! And Superintendent Morris gave him a light.

The police officers and the two solicitors went into a huddle. Then the colonel walked over to Higgins.

"Look here," he said bluffly, "I'm going to say something that won't be put on the record. You've done a decent thing, Higgins. You know very well I haven't the power to make any promises, or to keep them if I did, but we shan't forget this. We'll see that the—er—proper authorities are told about it. Damn it, man, I don't want to preach, but you did your bit in the war. Since then your record stinks, but if you want to go straight when you've had whatever may be coming to you, we'll see that you get a damn good chance to do it."

Snake met his gaze without flinching.

"Thanks, Guv," he said quietly. "I'll think about it."

The others chatted desultorily for what seemed a long time, but was really a short one.

Then Hughes came back, and Snake watched curiously

while the police officers examined as well as they could, under the desk-light, the Webley air pistol he had brought with him.

After a further consultation the deputy governor rang his bell and a prison officer came in.

"Higgins is not feeling very well," the deputy governor said. "Take him back to his cell. It's nothing serious, but see that he's comfortable, will you?"

Whatever that talismanic phrase signified in prison language, the prison officer replied smartly:

"Very good, sir," but he exchanged a grin with Snake as he motioned to him to follow.

Snake, passing Inspector Hughes, whispered:

"Wot abaht the other things in my room?"

"I didn't have time to look, boy *bach*," the inspector replied.

Snake chuckled as he went out.

The shorthand writer having been sent off to type out his notes for approval and signature, the others let their hair down.

The deputy governor relaxed, produced a bottle from his cupboard, and sent for additional glasses.

"Well," the colonel said, "that seems to be that. What do you think, Jenkins?"

The police-solicitor, a dapper man regarded as the cleverest criminal lawyer and the best judge of port in local legal circles, shook his head.

"We've had it," he answered. "You'll have to withdraw the case, Colonel. Even if we went to court, no jury would convict in face of what Higgins has told us."

"I agree," the colonel declared.

Ash whispered to the deputy governor, who nodded, took him to the door, and pointed down the corridor.

"Then I suppose you don't object if we tell Trevone now?" Dermot Lloyd asked.

"Of course not," Jenkins agreed. "We'll have him brought up immediately the court opens tomorrow, and I'll formally withdraw the charge."

"Thanks, but something ought to be said about the police being fully satisfied, and all that."

"Yes, that's only fair, don't you think so, Colonel?"

"Certainly, and I'm damn glad the boy's out of it—though it means we've got to start all over again."

"I'm glad, too, sir," Morris observed, "for young Trevone's sake; but as it seems he couldn't have done it, someone must have tried to frame him."

Bryn Jenkins frowned. "It certainly looks like it," he said, "but I can't see any reason for it. There was a definite motive in the quarrel between Trevone and Upwey, but once you take that away, what have you left?"

"I don't know," Morris retorted, "but nobody does anything without a motive, and when we find the motive we'll find the man."

"Or the woman," Inspector Hughes murmured.

"The woman?" Jenkins exclaimed. "What on earth do you mean? It's not a woman's crime, man! At least," he added uncertainly, "it doesn't look like one."

"I was only thinking that anything's possible until it's proved to be impossible," Hughes answered. "I am not saying it's likely."

"Well, thank goodness, it's a job for you, not for me."

"And for Mr. Ash," said Morris, as the Yard man came in from the corridor.

"I think," the deputy governor put in, "we're rather forgetting the person most concerned. I don't suppose Trevone is sleeping very soundly."

He was right.

When the door of his cell was unlocked Miles Trevone sat up in his bed and stared at them in dismay. He had been dreaming that he was in a condemned cell and the prison governor had come to tell him that a petition for his reprieve had been dismissed.

"It's all right, Miles," said Dermot Lloyd. "Good news, my boy. Fresh evidence has turned up and the case is being withdrawn. You'll be discharged tomorrow."

Miles rubbed his eyes.

"Thank God!" he muttered.

There ensued polite congratulations.

The deputy governor, an observer by experience and inclination, had not failed to notice the young man's shaking hands.

"We keep early hours here," he said. "Mr. Trevone will be up with the lark, so shall we leave him to enjoy what I hope will be a better night's sleep than he's had lately?"

Dermot Lloyd was leading a tactful laugh when Trevone
drew him aside.

"You'll let Kate know?" he begged.

Superintendent Ash was standing behind them.

"I had occasion to speak to Miss Dermot Lloyd on the
telephone a few minutes ago," he said, "and I told her what
had happened. I thought she might be interested."

CHAPTER VII

WHILE Superintendent Ash was pondering the Welsh idiom,
and the problem of who had killed Guy Upwey, in London
things were happening in which, although he did not know it,
he was soon to be very much interested.

Among other people who were also to be surprised and
interested was a certain Mr. Barnabas Darley Kair, Doctor of
Philosophy, Bachelor of Arts and Science, and bachelor
resident in Canton Court, a large block of flats in the crowded
north-western area bounded on three sides by Edgware Road,
Marylebone Road and Regent's Park.

Barnabas Kair was something of an enigma to most
people who knew him; but then, very few people could claim
to know him really well. Aged fifty, he was tall and spare. His
clean-shaven, sallowish face was long, with high cheekbones,
straight nose and wide mouth. His hair was grey, and over his
lustrous dark eyes heavy black brows almost met in a level
line.

Schooled at Marlborough, he went up to Oxford, where he
caused no stir either in academic or other circles. The few
people to whom he accorded more than the slightest acquaintanceship declared that he was shy and eccentric; the rest
said he was just damned lazy.

None of these descriptions was, in fact, wholly justified.

Kair was reticent, but rather self-sufficient than selfish. He
made few friends; and yet, oddly enough, he was not un-
popular.

Some years after he had left the university his widowed
father died. It was a heavy blow, for they had enjoyed a rare
intimacy of companionship. Kair, who knew of no living

relatives, stayed on for a time in the old house in St. John's Wood, but when Canton Court opened he moved there with Cradoc, his butler-valet, and Mrs. Cradoc, his housekeeper, both of whom had been with his father for many years.

The elder Kair had been wealthy, and even now, with post-war taxation, his son had no financial worries to distract him from his labours. He had never married; women he regarded as interesting—and sometimes amusing, though more often rather unpleasant—studies in emotionalism, a view that did not greatly endear him to the opposite sex.

While he was still at Oxford he became interested in sociological problems, and when he came down from Oxford his father encouraged him to continue. A few tentative articles he wrote were readily published, and his first book, *The Mind of the Misfit*, made his name. It was an unexpectedly popular success because its clear and simple style appealed to the man in the street, and even some eminent alienists and expensive psycho-analysts grudgingly admitted that a few of his ideas were worthy of consideration. *The Cruelty of Crime* and other books followed and Kair was repeatedly offered lecture tours and radio broadcasts. To the agony of his literary agent he refused to be lionised.

When the spirit moved him he worked furiously; when it did not, he drank.

For weeks he would work almost day and night; revising and polishing half a dozen times what he had written; sleeping at odd hours and disregarding mealtimes until he was almost forcibly fed by his exasperated housekeeper.

The work done, he would sink into an apathy lightened at intervals by a game of bridge, but more often darkened by long bouts of steady drinking during which he was never quite drunk and never completely sober. He would consume with equal readiness wine in a West End club or beer in a riverside pub, listening with silent courtesy to the conversation of his neighbours. He was never violent or offensive in his cups, but there were moments when he was uneasily conscious of a sudden cold anger for which he was unable to account and which he subdued with difficulty.

He presented to himself a problem as interesting as any of those he described in his writings, but for which he had so far failed to find a solution. . . .

Kair had read the authoritative literature of criminology, and a good deal of more speculative matter as well, because the mentality of the criminal must necessarily enter largely into any study of the nature of human society and the laws governing its development. His interest was not in crime as such, but in its effects on those who committed it, gained or suffered by it, or were concerned with its investigation.

Rejected for active service owing to defective sight—he wore horn-rimmed spectacles with thick lenses—he had at first worked as a cipher clerk in Military Intelligence during the war, but had soon been entrusted with duties of an equally confidential but considerably more responsible kind.

It was while he was with M.I. that Kair first met George Muir. He had taken a liking to the well-dressed and well-mannered policeman who was doing *liaison* work between the Yard and the Service departments. The fact that both had been Marlborough boys, though at different times, was an unexpected link. Also, both played good bridge.

Muir, the son of a Wiltshire doctor, had not been sufficiently attracted by medicine to qualify and eventually take over the comfortable country practice. Entering the Metropolitan police force, he had done his preliminary training at Peel House and tramped a constable's beat until his chance came to transfer to the detective branch. He climbed by the hard road, and when he became a detective-superintendent he was the youngest officer of that rank in the C.I.D. records.

Muir's introductions to colleagues and other people had helped Kair a good deal when he was able to take up his private work again.

That evening Kair had dined alone in his flat.

He drank half a bottle of Burgundy with the meal and a glass of port after it, and he had two brandies with his coffee in the lounge. He picked up a new book which he had promised to review for one of the quarterly magazines, but after turning a few pages he found that he was merely reading the words without appreciating their value.

It was not the effect of the wine; he had often taken as much and then worked on a book or an article until the small hours.

He was restless. Putting down the book, he rang for Cradoc.

"I'm going for a walk," he said. "If anyone telephones, say you don't know when I'll be back."

Cradoc went out, and returned with hat, stick and a light overcoat.

"What the devil do you think I want with a coat on a night like this?" Kair demanded irritably.

"You'll probably be late," the imperturbable butler responded. "Ne'er shed a clout till May be out."

Cradoc's addiction to *clichés* was incurable.

Kair shrugged, took the hat and stick, and went out.

It was a fine night, with the comfortable warmth that the middle of an English May sometimes brings.

Kair liked walking, especially by night. He was not particularly fond of the countryside, but he would stroll for hours through the streets of any city; if they were thronged, he studied the people in them; if empty, he peopled them and their buildings with characters he imagined.

Sometimes, too, when he had sat at his desk for hours, trying to express a nebulous idea in precise terms, he would throw down his pen, go out, and tramp until the right words came to him.

Leaving Canton Court by a back door provided for the convenience of tenants who kept their cars in the big underground garage beneath the Jade wing (each wing of the block bore an Eastern name), he cut through side streets and emerged into Marylebone Road. Turning right, he came presently to Edgware Road and followed that broad thoroughfare to Hyde Park.

He went into the park and loitered for a few minutes, watching one of the hoarse-voiced orators lashing himself into a frenzy over the iniquity of his favourite political villain; then he turned away and took the broad path leading to Kensington Gardens.

After walking steadily for some time he left the sylvan scene, crossed the Bayswater Road near Queensway, and entered the area of bomb-damaged streets and squares that lay between the gardens and Paddington railway station.

In a once fashionable but now shabby square stood a tall old house; on the pillars of its porch were painted the words

LIBERATION CLUB

The house, abandoned by its owner at the beginning of the war, had been requisitioned and used as something between a clearing-house and a social centre for foreign refugees. Several exiled governments had allotted such funds as they could and the British authorities and public had been generous, and the centre had become so popular that it was eventually established as a club and allowed to continue its existence when the war ended.

It was a place of many tongues and much tolerance; a neutral ground on which Christian and Jew, Moslem and Greek Orthodox wrangled without rancour over the problems of their countries and of the world. There was only one qualification without which no man or woman was admitted to membership, and it was the link that bound them together; their avowed and implacable hatred of Communism. They loathed and feared the Red Wolves—as they called the men in the Kremlin—even more bitterly than they had formerly loathed and feared the Fascists or Nazis under whose rule so many of them or their friends had suffered.

There was also a handful of honorary members, chiefly government officials who had been concerned with supervision of the original centre, and sympathisers—of whom Kair was one—who had contributed to its funds.

For a considerable time, however, the Liberation Club, to give it its new name, had been a registered and self-supporting institution. It possessed a committee, solemnly elected by the members, but no committeeman would have dreamed of interfering in the management or of disputing the authority of the secretary, manager, and general master of the revels, Pasquale Vico.

Most *maîtres d'hotel* like to be known by their first name; perhaps it was for that reason that Vico preferred to use his second. Vico liked to be different.

Few people even knew his first name. "That jolly little fat Italian," they called him, but in fact he had been born in Corsica. He had lived in half a dozen countries and spoke as many languages with fluent inaccuracy. He had been sailor, steward, barman, waiter, restaurant manager, and several other things, including smuggler. He was cheerfully unscrupulous, but his code forbade him to cheat his employer so long as his salary was paid. His flair for management had cleared the debts of the club and turned it into a profitable concern.

Kair left his hat and stick in the cloakroom and went downstairs. Almost the whole basement had been made into one room, with a bar at one end, a dais at the other, and tables surrounding a strip of floor left free for dancers. The walls had been decorated by artistic members, each section representing a scene from the painter's native land.

He sat down at a table in a recess near the bar. There were not many people in the room; a few were eating a late dinner or an early supper, and two or three couples moved slowly to the gentle music of the small orchestra on the dais. There were other people in the rooms reserved for those who wished to read, write, or play chess or cards, but as a rule the club was not crowded until later in the evening.

Kair lit a cigarette and began to drink the tankard of beer he had ordered. He felt pleasantly tired, and his surroundings were restful. Vico knew exactly how much light a room needed, and had explained acidly to his orchestra that they could produce agreeable music without necessarily making a loud noise.

"Good evening, Vico," said Kair, as the secretary appeared at his table.

Vico had a way of appearing from nowhere in particular, as though he had reversed the Indian rope trick.

Vico, bowing and smiling, was enchanted to see again so valued a member as Mr. Kair after an absence of—yes, truly, it was almost four weeks. And Mr. Kair kept himself well? That was very good. A little supper? A lobster, with a glass of white wine? . . . Mr. Kair had already dined? *Bien!* Later, perhaps, a Welsh rarebit . . . ah, a party arrived. Mr. Kair would excuse him for an instant. . . .

Kair was surprised that the party was being introduced by Meg Milcote, whom he knew slightly. Then he remembered that her uncle, Mr. Alfred Ingrow, had had some official connection with the place in its earlier days, and no doubt he and his family had been made honorary members. Ingrow's widowed sister, Mrs. Agatha Milcote, shared his Canton Court flat and kept house for him.

Meg had brought her brother Jack, and two other men and a couple of girls whose appearance suggested the art student.

Vico received them as though they had been Royal Acade-
micians of royal blood and began to exhibit with pride the
decorated walls.

Kair rose as they reached his table, and was introduced.

"I'm showing them the murals," Meg explained.

"But too wonderful!" one of the girls breathed, and a youth
who appeared to eschew hairbrushes admitted that they
were really rather divine.

Jack, catching Kair's eye, grinned sourly. He was a lusty
fellow.

Vico swept them on, and when the grand tour was completed settled them at a table and signalled a waiter.

Kair watched with mild amusement as the unbrushed youth
flung back his wayward locks and oracularly expounded the
composition of the nearest mural, overriding interruption
with a *"Darlings*, how *right!* But don't you *see*——"

The room was beginning to fill now, and Meg tactfully
induced the unbrushed to lower his voice, devote himself to his
beer, and allow the conversation to become general.

Into this peaceful scene there burst a miniature cyclone.

A short, bald-headed man with a spade-shaped black beard
appeared, darted to the bar, and seized the hand of the swarthy
Basque barman.

It was Dr. Joseph Ostrod, a Pole, who also lived in Canton
Court, and he was distinctly tight. His usually dead white
cheeks were flushed and his greenish eyes bulged behind the
thick lenses of his horn-rimmed spectacles.

"Henri!" he cried, climbing on to a high stool. "Henri, my
excellent friend, I am very happy! I wish you also to be very
happy. Let us drink together your beautiful brandy. *Vite*,
Henri, *vite!*"

The Basque grinned, poured out the drink and pushed it
across the counter. For himself he half filled a glass from a
bottle of coloured water kept for such emergencies. Vico took
a poor view of employees who got drunk on duty, but allowed
them to pocket the money instead.

Ostrod drank a third of his brandy at a gulp, and hic-
coughed slightly.

"Pardon," he said gravely. "The truth is that I am very
happy, Henri."

The Basque expressed his joy at this announcement.

"Very happy," Ostrod repeated. "I wish to make everyone else happy too!"

Pivoting, he regarded the assembly.

Kair began to edge into a corner of his recess, but was too late. Ostrod caught his eye, bowed, and fell off his stool. He was up again like a bouncing ball, laughed gaily, seized his glass from the counter, and made his way to Kair's table.

"My dear Mr. Kair," he said, "I am so glad that you are here. I am very happy. Please, I wish you also to be happy and to drink with me, yes?"

"Thank you," Kair responded, concealing his annoyance, "but I've got one already. Another time, perhaps."

He was surprised. As far as he knew, Ostrod was a quiet sort of fellow. As a rule he spoke almost meticulously careful English, in a curiously low tone, but now his tongue seemed to have run away with him.

"You do not understand, _hein?_" the little man went on, swaying slightly. "But you will permit that I explain, yes? I thank you." He refreshed himself from his glass. "Listen, please. You know that I have a business of teaching languages? Very well. There is a rich man who has a daughter. I go to his house to teach her French. He is a pig and she is a cow, and both are of an incredible vulgarness. But, I ask myself, what does it matter? He pays through his pig-snout because I speak of the important people I know, and he thinks that his cow daughter will learn some good manners from me. Ah, he is vulgar," Ostrod explained, much amused, "but he is also cunning. You understand?"

"Certainly," Kair agreed.

"You understand because you are intelligent, because you have the big mind. But wait! Now I will tell you why I am so happy. This Pig-snout is a—how do you say?—he makes books."

"You mean he's an author?"

"No, no!" Ostrod was transported with merriment at the idea. "He is not like you, ha ha! He makes books on the racehorse."

"Oh, you mean a bookmaker!"

"Yes. Well, I will admit that Pig-snout has his moments of generosity. A week ago I am at his house. He offers me a glass of brandy. It is a good brandy. I accept. I perceive that he is a little _tête montée_. He explains that he has had a good time—a good day. He has made very much money."

Ostrod emptied his glass and called a waiter.

"You will bring two brandies," he said. "No, no! I beg that you will not refuse," he added as Kair protested. "You will permit me to sit with you for an instant?"

Kair shrugged and made room for him on the cushioned seat against the wall; it was better, he thought, to let the excited little man talk himself out than to risk a scene.

The waiter brought the drinks and Ostrod tossed him a pound note and waved him away.

"*Santé!*" Ostrod said, raising his glass.

"*Santé!*" Kair responded, wondering whether the other had used his Gallic phraseology, and had chosen that greeting rather than one in his native tongue, because of an association with the language in which he was instructing the cow girl. "What happened then?"

"Ah, you recall me! Pig-snout gives me another brandy. He also takes another brandy. I felicitate him on having made so much money. I say that I am a poor man, but I am glad that a good fellow should have better fortune than I have. Pig-snout replies that I, too, am a good fellow. I do not deny it. He says that he wishes me also to have good fortune. I demand how that can arrive. He says that he knows of a horse. . . . Ah, ha! I look down my nose at that. He laughs. It is not what I think, he assures me. He knows of a horse which is to win a certain race. It is an arrangement, a very secret arrangement, so secret that he does not wish to tell me the name of the animal. If I wish to give him a pound, ten pounds, fifty pounds, he will see that I receive the profit when the horse wins. If the horse does *not* win, he will pay me double for my lessons until my loss is repaid. But I must pay money to him first so that his accounts may be clear. You comprehend?"

Kair nodded.

"Good! What do I do? I think a great deal, but very rapidly. I say to myself that this man cannot wish to ruin me, and I am too poor to be worth making a victim. For years I have been prudent, and I am still poor: for once I will be reckless! What arrives? I go home, I consult my bankbook, I consider my affairs. I resolve to risk fifty pounds. I take it to Pig-snout. He tells me to have no fear. I go away. At once I regret what I have done. It is a week of agony. Today the horse is to race. I know it, but do I dare to look at a newspaper? No!

I sit in my office. The telephone rings. I answer. It is Pig-snout. He tells me that the horse has won! Trembling, I demand to know my profit—a hundred pounds, perhaps, or even two hundred? Pig-snout laughs. Two hundred? He is sending me, he says, a cheque for *two thousand pounds*! My friend, I am unable to speak! At last I ask him if he is making a joke. He replies that he does not make jokes about money. It is true. Pig-snout is *canaille*, but he is honest. So now, my friend," Ostrod concluded, dropping a tear into his glass, "you know why I am so happy!"

"Congratulations," Kair replied. "Very glad you were lucky, but I shouldn't advise you to——"

He broke off.

Ostrod had seen Meg Milcote's party, and before Kair could detain him he was weaving his way to the girl's table.

"The beautiful Miss Milcote," he exclaimed, bowing from the waist. "But how amiable of you to come! Our little club is honoured. I have had the honour to play bridge with your distinguished uncle. I am very happy! I have had good fortune today, and I wish that all my friends should share it. You will permit, you and your friends? Waiter, bring champagne for these ladies and gentlemen. And meanwhile you will do me the honour to dance with me?"

Without waiting for a reply he seized the girl's hand and almost pulled her to her feet.

Jack half rose, but Meg waved him back into his chair. Like Kair, she thought it best to humour the little man.

Ostrod swept her on to the dance floor. Fortunately it was still not uncomfortably crowded. He was evidently a good dancer, and despite his condition he managed to avoid collisions.

Meg thought that after a round or two she would be able to induce him to return to the table, but Ostrod had metaphorically taken the bit in his teeth. Signalling to the smiling Czech conductor to increase the tempo, he began to execute ridiculous steps, keeping his balance by some miracle.

Meg could not help laughing as she protested that they really must stop.

"Once more round, lovely lady!" Ostrod cried. They were passing the table at the moment, and he saw Jack scowling at him. Steadying himself and the girl, he rumpled Jack's hair over his face, and unfortunately upset a tankard of beer over the young man's legs in the effort.

Jack sprang up and pulled Meg away.

"Clumsy swine!" he exclaimed. "You'd better clear out, unless you want me to throw you out!"

Ostrod stood staring at him, swaying slightly.

"Swine?" he repeated thickly. "Swine?" He burst into a torrent of Slavonic insults and slapped the lad's face.

Jack knocked him down.

Ostrod got to his feet and seized a bottle from a passing waiter's tray.

Kair was half-way across the room by this time, but Vico got there first and struck Ostrod's forearm neatly with the edge of his open hand. The bottle crashed to the floor, the contents deluging Ostrod's shoes.

"A thousand pardons," Vico said. "An unfortunate accident, my dear sir. One can see that you are not very well. If you will come to my room——"

Ostrod gave him a push that sent him reeling back. "Go away," he said loftily; "you are a common fellow, and I dislike common fellows."

Vico flushed.

"I am sorry, Dr. Ostrod," he said coldly, "but I must ask you to leave. I cannot allow you to behave like this."

For some reason that amused Ostrod, and he laughed unexpectedly.

"You cannot allow!" he chuckled. "Dear Mr. Kair, this animal is funny! He dares to tell me, Joseph Ostrod, that *he* cannot allow——! But let us forget all this nonsense and be happy. Waiter, champagne quickly! You will join us, Mr. Kair?"

"With pleasure," Kair smiled. "But a word in your ear first. There is a telephone message for you. I think it may be from your friend Pig-snout. Shall we go and find out?"

Ostrod drew himself up.

"I am a man of affairs," he proclaimed. "It is no doubt a matter of importance. Ladies and gentlemen, you will forgive me. I will return in an instant."

He kissed the tips of his fingers to Meg, made a sweeping bow, and accepted Kair's steadying arm.

As they passed Vico, however, he leaned forward, whispered something, and deliberately spat in the Corsican's face.

Vico grew livid and his hand flew to a pocket, but Kair gripped his arm and shoved him aside.

Ostrod allowed himself to be led away.

At the door Kair looked back and saw Vico staring after them with a hatred that made him shiver.

CHAPTER VIII

CRADOC pulled the curtains apart. The light streamed in and awakened Kair.

"What's the time?" he asked sleepily.

"Just gone eight."

"Eight? Dammit, Cradoc, I left a note on your pad telling you to call me at nine."

"I know, Mr. Barnabas, but there's someone to see you."

"Don't be silly. I don't see visitors at eight o'clock in the morning."

"You'll see this one," the old man replied, picking up a dressing-gown. "It's Mr. Muir, from Scotland Yard."

Kair sat up. "Funny time for him to call. I wonder what he wants."

"It'll be about the murder, I expect," Cradoc opined with gloomy relish.

"Murder?" Kair repeated, half out of bed. "What murder?"

"That Russian. The man with the square beard. Lived in the Jade Wing."

"You mean Dr. Ostrod? What happened to him?"

"Porter found him in the courtyard early this morning, with his head bashed in. That's what they say. I didn't see him myself," Cradoc explained as casually as though violent death had been part of the daily routine at Canton Court. "What suit will you wear? Oh, and Mr. Muir said to tell you not to hurry; he said he could wait till you got dressed."

"Tell him I'll be with him in ten minutes," Kair said, making for the bathroom. "Give him the morning papers and get breakfast for us both. He may not have had any."

"He hasn't," Cradoc remarked. "I asked him." He departed, reflecting aloud that in the midst of life we are in death.

Most people regarded Kair as a sluggish fellow, but he could move quickly enough when he liked, and in little more than the ten minutes he had bathed, shaved and dressed and was greeting the chief superintendent in the lounge.

"Sorry to disturb you so early——" Muir began, but Kair cut him short.

"Very glad to see you at any time. Had breakfast?"

"Not yet, but——"

"Then come and have it with me."

"Thank you. I won't say no to that. I was out pretty early."

"Cradoc's full of some story about Joseph Ostrod being murdered. Is it true, or has he been listening to gossip?" Kair asked as he led the way to the dining-room.

"It's true enough. That's why I've come to bother you. I'm hoping you may be able to help me."

Kair laughed as they sat down.

"Sounds ominous," he said. "That's the sort of thing one reads in the paper. 'The police are anxious to interview a man in connection with the death of so-and-so. They hope he can help them. . . .' Then they run him in."

"You'll be duly cautioned before you're charged," Muir smiled, "and of course you can have legal assistance. Seriously I've been picking up what information I can, and I hear Ostred got into a row at the Liberation Club last night. I'm told you were there."

"I certainly was. I saw the whole thing. But look here, you must be starving. I'm dying to ask you questions, but I'll postpone them until you've fed. Then we can go into the other room and talk comfortably."

Muir agreed. The two men chatted casually, to the disappointment of Cradoc, who had been charged by Mrs. Cradoc to obtain for her a full, true and particular account of the crime and of all matters and persons concerned therewith.

The meal over, Kair took his guest back to the lounge and they lit their pipes.

"I said just now that I was dying to ask you questions," Kair recalled. "I am, but I won't."

"Why not?"

"Because it's occurred to me that it's *your* job to ask questions, not mine. I'm not going to presume on the fact that you've eaten my bread and salt. I'll be very glad to help in any way I can, but I don't want to be a nuisance."

"I don't think you're likely to be that; in fact, I was going to ask you to let me make use of you. I needn't remind you that whatever we may say in these four walls is to be kept under your hat."

"Of course. Before we go any further, would you tell me just what *has* happened? All I've heard is Cradoc's version, and that was second-hand. He said he'd heard that a porter found Ostrod lying in the courtyard with his head bashed in."

"That isn't quite right. We haven't got a proper picture yet, but we've got the main outlines and our people are trying to fill in the details. Ordinarily the case would be handled by the local divisional detective-inspector, a very good chap called Gatley, but sometimes there are reasons for putting a Central man in charge. When Gatley's first report came in a message was telephoned to me at home. I 'phoned the Assistant Commissioner, and it was decided that I should handle it."

Kair smiled, but offered no comment. He knew that chief superintendents did not usually perform the preliminary duties of a D.D.-I.

Muir took some papers from his pocket, placed them on the broad arm of his chair for handy reference, and went on:

"Putting the bits and pieces together, here's the position as we see it: At about six o'clock this morning an assistant night porter, Samuel Sparks, was walking round the Cloister that runs round the interior court when he saw a body lying beside the little pond with the fountain that stands in the middle of the courtyard. He went across and recognised Joseph Ostrod. He says he touched the body and was sure Ostrod was dead. He's an old soldier and his remark was that he'd seen enough stiffs in his time to know one when he saw it. He had, or says he had, the sense not to move the body. He ran to the main entrance and told the chief night porter, John Wilkins. Then he went back to the body and stood by it. Wilkins telephoned to the police. They came and brought a doctor. Gatley was sent for and the Finger-print Branch was notified. Photographs were taken and the usual routine jobs done. The body was taken away."

Muir paused and consulted his papers.

"According to the records Joseph Ostrod was forty-four years old. He was the son of a Polish professor who was killed in the Warsaw political riots of 1926. Joseph, who had just taken his degree as Doctor of Philosophy, went to Switzerland. He took a law degree there, and friends helped him to get a job teaching languages. In 1929 he came to England and taught at several minor schools. Then he opened a translation bureau near Holborn, and also gave private lessons in German, French and other languages. He seems to have been a very good linguist. Sometimes he'd act as interpreter at one of the law courts. After he'd lived here for the necessary five years he applied for naturalisation as a British subject, and was granted his certificate in 1935. He was allowed a small flat here, rent free, because the Foreign Office sometimes employed him as an interpreter and guide for distinguished visitors from abroad.

"Now, as to his death. There was an injury to his right temple, but the doctor says it was caused by his head striking the stone rim of the pond when he fell, and it would not have been fatal. Death was due to a stab——"

He paused as Kair started, but the latter signed to him to continue.

"A *post mortem* will be made later today, but meanwhile the doctor who made the first examination says he believes Ostrod was stabbed with a thin, narrow blade driven downwards into his shoulder behind the collarbone, cutting the carotid artery. Death could follow in less than a minute. The doctor thinks the murderer stood behind Ostrod, and a little to his left, when he struck.

"We're going into Ostrod's affairs, of course, and we've got some other irons in the fire, but meanwhile I'd like you to tell me exactly what happened at the Liberation Club last night."

Kair told him, making his account as factual and unbiased as he could.

"Thanks," Muir said. "We've sent a man to make inquiries, and I'll probably look in and see this Italian chap myself later on."

"Pasquale Vico? He's a Corsican, as it happens, though I don't suppose it matters."

"Corsican, is he? They're as handy with a knife as the

Italians are—some of them, I mean, of course. So you couldn't catch what it was Ostrod said to him when he spat in his face? It's a pity, but perhaps Vico will tell us."

Kair hesitated. "I said I couldn't catch it," he answered, "because I'm not absolutely certain."

"You mean you could make a guess?"

"Yes, but you don't want guesses, do you?"

"I want everything I can get. Half the things people tell us are guesses, though they don't often admit it, but sometimes they turn out to be right. What's your guess?"

"Well, I thought Ostrod said 'Trade' or 'Trader', or something like that."

"That's interesting," Muir smiled. "Do you think it could have been *traditore*?"

Kair sat up. "I believe you've got it!" he exclaimed. "Why on earth didn't I think of that before? Of course," he added, "I can't swear to it——"

"I'm not asking you to," the chief superintendent assured him. "What happened when you'd got Ostrod out of the room?"

"I persuaded him to let me take him home."

"That was kind of you."

"Oh, I don't know. I was coming here myself in any case. I'd had enough of the club; I really only went in for a drink."

"And Ostrod didn't give you any trouble?"

"No. I got him into a taxi and he spent most of the time singing songs in two or three languages, and occasionally hanging out of the window and telling the world how happy he was. When we got here he insisted on telling Wilkins and Sparks about his good luck. At last we persuaded him to go to bed. Sparks wanted to see him to his flat, but he insisted that he was quite able to go there by himself, and we thought it best to let him do as he liked. As a matter of fact, he'd sobered up a good bit by that time, though he was still very jolly. He shook hands with us all about six times, and went off along the Cloisters, singing that song about the Volga boatmen. There are no porters on duty in the Jade Wing after six in the evening, but there are automatic lifts, and he seemed quite able to cope. I thought he'd go to bed and sleep like a top. I came up here and worked pretty late, and I was amazed this morning when Cradoc told me about him. I can't understand why he should have come down to the courtyard in the middle of the night. I wish I'd insisted on seeing him up to bed."

"It wouldn't have mattered," Muir declared. "I've had a talk with the two night porters. They saw him again soon after you'd come up here."

"Did they, indeed? What was he doing?"

"He turned up at their office off the main hall with a bottle of brandy, and said he wanted them to drink his health. They say they refused, being on duty, but as they're both old sweats—served in the same infantry battalion in the 1914–18 war—I have my doubts. Then, according to them, he said he must go and tell his good news to the night attendant on duty in the garage. That seems to be true. Frant, the garage man, says Ostrod turned up there and insisted on telling him about the bet. He offered Frant a drink, but Frant says he refused. Frant remarked that he had enough to do looking after residents who drove in during the night without worrying about what he described as boozed bloody refugees."

Kair laughed. "Just what Frant would say," he remarked. "He's not a bad chap really, but he doesn't like foreigners."

"Wilkins says the night porters have a fixed routine; the senior—that's himself—stays in the office and attends to the telephone and the main door; the junior is available for messages and he is supposed to make a round of the Cloister at 2 a.m., 4 a.m. and 6 a.m. Sparks says he made his rounds as usual; we've only got his word for that, but it's fair to admit that at two and four he might have failed to see Ostrod's body, the fountain being a fair distance from the Cloister."

"Can you fix the time of death?" Kair asked.

"Doctors hate to commit themselves on that point, and I don't much blame them; there are so many things to be considered—temperature, state of body, and so on. The doctor—he's the divisional police-surgeon, so he's had a little experience—made a rough calculation for me to go on with, and he thinks it's probable that Ostrod died somewhere between midnight and 3 a.m. The *post mortem* should help us."

"It couldn't have been much after ten when I left him," Kair remarked.

"The porters agree with you. There's one thing that surprises me in that connection."

"What?"

"I take it Canton Court isn't what you'd call a rowdy sort of place, and you'd think that a man singing songs in the courtyard late at night would have attracted some attention."

"Perhaps I can explain that. Ostrod always spoke in a curiously low, clear tone. When I said he was singing I didn't mean that he was roaring like a fuddled 'Varsity undergrad on boatrace night. He had rather a nice tenor voice, and he kept it well down. Anybody who heard him might have thought it was a radio programme coming through an open window."

"That's interesting," Muir said. "It——"

He broke off as the door opened and Cradoc appeared.

"You told me you didn't want to be disturbed," he said, "but Mr. Ingrow's on the 'phone. He says it's about the murder, and it's urgent."

"All right," Kair answered. "Excuse me, Muir, I'll just see what Ingrow wants."

He went into his workroom—he refused to call it a library—next door, and came back almost at once.

"Ingrow says he got on to the Yard and was told that you were here," he explained. "He wants to talk to you. He says it's very important. I told him to hold on."

Muir nodded. "Before I speak to him," he said, "I want to ask a favour of you."

"Only too glad——"

"Half a minute. You may not like it when you hear what it is. The manager offered me the use of one of his office rooms, but at this stage I want to keep things as informal as I can. That may sound odd, but I've got my reasons. There are people I want to talk to in a friendly way—people you know—and I'd like you to be in on it. I was wondering whether you'd mind if we had a sort of round table conference here. I couldn't very well invite you to be present at a strictly official conference——"

"Of course I wouldn't mind," Kair interrupted. "Do exactly as you like. You've only got to say what you want."

"Thank you very much. Shall we say eleven o'clock, then? I'll have the people I want notified. And now I'd better go and talk to Mr. Ingrow."

.　　　.　　　.　　　.　　　.

At quarter to eleven Kair and Muir were in the lounge, waiting for their visitors. With them was Chief Inspector Joe Marshall, a placid, elderly man who was Muir's assistant, and had been his colleague in many inquiries when they were both younger and of less exalted rank.

Cradoc had brought in extra chairs, but they had been carefully arranged so as to avoid any suggestion of a formal gathering. In a corner there was a small table at which Marshall could take notes.

Kair had made hospitable suggestions, but Muir had vetoed drinks, though he made no objection when Kair opened a new box of cigarettes.

The visitors were punctual.

When the clock of a neighbouring church chimed the hour there were present:

> Kair
> Alfred Ingrow
> Meg Milcote
> Jack Milcote
> Curtis Frost
> Chief Superintendent Muir
> Chief Inspector Marshall
>   and
> Mrs. Agatha Milcote, who had not been in-
>   vited, but had insisted
>   on accompanying her
>   daughter.

Kair recognised Mr. Curtis Frost as one of the men who had been in Meg's party at the Liberation Club. He was in the early thirties, and although his hair was curly he was distinctly not of the long-haired type. Nearly six feet tall, with broad shoulders and narrow hips, he was blond, blue-eyed and clean-shaven. His speech was that of a travelled American and his manners were easily good. Kair noticed that he contrived to sit next to Meg, a grey-eyed, slim, nineteen-year-old art student who had not abandoned her tennis racquet when she took to the paintbrush.

Kair welcomed the visitors as easily as though they had come to play gin-rummy or to discuss plans for a bridge tournament. He found them seats, handed round cigarettes, and then relievedly left the stage to Muir.

"I am much obliged to you all for coming here at such short notice," the chief superintendent began in his pleasant way, "and I'm very grateful to Mr. Kair for letting us use this room. I want to explain that this is an informal talk. If it should be necessary to take formal statements I'll let you know, and of course if you'd rather not say anything at all just now there's no reason why you should. As you know, I'm making inquiries about the death of Dr. Joseph Ostrod. I think most of you knew him, and some of you saw him last night, and I'm sure you'll want to help me if you can. I thought you'd prefer me to talk things over with you here than to ask you to attend an official inquiry at which it might turn out that you weren't really needed."

There was a pause.

"Very considerate," said Mr. Ingrow approvingly.

"That's all very well," Mrs. Milcote declared, "and I'm sure I don't want to be difficult, but what I want to know is: do you suspect any of us?"

She was a tall, fair woman with a prancing manner that irresistibly reminded Muir of a rocking-horse.

"Don't be absurd, Agatha!" her brother snapped.

The rocking-horse rocked determinedly.

"I'm not being at all absurd, Alfred," she retorted. "It's very nice of Mr. Muir to be so—so civil, and I don't want to be rude, but that man in the corner seems to be ready to write down everything we say, and I don't see why we should be trapped into saying things we might not want repeated outside."

"Mother!" Meg protested.

"Be quiet, Meg!"

Ingrow began to speak, but Muir held up a hand.

"One moment, please," he said patiently. "I hoped I'd made it clear that you can all say as much or as little as you like. Chief Inspector Marshall will make brief notes of any points that may help me in my inquiries. If it seems necessary, we can then take any formal statements required. I didn't invite you to come, Mrs. Milcote——"

"If my daughter's going to be questioned, I've a right to be present."

"We needn't go into that. I was going to say that I'm glad you *have* come, so that you can be quite satisfied as to what goes on. If anything that is said here should be repeated outside, it will be repeated by one of yourselves, not by me."

"Now that my sister has made her point, and you've answered it," Ingrow said drily, "can we get on with the business?"

There was a murmur of agreement. Mrs. Milcote flushed and rocked.

"So long as we know where we stand," she muttered ungraciously. "I'm sure I don't want to make difficulties."

"Thank you," Muir replied. "To come to what happened last night," he went on. "Mr. Kair happened to be at the Liberation Club and he has told me about a scene in which Dr. Ostrod, Miss Milcote and her brother were concerned——"

"Ostrod was tight," Jack broke in. "He started mucking about, and we stood it as long as we could. Then he went too far, and I had to knock him for six, and Mr. Kair and the secretary got him out of the room. That's all there was to it."

"Did you know Dr. Ostrod well?"

"Hardly at all. We nodded when we met, but I don't suppose I'd said a dozen words to him before last night."

"It wasn't Jack's fault," Meg said quickly; "about last night, I mean. I'd taken him and some friends to see the murals at the Liberation Club. They're supposed to be rather good. Soon after we got there Dr. Ostrod came over to our table. I could see he'd had several over the eight. I knew Uncle Alfred had played bridge with him, and I'd met him a few times at the bar downstairs, so I couldn't very well tell him to go away. He asked me to dance, and I thought that if I did he'd be satisfied and go away without any fuss. But he wouldn't stop when I asked him to, and he knocked Jack's beer over. Jack was afraid he'd get really violent, so he——"

"Knocked him for six?" Muir smiled as the girl paused.

"Well, he *did* hit him rather hard, I'm afraid; but he'd absolutely asked for it, you know."

"Had Dr. Ostrod ever been rude to you before?"

"Oh no! He was always most polite."

"Let me make it clear," Agatha Milcote interposed in her most frigidly social manner, "that my brother and I had occasionally played with Dr. Ostrod at the Bridge Club. Dr. Ostrod did not visit us; he was not the type of person I invite to my home."

"*De mortuis*, Agatha," said her brother smugly.

"Nonsense, Alfred! The fact that the man's dead is no reason why I shouldn't say what I think. Why all these foreigners aren't made to go back to wherever they came from is more than I can understand."

"Dr. Ostrod happened to be a British subject," Muir remarked mildly.

"Well, he didn't look like one," rocked the unconquerable rocking-horse defiantly, and Muir let it go at that.

"What time did you leave the Liberation Club?" he asked Meg.

"We stayed for about quarter or half an hour after Dr. Ostrod left, I think," she answered.

"That's right," Jack agreed. "I looked at my watch at ten, and we talked a bit longer and then left."

Meg unconsciously saved Muir the necessity of asking the next question.

"Some of our friends," she explained, "had promised to look in at a late party at a studio in Chelsea. They wanted us to go with them, but I thought it might be a bit hectic, so we refused. Jack had his car and we dropped Mr. Frost at his hotel and then drove back here. I waited while he put the car away—Frant was busy with some other people who had come in just before us—and then we went up to our flat. We told Mother about Dr. Ostrod and she was awfully annoyed."

"Naturally!" rocked that lady.

"I rather wanted to tell Uncle Alfred what had happened," Jack added, "but he was out, so I said good night and went to bed."

"You didn't see Dr. Ostrod again after he left the Liberation Club?"

"No." The significance of the question seemed to strike Jack suddenly. "No," he repeated, "I didn't. Why should I?"

"I asked," Muir explained, "because Ostrod was seen walking about the courtyard after Mr. Kair had left him. He had gone up to his flat and come down again. As he and Mr. Ingrow both lived in the Jade Wing I thought it just possible you might have gone out for a stroll and seen him in the Cloister or the courtyard."

"Well, I didn't," Jack replied curtly. "I didn't go out. I had a final drink and went to bed."

"I heard about it this morning," Ingrow put in. "When I got to my office I thought the best thing I could do was to telephone you at Scotland Yard. They told me you were here, so I asked Mr. Kair to put me in touch with you."

"It was very sensible of you, if I may say so," Muir replied. "Now, Mr. Ingrow, you told me on the telephone that you thought you could help us, and I'm much obliged to you for coming along."

Ingrow cleared his throat.

"It is the duty of the public to assist the police in every possible way," he said pompously, "and that duty is particularly incumbent on responsible government officials such as myself." He paused and glanced at his sister, who rocked her approval. "Last evening," he went on impressively, "I dined with the director of my department. As you may be aware, I am the Principal Assistant Director of the Directorate of Departmental Intelligence. He had invited also two gentlemen who are important officials respectively of the Home Office and the Foreign Office. It was not a mere social gathering. It followed a day of conferences on certain interdepartmental matters which need not concern us here. It is enough to say that they were matters of considerable importance, and my director was good enough to suggest that I should give them the benefit of my experience—I will not say advice—in an atmosphere less formal than that of an official conference."

He coughed, crossed his legs and adjusted the knife-like crease of a striped trouser. Muir wondered whether he wrote his official minutes in the verbose style of his conversation.

"We broke up about eleven, I think," he went on. "The director lives in St. John's Wood and one of my fellow guests, who had come in his car, offered me a lift, but I preferred to walk. It was a nice night, and I wanted to consider some of the points raised during our consultation. The distance, as you know, is not great. As I was not in a hurry I prolonged my stroll a little and eventually reached Canton Court from the Marylebone Road side. I came in by the garage entrance, which is, of course, nearest for the Jade Wing. There was still one point of procedure to be settled in my mind, and I thought I would take a turn round the Cloister before going up to my flat.

"Suddenly I was surprised to hear someone singing. It was a man's voice, and he was coming towards me. After eleven o'clock about half the electric globes in the Cloister are turned off, but enough are left on to enable people to see their way without difficulty. I saw that the man was Dr. Ostrod, and it was evident from his gait that he had been drinking. I had seen him once before in a similar state after an official dinner, and I knew that if he recognised me I should find it difficult to shake him off. I drew back into a patch of shadow, and he passed without noticing me."

"Was he going in the direction of his flat or away from it?" Muir put in.

"Towards it. I went the other way, thinking that by the time I had made the fairly long circuit of the Cloister he would have gone up to his flat. I looked over my shoulder once, and I am sure I saw a man who seemed also to be looking after Ostrod. I hesitated, and then it occurred to me that no doubt it was some resident who was avoiding Ostrod for the same reason as myself. I walked on, and when I had made the circuit and returned to the same place neither Ostrod nor the other man was to be seen.

"I thought no more of the matter; my mind was too much occupied with more important things. It was not until after I had heard of Ostrod's death that I remembered the second man. It may or may not be important; that is for you to judge. Unfortunately I did not see the man's face, and I'm afraid I could not identify him if he were standing here now. I have a vague impression that he was short and that he wore dark clothes and a black hat, but that might have been a trick of the light. I walked round the Cloister once more before going up to my flat. My sister and Meg and Jack had gone to bed, so I heard nothing about the scene at the Liberation Club until this morning."

He looked round him with the air of a man who has finished his speech and awaits deserved applause.

"Thank you," Muir said. "Is there anything else you can tell us?"

"There is nothing else I can tell you," Mr. Ingrow replied

D

regretfully. He turned to Kair and added suavely, "To Mr. Kair, however, my sister and I wish to express our thanks for having extricated Meg from an unpleasant situation for which she was certainly not responsible."

"Not at all," Kair murmured.

Jack said: "Of course she wasn't responsible, so I suppose that crack was meant for me. Perhaps you think I ought to have let her be pawed by that drunken——"

"That'll do," his uncle interrupted. "The plain truth is that you lost your temper. I don't say there wasn't some excuse for you, but fortunately Meg and Mr. Kair kept their heads. I don't suppose Ostrod realised what a nuisance he was; anyhow, he's dead now, so I think we can afford to forget it."

Jack scowled, but subsided.

The calm voice of Curtis Frost cut across the silence that followed.

"I agree, up to a point," he said. "From what little I've heard, Ostrod seems to have been killed without much trouble. I mean, no one seems to have heard him calling for help."

"What's the connection?" Kair inquired.

"The connection is that if Ostrod hadn't been drunk he'd probably have put up a heck of a fight. That makes one wonder whether anyone had an interest in making him drunk."

"But he was drunk because he'd won a lot of money on a race," Meg exclaimed. "He told us all about it, you know. He kept on saying that he was very happy——"

"He told Frant the same thing," said Kair.

"That doesn't necessarily discount my suggestion," Frost suggested. "What do you think, Mr. Muir?"

"It's a very interesting suggestion," the chief superintendent replied encouragingly.

His object had been to get these people to talk; they were talking, and he was prepared to listen indefinitely in the hope of hearing something useful. Patience was his long suit, but it was not Agatha Milcote's long suit. It was her impatience, indeed, that kept her out of the top class at bridge.

"It seems to me," she declared, "that we're just wasting time. It's unfortunate that Dr. Ostrod should have been killed just after he'd involved my daughter in a scene at that horrid club, but I don't see why we should be mixed up in it. Some wretched reporter came bothering us to let him take her photograph, but I told him I'd give him in charge if he didn't go away. I must say I think the police might protect decent people from that sort of thing. I don't know about the rest of you, but I've got a luncheon engagement, and several things to do before I go, and——"

"Please don't let me keep you," Muir interposed. "Mr. Ingrow, I know you're a busy man——"

"I have had to postpone two conferences this morning."

"I'm sorry. I'll have to get you and Miss Milcote to make statements for our records, but we can arrange that at your convenience."

"I think our solicitor should be present," Mrs. Milcote rocked.

"Agatha," said her brother, "I am sorry to have to ask you again not to be absurd. Please leave this to me. Mr. Muir, my niece and I will keep any appointment you like to make. Come, Agatha. Come, Meg. Come, Jack."

He divided a stiff bow between Kair and the others and shepherded his family out of the room.

"What about me?" Frost asked.

"I'm very much obliged to you for coming," Muir said. "As an American citizen——"

"The hell with that," Frost interrupted pleasantly. "As I told you when you 'phoned the hotel, I'd certainly be glad to help if I could. Meg Milcote's a nice child, and it's tough on her and her brother getting mixed up in this thing."

"To say nothing of her mother," Kair observed.

Frost laughed. "I guess she can take it," he answered. "You know them all pretty well, I expect?"

Kair scented the possible suitor a league off.

"Not really well," he replied. "I met Mrs. Milcote and her brother at the bridge club here, and I've run across them all in the public lounge now and then when I've looked in for a drink. The young people are rather nice. Jack's learning the publishing business, and Meg's at an art school."

"That's how I came to know her," Frost explained. "She's been giving spare-time lessons to the kids at a sort of club called the Teeners. It was started by a woman called Mrs. Jake Sweeney, and let me tell you she's done a grand job. When I came over here on business I had an introduction to her, and she showed me around. Seemed to me she deserved all the backing she could get, so I chipped in with a few dollars, not being of much use any other way. I guess the Teeners wouldn't be interested in antiques," he added, grinning.

"You're an expert in that line, I take it?"

"Expert, my foot! What I don't know about them would fill a national library and leave enough over for seven branches.

"Look, Mr. Kair, here's my idea: over in the States there's a heck of a lot of people who like to have nice things just because they *are* nice. Those people aren't millionaires; they can't buy real honest-to-goodness antiques, and they don't want cheap fakes. But say you go to Paris and look at the pictures in the Louvre. You can't buy the Mona Lisa or a Titian or a Meissonnier, but you can pay a real good artist to copy them, and hang the copies in your house and enjoy looking at them. But even that sort of copying costs biggish money if it's going to be really good. There's a lot of old stuff in this country—chairs, tables, beds, cupboards and smaller things—that's useful as well as beautiful. Some of it gets copied and sold by crooks as the real goods. What I'm aiming to do is to make good copies and *sell* them as good copies, at prices that won't lift the hair off the plain man's head. Right now I'm only in the stage of looking for the best things to copy, but when I've found enough I'll have copies made, or buy the originals and send them to the States. There's some pretty big people over there who've got interested in my idea, and they're going to put it across in a big way. You get me now, Mr. Kair?"

"Of course. I hope you'll be very successful," Kair assured him.

Frost looked at his wrist-watch.

"Thanks," he said, "but I guess I've been talking too much and wasting Mr. Muir's time."

"Not a bit," the chief superintendent replied, "and I mustn't waste any more of yours, either. You heard what the other people told us about the Liberation Club row. Is there anything you'd like to add?"

"Not a thing—except that if young Milcote hadn't socked that greasy Polack I'd probably have done it myself. Of course I didn't tell him that. On the way to my hotel I improved the shining hour by explaining to Jack that he'd never grow up to be great and good if he took a poke at every guy who got fresh when he was a bit high. I didn't say it *de haut en bas*," Frost explained, giving the French words an excellent accent, "but just as one man of the world to another."

He joined in the others' laughter.

"Speaking also as one man of the world to another," said Kair, "what about a drink?"

"No, thanks. I'd be glad to, but right now I'm behind on a date with a man who's said he's got some candlesticks that'll interest me, and I don't want to miss the chance. So, if Mr. Muir doesn't want me any more, I'll get along." He took a card from his wallet and handed it to the chief superintendent. "That's my address in the country, and I always stay at the Everyland Hotel when I'm in London."

"Thanks," Muir responded. "I hope I shan't have to bother you again."

Frost shook hands all round and Kair took him to the door of the flat.

"I hope we'll meet again," he said.

"Sure," Frost answered eagerly. "I'll get Meg to fix it up."

Kair returned to the lounge.

"Thanks for your help," Muir said. "The next thing——"

"The next thing," Kair interrupted, "is a drink to take away the taste of Agatha Milcote, and don't give me that stuff about you and Marshall being on duty."

Muir didn't.

CHAPTER IX

KAIR tried to persuade the two police officers to stay to lunch, but the chief superintendent replied that if he did not pay for his meals occasionally he would have no excuse for sending in an expense account, which would be bad for C.I.D. morale. Kair laughed and did not press the invitation.

Canton Court was one of the biggest blocks of flats in London.

It had been the dream-child of an old man who had made a large fortune as a trader in China. Returning to London in 1938, he was amazed by the size of the residential buildings which had sprung up during his long absence. Nothing daunted, he went in search of a site. To choose a location for so large an enterprise was comparatively easy; to acquire it was another matter; but the old merchant began his negotiations with the patient secrecy he had learned in the East, buying a lease here and an option there as opportunity served. He was not to know that German bombs would soon make drastic changes in the landscape.

The outbreak of war halted his activities and he died before it ended, leaving to his heirs the task and the means of fulfilling his ambition. One of the heirs, an influential Government official, was able to obtain the necessary permits and materials before the housing restrictions became too oppressive. The architectural plans were passed and the most modern constructional methods employed.

One condition the old man had made, born of his affection for the country in which he had spent more than half his life. He had wished his creation to be the 'pearl' of London buildings of its type and he decreed that it should be named Canton Court in memory of the Canton (Pearl) River. It was a vast rectangular construction and its four blocks, built round a central courtyard, were to be named respectively the Coral, Sapphire, Crystal, and Jade Wings—the first three recalling the official buttons worn by three senior grades of the old mandarin, and the last in allusion to the collection of exquisite pieces which he had presented to a famous museum, to the despair of dealers whose almost unlimited offers he had refused.

Canton Court, in its original conception, was to have been a miniature world from which a tenant, once installed, need never again visit the outer world if he did not wish, even to purchase a collar-stud. Post-war difficulties had imposed their limitations, but despite them the place was excellently equipped and administered.

While each apartment was self-contained, there were many communal services for those who desired to reduce their house-keeping cares to the minimum. There were rooms for dining, dancing, writing, and lounging over a cocktail; a swimming pool and Turkish bath; squash and tennis courts, a billiards room, and a gymnasium; a secretarial bureau; an underground garage with full service. Most of these and other amenities were on the ground floor, where were also the managerial offices and a few carefully selected shops, including those of a hairdresser, a florist, a bookseller and newsagent, and a tobacconist. There was also a branch of one of the big banks.

The central courtyard was laid out as a garden with a tiny pond and a fountain in the centre, and was bordered by a colonnade, known as the Cloister, which enabled residents to go from one wing to another, or to the main entrance, under shelter in wet weather.

The larger, and most expensive, flats were on the first floor. On the second and third storeys the apartments varied in size and rent; there were bachelor flatlets on the fourth, and those members of the staff who lived in had their quarters on the fifth floor. There was a flat roof on which residents could sit during the summer months.

The apartment occupied by Kair on the first floor of the Coral Wing was among the best in the Court.

Muir and Marshall went across to the tiny flat Ostrod had occupied high up in the Jade Wing. They had been there before, and Muir had left Detective-Inspector Hunt and a man from the Finger-print Branch to search the apartment.

The place was shabby, but clean. Ostrod had employed no domestic help, except for an occasional hour's work by one of the Canton Court cleaners. He had learned to look after himself in much less comfortable surroundings. The flat was sparsely furnished with bits and pieces, mostly secondhand stuff. In an old-fashioned bureau were found a diary; an address book; a file of bills, nearly all receipted; and a bank pass book showing a credit in Ostrod's favour of £782 15s. 7d. There were, however, no letters or other private papers.

Hunt and the F.P. man knew their job, and Muir was satisfied that they were not likely to have missed any secret drawers or other hiding places. Apparently Ostrod either had no secrets or took care not to leave evidence of them lying about.

While Muir was talking to Hunt the telephone rang; Ostrod had been allowed that luxury at government expense, so that he could be called when his services were required unexpectedly.

The call was from the Yard. Ostrod's little office off Holborn had been searched, but nothing of apparent importance had been found. There were some neatly kept account books, and lists of pupils and of firms for whom he had done work. It had not been difficult to trace the bookmaker whose daughter had been one of Ostrod's pupils, and to whom he had ungratefully referred as Pig-snout. The sportsman had at first been badly scared; but when he found that he was not to be led away with gyves upon his wrists, as a preliminary to facing a judge in a black cap, he was ready enough to talk. It was quite true, he said, that Ostrod had been employed to teach his daughter French. He (Pig-snout) had been sorry for the poor little foreign bastard, who always behaved very civil and was grateful for a drink or a cigar. Elated, he admitted, by a run of luck, Pig-snout had offered to let Ostrod share in a good thing —nothing crooked, of course; just one of those jobs that . . . well, anyhow, it was all square as far as he (Pig-snout) was concerned, and there were his books to prove it. Ostrod had placed his bet at very good odds, and the money was waiting for him, not that the poor little bloke would ever be able to claim it now. . . .

So that was that, Muir reflected. Pig-snout had no apparent reason for lying; indeed, men in his walk of life were usually very glad to stand well with the police.

"We'll see this Corsican chap next," Muir decided. He gave Hunt some instructions; then he and Marshall went to the garage entrance, where a police car was waiting.

Pasquale Vico, forewarned by telephone, was waiting for them at the Liberation Club and took them to his office on the first floor. It was a businesslike room, plainly furnished. An elderly woman with horn-rimmed spectacles sat at a typewriter: she rose and placed chairs for the visitors and went out, closing the door behind her.

Vico offered cigarettes, took the swivel-chair at a flat-topped desk on which writing materials and papers were neatly arranged, and waited for his visitors to open the conversation. His manner was suitably grave, but he showed no sign of nervousness.

"You have been told," Muir began, "that Dr. Joseph Ostrod was found dead this morning at Canton Court. He had been murdered, and we are making inquiries."

Vico bowed. Yes, he had been told about it and was deeply distressed.

"Mr. Kair and other witnesses have told us about what happened here last night," the chief superintendent went on.

"We want to find out as much as we can about Dr. Ostrod and we hope you may be able to help us."

Vico recounted the events of the previous evening, and the others listened without interruption. They had anticipated a torrent of excited words, but Vico confined himself to an unvarnished statement that agreed with what Kair and the others had already said.

"Did you know Dr. Ostrod well?" Muir asked.

"No," Vico replied. "I am secretary and manager here and it is my duty to know the members of the club in the way of the business, you understand. Dr. Ostrod did not come very often. Sometimes he would be here two times or three times in a week; sometimes we would not see him for longer—perhaps a month."

"How did he behave, as a rule?"

"Behave? His manners were correct."

"I mean, did he get drunk? Was he quarrelsome?"

"Ah, I see. Last night was the first time I saw him drink so much. I do not think he had much money. As to making quarrels—no. He would have great arguments with other members, but that was nothing. The people who come here all enjoy very much having arguments. It is natural, since they are of many countries. They talk very loud and become very red, but the next moment it is a laugh and a shake of the hand, and so good night. You understand?"

Muir nodded.

"Now, Mr. Vico, I am going to ask you a question, but please understand that you need not answer it, or any other questions, if you don't want to."

"But why not? I am very willing."

"Very well. Have you ever had any personal quarrel with Dr. Ostrod?"

"Me?" Vico looked puzzled. "But no! Why should I? I hear the members say many things, and often I do not agree, but so what, as you say? I do not take sides. It is my job to manage the club and to be polite. If I should make myself unpleasant the committee would very quickly ask me to go. That is business, *hein*?"

"Quite so. But there is one point I'd like to clear up. I'm told that when Mr. Kair persuaded Ostrod to leave, Ostrod stopped and spat in your face."

Vico's swarthy face flushed.

"It is true," he answered. "If it had occurred in the street, I would have known what to do! But here, in the club, it was an affair of business. It is, perhaps, difficult for you to comprehend the discipline of an *hôtelier*; he is like a soldier who must not speak back to his officer—and the customer is his officer. It is hard, but one acquires the habit to control one's anger. Also, I respect Mr. Kair and was grateful to him for his help. What, then, I ask myself, must I do? There is only one answer: I master my fury, I accept the insult. Mr. Kair takes the Russian away, and I go out of the club to be quiet for a little while and recover myself."

Muir pretended to consult a note-book.

"Someone who was near," he said, "believes that Ostrod said something to you in a low voice. Do you remember that?"

Vico nodded. "I remember."

"Would it have been *traditore*?"

The Corsican's eyes narrowed; then he smiled.

"The someone who told you had the stick by the wrong end," he declared. "You speak Italian?"

"No."

"Then I will explain. The word *traditore* means a person who cannot be trusted; a dishonest one; even a traitor. That, of course, would be foolish. My books are examined by officials who report to the committee. My reputation is without stain."

"Then what——"

"A moment, please. Dr. Ostrod would not have said a thing so foolish, even in his drink. No, he was angry because I told him he must go. He wished to insult me, so he called me *trattóre*. A *trattóre* is the keeper of an eating-house. I am secretary and manager; I am, by consent, also an honorary member; I hold the rank of gentleman. Dr. Ostrod wished to dishonour me, to place me on a level with a common fellow in a greasy shirt serving dishes stinking of garlic in a dirty *trattória*! Does it surprise you that I, Pasquale Vico, had a difficulty to master my fury?"

"No," Muir agreed, "it doesn't surprise me."

Vico frowned.

"Nevertheless, I *did* control myself," he said quickly.

"Dr. Ostrod was drunk and I was sure that soon he would come to me and make his apology. I am not one to hold a— what do you say?—a grudge."

Muir thought there might be two opinions on that point, but made no comment.

"You said you left the club after Mr. Kair and Ostrod had gone," he remarked.

"Yes. I placed my head waiter in charge. He is a good man. I wished to get some fresh air. I find always that when I am annoyed, or worried about affairs, a walk in the fresh air restores me. I am a big walker."

"Where did you go?"

The Corsican shruggged. "Is it foolish to say that I do not exactly remember? I walked a long way beside the park to Marble Arch and from there along Park Lane. I turned into small streets and in a little public house I sat until they closed, drinking beer. After that I continued to walk and found myself in Piccadilly. I tried to get a taxi, but could not, so I walked back. The club was closed, but I came in to see that everything was all right. The staff had gone home——"

"Do you keep a night watchman?"

"No. The policeman on the beat keeps watch. We have never been robbed."

"Did you see the policeman?"

"No."

"And after that?"

"After that I went home to my flat, which is in the next street."

"What time would that be?"

Again Vico shrugged. "I did not look at my watch, and my alarm clock does not work. It was late. The club closes at eleven, and then the staff clear up."

"So you probably did not get home before midnight?"

"It is probable," Vico admitted calmly. If he attached any particular significance to the question, he did not show it.

Muir considered.

"Had Dr. Ostrod any special friends here?" he asked.

"I do not think so. He would talk to this member and that, but often he would sit by himself, reading a book or a paper."

"Did he owe the club any money?"

Vico smiled at that. "We do not allow people to owe us money," he explained. "They may come into the club, you understand, but if they order food or drink they must pay for it. We cannot afford to give credit. That is why we are not in debt, and even make a profit. I know my business, sir."

"No doubt," the chief superintendent replied drily, and stood up. "Thank you, Mr. Vico. I think that's all for the moment."

"You will allow me to offer you luncheon?"

Muir thanked him, but said that he had another engagement and was already late for it.

Vico saw them to their car.

"Cool chap, sir," Joe Marshall said tentatively as he drove to the Yard.

"Yes. Had himself well in hand."

"These foreigners generally talk too much," Marshall remarked.

Muir shrugged as eloquently as Vico might have done.

"These foreigners, as you call them, are very much like ourselves," he answered. "Whether a man's British or French or German or Greek, or anything else you like, he's got his own private personality and you've got to handle him accordingly. And the same things apply to women, Joe, only more so. If human beings were turned out to the same pattern, like Ford cars, we'd have an easier job. I've said that before, haven't I?"

"You have," Marshall admitted drily.

"Well, you know it's right. Vico may be telling the plain truth, or he may be covering up. It's too early to say. I didn't press him too much because I didn't want him to turn sullen. We'll see if we can find out anything about the long walk he says he took."

"What about that business of the Italian name he says Ostrod called him?"

"That was interesting. It could be true, of course. If it wasn't true, then Vico must either have expected the question, or else he was clever enough to make up the answer very quickly. I think it'll pay us to find out a bit more of his history. The Special Branch ought to be able to help."

When they reached the Yard he told Joe to get a meal. Going up to his room, he ordered coffee and sandwiches to be sent from the canteen, and settled down to a consideration of the reports already in from Hunt and the other men so far engaged on the inquiry.

He finished the reports and the sandwiches, lit a pipe and put his feet up on his desk.

He was not in the habit of allowing his imagination to obscure his judgment and he was too experienced to count his chickens before they were hatched, but his very experience had taught him to estimate the simplicity or complexity of a case almost from the beginning. Some people would have described it as an intuition; others would have called it a hunch; Muir himself could not have explained it any more exactly than a sea-captain could have put into precise words the dozen reasons that told him of the approach of a storm before even the barometer could give him warning.

He felt in his bones that the problem of the murder of Joseph Ostrod was going to prove as difficult as any he had ever undertaken.

The conviction neither elated nor depressed him. He would solve the problem if he could; if he failed, his superiors —and, what was more important, he himself—would know that he had done his best.

In this philosophical mood he began to review the facts so far discovered and to try to estimate their significance. He had set in motion the elaborate machinery of the Criminal Investigation Department. It would bring to him many expected or unexpected pieces of information; but it would be his task to give them their proper value and to put them together as the pieces of a jig-saw puzzle are put together to form a complete picture.

He began with the golden rule for investigation of a crime; the consideration of motive, opportunity, and means, and of the three the first was the most important.

The motive for Ostrod's murder might have been robbery. It was true that he had lived in comparatively humble style and that his bank credit had not been a large one, but it was possible that he had had an account at another bank under a different name, or had kept money or other valuables in a safe-deposit box the key of which had been stolen from him. Inquiries would be made along that line; at the Yard nothing was taken for granted.

On the other hand, the crime might have been a sexual one. Possibly Ostrod had been killed by a jealous rival or by the husband of some woman with whom he had been having a love affair. That was, of course, one of the commonest motives for murder.

A third possibility was that he had been the victim of a political intrigue. International quarrels had not ceased with the end of the war, though personal differences did not often result in murder, at least in Britain. So far there was no indication that Ostrod had taken an active part in politics, but there, again, investigation would be necessary.

Alfred Ingrow's evidence had been interesting. Pompous though he had appeared, he was no fool, and he had been careful to point out that he would not be able to identify the unknown man in the Cloister. That impressed Muir. Ingrow had had too long an official training to make rash statements; he might be inaccurate in his observations, or wrong in his judgment, but he would never be casual.

One difficulty was that the dark figure Ingrow had seen need not necessarily have been that of a resident in the Court. The garage attendant, Frant, had readily admitted that it was possible for a stranger to come in without being noticed. Frant had said that sometimes two or three cars would arrive at the same time and he would have his hands full attending to them. There was a larger staff on duty in the daytime, for minor repair work, cleaning and so on, and Frant remarked bitterly that he had more than once complained to the manager about being overworked at night. It was, Muir suspected, an old grievance.

The fact remained that, however alert Frant might be, he could not be in two places at once, and it would be quite possible for a stranger to be within the gates without his knowledge.

Muir had taken the point up with the manager, who had assured him that in future Frant would have an assistant at night.

That, however, was locking the stable door after the horse had bolted.

Decidedly, Muir reflected as he knocked out his pipe and began to tidy the papers on his desk, this was going to be one of those infernally annoying cases in which everyone concerned was eager to help and was completely unhelpful.

CHAPTER X

KAIR spent the early afternoon in his workroom, trying to persuade himself that he was working; at last he gave in, and tried to settle down with a book.

It was no use. His eyes read the printed words and part of his brain recorded their meaning, but the other part obstinately insisted on concerning itself with the life and death of Joseph Ostrod. He replaced the book on its shelf and went into the lounge. Cradoc, coming in with tea, found him pacing the room. He had what the butler and his wife were accustomed to describe as *that look* on his face, which meant that conversation was definitely not indicated. Cradoc could never be called garrulous, but *that look* rendered him temporarily dumb. He put the tray down and departed.

If the killing of Joseph Ostrod had been just another documented example to be used in a treatise on homicide in relation to communal life Kair would have allotted the right number of polished sentences to it and passed on to the next point; but now that stark murder had been committed almost on his doorstep, with the victim a man he had known, it was a different matter.

He imagined Chief Superintendent Muir calmly surveying the field of the problem, picking out the basic point, and from that base moving along an undeviating path to the solution.

Why could not his own trained brain do the same thing, instead of darting into alleys of speculation and suspicion, all of which led eventually to the same *cul-de-sac* of bewilderment?

Irritably he poured the tea. It was cold. Still more irritably he ate a morsel of the leathery buttered toast. He rang the bell.

"Take this stuff away," he said when Cradoc appeared. "Bring me a drink. Gin. And tell Mrs. Cradoc I'll have dinner as early as she can get it. I'm going out afterwards."

He remembered that he had refused to eat any lunch, and now he felt hungry.

He resumed his restless pacing.

Once more he tried to recall every detail he had learned about the murder, and what he had heard each person say that morning.

But all the time there was something nagging at him like a

toothache, something that he was vainly trying to drag up from the depths of his memory.

It was something about Ostrod. He was sure of that, but he had no idea whether it was something he had known about the man, something he had observed without realising it, or something he had heard. It might be important; it might be of no consequence whatever; but the fact that he could not recall it annoyed him.

He ate his dinner with *The Times* beside him and forced himself to concentrate on the crossword puzzle, but had completed only one corner when Cradoc brought in coffee.

"I don't know whether I'll be back tonight," he said. "If anyone except Mr. Muir calls or rings up, say you don't know where I am. If Mr. Muir should ring, take a message and say I'll be back either late tonight or early tomorrow. If it's very urgent, telephone to Mrs. Flimby."

From Canton Court he walked to Baker Street station, where he took a bus that went along Marylebone Road and Euston Road. He got off near St. Pancras Station. Crossing the road, he cut through the network of streets and squares between the Euston Road and Bloomsbury.

In a shabby, war-battered street stood an old house which had escaped more than minor bomb damage. A brass plate on the front door bore the name:

FLIMBY

The house was externally as shabby as the street, but the brass plate shone like gold and the curtains at the windows were clean.

This was the residence of Mrs. Jane Flimby, widow, who provided bed and somewhat Spartan board for the poorer class of students enrolled at the great university or the medical school not very far away.

Jane Flimby had been Kair's Nannie and she had stayed on with the family until her marriage. When her husband died, leaving her a tiny income and a long lease of the house, she sturdily refused the pension the elder Kair offered her and turned the place into a boarding-house. Now she was white-haired, but as erect as a Guardsman, and she ruled her lodgers with iron discipline. They quailed at a glance from the fierce eyes behind her steel-rimmed spectacles, told her their troubles and triumphs, and proclaimed her virtues to envious comrades less fortunately placed.

To Kair she was always Nannie, and to her he was Master Barnabas.

He rented two back rooms in the basement. They had nearly quarrelled because he wanted to pay a fantastic rent, but his threat to go elsewhere prevailed and they compromised on a sum which she still considered excessive but was a comfortable addition to her income.

Kair's rooms had the advantage of a separate entrance from an alley behind the house. He could come and go at any hour without meeting the other inmates.

The idea of taking the rooms had first occurred to him when he was gathering material for one of his earlier books. He would put on shabby clothes and wander about poor areas, scraping acquaintance with workers, idlers, down-and-outs and crooks. To have left Canton Court in evening dress and returned in the small hours dressed as a dock labourer would have provided the hall porters with matter for spicy speculation.

There were times, too, when he felt he must break out of the circle of his well-ordered life—his bridge-playing circle, his clubs and the ministrations of the efficient Cradocs. Then he would retreat to his Bloomsbury cavern and think, read, idle and drink until the fit passed.

For Nannie he could do no wrong. She knew that he wrote deep books—none of which she had read—and was famous, and she was convinced that what in lesser mortals might have been dubious eccentricity was for Master Barnabas the right and proper expression of his genius.

Kair found this mildly amusing, and very convenient.

Nannie had a key to the door which barred the stairs from the house to his rooms and was allowed to enter them occasionally in his absence to air and clean them, but even she dared not alter the position of a piece of furniture or fail to replace a book or other object in its appointed place; and there were certain locked cupboards and a desk to which only he possessed keys.

Kair let himself into his rooms by the alley door. Going

into the bedroom, he opened a big wardrobe in which he kept
a variety of garments.

On one of his visits to the Yard during the war he had
chatted with a Special Branch man while they both waited to
be called, if necessary, into a conference which was in progress,
and he had picked up some hints on disguise. The popular idea
that every detective carried a false beard and moustache
ready for instant use was derived from old-fashioned melodrama, though a well-made wig or other hirsute adornment
might still be resorted to in very exceptional circumstances.
The art, he was told, lay in the detective's choice of clothes
suitable to the environment in which they were to be worn,
and still more so in his ability to wear them, not as a disguise,
but as though he wore them every day and sometimes slept in
them. "If you want to look like a dustman," said his informant, "you've got to *feel* like a dustman. You can't go
smoking Turkish cigarettes when you ought to be using shag
in a clay pipe. That's a crude example, but you see what I
mean, don't you?"

Kair had seen, and later on he had amused himself by
practising what the Yard man had preached.

Now he chose from his wardrobe a black jacket and waistcoat. The coat was shiny at the elbows and seams and there
was dandruff on the greasy collar. One of its buttons was
missing, as was one from the stained waistcoat. Next came a
pair of grey striped trousers which a K.C. might have worn
with credit when they were new; now the seat was shiny, one
leg had been torn and not too skilfully mended, and the
bottoms had worn into ragged fringes.

Stripping off his clothes, he put on the trousers. He did not
need to change his white shirt, for clean linen was part of the
dress of his rôle, but he took from a drawer a freshly laundered
but frayed wing collar, and fastened round it a made-up black
bow tie. A pair of well-polished but cracked black shoes,
and a shabby black felt hat with a wide brim, completed his
costume.

From a make-up box he took a pair of short grey side-
burns and affixed them with spirit-gum so that they prolonged the hair at his temples.

He exchanged his horn-rimmed spectacles for a pair that
had one of the side pieces wrapped with adhesive tape, to

suggest a break which the owner was either too poor or too parsimonious to have repaired.

In the sitting-room he jammed old books into a brief-case of worn black leather until it bulged. The lock was broken, and he passed a brown leather strap round the case. The flap did not quite cover the books. Three other books he tied together with string and then tied them to the handle of the brief-case.

Picking up a heavy ash stick with a rubber tip covering the ferrule, he let himself out, locking the door behind him.

He was now Mr. Barney, a man who had formerly kept his own bookshop, but had been bombed out during the war. Nowadays Mr. Barney lived 'on the other side of the river' and eked out the small income from his savings by peddling books to some of his old customers and such new ones as he could find.

Leaning on his stick, he walked steadily in the direction of Tottenham Court Road.

Crossing that busy thoroughfare, he made his way to Charlotte Street, and from there to a narrower street in which stood a public house named the 'Cornish Wrestler'.

It was not one of those houses in which a long-haired aesthete with dirty hands pounded a piano, perverts prattled petulantly, brawny young women of sullen aspect argued with bearded pedants, and a fringe of respectables from the outer world observed these proceedings in the delicious belief that they were at last beholding a great city's evilness in its most sordid setting.

The saloon bar of the 'Cornish Wrestler' was furnished with an eye to homely comfort rather than luxury. The whole place was spotlessly clean, the lighting was not too bright for tired eyes, and the radio was restricted to the announcement of news bulletins. A white-coated barman and a barmaid in a high-necked dress served customers under the watchful eye of a stocky man with a red face and blue eyes who looked as though he had been a sailor. The red-faced man was the landlord; he was Dan Gurney, he had been a sailor, and he was a Cornishman who shared with most of his fellow-countrymen the conviction that the Almighty had made Cornwall and then, finding some land left over, had fashioned it—rather than waste it—into the rest of England and those odd places known as Wales and Scotland.

Kair entered the saloon bar, obtained a pint of bitter, and carried it to a small wooden table in the corner formed by the L-bend of the long bar. It was a quiet and rather dark corner and he liked to sit there and watch the people who sat on the stools at the bar or on the benches and chairs along the wall.

He had hardly settled himself when another customer came in, ordered a pint of beer, and took possession of the vacant chair at Kair's table, nodding civilly as he did so. The newcomer was a youngish, clean-shaven, fair-haired fellow with a pleasant expression. He wore a sports jacket and flannel trousers and looked like a newly fledged medico doing his first job as a house physician or house surgeon at a neighbouring hospital.

"Perhaps you were hoping to keep this seat for someone?" Kair asked, thinking that a pretty nurse or probationer might be in the offing.

"I was not, then, thank y'all the same," the other replied in a rich brogue.

At that moment the landlord appeared beside them.

"Good evening, Mr. Barney," he said. "I see the bag's full. Anything in it for me tonight?"

"Not tonight, Mr. Gurney, I'm afraid," Kair replied. "I think you must have had nearly everything that's been written about Cornwall, but I keep on trying."

"That's right, m'dear," Dan chuckled; "'tis my great joy, as you do know, and I'll never get tired of it. Empty your can, Mr. Barney, and let me send the lad over with a full one. I'll be seein' you again."

He nodded and rolled back to the bar, whence his aide presently brought a full pint pot and put it beside the one Kair had not yet emptied.

"Mr. Gurney thinks there's no country in the world like his own," Kair explained to his companion. "He's Cornish."

"Well, fancy that, now!" exclaimed the young man in mock surprise. "I thought he had the least bit of an accent. Sure, some people never lose it," he added, smiling.

Kair looked expressively at the other's old school tie. "A few years at a public school and a few more in London usually make a difference even to a Cork brogue," he said drily.

The young man coloured.

"How right you are," he answered in a different tone; "just as spectacles and shabby clothes can alter a man's appearance if he knows how to wear them, Mr. Kair. I admit my tie was a mistake that I shan't make again."

"My own little effort doesn't seem to be too successful."

"It's quite good, really, but I happen to have seen you more than once before."

"Indeed? Where?"

The other took an engraved visiting-card from his pocket and handed it to Kair, who read:

CHIEF DETECTIVE-INSPECTOR LAWRENCE DOYLE
New Scotland Yard

"I'm Special Branch," Doyle explained. "I believe you know some of our Great Ones at the Yard pretty well?"

"Only a few, and not intimately. But look here, am I in the way? I mean, if you'd rather be alone——"

"Not a bit. Please don't move. I often come here when I want to have a pint in peace and quiet; it's a decent place and decent people use it."

"Including 'busies' in plain clothes and authors posing as book pedlars," Kair suggested. "Does Gurney know you're a bobby?"

"What does he know of Gurney who only Gurney knows?" parodied Doyle, smiling. "He keeps his eyes open and his mouth shut; you've got to, if you want to run a pub in the western section of this fair city."

"You give me furiously to think. I'm by way of studying my fellow-man——"

"And to some purpose," Doyle put in with obvious sincerity.

"Thanks. Well, I thought I'd better have some excuse for living, as you might say; it saves explanations. I had a devil of a job to get hold of a couple of Cornish histories for Gurney, and he thinks I'm marvellous. They cost me pounds and I sold them to him for three half-crowns."

"No wonder he thinks you're marvellous! But if he's so keen on that sort of stuff he's probably tried big dealers who'd charge him much more. Perhaps he thinks you stole them?"

"Oh no. I explained that they belonged to a man I'd known

in the days when I had my own shop, and when he died I got them from his widow for a song."

Doyle laughed. "You ought to be writing thrillers," he said. "I'm not sure that I oughtn't to ask you to accompany me to the police station and have your bag examined."

"It contains stolen jewels, half a pound of cocaine in small packets, and some portions of the body of the last man I murdered. I'll come quietly, but I must insist on having legal advice."

"By all means, but what about having another pint first?"

He collected the three pots, took them to the bar, and returned with two full ones.

They exchanged salutations.

Doyle noticed that Kair's can stopped for an instant on its way to his lips, then completed its journey. He followed the direction of Kair's glance and saw the man who had just entered.

"Know that fellow?" he asked.

"As it happens, I do. Man called Vico."

They watched Vico order a large gin and vermouth and carry it to a seat. Vico gave them a casual glance, but did not appear to recognise Kair.

After a moment Kair said:

"Look here, Doyle, will you think me offensive if I ask you to show me your warrant card?"

"Not at all." The detective took from an inside pocket a small leather case containing the official card which is issued to every member of the Metropolitan Police, is signed by the Commissioner and is the holder's evidence of identity and his authority to carry out his duties.

"Thanks," Kair said. "I just wanted——"

"You were perfectly right," Doyle interrupted, putting the case away. "Any crook could have an ordinary card printed, like the one I first showed you. Anything you wanted to tell me, or shall we leave it at that?"

"You know Vico too, I suppose?"

"I know a bit about him. I don't think he knows me."

"Do you know about the murder of a man called Ostrod, at Canton Court?"

"Yes. Our Branch has been told to help Chief Superintendent Muir in the case. You know him, I think?"

"I do, and I like him. Now, I don't want to butt in where I'm not wanted, so if I ask any question I shouldn't, just tell me to mind my own business."

"Go ahead."

"First of all I'd better make it clear how I came to be mixed up in the Ostrod business——"

He gave a brief account of his visit to the Liberation Club and of the subsequent conference which had been held in his flat.

"I'd heard something of the case," Doyle said, "but not as much as you've just told me. Did you expect to see Vico here?"

"No. I should have thought this place was rather off his beat." He hesitated. "You'll probably think I'm talking nonsense when I say that I came here to look for something, without knowing what I was looking for."

"I haven't met you before," Doyle answered, "but I've read some of your books. There wasn't much nonsense in them. I take it you mean you've got a vague idea about something, but you haven't been able to tie it up with anything else?"

"Exactly!"

"That happens to us very often. Sometimes it works out all right, and sometimes it doesn't. Do you care to tell me more about it?"

"I'd like to. It's about Ostrod. I'd met him a few times, but I really knew very little about him. And yet I've got a feeling I've seen him somewhere—not at Canton Court."

"Here, do you think?"

"That's what I can't remember. You know how associations stir one's memory—a place, a book, a piece of music, or a perfume? I came here to see whether this place would remind me of anything. It was just a hundred-to-one chance."

"Any luck?"

"Not so far."

"Would it have had anything to do with Vico?"

"No, I'm pretty sure of that. I got a start when Vico came in, but I think that was only the coincidence of his turning up just now. He didn't seem to recognise me, by the way."

"Your get-up is good, but of course he may think it tactful to pretend he hasn't spotted you."

"I'm still wondering what Vico's doing here."

"So am I," said Doyle. "Hullo! He's clearing out."

As they watched the Corsican leave, Kair found himself thinking about the Special Branch inspector. He remembered now that he had once heard 'young Larry Doyle' mentioned as a coming man, though in what connection he could not recall. It was quite likely that he was entitled to wear the Marlborough tie: Chief Superintendent Muir had been a Marlborough boy who had surprised and rather disappointed his doctor father by preferring a policeman's baton to a surgeon's knife. The Special Branch men spoke from one to half a dozen foreign languages and their backgrounds were as varied as their experiences. It was odd that he should have met Doyle on that particular evening. Or was it? Doyle had complimented him on his disguise, but had apparently had no difficulty in penetrating it. On the other hand, Doyle could not have followed him to the 'Cornish Wrestler', or could he . . . ?

Looking up, he caught Doyle smiling.

"You're wondering what the devil I'm really doing here, aren't you?" the Special Branch man asked. "As a matter of fact, I've come to fetch you."

Kair stared at him in astonishment.

"I must apologise for having been a bit theatrical about it," Doyle went on, "but when I saw you dressed up like that I couldn't help pulling your leg. Not but what," he admitted fairly, "you caught me out over this damned tie."

"But how did you know where to find me? I told Cradoc ____"

"Your man did what I've no doubt you wanted him to do. When he told me you'd gone out and he couldn't say when you'd be back I did some telephoning. As I expected, you'd gone to Mrs. Flimby's, so I picked you up and followed you here."

"Are you having me watched?" Kair demanded.

"Good heavens, no! Sorry if I gave you that impression. You see, this particular quarter of our fair city happens to be rather my pigeon. As you probably know, some queerish birds make their nests here, and we keep an eye on them for various reasons. Our local people know all about the fierce but kindly Mrs. Flimby—*and* her tenants. That's all there is to it."

Kair laughed.

"Talk about the Gestapo, and the Abominable Snowmen,

and such creatures—they're not in the same street with you!"
he declared. "But you said you'd come to fetch me; am I
allowed to ask why?"

"Of course. Mr. Muir sends his compliments and would be
grateful if you'd spare half an hour for a chat with him."

"I can almost feel the handcuffs on my wrists!"

"I shouldn't worry about that," Doyle answered quietly,
"but I fancy the idea is that you might be able to help us to
put them on someone else."

"Who's the proposed victim?"

"Sorry. I'm only an understrapper——"

"With the rank of chief inspector."

"Oh, that was just luck. Seriously, I don't know what the
Chief wants——"

"And if you did, you wouldn't tell me."

"The question doesn't arise, as the legal blokes say."

"All right. Hadn't we better be moving? I don't suppose
His Chieftainship will be greatly pleased at being kept waiting
while we indulge in this airy badinage."

"He's not exactly champing his bit," Doyle explained.
"More likely to be champing a late meal kept hot for him by
Mrs. Muir. Rotten job, being a policeman's wife. I've been
watching the clock and we've still more than half an hour to
spare. Unless, of course," he added maliciously, "you'd like to
make some slight change in your dress——?"

Kair laughed and emptied his tankard.

"Damn your eyes!" he retorted. "Come along to my
Nannie's and watch me make myself respectable."

They left the public house, but had walked only a short
distance when an unobtrusive car, driven by a policeman in
plain clothes, sidled up to the kerb and stopped.

"Hop in," said Doyle, who had evidently worked out his
time-table with care.

The car waited outside the Flimby house while Kair, who
took Doyle in with him, resumed his normal appearance. That
did not take long, and they were soon rolling in the direction
of the Embankment.

"Hullo!" said Kair presently, as the car took a direction
he had not expected. "Aren't we going to the Yard?"

"No," Doyle replied. "The conspirators assemble at Mr.
Muir's private house in Buckingham Gate."

He said it with the same cheerful good humour he had adopted since they met, but something in his tone made Kair feel that further direct questions would not be in order.

"Nice part, Buckingham Gate," Kair remarked casually. "Our Mr. Muir does himself well."

"He can afford it. Haven't you heard of his romance?"

"No. I certainly wouldn't have described him as a romantic."

"He isn't," Doyle grinned, "but it's a romantic story, all the same. From what the old hands tell me, Muir was always regarded as the toughest bachelor in the C.I.D., not to be tempted by the three Graces and a *Folies Bergère* chorus put together. Then one fine day—all in the line of duty, as the Yanks say—he finds the young, rich and beautiful Miss Gloria Gale mixed up in a murder case,[1] and rescues her from an 'orrid death."

"And they lived happily ever after?"

"Yes—but the same old hands declare that the lady almost had to handcuff him before she could drag him to the altar. Poor (though he's not exactly that) but proud police officer refuses wealth of grateful heiress, and that sort of thing. Fortunately she was able to make him see reason. He thinks she's the most wonderful person in the world, and she's convinced that Scotland Yard would have to shut up shop if he resigned. And I don't mind telling you," Mr. Doyle added with a certain warmth, "that for once I find myself in respectful agreement with my superior officer."

"Wait till *your* most wonderful person comes round the corner."

"I'm waiting. I'm the world's most disappointed cornerboy, but I never give up hope."

The car stopped outside a small, compact house, and they got out. The sound of Big Ben chiming a half-hour made Doyle nod; they were evidently exactly punctual.

He rang the bell and a maid opened the door, but as she took Kair's hat George Muir appeared, unfamiliarly at ease in well-worn smoking-jacket and slippers.

"This is very good of you, Kair," he said. "I hope I haven't interrupted you in your work?"

"No, I was at a loose end. I was sinking into the depths of boredom—which means fuddling myself with alcohol—when a

[1] See *The Ink Street Murder.*

messenger from the gods, in the form of Mr. Doyle, appeared and rescued me."

Both men laughed, and Larry Doyle said formally:

"Good night, sir. Good night, Mr. Kair," and turned towards the door.

"What's your hurry? Got another job on?" Muir asked.

"No, sir."

"Then come and help me to fuddle Mr. Kair a bit more. Your head is stronger than mine."

Doyle grinned, but Kair thought he seemed greatly pleased as they followed their host into a tidily untidy room that was something between a library and an office. There were leather easy chairs, a good many books, and a big writing-table. There was also a trolley with fuddling materials.

When Muir had gone through the motions of hospitality and had lighted his pipe he said:

"Look here, Kair. I'm going to be plain with you—or at least as plain as I'm allowed to be. That sounds rather rude, but you had a lot to do with us in the war and I don't think you'll take it that way."

"Of course not."

"Thanks. It's because of the good job you did then that I've been allowed to ask you to help us again now."

"I did what I was told," Kair answered shortly. "There was nothing particularly clever in that."

He had always resented having been chained to a desk instead of being allowed to serve in the ranks, declaring that even a man with glasses could learn to drive a tank, or chuck at least one hand-grenade at the enemy before he got scuppered. He had, indeed, mulishly refused the quite important and fully deserved civilian decoration offered to him.

Muir, who knew that, said tactfully:

"I wish the Commissioner would have those golden words circulated in Police Orders. Some of our people might find them instructive."

Doyle chuckled, and Kair had the decency to colour.

"I asked for that," he admitted. "Please go on."

"We want you," Muir said deliberately, "to help us in the Ostrod case."

Kair hesitated—not from any doubt as to his reply, but from sheer astonishment.

"I'll be only too glad to help," he said, "but may I ask a question?"

"Yes, though I can't promise to answer it. What's the point?"

"Well, I don't know much about the Yard, but I do know that you fellows are not in the habit of asking members of the public to help you to catch an ordinary murderer. I'm not asking to be told secrets, but am I right in thinking that there may be more behind the murder of Ostrod than, shall we say, has appeared in the newspapers?"

Muir knocked out his pipe, refilled and lit it before he replied.

"There may be a hell of a lot behind it," he answered. "I can't go into details. The truth is, we think there may be a political reason for his death. That's one reason why I suggested to Sir Justin that you might be useful. You're not a policeman, you know a lot of people, and you've had enough war experience to realise the harm that can be done by casual talk. Anything else you want to know?"

"Lots, but I might ask the wrong things, so I'd better listen instead."

"Good. To put it brutally, Kair, if you're going to be any use to us you'll have to do what you're told and keep your mouth shut. You may be asked to do things that seem damn silly. You'll get no limelight and no pay, and you may find the job boring, or unpleasant, or even dangerous. Whatever you may see, or hear, or be told will be reported to us, and you won't speak of it to anyone else without our consent. There's the proposition. If you don't like it, don't hesitate to say so."

"No complaints."

"Thanks."

"When do I start?"

"Consider yourself started, but if you don't hear anything from me for a bit don't think we've forgotten you."

"Would you like me to report at the Yard every day in case I'm wanted?"

"Good heavens, no! It wouldn't do for you to be seen hanging about there. You'll be told when and where to go when the time comes. Meanwhile, there's one thing you might do."

"What's that?"

"You remember Miss Milcote talking about the Teeners' Club?"

"Yes."

"Could you get her to take you there?"

"Easily. As a matter of fact, I've asked her. It sounds like the sort of show that interests me. She says that chap Frost is giving a party for some of the workers and she can get me invited. He's taking them down to a place he has in the country. Doing it in style, too; a private 'plane to Bristol, or somewhere near there, and then a fleet of cars. But tell me, is there anything crooked about the Teeners mob?"

"That's what we want to know. Most of the people who run it are just honest-to-goodness social workers, but there may be things going on that they don't know about. It's just an idea," Muir added casually. "So keep your eyes open, but for goodness' sake don't let them think you're doing anything more than getting material for a new book."

"I'll be careful. Any other instructions for a humble nark?"

Muir smiled at the expression, but his tone was grave enough as he answered:

"Yes. I don't want to come the heavy stuff, but it's only fair to tell you that this is a sticky job, and it may be stickier presently. When you go out, especially at night, watch your step and carry a stick."

"Meaning——?"

"Meaning that I don't want you to get a crack on the head with a cosh, or a knife in your ribs, or be run over by a fast car when you're crossing the street. Have you got a police whistle?"

"No."

"I'll give you one. Have you got a gun?"

"No. I was given one when I was on secret work, but I turned it in after the war."

"I don't think there's any need for it at present. We can arrange for you to have one if it seems necessary later on. Are you a shot?"

"No. I was shown how to use the thing, and I fired a few rounds at a target, but I don't think I could hit anything more than a few feet away."

"That might be enough," Muir said drily, "but firearms are chancy things unless you're used to them. Now, another thing. I want you to get into the habit of keeping eyes in the back of your head, so to speak. I don't mean walking about with your head twisted over your shoulder. An occasional look into a shop window, or a casual glance round when you come to a corner—that sort of thing."

"In case I'm being followed?"

"Yes. Suppose you're in a Tube or a bus. You see a man with a pimple on his chin. If you see him again it may be a coincidence, but if you see him two or three times it probably isn't. That's crude, but you get the idea?"

"Of course; but am I as important as that?"

"No, but the people you know may be."

"*Touché!*" Kair laughed. "The cog in the machinery."

"A cog out of place may stop the machinery. We're all cogs, you know, from the A.C. downwards. That's how the machinery works."

"Well, this little cog will try to keep its place, in more senses than one. You won't find me talking out of turn."

"We know that," Muir replied readily. "But that doesn't mean that we won't be glad to hear any ideas or suggestions you may have."

"You mean that? Or are you just being decent?"

"I certainly do mean it. Have you got any to offer?"

"I don't know about suggestions, but I've some ideas."

"Let's hear them."

"Looking at it simply from the point of view of the man in the street," Kair said, "the fact that Ostrod was killed so near his own flat suggests that the murderer hadn't planned the crime beforehand; at least, he may have decided to kill Ostrod, but not in such a hurry. He had to risk being seen by someone, and it was a fairly big risk. You agree?"

"Yes."

"Then something must have happened to make him change his mind. May I ask whether you know how Ostrod spent the time between hearing of his good luck and turning up at the Liberation Club?"

"No, we haven't filled in that gap so far. It's obvious that he must have been drinking, as he was well on when he got to the club, but he might have been on a general pub-crawl."

"Quite," Kair assented. "Well, he arrives at the club and has a row with young Milcote and Vico, but I can't see either of them murdering him on that account. May I ask another question?"

"What is it?"

"Do you know anything about Ostrod's sex life?"

"No. So far nothing has turned up in that line. We're working on it, of course, but we haven't found anything that suggests he was a womaniser. He couldn't afford to keep an expensive mistress, from the look of his bank book. He didn't keep a secretary, by the way. His office was just one room, and he seems to have typed his etters himself. Sometimes he'd have longer jobs—translations and so on—done by a type-writing agency in the same building. The caretaker says he used to have an office boy, but the lad left him about a year ago; he told the caretaker that Ostrod said he couldn't afford to raise his wages. The caretaker says he doesn't remember seeing women come to Ostrod's office—or many men either, for that matter."

"All the same," Kair pursued, "he might have been having an affair with some woman you haven't heard about yet. He wasn't what I'd call an attractive bloke, but there's no account-ing for feminine tastes."

"True enough; but are you suggesting that a woman killed him?"

"No; but do you think it's possible that he might have been killed by a husband, or some other man who was jealous of him?"

"It's possible."

"Which," Kair remarked blandly, "of course explains why I must carry a stick and look over my shoulder when I take my walks abroad."

Muir ignored the thrust.

"How's the second-hand book trade going?" he inquired. "Nice little pub, the 'Cornish Wrestler'. Our divisional people say Gurney has a clean sheet with them."

Kair laughed. "All right. I can take a hint as well as the next man. But you asked me to give you my ideas. I'll give you one more before I shut up. You said there might be a political motive behind this crime. That, if I may say so, is sticking out a mile. I don't pretend to know what it is, and I'm not going to ask; I'm content to wait till you're prepared to tell me. Meanwhile I'm ready to do anything from running errands to cleaning your shoes."

"Thanks," Muir smiled. "That tankard of yours looks very empty. Let me fill it. . . ."

The remainder of the visit was strictly social, especially when Muir called Gloria to join them.

CHAPTER XI

SUPERINTENDENT ASH caught a morning train from Treporth, lunched in the restaurant car, and had time to call at his flat for a few things he wanted before going to the Yard.

On the previous evening he had received a curt message instructing him to return and report to Chief Superintendent Muir.

When he entered Muir's room he found that officer and Chief Inspector Marshall busy with some papers.

"Hullo, Andrew," Muir said, looking up. "Take a pew, will you? We shan't be long."

Ash sat down.

Muir continued to read a document, while Marshall sucked an acid drop as silently as possible. The chief inspector was popularly known as 'Acid Drop Joe' because of his confirmed addiction to that sweetmeat.

"All right, we'll leave it at that," Muir said presently. "Put a good man on it."

Marshall nodded, gathered up the papers, and left the room.

Muir lit a cigarette.

"Well," he said, "how are things going? I suppose you speak Welsh fluently by this time, by damn?"

He spoke cheerfully enough, but the superintendent knew him well enough to detect a certain strain under his chief's cool manner.

"Not quite," he replied, "but my friend, Inspector Haydn Hughes, has promised to learn me when he have time, see. He do say that I am quick in the uptake, for a chap from London."

Muir laughed. "From such a source, that's a compliment. Well, I expect you're wondering why I sent for you in such a hurry. To tell you the truth, so am I. All I know is that there's some sort of a high-power conference on this afternoon, and Sir Justin told me to get you here in time to attend it. I don't even know who's coming, apart from our lot, and Sir Justin's attitude didn't exactly encourage questions."

Ash nodded. He knew those moods of the Assistant Commissioner, who could change in a moment from the scholarly courtliness of an Oxford don to a phraseology that would have made a Thames bargee bow his head in silent awe.

"I've read your reports, of course," Muir went on. "That chap Trevone seems to be in the clear, then?"

"Yes. I was never satisfied about him, though the case against him looked good enough."

"Who's next on the list of suspects?"

"I don't know, sir," Ash declared frankly. "Miles Trevone seems to be the only one who had a motive for killing Upwey." He hesitated. "There's something queer about the whole set-up—at least, that's how I feel, though I can't give you any good reason for it."

"You feel like that, do you?" Muir answered thoughtfully. "That's interesting, very interesting."

"Why?"

"Look, Andrew. I've got to say something that's a bit difficult, but I know you'll take it the right way. It's the first time I've ever known a senior officer to be put on a case without being told all the facts. I couldn't help it. I had my orders from the A.C. himself, and he was quite definite—in fact, damned definite. As a matter of fact, I don't know very much more than do you, except for a hint here and there, but I expect we'll be told a good deal at the palaver presently. You were sent to Treporth to see what you thought of what looked like an ordinary crime of jealousy. By the way, how did you get on with the Chief Constable?"

"Very well, but I couldn't help wondering whether he knew more than he admitted."

"He did, but he'd been told by high authority, *very* high authority, to keep his mouth shut. I do know this much: Sergeant Upwey was an ambitious bloke. He thought he'd got on the track of an international gang. Instead of reporting to his own chiefs, he wrote privately to a man he knew in the Special Branch, asking for some information. It was most

E

improper, of course, and the S.B. man reported it. Upwey was evidently hoping to pull off a big *coup* on his own and scoff the credit. It was decided that Colonel Bassenthwaite Lake had a right to know about it, but he was pledged not to tell his own officers or to discuss it with you."

"Then why send me there?" Ash asked bluntly.

"Sir Justin said he wanted your unbiased opinion—I'm not giving you soft soap—because Upwey's death might have been a political murder, or just an ordinary crime, and he knew he could rely on your judgment, even though you were partly in the dark. You can take it from me, Andrew, that so far from being a reflection on you, it was the very reverse. Between ourselves, I think Sir Justin is as much under the orders of V.I.P.s in this matter as we are under his."

Ash digested that. It was not usual for C.I.D. men, even of his rank, to be offered what was virtually an apology by their superiors, and he and Muir had been friends as well as colleagues too long for him to doubt his chief's sincerity.

"Thanks for telling me," he said.

"Right," Muir answered. "Tell me, what do you make of the Fersens?"

"I told you in my report about Oscar's stick. Nothing doing there. Besides, I can't find any hint of motive. He seems to have done his best to stop the row between Trevone and Upwey. Since my last report I've met his brother, Axel Ferson. He's a quaint bird. The sort of scientist you read about in romances but don't expect to meet in real life. He stands over six feet, gaunt, clean-shaven, with a mass of white hair. He is casual in his dress, but not snuffy or dirty, and his manners are charming. But when you talk to him you feel he's had to make an effort to pull his mind away from some scientific calculation. Once he's done it, he's a very pleasant host, and I believe he plays a good game of bridge. He and Oscar belong to a little circle of bridge players. There's a Mrs. Jake Sweeney, and a man named Ingrow, a civil servant——"

"We know them both. Ingrow's pompous, but he's got brains, and he'll be the new Director of Departmental Intelligence when his chief retires soon."

"He's got a cottage near Treporth. Does a bit of fishing."

"Yes, he's very keen on that. You might get in touch with him, Andrew. He probably won't say anything private to

you unless you give him a lead, but you may find him useful.
I'm told he's regarded as a very shrewd bird. I've met him
myself. He's a climber, and very touchy about his official
status and all that, but he's no fool and he was really responsible for building up this new Department of Departmental
Intelligence."

"What does it do?"

"It keeps the different government departments informed
of matters that may affect them. It's all very confidential and
calls for a good deal of tact, because there are a lot of things
that have to be kept secret, and that makes for jealousy among
people who aren't allowed to be in the know." Muir looked at
the clock and rose. "We'll have to get along to the A.C.'s
room now," he said, "but when the palaver's over I want to
have another talk with you, Andrew. There's still a lot you
don't know."

Ash did not have to be told that. More than once during
the conversation his gaze had gone to a side table on which,
half hidden by some folders, lay a pair of socks. They were
hand-knitted, with gaily coloured tops, and Ash thought they
looked remarkably like the socks he had seen Mrs. Jake
Sweeney placidly knitting in her house at Pentref. He followed
Muir out of the room without comment.

A select company assembled in the office of the Assistant
Commissioner, Criminal Investigation Department, at New
Scotland Yard.

The venue of the meeting had not been Sir Justin's choice.
For one thing, his room—a comfortably furnished apartment
overlooking the River Thames—was adequate for his usual
needs, but was not of vast proportions. He could, of course,
have commandeered one of the large rooms used for lectures
and other purposes, but that would have created an atmosphere of formality which he was most anxious to avoid. He
was well aware of the jealousies existing between the various
governmental departments and he wished that some other
place had been chosen for the meeting, but High Authority
had decreed that it should take place on the supposedly
neutral ground of the Yard. He had already accompanied the
Commissioner of Police to No. 10 Downing Street, where the
Prime Minister, the Foreign Secretary, the Home Secretary,

the Secretary for War, and other exalted persons had metaphorically let their hair down and talked with a freedom in
refreshing contrast to their mellifluously guarded utterances
in that temple of free speech the House of Commons.

Sir Justin had, so to speak, been given his brief, and with it
a gracious expression of confidence in his sagacity and tact.
He had received both with an impassivity which had made the
Commissioner suppress a smile, and while returning in the
police car he had relieved his feelings with a burst of profanity
which might have awed even the toughest members of the
Cabinet.

Back at the Yard, he had explained the situation to his
confidential secretary and directed her to cope with the
matter. The confidential secretary, a pleasant woman agree-
ably free from the acerbity so often displayed by members of
her professional sisterhood, had coped. She would have coped
as tranquilly with the slight confusion to be expected after the
sounding of the Last Trump.

The result was adequate seating accommodation so disposed as to suggest the imminent arrival of guests eager to
congratulate the Assistant Commissioner on the attainment of
another birthday. Sir Justin grinned as he observed the number
of ashtrays borrowed from other rooms. There were, however, no drinking utensils except the tumbler over the water
carafe on his desk. It was, after all, an official conference. . . .

The guests arrived.

The Yard contingent consisted of the Assistant Commissioner (whose deputy assistant was absent on sick leave),
the Commander (Crime), the Deputy Commander in charge of
the Special Branch, Chief Superintendent George Muir,
Superintendent Andrew Ash and Chief Detective-Inspector
Larry Doyle. The two latter officers had been surprised to
find themselves bidden to such a superior feast of reason, but
Sir Justin's methods were as unpredictable as his decisions were
absolute.

The War Office had sent a colonel and a major, both in
Military Intelligence. They gravitated naturally towards the
captain R.N. and the wing commander who represented respectively the intelligence departments of the Admiralty and
the Royal Air Force. The four officers wore civilian clothes.

The Foreign Office and the Home Office had each con-

tributed a principal assistant, and the party was completed
by the Director of Departmental Intelligence, an amiable
veteran much pleased and a little astonished by his good luck
in receiving directorial rank before his approaching retirement.

Almost all the visitors arrived a few minutes before the
appointed time, and Sir Justin welcomed them and made
introductions where necessary. Most of them, however, had
already met at least some of the others.

Big Ben began to boom the hour as the door opened and
the representative of His Majesty's Principal Secretary of
State for Foreign Affairs made an effective entrance.

Foreign Office, impeccable in dress and suave in manner,
acknowledged his introduction to the assembled mob with a
little bow that subtly hinted his permission for them to remain
seated and his willingness to mingle for a space, in the national
interest, with the sturdy yeomanry of his country.

Chief Inspector Doyle mastered a temptation to hum the
National Anthem.

Home Office sniffed.

Army, Navy and Air Force made polite noises and thought
longingly of the more severe aspects of recruits' training.

The police officers smiled woodenly and the Director of
Departmental Intelligence blew his nose with a trumpeting
sound.

Sir Justin lowered his corpulence into the swivel chair
beside his desk, crossed his legs and polished his monocle.

"Gentlemen," he began, "I find myself in a situation of
some embarrassment."

The police officers smiled—but inwardly this time. They
had seen the Assistant Commissioner in many situations and
moods, but they had never known him to be embarrassed;
and they knew that purring note in his voice. Watch your
step and look out for the claws when Old Just-in-Time starts
purring was a Yard axiom.

"The Commissioner of Police," Sir Justin went on, "was
sent for by the Prime Minister to attend a conference at which
the Foreign Secretary, the Home Secretary, and other
Ministers were present. I was directed to accompany the
Commissioner—in quite a minor capacity, of course."

Foreign Office tried to look unimpressed, and failed. He
had never attained Downing Street.

"One of the results of the conference," Sir Justin continued, "was the decision to ask you all to meet me here, so please don't regard me as the chairman of a formal meeting, but only as a human gramophone repeating the instructions given to me. The Prime Minister particularly wished me to make it clear that you gentlemen from other departments have been chosen by your respective chiefs because they have complete confidence in your abilities and your discretion. The same principle has guided me in my choice of the police officers who are with us now."

Foreign Office made an unexpected gesture.

"Thank you, Sir Justin," he interposed. "I'm sure what you've just said applies to the others, but in my case I ought to explain that I'm only here as a temporary substitute for a senior officer of the Secret Service section of my ministry. He has been making certain inquiries abroad and was due back this morning. Unfortunately he's been delayed, and I am to make a report to him when he arrives."

"I knew that," the Assistant Commissioner answered, smiling, "but I was also told enough about you to make me very glad to have you with us."

Foreign Office bowed, and was annoyed to find himself colouring.

The colonel chuckled and said:

"All right, Soames. Most of us know you and we're not jealous, so let's cut out the genteel stuff and get down to things that matter."

"By all means," Sir Justin agreed promptly. "Here's the position, then, and you'll forgive me if I go over matters that some of you know already, for the benefit of those who don't know quite so much. The Cabinet are taking a very grave view of what is popularly known as the Communist menace——"

"About time, too!" the colonel cut in. "We've been taking that view for a long while. But are they really going to *do* anything about it?"

"They are, and that's what we're here for. So far there's been quite a lot of work done in different directions, but the P.M.'s idea is that there should be closer co-operation between departments, with some sort of central bureau to prevent overlapping."

"This central bureau being located in Scotland Yard, no doubt?" the captain R.N. suggested.

"The P.M. did throw out a hint to that effect," Sir Justin replied acidly, "but if you think it would function better from the bridge of a battleship or in a submarine, we'll be only too glad to hand the job over to you. We've enough on our plate as it is."

"But I didn't mean anything like that," the sailor protested. "Sorry I put it so badly. I meant the Yard is the obvious place to choose, if you're willing to take it on."

"Oh, I see. But perhaps someone else has a different view?"

"We certainly haven't," grinned the wing commander. "I was told to say that my mob's ready to jump when you give the word."

(The irrepressible Larry Doyle, sitting in a corner beside Andrew Ash, scribbled, "Oh, wizard prang!" on his note-pad and held the pad where Ash could see it.)

Sir Justin looked inquiringly at Foreign Office, who observed that he was empowered by his Ministry to promise its co-operation.

"Very well," said the Assistant Commissioner, who had been exhibiting a restraint at which his staff marvelled, "since we seem to be in general agreement I propose to release Chief Superintendent Muir from his present duties and appoint him *liaison* officer. . . ."

George Muir sat up in astonishment, for Sir Justin had given him no hint of his intention.

"I think that, if you agree, Mr. Muir should be given a fairly free hand. He did a *liaison* job between the Yard and the Services during the war——"

"And did it damn well," the colonel commented.

"Thank you, Colonel. Mr. Muir will be directly responsible to me. It will be his job to keep in touch with us all, collect as much information as he can, and make suggestions for joint action. Such suggestions will be put before you and we can then meet to discuss them. Mr. Muir will have Superintendent Ash and Chief Inspector Doyle as his personal assistants. I think this arrangement ought to save a good deal of time and prevent possible misunderstandings. May I take it that you agree?"

Everyone agreed—except Muir, who was not asked.

"That's settled, then," Sir Justin said with relief. "Now let's get down, as the colonel put it, to the things that matter, and I don't have to remind you how very much they do matter.

"There seems to be no doubt that the Reds are getting ready for a big push, especially in this country. When the war was over they thought they were going to sweep the board in most of the European countries. Instead of that, they were badly disappointed in France and Italy—to mention only two examples—and they found their stock going down almost everywhere."

"Nasty medicine for Moscow to swallow," the major commented.

"Yes. It was fairly easy for the leaders in the Kremlin while they only had to run Russia. They had everything taped and they could stamp out any local revolt before it got big enough to be dangerous. But when they had to deal with men who'd been cock of their own dungheap in the satellite states behind the Iron Curtain I fancy the Kremlin lads found they'd taken rather a lot on their plate, and what they'd swallowed was giving them a bit of indigestion. However," Sir Justin remarked apologetically, "our friend from the Foreign Office knows more about that than I do and I'm not going to poach on his preserves. I'm only concerned with what goes on in this country, but I do want to make this point: a lot of people believe that the Communist movement here was not only started and financed by Russia, but is still being run entirely under direct orders from Moscow. We—I'm speaking for the Yard—don't altogether agree with that view."

"What *is* your view, then?" inquired the captain R.N., deeply interested. "I've always understood that Russia regarded the British Commonwealth as the worst snag in her plans for eventually bossing the whole world."

"So she does, and she'd like nothing more than to start a real bloody revolution over here. But conditions have changed since the saintly Lenin and his friends murdered the Tsar and started the Soviet system of government, and especially since the war. The Communist leaders in every country are willing enough to take money and other help from Moscow, but if they can get into power they may not be quite so willing to divide their loot with the Kremlin crowd. But apart from that, we believe that all the Red money in this country isn't coming from Russia. There are a good many people all over the world who wouldn't be sorry to see Royalty wiped out, British military and economic power destroyed, and the Commonwealth split into morsels that could be gobbled up one by one. Take Germany, for instance. We know the Nazis salted away a lot of money in other countries when they saw things weren't going well, and they planted agents here and there to look after it until such time as it might be needed, either for themselves or for their party——"

"Sorry, but I don't get that," the wing commander interrupted. "Surely the Nazis hated the Communists like poison and did their best to scupper them?"

"Certainly, but there's not really a lot of difference between Nazis and Reds: both want to be dictators. And the men at the top in both parties want to grab the best jobs and as big a share of the pickings as they can. That's human nature."

"Fair enough," the wing commander agreed, grinning. "So you think there's German money in the comrades' pockets?"

"Yes, mixed up with other currencies, but all good for spending. So far the comrades have been spending it with more enthusiasm than success, but we think someone's been cracking the whip lately. They've built up quite a big underground organisation, climbed on the back of the Socialist wagon, planted agents in the trades unions and in the armed forces as well as in the Civil Service, and engineered a lot of strikes and sabotage. But now it looks as though they were going to take the gloves off. As we're speaking in confidence, I may say that we've thought it advisable to take more than ordinary steps to protect members of the Cabinet and certain other prominent people whose names I need not mention."

There was a short silence. Then the captain R.N. said:

"We knew, of course, about the attempts to start mutinies in the Navy. That sort of thing isn't new, and we've been able to handle it pretty well so far. But you remarked that you thought the Reds were going to take their gloves off. I take it you mean open violence?"

"Quite possibly."

"May I ask whether you're speaking generally, or whether you've discovered some particular plot?"

Sir Justin hesitated. Ordinarily he would have refused to

be drawn, but in the circumstances the question was a fair one and he could not refuse to answer it.

"You've probably seen in the newspapers," he replied, "some reference to the murder of a man named Joseph Ostrod."

"The chap who was knifed in Canton Court? Yes, I read about it. Was he a Red?"

"We think not. Frankly, we don't know a lot about him, but we imagine he was in the opposite camp."

"Then the Reds did him in?"

"We're not sure, but we believe it's possible. I'm sorry to be so vague, but we haven't a lot to go on so far. Ostrod doesn't seem to have been of much importance, but if we can find out who killed him we may be able to get a line on that underground organisation I spoke of just now."

"But I take it you know some of these Red agents?"

"Oh yes, plenty. We could pull in a lot of them in a few hours, but that would do more harm than good. We want the big fish, not the little ones, and it's no good frightening them by stirring up the pond too soon. We've taken some pains to spread the impression that we're a lot of blundering silly fools, and we hope they'll believe it until it's too late for them to do anything about it."

"Good!" said the colonel, knocking the ashes out of his pipe. "It's an old game, but it's amazing how often it comes off. Well, thanks for telling us all this. I take it we'll hear from Mr. Muir as soon as——"

The buzz of the telephone interrupted him.

With a gesture of apology the Assistant Commissioner lifted the receiver and listened, making only an occasional brief comment. Replacing the receiver, he turned to the others.

"At least one glove seems to have been removed," he said. "An attempt has just been made to assassinate the Home Secretary."

The others sat up. Home Office emitted a startled noise and even Foreign Office permitted himself to utter a profane word.

"It was unsuccessful," Sir Justin explained. "As the minister was leaving his house a young man ran across the road and fired twice at him with a revolver. One shot went through the minister's hat, but one of our two men there knocked his arm up and the other shot went wild. Our fellows collared him, but before they could get the pistol away he tried to put a bullet into his own head."

"Dead, sir?" asked the Commander (Crime).

Sir Justin shook his head.

"That's good," the wing commander remarked. "You may get him to talk."

Sir Justin shrugged. "I doubt it. He'll probably go down in the records as the usual fanatical foreign student with a general grudge against authority. The Reds know how to pick their men. We'll do what we can, of course. . . . And now, gentlemen, unless anybody has any further questions or suggestions, perhaps you'd care for a cup of tea?"

They cared for it.

CHAPTER XII

On the morning of Curtis Frost's party Kair drove Meg Milcote to the Teeners' headquarters on the Swiss Cottage side of Hampstead.

The girl was obviously delighted at having secured such a literary lion for the occasion, and she chattered so readily about the organisation that Kair had only to put in an occasional word to obtain the preliminary information he wanted.

Meg was a devotee of Mrs. Jake Sweeney and regarded that lady's absence from the gathering as the only cloud in what promised to be otherwise a perfect day. Most of the other leading helpers would, however, be there, either to take part in the excursion or to give the voyagers a send-off. They included the vicar and the Roman Catholic *padre*.

"We bar religion and politics," Meg explained. "I mean, we never try to force any brand of religion on the Teeners, but the vicar and the *padre* help us to get hold of youngsters who need looking after."

"Very helpful," Kair agreed, secretly amused, but a good deal impressed by the maturely earnest air of this girl who was still in her own teens.

"The vicar's a wonder with his hands, too," she went on, "and he teaches carpentry. Then there's a very jolly police inspector named Vance; he teaches the boys to box, and is he popular! Of course there are lots of others, like the man who keeps the accounts—he's a bank manager, I think—but Mrs. Sweeney's right hand man in the show is a dark Welshman named David Jones. He's a working man and it's really awfully decent of him to give us practically all his spare time."

"What is his job?"

"He's a foreman printer. We got hold of a small second-hand printing press—I'm not technical enough to describe it, but I'll show it to you presently—and we print our own little magazine. His daughter, Myfanwy, is a typist and she takes classes in shorthand. I've only mentioned them as examples, but we have circles for art, crafts, sports and games, acting, music, even languages. And that reminds me: poor Dr. Ostrod used to have a class for French. We were shocked when we heard of his death."

"Ostrod? How did he come to row in this galley?"

"Pasquale Vico. . . ."

"Vico? Is he in it too?"

"Isn't he a funny little soul? He's a marvellous cook, you know, and he loves teaching the boys and girls how to cook simple dishes and wait at table, and so on. He persuaded Dr. Ostrod to come and help us. Of course," Meg added apologetically, "it's all on a very small scale, and no doubt you're thinking that the county councils run much better classes, with much better equipment and properly qualified teachers. We always point that out to the Teeners, but the difficulty is that they don't like rules and regulations and they won't be punctual and attend regularly. With us, they can come or stay away as they like, try one class and go on to something else next time— just please themselves. And a good many don't do anything but play indoor games or read magazines and papers when it's too wet or cold to be outdoors."

"Do you have any difficulty in keeping order?"

"We did at first, especially when we started little branches in various places, but we don't now. Mrs. Sweeney put it up to the Teeners themselves. Those who were really interested in their classes didn't like being pushed around by young hooligans, so she let them elect their own committees. There are several of the bigger lads responsible for keeping order, and they certainly do it! You'd be surprised how seldom the helpers have to interfere."

When they reached the big, old-fashioned house she took him on a tour of inspection.

Mrs. Sweeney, it appeared, had had her own rooms on the first floor. The servants lived on the second floor, where a kitchen and an additional bathroom had been installed. The attics included storerooms and a couple of small bedrooms in which Teeners could be put up for a night or two in cases of exceptional hardship.

On the ground floor, the two large rooms on one side of the hall had been made into one. This was the general meeting place, where draughts, darts and other games were played. There was a small stage at one end, with a piano. On the opposite side of the hall there was a reading and writing room, and behind it another room sub-divided into small classrooms.

The cellars were spacious. There was a miniature gymnasium in one; another was fitted up for carpentry and the simpler forms of metal-working. In a third stood an old-fashioned, but quite serviceable, flat-bed printing machine, with cases of type and other accessories. The machine was used only under the supervision of David Jones, who also gave talks on bookbinding and kindred subjects. He was, it appeared, a highly skilled man, and Meg remarked with pride that several lads who had been grounded by him were now in steady employment.

The washrooms and lavatories were in the basement where the kitchens and larders had been when the house had been occupied by a large family.

By the time they had finished looking round most of the party had assembled, and Kair was introduced to the clerical gentlemen; to David Jones, a dark man with the eyes of a fanatic, and his dark, vivacious daughter; to the big, genial Inspector Vance of the uniformed branch; and to other leaders and a few selected senior Teeners who had been included in the festivities.

Curtis Frost welcomed Kair and waved aside his thanks for the invitation.

"I'm proud to have you with us," he declared. "I don't have to say I've read your books. Everybody has—everybody who's interested in what's going to happen to this world of ours, that is. You're trying to do something that will help people."

"It seems to me you're doing a good deal yourself," Kair replied.

Frost shrugged. "This is nothing," he answered. "I've rented a house near Normansea, on the Somerset coast, and it seemed a good idea to ask a few of the Teeners gang to sniff a bit of sea air. I put the idea up to Mrs. Sweeney and the others and they seemed to think it was worth while."

Much activity ensued. Meg was rushing about, with Frost in attendance. David Jones and his daughter were checking lists of names. Inspector Vance was shepherding sedate elders and excited youngsters into the waiting motor-coaches with the genial efficiency of long practice.

The Teeners were noisy, and some of them—both youths and girls—looked decidedly tough; but their jostlings were playful, and Kair was struck by the alacrity with which they obeyed the directions of their elected leaders. Remarkable discipline, he thought, and the more so because its subjects did not realise that they were being disciplined.

Kair contrived to get a few words with the vicar, who had come to see the party off.

"Frost seems a pleasant fellow," he remarked, "though he's the nearest thing to a playboy in a Hollywood film I've ever seen."

The vicar chuckled.

"A very good description," he agreed, "but I must say I like him. More money than brains, I fancy, but he has the decency to admit it. I'm told that his father left him quite a lot of money and he's tried his hand at all sorts of things, including films—producing, not acting—and lost a packet on most of them. But he seems quite happy; he says he's willing to try almost everything once."

"Including the hazards of warfare?"

"That's the only thing I've ever seen him get angry about. He says his doctor told the American army doctor that he was afraid he had something the matter with his lungs— Frost's lungs, I mean—so they wouldn't take him. Frost insists it was all nonsense. He went to California, or somewhere, to get cured. He was supposed to have T.B., but it cleared up. By that time it was too late for him to join up. I'm only repeating what he told us, of course. Anyhow, he's been pretty generous to the Teeners. It appears that his father knew Mrs. Sweeney's husband, and when Frost heard of what Mrs. Sweeney was doing he said he'd like to help. Hence this joyride. That's really all I know about him. As you said, he looks like a film playboy, but he's pretty good at games and so forth, and he doesn't brag about his money."

The conversation was ended by the departure, amid cheers, of the laden coaches, bound for the airfield from which the party would fly westward.

Frost, it appeared, was to drive his luxurious Lincoln, with Meg, Kair, Inspector Vance and David Jones as his passengers. Kair was not surprised to find that Meg was installed beside Frost, the others occupying the back seat.

Kair did not find the journey tedious. Inspector Vance, at ease in sports jacket and flannels, told some amusing tales of his constable days on the beat, and David Jones contributed reminiscences of his apprenticeship in a small Welsh firm that published a weekly newspaper as well as doing a thriving business in jobbing printing. Jones' best story was of a correspondent in a rural neighbourhood who sent in a long account of the funeral of a local notable. It happened that just as the coffin was being lowered into the grave one of the mourners suffered a heart attack and dropped dead beside it. "And this," wrote the correspondent, "cast an unfortunate gloom over the proceedings."

It was a story which, as Kair happened to know, was true, but it had been round the world at least twice, ascribed to a hundred different localities; nevertheless Jones told it, in his Welsh intonation, with a dry humour that gained the applause it deserved.

The flight in the big aeroplane which Frost had chartered was a new experience for most of the party, but no one was airsick, and everyone was in high spirits when the machine touched down at the landing-field at which other motor-coaches were ready to take them to Frost's house.

It was still fairly early in the day when the leading coach, turning out of a main road, passed through the gateway of the drive and across the extensive ground that surrounded Five Towers, an old stone mansion set high on a shelf in the cliff overlooking the sea, not far from the historic town of Normansea.

It had been the country seat of a famous family generations

before, but had passed into other hands, and Frost had leased it, furniture and all, from its present owners. It was called Five Towers because there was one at each corner of the square main building, and a fifth surmounted a wing built out at the back.

Frost might not, as he admitted, have conducted his business ventures very successfully, but as a host he left nothing to be desired. He assembled the mob on the lawn before the house and announced the day's programme.

His own cabin cruiser and a number of hired motor-boats awaited those who cared to brave the waters of the Bristol Channel (at the moment fortunately calm). The coaches would then tour historic and beautiful spots in the neighbourhood for the benefit of the less adventurous people, and the whole party would return to Five Towers in time for luncheon at half past one.

In the afternoon a concert party would perform in a big marquee, and then an orchestra would provide music for dancing. For the younger folk games of various kinds would be organised.

The festivities would end with an early 'high tea', sufficiently substantial to enable the party to endure the fatigue of the return journey.

Frost's announcement was received with what a local newspaper reporter, who had heard of the affair from the caterers concerned, described as loud and prolonged applause.

When the laden coaches had departed there remained Meg Milcote, Kair, Vance and a few others, none of whom thirsted to sail the seas or to muse upon the relics of an earlier age. Frost suggested that thirst of another kind should be assuaged with a glass of sherry or a cocktail 'on the side', for it had been decided that alcohol should not be included in the general refreshments.

The suggestion was well received. They went into the house and were served by Skelton, a beefy man who looked as though he would have been more comfortable in shirt-sleeves than in his correct black coat. Skelton had been a policeman on the New York force until he was sacked for knocking out a sergeant whom he had considered too well provided with aces in a poker game. After trying various occupations, for he was an adaptable person, he had been taken on by Frost's father as an extra chauffeur, and had graduated into house service. He was, Frost remarked, a pretty bum butler and not so hot as a valet, but he was surprisingly honest and he certainly could throw a cocktail that made you feel good all the way down. With the latter statement Kair heartily concurred.

When he could not persuade anyone to have more drinks, Frost showed them the more interesting parts of the old building. His historical detail was remarkably accurate, and Kair said so.

The American grinned. "Don't let me fool you; I got nearly all this stuff out of guide-books," he confessed.

"Why not?" Meg demanded. "It doesn't matter where you got it so long as you're really interested—and you are, aren't you?"

"I'll say I am! I'm a hundred per cent American, and proud of it; but when you see places like this, where the ancestors of people like George Washington were living generations before there was such a thing as the United States to write a Constitution for, it certainly does something to you. Say, do you know there are big cellars here that were used by smugglers? Let me show you, before the gang gets back. They're called cellars, but at first they may have been practically caves, so the books say."

They went down to the basement and followed a narrow passage that led to the first of several great chambers which opened into each other. They were floored with fairly modern bricks, but the walls and roofs were of much older stone, and in each room there was a long stone table. Owing to the slope of the ground it had been possible to cut windows for lighting, and doors by which the caves could be entered from the grounds at the back of the house. Additional light was provided by electric globes, the current being obtained from the private plant which supplied light and power to the whole house. This plant had been installed in a smaller cave, and was at present run by Hank Peters, a lean and silent person who had once been a racing motorist and was now Frost's chauffeur, mechanic and general handyman.

Skelton and Peters were the only permanent members of his staff, Frost explained. A cook-housekeeper and some other women, recommended by the owners, came in daily, but did not sleep in the house. They had been allowed to take this day

off because a Normansea catering firm had been given *carte
blanche* to feed and entertain the Teener party.

"And I expect the housekeeper and the other women are
making a nice thing out of it," Vance commented. "What you
want is a real smart wife to take care of you."

"You've got something there," Frost agreed promptly.
"I've been thinking that myself, just lately."

He tried to catch Meg's eye, but that young lady was
showing such a respectful interest in the electrical plant that
even the saturnine Hank Peter's icy reserve was melted.

The two biggest caves had been handed over to the
caterers, who had transformed them into something between
an ancient banqueting hall and modern restaurant and were
now preparing for the onslaught of the famished guests.

Frost looked at his watch.

"We've got to hurry," he said, "but there's one more thing
I want you to see."

He led them to the farthest of the caves, where there was at
one end a carpenter's bench and tools and at the other a forge
and other appliances for working in metal.

"What do you know about that?" he asked with obvious
pride.

Two men in overalls were at work. Frost spoke to them in
German, and they smiled and bowed to the visitors.

"They're D.P.'s—Displaced Persons, you know," Frost
explained. "One's a Czech and the other's a Pole. Your Government let me have permits for them to make my models, and are
they dandy!"

He looked at his watch.

"But say, we'll have to beat it. The rest of the gang are
due back, and they'll be starving."

His prediction was correct. Mariners and motorists alike
fell on the food voraciously. Then, stomachs comfortably
distended, they trooped back to the grounds to dance, play
games, or listen to the professional entertainers in the marquee,
as seemed good to them.

Frost, aided by Meg, Kair and Vance, worked hard to get
things going. Then Frost took the girl off to dance.

Kair slipped away to a quiet corner of the grounds, lit his
pipe and promptly fell asleep.

He was apparently not the only one to enjoy a little folding of the hands to slumber, for when he awoke, reproaching himself for his desertion, he saw Inspector Vance crossing the lawn and hailed him.

"Ah, there you are," Kair greeted him. "I was just wondering where you'd got to."

"I slipped away and had a snooze," Vance confessed. "I was on duty late last night, and up early this morning. Well, I suppose I'd better go and help with the kids' games."

"Just a minute," Kair said. "Got some dust on the back of your coat," and he brushed the inspector's sports jacket with his hand.

Vance thanked him, and strolled away, lighting a cigarette.

The moments sped by inexorably, and at last Frost had to summon everybody into the caves for tea.

Then the coaches were loaded once more and the occupants sang songs all the way back to the airfield, and from there until they were finally decanted from the coaches at Swiss Cottage.

There David Jones thanked Curtis Frost on behalf of the party, and cheers were given.

Frost grinned, said something incoherent, and bolted into the house.

The Teeners and most of the helpers dispersed.

Frost offered to give Meg a lift home in his car, but found that Kair had forestalled him.

Vance shook Frost's hand.

"You've given us a great time," he said.

The others agreed.

Frost said a hasty good-bye all round, almost jumped into his Lincoln, and drove off.

Kair, taking Meg back to Canton Court, found himself wondering on what dusty couch Inspector Vance had reclined to enjoy his afternoon snooze.

CHAPTER XIII

KAIR was in his workroom about eleven o'clock the next morning when Muir telephoned.

"You know who is speaking?" the chief superintendent asked. "Right. My wife wondered whether you could come to tea this afternoon at four?"

The words were an invitation, but the tone was an order.

"There is only one answer to a royal command," Kair answered, "especially when it's such a welcome one."

"Thanks. You know my house. It's bit off the beaten track, so give yourself plenty of time in case you take a few wrong turnings. We'll expect you at four, then. Good-bye."

Kair replaced the receiver and considered the short conversation. He knew the chief superintendent's capacity for saying a good deal in a few words. Muir's caution did not necessarily mean that he suspected that the Canton Court operator was listening-in, but it certainly meant that he was taking no risks. That bit about allowing plenty of time in case he might take a wrong turning was an equally obvious warning to look out for followers. Finally, the 'we'll expect you' meant that he would not be the only guest.

What struck him most, however, was not what the chief superintendent had said, but the way in which he had said it. Muir had not been in the least dictatorial, or even curt; but there had been a hard note in his voice that Kair had not heard before.

Shrugging, he tried to put the matter out of his mind. He spent the rest of the morning consulting works of reference and generally making a great show of mental activity.

It was a great relief when Cradoc announced lunch, and he sat over the meal as long as he could.

At quarter to three he told Cradoc he was going out and he was not sure when he would be back. At his request the man telephoned to the hall-porter to pick up a taxi-cab.

When Kair arrived at the main entrance a few minutes later the porter had a cab waiting for him. He told the driver, rather loudly, to take him to the Imperium Club.

The Imperium, damaged by bombs during the war, had moved to a pleasant riverside site near Westminster Bridge, but on the Waterloo side of the Thames—the first of the big London clubs to dare such an innovation.

At the club he paid off the cabman. Going inside, he asked the hall-porter if there were any letters for him, chatted with the man for a few minutes, and then walked through to the spacious garden abutting on the river which was one of the club's most attractive features. At one end of the garden there was an alley used by tradesmen when delivering goods. By this alley Kair slipped out to the main road and walked briskly to Waterloo. There he took an underground train. Getting out at Trafalgar Square, he allowed all the passengers to leave the platform before he went to the escalator and ascended to street level.

During all these proceedings he had not seen the same face twice, but he knew that if he were really being followed it was probable that one trailer would relieve another.

Cutting across the Square, he strolled into St. James's Park and sat down on an isolated bench. He was timing his movements carefully.

There were not many people in the park, as it happened, and when he resumed his stroll he kept well in the open. He was fairly satisfied that he was either not being followed or had shaken off his pursuer. Leaving the park, he plunged into the maze of little streets behind Birdcage Walk, and at two minutes to four he reached Muir's house. Grinning at his own vanity, he waited until Big Ben began to strike the hour before he pressed the knob of the electric bell.

Muir opened the door himself, said, "Glad to see you. Come in," and led him to the living-room. Larry Doyle and Joe Marshall were there.

A maid brought in the materials for tea, including buttered toast, piping hot.

"Sybarite!" Kair smiled, taking two pieces.

Chat was general for a few minutes, but Kair was uncomfortably conscious of a certain tension.

When no one wanted any more toast or biscuits, Muir said:

"Now, Kair, we want some information from you."

"From me? What sort of information?"

"You'll soon see. If you'll excuse me, we're going to cross-examine you like a witness in the box."

"Go ahead," Kair responded, considerably astonished, "but I don't understand what you can have to cross-examine me about. Have I been doing something stupid?"

"Not at all. You've been very useful, though you don't know it. Coming down to brass tacks, you went to Normansea with the Teener party yesterday, I believe?"

"I did. Why?"

"Never mind that for the moment. Will you give us an account of the outing, starting from the time when you arrived

at Mrs. Sweeney's house in the morning? I know this sounds
very mysterious, but you'll see our point presently. We want
to get your impressions while they're fresh and before we tell
you the reason."

Kair shrugged. "You know best," he replied. "Do you
mean you want me to go into details? It'll take a bit of time,
you know."

"That's all right. We're not in a hurry."

Kair looked at the three gravely attentive faces, and without more ado proceeded to describe the events of the previous
day. He was surprised, once he began to speak, to find himself
recalling incidents which he had not consciously noted at the
time. Many of them seemed to him to be trivial, but he took
Muir at his word and recounted them. None of the three made
a single interruption, but Doyle occasionally scribbled a note
on a pad of paper. The narrative took, as Kair had predicted,
some time. When he had finished, Muir said:

"Thanks. You've given us a very good picture."

"May I ask——"

"Just a minute, please. This was your first visit to Mrs.
Sweeney's house, wasn't it?"

"Yes."

"You mentioned Inspector Vance. Did you have much talk
with him?"

"Not as much as I wanted. I took rather a shine to him. He
and David Jones and I had a chat on the way down, and Vance
told us about his early days as a constable."

"Did you see much of him when you got to Normansea?"

"No. He disappeared for a bit, and when I next saw him
he said he'd been having a nap."

Kair's face must have changed as he spoke, for Muir asked
quietly, "When was that?"

"After lunch."

"Were you surprised?"

"Not at first. He explained that he'd been on late duty the
night before, and he'd been rushing round a good deal yesterday, helping Curtis Frost."

"You said 'not at first'. Did anything occur to you afterwards, then?"

Kair hesitated. "Well, it may not be worth mention-
ing——"

"We'll judge of that. Please go on."

"It was only that I noticed that he'd got the back of his coat a bit dusty, and I wondered why. I mean, I wondered why he hadn't taken his nap on a sofa or in a deck-chair, or something like that."

"Did he explain that?"

"No. I brushed the dust off with my hand—there wasn't much, you know—and he thanked me and went off to play games with the smaller fry."

Muir nodded. "Was he in good spirits?"

"Good spirits? Of course. I should think he was about the most popular person in the whole show, after Frost. But frankly, Muir, I don't get all this. Why not ask Vance yourself?"

"Vance is dead," Muir said heavily.

Kair stared at him incredulously.

"Dead? But he seemed perfectly well when I said good-bye to him last night. I asked him to come to my place for a drink and a chat, but he said he wanted to get home. I'd have thought he was a very fit man."

"He was. Not long after he left Mrs. Sweeney's house he was found lying in a quiet road, with the back of his head smashed in."

"You mean he was murdered?"

"Yes."

"Couldn't it have been an accident? He might have been knocked down by a car——"

He stopped as the other shook his head.

"I'm afraid not," Muir replied. "Now you see why we wanted you to tell us as much as possible about what happened yesterday."

Kair nodded. "I liked Vance," he said slowly.

"So did we," Joe Marshall muttered.

"You knew him, then? I mean, he was in the uniformed branch——"

"We knew him very well," said Doyle, speaking for the first time, and something in his manner made Kair start.

"Vance was doing special duty for us," Muir explained. "We've been keeping you in the dark, Kair; not because we don't trust you, but because we didn't want to put ideas into your head too soon. Now I'm going to tell you several things, and I may say that I've again had to get special permission to do it. Three of us—Superintendent Ash, Doyle and myself—have been given a sort of *liaison* job to co-ordinate plans for dealing with what's believed to be the biggest Communist push we've ever had in this country. More than that I can't say at present, but I want you to realise that it's a damned serious matter. You've got to watch your step; as I told you before, a careless word might mean a bash on the head or a knife in your ribs, and what's more important—to be brutally frank—might put a lot of very dangerous people on their guard. It's not your job, after all, and I've been told to assure you again that no one will blame you if you decide to drop it——"

"Thanks for the offer," Kair interrupted, "but I think you know my answer already. I don't want to talk a lot of patriotic hot air. Anyone with a grain of sense, even the most convinced Socialist, must realise that a Red dictatorship would be more horrible than the worst things the Fascists or the Nazis ever planned. I'll only be taking the risks you fellows have to take every day, and if I get myself into a mess, that's my lookout. I've spent enough time writing tripe about the working of other people's minds, when I don't understand how my own works. Now, perhaps, I can do something really useful. Just tell me what you want me to do, and I'll have a damned good try at doing it."

"Right," Muir said quietly, but his smile said more. "We'll leave it at that. Before we go any farther, is there anything you want to ask me? I may not be able to say a lot, but if you're going to be useful you must have as clear a picture in your mind as possible. Any questions?"

"Yes, please. First, do I take it that Vance was keeping observation, or whatever you call it, on the Teeners organisation?"

"He was."

"Does that mean that Mrs. Sweeney is a Red?"

"No. She certainly did a lot of good work in the war, and since then the Teener movement has been quite a success in a small way. But the organisation is being used to train young Reds and spread propaganda—we're sure of that. We've checked up on Mrs. Sweeney, of course, but there's no doubt that her late husband had his fingers in a good many political pies in the States. Unfortunately, the Federal Bureau of Investigation can't give us anything definite about him. He seems to have kept well under cover. But Mrs. Sweeney certainly isn't the boss of the show."

"Am I allowed to ask who *is* the boss?"

"I wish I could tell you. Vance believed that the printer, David Jones, was one of the leading figures, and probably did the printing of pamphlets, faked passports, and so on, but Vance was sure there was a bigger man in the background. Of course, there are a lot of respectable people in the show—the rector, the R.C. *padre*, the man who audits the accounts, and others. On the other hand, you can never tell what a fanatic will do for his cause. We think that a lot of these people were encouraged to act as helpers because the very fact that they belonged to the organisation gave it a good name. It seemed a clever stroke to get Vance to give boxing lessons, but it wasn't quite clever enough. They thought they could fool him, but as a matter of fact we'd been trying to get a man into the organisation, and they played into our hands."

"But if they didn't suspect him, why on earth should they murder him?"

"That's just the point. We think that something happened yesterday that made them suspicious—or confirmed their suspicions, if they had some already. Your remark about that dust on his coat may be the answer."

"You mean he may have been doing a bit of snooping at Normansea?"

"Yes. We've been interested in Curtis Frost for some time. The American Embassy people have helped, but his papers are in order and his father was a strong Roosevelt man. It's true Curtis was in a Leftish set for a bit, but that's common enough with the sons of rich men. He seems to have got tired of it fairly soon and adopted his father's faith, though he didn't take any prominent part in politics."

"Apparently he was unfit for military service."

"Yes, so we are told."

"There's such a thing as buying a faked medical certificate."

"It could have been done, the Embassy people say, but it wasn't easy. So we have to give him the benefit of the doubt. But we're interested in Frost for a lot of reasons. For one thing, when he was a boy his name was Kurt Forst."

"A German!"

"Half a minute. There are millions of Americans whose people came from Europe. His father and mother left Germany and went to the States when they were newly married. Forst senior went into the office of an uncle who was in the real estate business. In due time the uncle died and Old Man Forst took over. He improved the business and also made some good speculations in property on his own account. He was a rich man when he died. Long before that he had taken out naturalisation papers and changed his name to Frost. Young Kurt, who was born in 1916, became Curtis. At fifteen the boy was sent to Europe. He went first to a French school and then to a German one. We think that the whole thing was arranged by his father in collusion with certain people in Germany. There's no doubt that Old Man Forst, later Frost, was in touch with the German Embassy in the States before the 1914–18 war. That was, of course, before he took American nationality. We've got very little to go on, but the Federal Bureau suspect that young Curtis was trained by the Nazis and was sent back to the States in 1936 to act as a secret agent there. Whether his father knew that is uncertain, and doesn't much matter."

"But if Frost is, or was, a Nazi, why should he back the Communists?"

"There's reason to believe that some people who want to see Germany a great nation again are trying to infiltrate the Communist Party, and encourage it to upset the Western Powers and Russia into the bargain. Then, when things are in complete confusion, they hope to step in and set up a much more powerful Nazi State than Hitler was able to do. You get the idea?"

"Yes, but it hardly seems possible that they could pull it off."

"That's what people said about Hitler before the war," Muir retorted. "However, we're not here to talk politics. Those are matters for my elders and betters. I'm just trying to explain where Curtis Frost comes in—or may come in, because most of it's guesswork so far."

'I understand. Thanks for telling me."

"'Right. Now let's get back to Vance. When he left you last night to go home, was he wearing a hat?"

"No."

"You're sure of that?"

"Quite. When we got into Frost's car to go to the airfield

Jones and I put our hats into a net arrangement fixed in the roof to hold light parcels. Vance remarked that as he had to spend so much of his time wearing a uniform cap he liked to go without a hat when he was having a holiday. Is the point important?"

"Very. Vance was a powerful man and a good boxer, but there was nothing to suggest that he'd put up a fight. What do you make of that?"

"Obviously that he was taken by surprise."

"Exactly. The police-surgeon says there were two blows; he thinks the first one stunned Vance and the second one finished him. I needn't go into the medical details. Briefly, this is our theory: Vance was walking along a quiet road. A car came up from behind and stopped at the kerb beside him. He was on the near side. Someone *he knew* was driving the car. The driver called out to Vance, and Vance put his head inside the window. The driver was holding a weapon—possibly a spanner, from the appearance of the wounds—in his right hand. As Vance leaned forward into the car the driver put his left hand on Vance's back, forcing his head down, and struck him with the spanner, or whatever it was, with his right hand The first blow knocked Vance out, and the driver was able to give the second and fatal blow with more care. Then he pushed the head so that Vance fell back on to the kerb, and the car was out of sight in a few seconds.

"You probably know that it's not difficult for a doctor to distinguish between various types of injuries, and in this case the police-surgeon's opinion is confirmed by"—he mentioned a specialist of European reputation. "We tried the thing out at the Yard this morning, using cars of different sizes. At first we doubted whether the driver would have enough room to strike sufficiently heavy blows, but we found it could be done. In fact, the man impersonating the murderer got a bit too enthusiastic and hit the victim a crack that nearly knocked him out. It was easiest, of course, when we used a big car with plenty of head room."

"Frost drives an enormous Lincoln," Kair put in.

"Yes, and Frost left Mrs. Sweeney's a few minutes after Vance had gone."

"There's one thing that's just occurred to me," Kair said. "I remember that Frost offered to drive Meg Milcote home, but she'd already arranged to go with me. I thought Frost was a bit annoyed."

"It's quite possible he had overheard you making that arrangement, and knew it was safe to make his own offer. He didn't offer you or anyone else a lift, did he?"

"No, he didn't. We thought he was embarrassed by being thanked for the party, and wanted to get away. Are you going to arrest him?"

"How the hell can I arrest him?" Muir demanded acidly. "If I pull him in he'll stand on his rights as an American citizen and yell to the Embassy for help, and they'll have to give it. I can't charge him with murder when I haven't a shred of evidence to produce, and I can't keep him in jug just because he looks like a Nazi in English tweeds. Besides, it would mean giving our whole game away. If I could prove that he killed Vance I'd have to pull him in at once, but I can't, and I'm hoping he doesn't think we suspect him."

"What about his car?" Kair asked. "Wouldn't there be bloodstains on the floor?"

"There might, but in such wounds bleeding is usually slight, and Frost could have laid a rug or a thick newspaper on the floor as a precaution. But that line is no good. We rushed a woman detective down to Normansea early this morning. She was supposed to be a saleswoman selling accessories for a motor firm. She saw Frost's chauffeur and produced samples and all that. Frost has a couple of other cars besides the Lincoln. The chauffeur wasn't interested in her samples, but he was fairly civil. She flattered him about the Lincoln and the care he took of it and he let her have a look inside. It was as clean as a new pin."

"I still don't understand Frost's game," Kair said. "He seemed quite enthusiastic about the work he was doing, and the things he'd had made were well finished."

"Of course they were. Do remember that we're dealing with people who've thought of the answers before you've had time to ask the questions. We believe Frost is running the munitions side of the organisation—smuggling in explosives and weapons, and making bombs. One of his amusements is dashing about in his big motor-boat, especially at night. He's friendly with a man named Muldoon, who lives in a cottage at Oastmarsh, a small town not very far from Normansea."

"I know the place," Kair remarked. "Very historic, quaint old houses, and all that."

"And also much concerned in the smuggling business in the old days," Muir said significantly. "We think Vance must have seen something he wasn't supposed to see at Frost's house, and been spotted by Frost or one of his men."

"It must have been something important, if that's why he was killed."

"Yes. It seems to have been a hurried job, though efficient, and it meant taking a definite risk."

Kair had an idea. "It was the same in Ostrod's case," he said. "Whoever killed Ostrod took a hell of a risk of being seen."

Muir nodded.

"Talking of Ostrod," Doyle put in, "we've found out one thing about Pasquale Vico that he didn't tell us. He spoke the truth when he said that after the row at the Liberation Club he took a long walk, and called in at a pub for a drink, but he didn't mention that he made a telephone call while he was there. We found the pub, and the landlord recognised Vico's photograph. It was a bit of luck. Vico asked for change, as he had no pennies. The landlord noticed that his hands were shaking. Unfortunately the 'phone is in a box in the corner of the bar, and it's a dial instrument, so we don't know the number Vico called. I haven't told him we know that, sir."

"Quite right." Muir looked at the clock. "Now, Doyle, you want to ask some questions, don't you?"

"Yes, sir." He turned to Kair. "You said that Miss Milcote showed you round the house?"

"Yes, the lower part."

"You didn't go upstairs?"

"No. She said Mrs. Sweeney and a couple of maids had lived up there. I don't know whether she retains the rooms or not."

"When you were downstairs, did you see anything that surprised you?"

Kair looked blank, and Doyle said, "I know that's vague, but I don't want to give you any lead."

"I don't know that I was exactly surprised," Kair explained after some reflection. "You must remember that I didn't know then what I know now, but I do remember thinking that the cellars seemed to be unusually large for a house of that size. Then I remembered being told that Mrs. Sweeney had had them fitted up as air-raid shelters and I concluded she'd had them enlarged."

"Did you go into the back garden?"

"No."

Doyle consulted his notes. "Going back to yesterday's doings: can you say where Frost was while Vance was supposed to be having a nap?"

"Frost was certainly in the marquee when the show began. I distinctly remember seeing him. I told you that when I'd done what I could to help I went off for a smoke in the grounds. I think—but I'm not sure—I saw Frost crossing the lawn in the direction of the house."

"When did you next see him?"

"After the concert. He was dancing with Meg. Then he danced with a lot of the other girls."

"While Vance was missing, did you see anything of Skelton, the butler, or Peters, the chauffeur?"

"I didn't see Skelton, but I saw Peters; he was standing at the back of the marquee, listening to the comedian of the concert party. I didn't notice him again until we were nearly ready to leave."

"Thank you. I think that's all, sir."

Muir looked inquiringly at Marshall.

"I'd like," said the chief inspector, "to hear Mr. Kair's impression of David Jones, the foreman printer."

"A very intelligent man, I thought," Kair responded. "He told me he was self-educated, and I said he'd made a good job of it. That seemed to amuse him. I don't suggest that he tried to show off, but it was quite evident that he'd not only read a lot of books, but had formed very definite opinions about them."

"Your own books, for instance?" Joe suggested slyly, and Muir and Doyle laughed.

"Yes, curse you," Kair retorted, "and he was kind enough to approve of them, if you want to know."

"A very intelligent man," Muir murmured.

"Did Jones mention his daughter at all?"

"No, I don't think so."

"Did he talk about anyone else in the Teener organisation?"

"Yes. He said how much they owed to Mrs. Sweeney for

letting them use her house and for all the other things she'd done, and how grateful they were to people like Miss Milcote and Inspector Vance for giving so much of their spare time to the work. Vance replied that he enjoyed it, and that they all knew how much Jones had done for the Teeners."

"Quite a mutual admiration society," Muir remarked.

"It sounds like it, but it was really all quite casual. Then Jones started to talk of his own young days and Vance followed suit, and they were both very interesting."

"Did either of them refer to Frost?"

"No; but Frost was sitting in front of us, driving, and they may not have cared to discuss him."

Muir nodded, and there was a short silence.

"There's one thing I'd like to say," Kair began with some hesitation, "if you won't think me too damned impertinent?"

"Go ahead," Muir encouraged him.

"I don't want to tread on forbidden ground, and, of course, I realise you know a great deal more than you've told me, but somehow I can't see Mrs. Sweeney and her associates as a very dangerous menace to our glorious commonwealth."

Kair had spoken lightly, but the others recognised the serious note behind his words.

"Why not?" Muir asked.

"The thing seems too small. They may be willing enough to wound . . ."

"But *not* afraid to strike," Muir altered the quotation.

"I agree, but how can they fight the Government and the Secret Service and the police? You talk about gun-running and bomb-making, and what-have-you, but can they do it on a big scale? It's true they seem to have money and if they murdered Ostrod and Vance they must be pretty ruthless, but how far can they get before you chuck them all into gaol? Forgive me if I say that, with all the resources you control, you ought to be able to knock hell out of them any time you like."

There was another silence, and Kair wondered if he had gone too far, but the others showed no sign of annoyance.

"I don't think," Muir said quietly, "you quite realise the situation, even now, and I don't altogether blame you. You're rather in the position of a barrister who's been given a brief with only half the facts of the case in it. But you've got to stop thinking in terms of a schoolboys' secret society. This thing is deadly serious. You mentioned Ostrod and Vance just now; but we have to produce enough hard evidence to convince a judge and a jury who, thank God, are still free to see that a prisoner has a fair trial. But Ostrod and Vance are not the only men who've been put away in the last few months. Who the others were doesn't matter at the moment, but you can take it from me that they were all parts of this jigsaw puzzle." He paused, then went on, choosing his words carefully: "You think this is a small organisation; we don't. I only wish we knew how big it really is. But I'll give you this hint: it's big enough to be able to get hold of information that should be known to perhaps only a score of people in the whole country.

"And yet," Muir added impressively, "we haven't discovered a single suspect who holds any official position or is in any way connected with Government circles. I don't mean those pink Reds who get weeded out every now and then and go about yelling for vengeance. I'm talking about the really dangerous men, the men who are clever enough to keep under cover. Time and again arrangements have been made to take some particular step; only a comparatively few people have been in the secret; and yet that secret has got out somehow. We'd decide, for instance, to arrest a man; when we went to pull him in we'd find he'd vanished. And yet all the people in the secret were—well, let's say they were above suspicion in every way. I know, of course, what you're thinking. You're thinking that one of them must have been a Judas. All right, that's fair enough," Muir declared savagely: "but the logical answer is that the Judas may be me, or Doyle, or the Prime Minister, or even that brilliant sociologist, Mr. Barnabas Darley Kair. So put that in your pipe and damn well smoke it!"

Again there was silence. Then Muir gave a short laugh.

"Sorry," he said. "I shouldn't have lost my temper, but now perhaps you'll have some idea of what we're up against. Well, I think we've talked enough—too much, as far as I'm concerned. I'm not going to insult you again by telling you to keep all this under your hat and watch your step; if you don't you probably won't have a head to put your hat on. Now Doyle and I've got things to do, but there's time for just one drink before we break up."

They had just one.

CHAPTER XIV

POLICE-CONSTABLE REDFERN was an intelligent and observant officer. It was only six months since he had completed his recruit's course at Peel House and been sent to the Swiss Cottage district to be broken in to street work, but already his sub-divisional inspector had decided that something might be made of young Redfern; it might be worth while giving him a chance one day, if a chance came along. Constable Redfern, of course, did not know that, for sub-divisional inspectors do not say such things to constables.

When the sub-divisional inspector was informed by his superintendent that a discreet eye was to be kept by the uniformed branch on the Sweeney house he gave the matter some thought. It appeared, he gathered from his superintendent, that those C.I.D. gods at the Yard, who moved in such mysterious way their wonders to perform, were anxious to avoid putting on plain clothes patrols or taking any other step which might, however careful were the men concerned, attract the attention of the Sweeney household. A uniformed constable, however, rather lazily pacing a quiet beat, was as much a common object of the seashore as a milkman or a postman.

The sub-divisional inspector summoned Constable Redfern and spoke with him. He did not say a great deal but he was satisfied that the young constable had put two and two together and had made four. It was obvious that Redfern could not be on duty for twenty-four hours consecutively, so the sub-divisional inspector tried him first on the afternoon turn of duty, making other arrangements for the remaining hours.

P.c. Redfern, then, was pacing with deliberate slowness the road in which Mrs. Sweeney lived when he saw a van stop at her house. It was about four o'clock. The van bore the name of a well-known furnishing firm. Redfern eased up, with the air of a bored constable glad of even the smallest incident to break the monotony of duty in a respectable neighbourhood in which nothing ever seemed to happen.

The rear doors of the van opened and two men emerged. One was tall and thin and the other short and stout. Both wore green baize aprons with bibs up to the collar; one of them had

F

a cap and the other a bowler. Between them they extracted a
roll of carpet from the van and carried it into the house.

Then the thin man returned and got into the van and its
driver drove it away.

What, Constable Redfern asked himself, had become of the
short, stout man, who had not returned to the van? He considered the point, strolled slowly to a telephone box and rang
up his station. As instructed, he asked for the sub-divisional
inspector; the sergeant was annoyed, but he also had his
instructions and could do nothing but put the call through. A
pretty state of affairs, the sergeant reflected, when a blasted
pup of a new p.c. could talk to the S.D.I. without so much as a
by-your-leave!

Redfern made his report, and added the remark that the
van was obviously an old one, but the name of the firm seemed
to have been newly painted on it.

"All right, Redfern; keep your eyes open," was all the sub-
divisional inspector said; but constables quickly learn the
idiosyncrasies of their superiors, and the young constable
caught an inflection in the S.D.I.'s voice that made his chest
strain at the buttons of his tunic.

The superintendent was out, so the sub-divisional inspector
got on to the Yard and was put through to Chief Inspector
Larry Doyle.

Larry thanked him, and made a telephone call before he
went to Muir's room and relayed the message.

"Interesting," Muir commented. "That constable seems to
have some brains. We might bear him in mind. Now, about this
bloke in the bowler hat?"

"Sounds rather like our friend Oscar Fersen, sir."

"It does. It's the first time we've traced him to Mrs.
Sweeney's house, isn't it?"

"Yes. He may have been there, of course, but we haven't
spotted him. That's the worst of having to be so careful."

"I know, but that's how it is. Once put them on their guard,
and they'll avoid the place like the plague."

"I believe you know about Oscar Fersen and his brother
Axel, sir?"

"Yes, a good deal; but I thought they were supposed to be
genuine Swedes and above suspicion?"

"They're Swedes all right. At first we believed they were

O.K., and we still think Axel, the inventor, may not know what's going on behind his back, but since we got that message from Sergeant Upwey we've been trying to find out more about Oscar. It hasn't been easy. He's covered his tracks pretty cleverly. Stays down in Wales most of the time, and when he has come to London he's generally stayed at the Everyland or some other good hotel. It's only in the last few weeks that we've got another line on him. We believe he's known to the London mob as 'The Captain', a retired sea-captain—which is true enough. He dresses the part, too, and does it well. He stays with a man called Evan Jenkin Pryse, who keeps a chemist's shop in a back street in Islington. Pryse is a genuine chemist, a member of the Pharmaceutical Society. He's a rigid Baptist; no funny business, no illegal drugs or abortions. Tall, thin type; wears spectacles and stoops. Looks consumptive, but isn't. He's got a rough tongue, but a good business; his poorer customers think he's better than any doctor."

"Think he was the thin man with the van?"

"Sounds like it, sir. It certainly wasn't Curtis Frost; Redfern told his inspector so. And I forgot to say that the van was definitely faked. I rang up the firm and they say they made no deliveries in that road today."

Muir considered. "Perhaps there was something hidden in the roll of carpet," he suggested.

"The inspector questioned Redfern about that. Redfern said he happened to be able to see the end of the thing and it seemed to be tightly rolled, so if there *was* anything hidden it couldn't have been anything bulky."

"Sounds reasonable," the chief superintendent admitted, "but they seem to have gone to a hell of a lot of trouble just to get the Captain from Islington to Swiss Cottage."

"If I may suggest——"

"Of course you may. That's what we're here for, isn't it?"

Larry Doyle grinned. "Thanks, sir. Well, it seems to me there are two explanations, or perhaps I ought to say one explanation in two parts. I think the Captain's very anxious to keep under cover, and the others are just as anxious that he shouldn't seem to have anything to do with them. Secondly, we—I mean the Special Branch, of course—have often noticed that foreigners are much fonder of the cloak-and-dagger business than our crooks are. That's not to say that people like the Captain don't know their job; they most certainly do; but if there's a chance for a bit of theatrical stuff they won't miss it. We've seen that happen time and again, and sometimes it's helped us a bit."

"I see your point, but if the Captain wants to keep under cover, why didn't one of the others go to see him, instead of bringing him to Swiss Cottage?"

"Pryse's shop is well known in its neighbourhood. The Captain is supposed to be his brother-in-law. The story Pryse put about is that when his sister died some time ago the Captain was heartbroken. He decided to retire, sold his house in Sweden, and came to stay with Pryse until he could make up his mind where to settle. Pryse, who's a widower too, lives over the shop. He's a morose sort of bloke and doesn't seem to have any intimate friends, so I imagine they thought that if people started calling there it would soon cause talk, and talk of any kind would be just what they'd want to avoid. Of course, that's only my guess. . . ."

"It's likely to be as good a guess as any other. You've seen the Captain yourself?"

"Yes, once."

"Does he know you?"

"I don't think so, but I can't be sure."

"No, I suppose not. I'd like to know whether he really is at the Sweeney house or not, but I can't take the risk of having you spotted. There isn't an empty house near, is there?"

"Not within a quarter of a mile, but I think we could manage it another way."

"How?"

"There's a narrow lane at the back of the house. If the Captain isn't going to stay all night he's more likely to come out that way than by the front door. They can't have a furniture van driving up to the house in the middle of the night."

"Well?"

"Suppose I wait until it's dark, nip up the lane and shin over the back wall of one of the houses across the lane. From there I could keep an eye on the garden door of the Sweeney house——"

"And have the occupants of the other house dialling 999 and shouting for the police to come and run in the sinister figure lurking in their backyard? It seems to me that'd be asking for trouble."

"I'd thought of that, sir," Larry replied with respectful obstinacy. "The house I have in mind is occupied by two old coves who spend nearly every evening playing chess, and you know what chess is! You could almost drop a bomb outside the house without their noticing it."

"Isn't there anyone else in the house?"

"Not at night. They're brothers, and bachelors, and they're looked after by a man and his wife who come in every day, but don't sleep in the house; they live with a married daughter and her family. They go home every night after they've served the old boys' dinner and cleared away."

"You seem to have gone into it pretty thoroughly."

"I thought something like this might happen, so I got as much dope about the neighbourhood as possible."

"Good work," Muir approved. "You Special Branch lads seem to justify your existence at times, after all. Have you any dope on the Buckingham Gate neighbourhood, by the way?"

"No, sir," Doyle assured him; "I haven't been put on that district so far."

"You relieve my mind," said the chief superintendent, and they both laughed.

"At the bottom of the old boys' garden," Doyle went on, "there's a row of trees that'll make good cover. And if the worst comes to the worst and I am spotted, I can always pull out my warrant card and say I thought I saw a burglar trying to get into the house."

"You mean you'd tell a deliberate lie?" Muir said with mock severity. "You Irishmen could coax a fox out of its den on a winter morning! I suppose I'll have to let you go. But seriously, Larry, you mustn't mess this up. We can't afford a mistake, and I'm trusting you not to make one."

Chief Inspector Doyle departed, treading on air. He had gained his point, and his chief superintendent, who was not noted for undue familiarity in professional relations, had called him by his Christian name. All, as the jocose sentry remarked, was remarkably well.

The shades of night, Larry observed to himself lyrically but incorrectly, had fallen fast as through a narrow alley passed a (by courtesy) youth whose cheek no fear could blanch, for he was of the Special Branch.

In plain words, Mr. Doyle was prepared for trouble but had taken every possible precaution to avoid it.

He wore a dark suit, a black hat pulled well down, and rubber-soled shoes. A navy blue silk handkerchief was knotted loosely round his throat and tucked inside his collar so that it could be raised to cover the whiteness of his face. He carried what appeared to be a plain ash stick with a curved handle.

A constable who had been instructed to meet him a little distance away had given a gruff response to his cheerful good night as he passed, but the response had informed him that the coast was clear.

Halfway up the lane he stopped and manipulated the implement he carried, a steel tube painted to resemble wood. He took the ferrule off and pulled out a telescopic rod, to which he clipped a hook. To the hook was attached a length of thin but strong rope, knotted at intervals. Placing the hook firmly over the top of the wall, he withdrew the rod, folded it up, and shinned up the rope. In a matter of seconds he was perched on a thick branch of a tree, with his back against the trunk, the rope back in his pocket and the counterfeit stick hooked to a smaller branch beside him.

Now began one of the commonest, but most wearisome, tasks that can fall to the lot of a detective officer: that of waiting for something to happen.

He knew that his vigil might last half an hour or half a dozen hours, and produce no result. He could not look forward to the arrival of a man to relieve him at an agreed time; he must not smoke; there was no light by which to read; and if he allowed himself to doze he would probably fall awkwardly and break a limb, besides running the risk of attracting attention. The most he would dare to do would be to move cautiously, at intervals, and alter his position to relax unbearably cramped muscles.

It did not occur to him, however, to bemoan his fate. In his walk of life there were comfortable jobs and uncomfortable ones, and this was one of the damned uncomfortable ones. A detective took the rough with the smooth; that was all there was to it—except that there was always the chance of pulling off something that might put him up a rung on the ladder of promotion, and give him the satisfaction of knowing that he had done something worth while.

He beguiled the time by thinking about this case in which he had had the luck, as he considered it, to be chosen to work with Superintendent Muir. A dozen times he went over all the facts known to him and considered the characters of the people he had met or hoped to meet. He tried to put himself in Muir's place. It was easy enough to plan bold strokes, mass arrests and dramatic confrontations, but this was not a novel or a film in which one could be comfortably satisfied that Vice would in the end be trampled (a little smugly) under the feet of triumphant Virtue. It was a deadly conflict between the forces of law, order and freedom on one side and on the other an enemy evil, ruthless and dangerously cunning. That, he told himself, might sound melodramatic, but it was the cold truth. If Fersen and the forces he represented should succeed in their aims, decent people would lie quaking in their beds at night, dreading the knock on the door that meant a summons to a tribunal from which there was no appeal and whose kindest decree would be a quick death. It was almost incredible, yet it had happened a million times in other countries; it must not happen here. . . .

The strains of the waltz died away.

Meg Milcote and Curtis Frost threaded their way back to a table at the edge of the dance floor. Frost signalled to a waiter to become active about the champagne supply.

"Say, Meg," he exclaimed, "that was something! I don't know whether angels dance, but if so they certainly haven't anything on you."

The girl laughed, but before she could reply a diminutive page-boy appeared.

"Beg pardon, Mr. Frost," he piped, "but you're wanted on the telephone. The caller won't give his name, sir, but he says it's urgent."

Frost frowned and hesitated.

"All right, sonny," he replied. "I'll be right along."

Apologising to Meg, he followed the boy out of the big room.

It was during the visit to Normansea that Frost had, not without some difficulty, persuaded the girl to dine and dance with him at the Everyland, enormous but irreproachably correct queen of West End hotels. She had stipulated, however, that they should leave at half past eleven.

The evening had gone well. Frost seemed to know everyone from the hall porters to the *maîtres d'hôtel*, and he received that service which is a tribute more to a customer's personality than to his readiness to pay.

Meg was pleasantly conscious that her hair was right and that the old gold frock she had been lucky enough to pick up in a sale at a small but smart shop she knew fitted her like a glove. She recognised the tact with which Frost expressed his frank but respectful admiration, without attempting to make love to her. It was a technique, she decided with amusement, acquired and perfected by long practice. Meg had practised more than art at her art school.

When the American returned he appeared even more annoyed than when he had left her. It had been a mistake, he explained. There was another man named Frost staying in the hotel and the receptionist had got them confused.

"Too maddening," she agreed. "I thought it was probably a business call."

"I don't get many business calls at this time of night. In fact," he smiled, "I don't get many business calls."

"Isn't it rather a pity?"

"A pity? I don't get you."

"Oh, nothing. It was awful cheek. Please forget it."

"But I don't want to forget it. Just what were you thinking?"

"Well, it seems a pity you should be wasting your time. You told me yourself about this antique scheme . . ."

"What's wrong with it?" he asked as she paused.

"Nothing at all, but is it *big* enough for you? I mean, you've got money and you've got brains—— Oh, dear, this is all frightfully impertinent of me! Do forgive me."

"Forgive? Listen, honey, it's just wonderful to think you take that much interest in a guy who hasn't been any good to himself or anybody else. Lots of people have reminded me that I've got money, and they sit up nights figuring out ways of prying it loose from me; but there hasn't been any delegation urging me to sit in on the village brains trust so far."

"Perhaps you didn't encourage them. I mean, men who do big things don't wait to be asked to do them."

Frost crushed his cigarette into a tray.

"Perhaps you've got something," he said slowly. "But where do we go from there? I'm not a painter, I couldn't write a book, I wouldn't be any good as a doctor, I couldn't even play the piano except by ear, and I haven't any parlour tricks. What's left for a guy like me?"

"There's always politics."

"Politics are dirty, especially in my country."

"Then why not try to clean them up? I've never been to America but I've read about plenty of Americans who started at the bottom and finished at the top."

"From Log Cabin to White House?"

"Don't laugh—and remember, you'd be starting halfway up."

"I'm not laughing," he assured her, "but trying to straighten out the political game would be like a man trying to knock down a brick wall with his head."

"If he *used* his head he'd knock the wall down with a bit of dynamite. If Hitler had taken your line there wouldn't have been a Third Reich."

"I thought you English hated Hitler?"

"Of course we hated him! Look at the horrible things he did, or allowed to be done. But anyone but a fool must realise that if Hitler and Mussolini hadn't gone mad through sheer vanity they could have done a lot for their own people and for the rest of the world as well. What I mean is: they were men who'd had no real education and knew practically nothing about other countries, and they didn't understand how to use power when they got it, but they *did* show what even one man can do by sheer personality and determination. But, good heavens!" Meg interrupted herself, "I'm talking like a soap-box orator in Hyde Park on a Sunday morning. Anybody'd think I was a student at the London School of Economics. Give me another cigarette, Curtis, and let's talk about something else, shall we?"

Frost gave her a cigarette and a light. Then he leaned forward and looked straight into her eyes.

"You're dead right," he said, his voice deepened by suppressed eagerness. "Hitler had a lot of what it takes, but he hadn't *enough*, if you get me. He tried to stand on top of the world, but he forgot that it keeps on turning round and he didn't have enough spikes in his shoes to keep him from slipping. Listen, honey, you've said enough to make me do some thinking. Right now I'm only going to say one thing: a guy can do a lot if he knows there's even one person who believes he can get somewhere if he tries hard enough. I guess I haven't any right to ask, but it'd make a big difference if I thought you could feel that way about me."

Meg felt herself colouring. She had not meant to let things reach that stage, and the unwavering gaze of his steel-blue eyes made her almost shiver. But she pulled herself together and smiled.

"I think you could do a lot of things if you wanted to," she answered. "Suppose you try? And now I really must fly—it's twenty to twelve."

He took her hand and pressed it as she rose.

"Thanks," he said quietly. "That's all I wanted to know."

Frost was staying at the Everyland that night. When Meg went to the ladies' cloakroom for her wrap he went up to his bedroom, took off his dinner-jacket, and buckled round him a shoulder-holster that carried a .38 automatic pistol. His jacket had been cleverly cut so that when he put it on again the holster, lying snugly against him, made no noticeable bulge. He was back in the hall in time to collect Meg. His car was garaged and a porter called a taxi.

Neither he nor the girl said much on the way to Canton Court. He did not attempt to kiss her. They sat, for the most part, in a companionable silence.

He stood bareheaded while she thanked him for the evening, and only then did he take her hand.

"It's been the best I've ever had," he said. And that was all. As she closed the door she heard him tell the driver to take him back to the Everyland.

She was very thoughtful as she undressed and it was some time before she slept.

A hundred yards from the flats Frost called to the taximan; he said he had changed his mind and he told the man to take him to the Swiss Cottage Underground station.

The driver accepted the change with the indifference of a man used to the vagaries of passengers, especially at night. The bloke's bit of fluff wouldn't let him come in, he told himself, so he's going to try another one and he doesn't want to give me her address.

At Swiss Cottage, however, Frost upset the philosopher's calculations by handing him his clocked fare and a generous tip and then disappearing into the station.

The philosopher shrugged his shoulders and drove away, but if he had waited a couple of minutes he would have seen the American come out of the station, glance up and down while he took out a cigarette and lit it, and walk away with the leisurely air of a man who was not in a hurry to reach his destination.

Presently Frost threw away his cigarette and quickened his pace. He passed Mrs. Sweeney's house without looking at it, turned a corner, and so reached a narrow lane running parallel with the road in which the Sweeney residence stood. On each side of the lane were the back gardens of the houses of two long roads. The walls were pierced with doors for the use of gardeners.

Frost stopped at one of these doors. It looked as though it had not been opened for years, but when he pressed a concealed knob the lock clicked and the door swung open on oiled hinges.

Shutting the door behind him, he crossed the garden obliquely and came to an oblong mound of earth with a wooden door at one end. This had been an outdoor shelter during the air raids, the roof being supported inside by thick wooden beams. The floor was lower than the ground outside and the walls were lined with matchboarding. He opened the door, which was fastened only by a latch, stepped down into the shelter, and closed the door. The place was used as a shed for gardening tools and for several odds and ends such as a battered bicycle, a broken gramophone and an old iron bedstead.

Frost produced a small electric torch and picked his way to the end of the shed. There were half a dozen rusty clotheshooks screwed to the matchboarding. He pulled one of these hooks four times at short intervals; after the fourth pull a strip of the woodwork swung inwards above a short flight of steps which led down to a passage. As he descended the steps, which were lighted by a shaded electric globe, the wooden panel swung back into its original place.

Bending a little under the low roof, he made his way along the passage, opened a door, and stepped into one of the original

cellars of Mrs. Sweeney's house. It was an extension of the
original cellars, but had been walled off from them. A second
door cleverly made to look like part of the brickwork gave
access to the cellar in which David Jones did his printing work.

The room was brightly lighted and was carpeted and comfortably furnished. Some bottles and glasses and a box of
cigars were on a table in a corner. An electric fire gave a glow
that was welcome, although the place was not damp.

Myfanwy Jones, in a high-backed chair, was sewing.

David Jones, in a similar chair opposite her, smoked shag
in a seasoned pipe. A glass of beer was within his reach.

In a deep armchair reclined a man in a double-breasted
suit of heavy blue serge; a bowler hat with a narrow brim lay
on a table beside him. A bottle of rum, a jug of water and a
half-filled glass were also on the table, and he was smoking a
dark-coloured cigar. It was Oscar Fersen.

When Curtis Frost burst upon this scene of homely comfort
Myfanwy looked up from her embroidery and said, "Well,
Curtis."

David Jones nodded and took a drink of beer.

Fersen emitted a cloud of smoke and said, "So, you have
come, then?"

The reception could not have been described as hearty, but
Frost did not appear abashed.

" 'Evening, folks," he said cheerfully as he threw his hat
and light overcoat on a sidetable, mixed a whisky-and-soda,
and sat down, casually moving his chair into a position from
which he could observe every movement of the other three
people. "I got your message at the Everyland," he went on,
"and when I'd taken my girl friend home I came along. What's
it all about?"

"We've been trying to find you all day, man," David Jones
remarked acidly.

"Well, you found me at last. How did you know where I
was, by the way?"

"Does that matter?" the girl retorted. "We can generally
find people when we want them."

"Especially when its someone who always stays at the
Everyland when he's in town," Frost agreed.

"Enough of this fooling," Fersen interposed harshly. "We
sent for you, and you have come——"

"Just a minute," Frost interrupted. "Where do you get that 'sent for' stuff? Your message *asked* me to come here to discuss important business."

The Captain's ruddy face became ruddier, but he controlled himself.

"Please listen, Mr. Frost," he said coolly. "We wish to speak with you about that policeman, Inspector Vance. You killed him?"

"Certainly," Frost replied with equal coolness.

"And why?"

"Because if I hadn't killed him then, he'd have got us all into the cooler—if not on to the scaffold. That's why."

"Please explain."

"Sure. When we were down at Normansea, Vance decided to do a bit of snooping. It was all right at first, but while Skelton and Peters were busy Vance slipped them and saw things he shouldn't have seen. How he found the door of the secret vault I don't know, but I *do* know he had blue dust on his coat when he came back. The only place he could have picked up that dust was in the vault. The Pole had been doing his experiments with explosives there. I saw that sourpuss Kair brushing the dust off Vance's coat."

"So you bumped him off," Fersen commented. "You didn't think it worth while to consult us first?"

"I certainly did not! Vance wasn't going home; he was going to make a report. If he'd made that report, you wouldn't have been sitting here now."

"A moment, please," the Swede interposed. "When you saw the dust on Vance's coat, what did you do?"

"What in heck d'you think I did? I told Skelton and Hank Peters to shift the stuff over to Muldoon's place as soon as we'd gone, of course."

"So that if the police had visited your house they would have found nothing?"

"Not a darned thing."

"Then why kill Vance?"

"Because he'd have made trouble for us. Even if the police hadn't found anything at Normansea they'd have believed what Vance said."

"You mean they'd have suspected you?"

"Sure."

"So you killed Vance to save yourself, not us?"

"Certainly," Frost agreed. "You'd have done the same thing——"

"Never mind what I would have done or would not have done. The point is that you acted without orders——"

"Orders?" the American snapped. "Who's giving orders around here?"

"I am."

"Is that so?"

"Yes, it is so," the Swede replied calmly. "It is time you realised that, my friend."

Frost's face hardened. "Listen, you," he retorted. "You may be a hell of a fellow when you're with your pals in Moscow, but over here you're just one of the mob. I'm willing to play ball with you folk, but I'm not standing for any heavy stuff. I didn't raise hell when you had Ostrod bumped off, though whoever did it was pretty clumsy. I did a much neater job though I hadn't much time to work it out, and those boneheads at Scotland Yard couldn't pin it on me in a thousand years."

"We'd been watching Ostrod for weeks," Myfanwy declared, "but it wasn't until he spoke to Vico when he was drunk that we were sure of him. Then he had to be put away at once."

"Who did it?"

"Never you mind who did it," David Jones exclaimed. "You ask too many questions, man. If you will mind your own business and do what the Captain tells you, it will be better for everybody."

Frost laughed unpleasantly. "Is that so? You people ought to be in Hollywood, making gangster films. What am I supposed to do? Ask the Big Shot's pardon and say I'll never do it again?"

"That might not be a bad idea," Myfanwy remarked. "In the gangster films I've seen, people who make trouble are apt to get rubbed out."

The Captain reached for a pocket. Frost's hand slipped inside his coat, but the Swede took out a box of matches, struck one and applied it to his cigar.

"We are not making a film," he said, "and this conversation is not funny. There are serious things to be said and it is for me to say them. You spoke of boneheads at Scotland Yard.

That was a foolish thing to say. There are men there who are
very clever——"

"They don't show it."

"That is where they are clever. They like other people to
think they are stupid—people like you, Mr. Frost."

David Jones chuckled, and his daughter smiled.

"Four days ago," Fersen went on, "there was a meeting at
Scotland Yard. There were important men there—men from
nearly all the Ministries, as well as policemen. The meeting was
arranged by order of the Prime Minister himself."

"How do you know all this?" Frost demanded, more impressed than he cared to admit. "You weren't there, I suppose?"

"No," the other replied, unmoved by the sarcasm, "but
I have in my pocket a list of the men who attended."

"Let's see it, then."

"Why? To prove that I am not lying to you? Don't be
stupid, my friend. I could write a dozen names on a piece of
paper to show you, and you would not know whether they
were correct."

"Sure," the American admitted unwillingly; "but I don't
see why you can't tell me who it is that can give you such inside
dope. You can't tell me you've got the Prime Minister or the
Police Commissioner on your payroll. This isn't Ruritania, or
even Russia!"

The Swede put down the glass he had lifted, leaned forward.
and gazed at the younger man, his eyes glittering.

"No," he answered grimly, "this is not Ruritania and it is
not Russia. Perhaps it is a good thing for you, Mr. Frost, that
it is not Russia. In that country they know how to deal with
people who wish to argue instead of doing what they are told
to do. Please don't make that mistake again. We have been
glad to let you help, but we are not going to let you spoil our
plans. You thought you could make use of us, to play us for
suckers, as you would say. That was not very clever of you.
Ostrod died because he thought he was clever; it would be a
pity if anything happened to you for the same reason."

"Film stuff!" Frost sneered.

"You know that it is not film stuff. You put on a front, but
you know that what I am saying is true. You spoke of me as
the big noise, but it is you who want to be the big noise

yourself. Don't be a fool! Neither of us is a big noise, as you call it. I have my orders and I give you the orders of my chiefs. It is true that I am for the moment directing the movement in this country. Ask Mr. Jones and the others. They will tell you that they accept my authority—they and many others you don't even know. I have been very patient with you because you have been useful and can still be useful, and if you are sensible you will not find us ungrateful. But no more killings, please. And another thing: do not be too friendly with the charming Miss Milcote.''

Frost flushed. "What the heck right have you to tell me how to choose my friends?'' he said angrily. "Leave Miss Milcote out of it; she's got nothing to do with this business.''

"That's what you think,'' the stout man responded calmly. "But we have talked enough and it is time I went away. You will please go first. I am sure that when you have had time to think over what I have said you will agree that it would be stupid for us to quarrel when we both serve the same cause. Good night—or rather, good morning, Mr. Frost.''

The American stared at him and began a furious retort, but thought better of it. Picking up his coat and hat, he kept his eyes on the three silent figures as he moved to the door, backed through it, and vanished into the tunnel.

Myfanwy rolled up her work.

"I'm still not sure it wouldn't have been better to rub him out at once,'' she said. "Father had made a hole and got the plaster ready to wall it up again.''

"I could call him back,'' the Welshman suggested, but Fersen shook his head.

"Not yet,'' he decided. "There are still things I want to know about that young man.''

"Well, you're the boss,'' Myfanwy conceded. "You'll be going now? Right. Then I'm for bed. I'm staying here tonight.''

She smiled as the gallant captain heaved his bulk up from his chair and bowed her out.

"A remarkable girl,'' the Swede observed as he emptied his glass and picked up his hat.

"Aye indeed, man,'' Mr. Jones agreed.

Larry Doyle, clinging uncomfortably to his perch, started at the sound of footsteps in the lane, and automatically glanced at the illuminated dial of his wrist-watch. He cursed the light clouds which now obscured what an hour before had been a starlit sky.

A tall figure stopped just below him. He was almost sure it was Curtis Frost. There was the click of a lock and he could hear the gentle closing of the garden door opposite. Then the dark shape crossed the garden and vanished into the toolshed Vance had described.

He stretched his cramped limbs as well as he could, and sighed with relief. At last something had happened. He would have liked to follow the newcomer into the Sweeney garden, but he resisted the temptation. A dozen times he looked at his watch.

Suddenly he stiffened. The door of the toolshed had opened and for a moment the beam of a torch shone on the face of a man who must have been momentarily careless. The next instant the light snapped off, but Larry had recognised the face of Curtis Frost. More footsteps, and quicker this time; the steps of someone impatient, angry, or perhaps afraid. The garden door opened and closed, and Frost strode away down the lane.

Again Larry was tempted to follow, but his business was with someone more important.

He had not long to wait. This time there was no incautious flash of light, and he was startled to see a short, heavy figure emerge from the garden door, moving with astonishing lightness for its bulk.

Larry allowed the man to get nearly to the end of the lane before he left his sheltering tree. There was no time to use his ladder. Hanging by his hands from the wall, he let himself drop, and landed almost silently.

Keeping close to the wall, he followed the figure ahead and saw it vanish. Cautiously he peered round the corner. The man was walking briskly along the side road.

Then Larry made the old mistake. He was too intent on his quarry to look behind him, and he did not see the second man come out of the Sweeney garden.

Larry had a difficult job. They were in a lighted road now, but he had tailed people before and he crossed the road and stole silently after the figure which continued to walk steadily without looking round.

Another turning gave Larry the chance he wanted. The

light of a street lamp fell on the man's face, and Larry knew that he had been right.

He heard the car behind him, but for a moment gave it no attention. It had come at a dangerous speed out of a side road and its driver jammed down the accelerator.

Larry glanced over his shoulder and jumped, but not in time. The car mounted the pavement, struck him with a force that threw him headlong against the wall, and roared away to where the burly man awaited it. . . .

When he came to himself he was lying in a hospital bed. There were several people standing round him. After what seemed a long time he discovered that the two nearest were Chief Superintendent Muir and Chief Inspector Marshall.

A flash of recollection came and he believed that he shouted at them, but in fact it was a faint whisper.

"All right, lad," he heard Muir saying. "Don't try to talk."

But he *had* to talk. He knew what he wanted to say, if he could only think of the words. Suddenly they came.

"It—was the Captain—Frost there, too——"

Then somebody, he thought, stuck a pin into his arm. Silly thing to do.

The faces that smiled at him grew blurred and the voices that had seemed to be saying vaguely reassuring things died away.

"Clear out, please," said the brisk surgeon.

Muir said in his most official tone, "Will he——" and stopped abruptly.

"He'll be all right," the white-coated man replied; "he's had a nasty swipe, but we'll put the bits together again for you. Now, if you'll excuse me . . ."

"Come on, Joe," said Muir.

CHAPTER XV

MR. CONSTANTINE MULDOON stood at the door of his cottage and surveyed the prospect approvingly. Before him lay the wide marshes, intersected by the river that crept like a sluggish serpent to the sea a few miles away. Beside the river ran the broad road to the small but ancient town of Oastmarsh a brisk ten minutes' walk away.

In Oastmarsh eyes all persons not resident in, or at least connected with, the town for at least twenty years were foreigners, persons to be treated with wary civility pending leisurely judgment of their merits and demerits.

When Con Muldoon had rented the picturesque old cottage he had forestalled the inquiries of curious gossips. Over his tankard at the local inn, and his glass in the more pretentious saloon bars of the town, he had with artless simplicity recounted his past career, his present pursuits, and his plans for the future. It was not long before the burly, red-bearded, blue-eyed man with the heart-warming laugh and the Irish brogue that years of travel had not wholly eradicated was received with a guarded approval that admitted him to the outer circle of the local freemasonry of conviviality.

That was all that he desired.

According to Mr. Muldoon, he was the son of a successful but improvident Dublin solicitor. Quarrelling with his father, he roamed the world, trying his hand at most things from gold-mining to playing the piano in cheap waterfront dives, until a legacy from a rich uncle enabled him, at forty, to settle down in modest comfort and recall with amusement the vicissitudes of his earlier years.

In cold fact, Con's father had kept an ale-house of ill-repute, had been steeped to the eyebrows in political intrigues, and had been shot during the 'Troubles' for betraying a rebel leader to the police. Con's meagre schooling had been supplemented by his mother's brother, a scholarly parish priest whose integrity had won him the trust of both sides. Con had been embroiled in his father's intrigues, and when the elder Muldoon's career came to a sudden end his priestly brother-in-law got Con out of the country, equipped with a little money, a smattering of education, and a boundless confidence in his ability to open the world's oyster. He was physically powerful, brutally courageous, and ready at any time to steal his best friend's last half crown or take the pennies out of a blind man's box if he felt sure he would not be caught.

In one particular, however, his accounting to the Oastmarsh populace was perfectly true. He had a hobby; it amounted, indeed, to a passion; it was photography. He was a wizard with the camera and he could have shown his work with credit in the best exhibitions. He could have sold his work, too, but he would accept no paid commissions, though he was always ready to make a picture for a friend or to present half a dozen to be sold at a bazaar or fête for charity.

He did no portraiture, but his studies of landscapes and ancient buildings were superb.

It did not, therefore, surprise his acquaintances when he spent hours tramping the marshes or floating in his little boat on the river, with a camera slung over his shoulder, waiting for the dawn that would enable him to get the effect he wanted.

The idea that his quite genuine hobby might cover other and more sinister activities would have been ridiculed by the cronies with whom he consumed vast quantities of beer and exchanged racy stories.

Mr. Muldoon, then, stood at the cottage door, surveyed the prospect, and decided that it was good both artistically and materially.

He had eaten an early lunch (he was a good cook and his spotless bachelor home would have shamed shiftless wives if they had been allowed to cross the threshold), his pipe was drawing well, and he had that morning developed in his dark room a picture of wild ducks in flight that satisfied even his critical taste.

Into this sylvan place there came Fury with a capital F.

The rapid beat of a boat's engine faded as a cabin cruiser tied up to a mooring in the river. Curtis Frost sprang ashore and strode up the path leading to the cottage.

"Now, I wonder," Mr. Muldoon reflected, "what's the matter with the young man today? By the look on his face he's in the divil of a temper."

Frost's usually cheerful countenance was set in hard lines. Barely returning Muldoon's greeting, he pushed past him into the sitting-room, and dropped into a chair.

His host followed, silently produced a bottle, a syphon and two glasses and set them on a table.

Frost poured out a stiff whisky, added a dash of soda, and half emptied the glass.

Con Muldoon waited; he had always found it good policy in business conversations to let the other man speak first.

"It's come to a show-down," Frost said abruptly.

Con's eyes narrowed. He mixed a moderate drink for himself and drank a little of it, but said nothing.

"It's that son of a bitch they call the Captain," Frost went on. "He had the gall to try to tell me where I get off!"

"Fancy that, now," Con responded calmly.

Briefly, but with mounting anger, Frost described the killing of Inspector Vance and the midnight conference at Mrs. Sweeney's house.

"I told that bit of scum from the Kremlin sewers," he concluded, "that if he thought he was the Grand High Muckamuck of this show he'd better take another quick think and change his mind. So he can put that in his samovar and boil it up and drink it, and I hope it chokes him!"

Con tapped the dottle from his pipe neatly into a large glass ashtray. When thieves fell out, he reflected, honest men had an awkward way of coming by their own; but he kept that reflection to himself.

"So you told him that, did you?" he said. "Fancy that, now."

"Stop saying, 'Fancy that, now,' for the love of Mike!" Frost burst out. "This is serious, Con."

"Serious? Did y'think I was after taking it for a joke? I'm as serious as a mourner who hasn't had a drink at the funeral. And by the same token, we don't want any funeral on our side of the fence."

"Just what do you mean by that?" Frost demanded. "Not turning yellow, are you?"

"The only time I ever turned yellow was when I had the jaundice," Muldoon answered evenly. "I'll thank you to take that back, if you and me are going to do any more business together."

Frost saw the red light.

"Sorry," he said. "Of course I didn't really mean it. It's only that—— Hell, Con, that Swede's got me so riled I could kick his teeth down his neck."

"Take it easy. Perhaps you'll get a chance to do it some-time, but just now there's bigger things to think about."

"You're dead right there are, and I'm not going to let Ferson wipe his dirty snow-shoes on my mat." He proceeded to express some further opinions about the Swede in pungent terms. The Irishman waited patiently until the tirade ended; then he said:

"Now you've got that off your chest you'll feel better. If there's nothing else you want to call him we might begin considering what's going to happen next."

Frost hesitated, grinned, and finished his whisky.

"That's better," Con approved. "Give yourself another drink and let's get to the bottom of this thing, as the drunk said when he jumped into the lift that wasn't there. The trouble with you and the Captain is that you both want the ship to go the same way, but neither of you trusts the other to hold the wheel. You can't run a railway that way, as the signalman said when he saw the up train hit the down one."

"So what? Are you trying to tell me I'm to——"

"Will y'wait a minit, now, and let me have my say? The Captain may be all you've said, and several things you forgot to mention, but you've got to admit he's clever. Those buckos in Moscow don't pick mugs to do their big jobs, and they've never tackled a bigger one than this. Then there's Black David with his crazy Celtic notions, but not too crazy to keep his neck out of a rope. They're a cunning lot, and they've got something you haven't got yet—a big organisation behind them."

"I have the New Germany behind me," Frost declared, and his hand went out in the old Nazi salute.

Muldoon lifted his glass to his lips to conceal a smile.

"I'm not denying it," he replied, "but the New Germany's a hell of a long way away. Most of it's over in the States, putting up the money, but leaving you to do the work."

"They chose me because I am a German by birth and tradition," Frost retorted proudly, "and because they know that I would give my life for the cause I serve."

"Sure, I believe you would," Con agreed, his eyes twinkling, "but it'd be better for you and the cause if you kept on being alive till the job's done."

Frost scowled. Then the sense of humour acquired in a free country got the better of his Prussian dignity and he laughed.

"You've got something there," he admitted.

"Of course I have," Con declared. "You can't do without the Captain and his mob just yet. Plenty of time to hit him a kick when he turns his back. Let him alone for a bit until you both cool down. I wouldn't be surprised if the Captain isn't feeling sorry for the way he talked. Maybe it'll do him good to wipe the snow out of his eyes and take a good look at a man who isn't afraid of him. It's not for me to tell you what to do; you're the boss and what you say goes for me too; but if you asked my advice I'd say you ought to lie low for a bit and let the next move come from the other side. They can't do without you, and they know it."

"Thanks, Con," Frost said, getting up. "I certainly believe you're right. Now I'll be getting back to Normansea. Did you pick up that old bureau for me?"

"I did indeed. It's in the next room, and a nice price the old dealer made me pay for it. Speaking of that, I've had a bit of expense lately, one way and another. Could I be troubling you for a bit of money?"

"Surely." Frost produced a bulky wallet, extracted a wad of five-pound notes, and handed ten of them to the Irishman. "That suit you?"

" 'Tis generous," Con assured him. "You can always tell a real big man by the way he treats the people that work for him."

"That's nothing. One day I'll show you what I can do for a man who serves you well. You'll be surprised. Now where's that bureau?"

Together they carried the piece to the boat. They took their time about it, for the benefit of casual observers. It was known that Con Muldoon had a standing commission to pick up antiques for his wealthy American friend.

When the cabin cruiser had chugged its way down the river Con returned to the cottage. From a locked desk he took a telegram he had received that morning and a large-scale map. After studying the map for some time he locked the cottage door, went to a shed that served as a garage, and started his car. It was small and looked shabby, but it had a surprising turn of speed.

It was fortunate, he thought, that he had lunched early and that Frost had not stayed long. He had a fairly long run to the airport where he would pick up one of the ordinary planes on the passenger service to London.

He was going to meet a girl. She would be at a named point in the gardens of the old palace at Hampton Court between four and half past; if he had not arrived by that time she would go to a small teashop not far away. The open air rendezvous was preferred.

Con timed his journey well. At four fifteen he was sauntering through the gardens.

In a secluded corner there was a bench, so placed that its occupant could see anyone approaching. It was sheltered in the angle formed by two high hedges, but far enough from them to defeat eavesdroppers. At one end of the bench a girl was sitting with an open book on her lap.

It was the darkly pretty Myfanwy Jones, daughter of Black David, as Con had called the foreman printer.

The girl had telephoned that morning to the offices in which she was employed. She explained that on the previous evening she had been preparing a meal for herself and her father, who was a widower, when she had a slight accident. She was cutting bread. The knife slipped and gashed her hand. At the hospital she had the wound dressed; the doctor had told her that it was not serious, but it would be better for her not to do any typewriting for a day or two while the cut healed. With that attention to detail which characterised the proceedings of the Captain's employees, Myfanwy's left hand was bandaged.

Con looked at the girl, who was apparently engrossed in her book. He adjusted his tie and cocked his hat in the manner of a gay Lothario bent on romantic adventure, and sat down at the other end of the bench. Presently he raised his hat and spoke. She looked at him critically, smiled, and replied. He moved nearer to her. The pick-up, any spectator would have thought, was accomplished.

"You've seen Frost?" she asked, without preamble.

"Yes. He came over in his boat. Couldn't have had a lot of sleep."

"The Captain was sure he'd go to see you. He wants to know what happened."

Con offered her a cigarette and took one himself.

"The boyo was fit to be tied," he answered, chuckling as he recalled the scene. "He told me all about last night. It's a mercy he didn't tear the Captain's tongue out with his bare hands."

"It's a mercy for him he didn't try," the girl said shortly. "Mr. Curtis Frost's got too big for his boots. It's time he learned manners. He thinks every girl's waiting for his nod, but one of these days he'll find he's made a mistake."

She had spoken with sudden vehemence, and as she met Con's astonished look she coloured and went on quickly.

"Did he tell you what he's going to do next?"

"He thinks he did, but 'twas I told him what to do. He's going to keep quiet and see what the Captain does. I put the wind up him and made him see reason. What's the Captain going to do?"

"I don't know, and I wouldn't tell you if I did. Keep your place, Con Muldoon."

"I know the place I'd like to keep, and the girl, too," the Irishman replied. "A nice little place with you in it——"

"And don't hand me that line, either," interrupted Miss Jones, who did not disdain the cinema. "Now, listen: the Captain says you're to watch Frost closer than ever, and report what he does and says. The Captain'll send you fresh orders soon, so don't be away from the cottage more than a few hours at a time."

"Is that all?"

"No. Here's something for you."

She handed him an envelope and added: "You'd better go now. I want to get back."

"Can't I go with you a bit of the way home?"

"No, you can't. I'll go back the same way as I came. That's the Captain's order."

"All right, Beautiful," Muldoon said as he rose. "Come down and see me sometime. I've some nice pictures I'd like to show you. Sleep well and dream of your faithful Con who thinks of you night and day."

The girl smiled despite herself.

"You're the biggest liar unhung," she declared. "Clear out before I call a keeper and give you in charge for molesting an innocent girl."

He laughed, blew her a kiss, and strolled away.

When he had found an empty taxicab he opened the envelope the girl had given to him, and counted the money it contained. There were twenty one-pound notes.

"The stingy swine!" he muttered. "My old man always said it was better to work for a fool than a knave, and by this and that he was right."

CHAPTER XVI

CHIEF SUPERINTENDENT MUIR nodded to the man who had risen to his feet as Muir entered the interrogation room with Chief Inspector Joe Marshall.

"Sit down, please," he said. "I am told you understand and speak English?"

The man bowed and took a seat.

"Would you like to have an interpreter in case anything isn't clear?"

"There is no need."

"Very well. You know, I suppose, that while you are in this country you are subject to its laws and that you can be tried on a charge of committing, or attempting to commit, a criminal offence?"

"I know."

"You have been asked whether you would like to have legal advice and I understand you refused. Is that so?"

"It is so."

"Do you wish to change your mind?"

"I do not wish to change my mind."

Muir sat back and studied the thickset, fair fellow with the untidy mop of hair, who had answered his questions with a dull patience that was rather indifferent than uncivil. Between twenty-five and thirty, Muir thought; the face would have expressed stupidity but for the alert eyes.

"There's another point," the superintendent went on. "When you were charged you were cautioned that anything you might say would be taken down and might be used in evidence. You made no reply. I want to be quite sure you understood what was meant."

"I understood."

"I have had you brought here because I propose to ask you some questions, but you need not answer them, or say anything at all, unless you like. If you do, Inspector Marshall will make notes of what is said."

"I do not mind."

Muir took some papers from his brief-case.

"I have here," he said, "a document found in your pocket. Do you recognize it?"

"Yes, it is my passport."

"It states that you are a Dutch subject named Lonneker, born and resident in Rotterdam. Attached to it is a letter, supposed to have been written by a professor at a Dutch university; it states that your object in coming to England was to take history classes at London University, after which you would return to Holland, where you hoped to take a degree."

Lonneker bowed.

"We have been informed by the Dutch police," Muir continued, "that this passport is a false one, that they can trace no one of your name in Rotterdam or at any Dutch university, and that this letter is also a forgery."

Muir did not mention that the Dutch police had added that, as a glance at the map would show, Lonneker was the name of a place in North Holland, near the German border.

Lonneker, to give him the name he used, said nothing.

"What is your real name?"

"You do not believe what is on that paper," the other replied, "so there is no reason why you should believe me if I give you another name. Anyhow, it does not matter." He waved his hand as though dismissing a point of no importance.

"Why did you come to London?"

"To do what I tried to do—to kill a Minister."

"Any Minister, or one in particular?"

"Any one—or more, if I could get away after the first one."

"Then it was not a personal grievance against anyone?"

"No. I wished to awaken your people to the wickedness of their Government. I will explain all that when I am tried in the public court, so that you policemen cannot make a secret of it."

"There's no question of secrets. The judge will see that you get a fair hearing."

"I know," Lonneker agreed, showing his first sign of animation. "It is not like in my——" He stopped abruptly.

"In your country, you mean?" Muir suggested. "Where is that?"

Lonneker ignored the question, and the chief superintendent went on:

"You have been living in a boarding-house in Bloomsbury

where other students live. I'm told you didn't make friends with any of them."

"Is that a crime?"

"Oh no; but students generally make friends with each other."

"I have no friends."

"None at all?"

"No. I do not wish friends."

"You know the Liberation Club?"

"I have heard of it."

"You are not a member?"

"No."

"I should have thought you'd have liked to go there. You might have met someone you know."

Lonneker conveyed with a shrug that what the chief superintendent thought was unimportant.

"Do you know Pasquale Vico, the secretary of the club?"

"I have heard of him."

"That wasn't what I asked you. Do you know him?"

"No. I have told you I have no friends."

"So you say. Do you know a man named Joseph Ostrod?"

Lonneker had been sitting with his legs crossed, one foot swinging slowly. At Muir's question the foot stopped swinging.

"No," he answered, "I did not know him."

"Why do you say 'did'? If you didn't know him, how do you know he's dead?"

"I read about him in a newspaper," Lonneker replied woodenly.

Muir showed no sign of his annoyance. He had not expected the man to be easy.

"If I told you that you were seen talking to Ostrod shortly before his death, what would you say?"

There was a perceptible pause before the answer came.

"I would say that it might be so. It has happened sometimes that people have spoken to me, it might be in a café, but I did not know them. I have replied, because I did not wish to make offence, and presently I have gone away."

"Ostrod's photograph was in all the papers; if you read about him you must have seen it. Did you recognise him?"

"No."

"Isn't that rather strange? You've told me you never made

friends, so one would think you'd remember people who spoke to you."

"I do not see why that should be," Lonneker said; "I would be more likely to remember a friend than a person who spoke to me for perhaps two or three minutes."

It was, of course, quite true, which was all the more aggravating. Muir felt that so far the Dutchman—if he were really Dutch—had had the best of the battle. One could not call it a battle of wits; he had taken refuge in a mulish, but effective, obstinacy of denial. Yet Muir was sure that Ostrod's name had come as a surprise to his adversary.

"Have you ever been to Switzerland?" he asked.

"I have made a holiday there many years ago."

"Did you meet Ostrod there?"

"No. I was a boy then."

"You might have met him, all the same."

"I did not meet him."

"You know what Ostrod's job was—the sort of work he did here, I mean?"

"I read that he was a translator of languages."

"Did you know that he had a very wide circle of acquaintances among the foreigners in London?"

"Also I read that."

"You seem to have read a lot about the case. Why were you so interested, if you didn't know him?"

"It is always interesting to read about the killings of people."

"You find it so, do you?"

"Why not? There are two important things in this world: Life and Death. You also are interested in death, no?"

"That's my business, so to speak," Muir countered.

"It is everyone's business, I think."

"You seem to have made it yours, anyhow," the chief superintendent said with deliberate brutality.

"Please?"

"You made it your business to try to kill the Home Secretary, who hadn't done you any harm?"

A faint flush rose in the man's sallow cheeks.

"You do not understand, or perhaps you do not wish to understand," he declared. "For the man as a man I had no— what do you say?—grudge. For the man as a Minister I had a hatred."

"Why? He was a good Minister. His job was to uphold law and order and help to see that everybody had a chance to live in peace and quiet," Muir said, feeling uncomfortably as though he were addressing the children in a Sunday-school.

"And he was, of course, your chief," Lonneker remarked with a shade of irony in his tone.

"Yes, he was my chief, but that has nothing to do with it. But let's get back to Ostrod. Do you know a pub—a public house called the 'Cornish Wrestler'?"

"I have been there. It is respectable."

"Very respectable. Do you know that Ostrod used to go there?"

"How should I know?"

"I'm asking the questions. Did you know?"

"I did not know."

"Are you sure you didn't meet him and talk to him there?"

"I have said that it has happened that people I did not know have spoken to me. This Ostrod may have been one of them."

"Did you discuss political questions with him?"

"I did not."

"If you didn't know him, how can you be so sure?"

"Because I did not discuss such things with anyone. I did not wish to find myself in a disturbance—a quarrel."

"If you had joined the Liberation Club you could have discussed anything you liked without much fear of that."

"Perhaps. But I did not wish to discuss. I wished to go about my affairs quietly."

"You must have felt lonely."

"Why? I had my books, my studies."

"You used to take long walks, too, didn't you?"

"Sometimes. It was good for my health."

"Especially at night."

"Naturally. In the daytime I had my classes."

"Yes, you attended your classes, but I'm told you were not exactly a brilliant student."

"Unfortunately I am a little stupid," Lonneker admitted, and again there was that note of irony in his voice.

Muir regarded him as a housewife might have regarded a cockroach in her spotless kitchen.

"You're not at all stupid, Lonneker," he retorted, "but

you'd like me to think you are. Where did you go when you took those walks at night?"

"Many places. Your London is very interesting."

"I can quite believe you found it interesting," Muir assented drily. "What parts interested you most?"

"Your ancient buildings. The Tower, the Guildhall——"

"You can't go into them at night."

"I liked also to walk in the streets."

"Especially the quiet streets?"

"All kinds. Streets with people, and streets empty and quiet."

"Let me mention a few places and see whether you know them. Hyde Park?"

"Of course."

"Baker Street?"

"Yes."

"Sloane Square?"

"Yes."

"Swiss Cottage?"

"Yes," Lonneker answered without hesitation or any change of expression that Muir or Joe Marshall could detect.

"Do you know anyone who lives in any of the places I've just mentioned?"

"No."

"You know, I suppose, a big public house near Swiss Cottage Underground station? It's a well-known place."

"Yes, I know it. It is nice. I have taken beer there."

"If I said that you had been seen entering a private house near the pub, would that be true?"

"It would not."

Quite right, Muir thought; at least, not by anyone we can discover. "Did you meet anyone you knew in that pub?" he asked.

"Yes, one time."

"Who was that?"

"He is a porter at the university. I do not know his name. He is big and wears medals. When I was new and did not know my way he was kind and directed me. So when I met him one night in the public house I asked that I might buy some beer for him. I have not again met him, except at the university, when we say good day to each other."

"Can you describe him to me?"

"He is big and tall and he has a moustache, he wears two rows of medals. On the left side of his neck there is the mark of a wound that has healed. I have heard students call him Toffee—no, Taffy—but I think that is a joking name."

"A nickname, you mean?"

"Yes. You can find him easily now?" and he smiled faintly.

"We can find him," Muir agreed, thinking glumly that it would not matter when they did find the man. Lonneker was too clever to have invented the story. He replaced the papers in his case.

"Well," he said, "it's not my business to give you advice, and I've no power to make any promises, but don't forget that if you change your mind and decide to make a statement, you can send me a message at any time. As I say, I'm making no promises, and I'm not trying to influence you, but it might make a difference when you come up for trial."

That was as far as he could go, and he awaited the result with more interest than he allowed to appear.

Lonneker smiled.

"Thank you," he answered. "You are kind. Everyone has been kind. I will think over what you have said. May I ask for a favour, a small thing?"

"What is it?"

"I have much to consider and I wish to arrange my thoughts by writing them down."

"Of course you can do that. You're on remand and you're entitled to certain privileges. Instructions were given that you are to have pens and ink and paper——"

"Oh yes," the other interrupted. "I have them, but I do not like to write with a pen that you dip in the ink. When I was searched they took some things from me—my little penknife and my fountain-pen. I would like, please, to have my fountain-pen again."

Muir smiled.

"Certainly," he agreed. "You shall have your fountain-pen at once. I am sorry they forgot to return it."

Lonneker sighed with obvious relief.

"Thank you very much, sir," he said humbly.

"You're welcome," Muir assured him. "By the way, we found the poison you'd hidden in the pen, and we've taken it out. We wouldn't like you to do yourself any harm while you're in our care, you know.''

Lonneker caught his breath, his face contorted with fury.

For a moment he sat motionless; then he leaned across the table and spat in Muir's face.

Joe Marshall's big fist knocked him back into his chair.

Muir took out his handkerchief and wiped his cheek. With a restraint that Marshall admired he kept his hands off the man. Calling in the constable on duty outside, he said:

"Take this man back to his cell. Be careful; he's inclined to lose his temper and do silly things."

Beckoning to Marshall, he walked out.

"Come on, you," said the constable, "and don't try any funny games unless you want me to knock your block off!"

Back in his room at the Yard, Muir pitched his case on to his desk, sat down and lit his pipe.

Joe Marshall sat opposite to him and said nothing. Joe was very good at saying nothing at the right moment.

The two were old friends, although Muir had out-distanced the older man, as well as Andrew Ash, in the promotion stakes. When Muir had been a chief inspector Joe had been his sergeant when they hunted in couples; now the sergeant had become a chief inspector and was the chief superintendent's assistant.

"Blast that Lonneker man!" Muir exploded. "I tried him every way I could think of, but I might as well have talked about the weather for all I got out of him."

"Difficult bloke," Joe agreed. "Like pumping a dry well."

"Worse. At least you know there's nothing in the well, but there's a hell of a lot inside that fat Dutch head if I could only get at it."

"If he *is* Dutch."

"Yes. He might be anything. He talks the careful English of an educated foreigner, and his accent isn't marked enough to place him. Do you think I missed any chances, Joe?"

Muir never disdained the opinions of his subordinates and he had a considerable respect for Marshall's judgment.

Joe shifted his acid drop from one cheek to the other and considered the point.

"No," he answered. "You gave him all the right leads, but

he was too clever to follow them. He had his brief and he stuck to it."

"I'd like to know who drew it for him. The people behind him weren't born yesterday."

"I wonder how he got over here."

"Probably another hardy mariner," Muir said, alluding to aliens who arrived hidden in big Thames barges, or were brought across the water in speedboats, landed by night at quiet spots on the English coast, and picked up by confederates who had been warned to expect them. Such unwelcome visitors included smugglers of gems and drugs, criminals evading the police of their own country, and spies.

"Curtis Frost has a fast boat," the inspector remarked.

"Yes, I thought of him, but I fancy Lonneker's one of the Captain's mob, and the wily skipper doesn't seem to trust Frost farther than he can see him. I wish we could catch Frost at his games. There's no doubt he's responsible for bringing in the weapons and explosives, but the Customs people haven't been able to pin it on him. They're pretty smart, too, but they've been a bit hampered by being told not to let him think he's suspected. Damn it, Joe, I wish you and I could go out after a real, honest-to-goodness murderer instead of this Ku-Klux-Klan stuff. Why can't the Special Branch do its own dirty work?"

If other people had been present Muir would have been the correctly professional chief detective-superintendent, but their privacy allowed him metaphorically to let his hair down and beat his breast.

"It was the A.C. who picked you for the job," Joe reminded him. "There's a good many in the Yard who wouldn't mind being in your shoes."

"I wish Sir Justin had picked one of them instead of me."

"No, you don't," Joe contradicted him calmly, "and you'd better not let Mrs. Muir hear you talk like that when you get home. She'd give you hell, and quite right, too."

Muir smiled. Joe's devotion to Gloria, whose life he had helped to save, was a matter of history.

"I know I'm just being a damn fool," he said, "but I've never seen Old Just-in-Time come so near to being excited about anything before, and I don't want to let him down."

"You won't. I wish I was as sure of anything for the

Derby as I am of you; I'd put six months' pay on it and retire on my winnings."

Muir looked at the burly fellow whose pleasant stolidity concealed a shrewdness that such good judges as Sir Justin Soames had long recognised. The mills of the chief inspector's brain might grind slowly, but they ground exceedingly small.

"Thanks, Joe," he said quietly. "Sorry I talked such rot. Forget it, will you. Now, about——"

A buzz on his telephone interrupted him. He listened and replied.

"That was York," he explained. "I've told him to come along."

Inspector Robert York came in. "I found your message on my desk, sir," he said.

"Sit down. You've got a new job, or partly new. Sir Justin's let me pinch you. There was talk of giving me another Special Branch man in place of Larry Doyle, but I got the A.C. to agree to let me have you instead. You'll be taken off all other duties, except the Ostrod case, of course. That's really part of our show."

"Right, sir," York responded with his habitual cheerfulness.

"I've been talking to Lonneker," Muir went on.

"Get anything out of him?"

"Not a damn thing." He gave the inspector a pithy account of the interview.

"Sounds as though he *did* know Ostrod, although he denies it," York commented.

"I'm convinced he knew the Captain, too, but I was afraid to give him too much of a lead in that direction. Talking of the Captain, any luck about the car that hit Doyle?"

"No. We got a look at David Jones' car. He keeps it in a garage near where he and his daughter live. He doesn't use it much except at week-ends. There wasn't a mark on it of any use to us—just the ordinary wear and tear you'd expect. It's an ordinary blue Austin four-seater. There are strong bumpers back and front and I think there's no doubt Doyle was hit by the front bumper."

"Who went to the garage for you?"

"Sergeant Hunt, sir."

"He didn't let the garage people know what he was after?"

"Oh no. I warned him to be very careful. He said he was making inquiries about a car that had been stolen and might have been faked up to look different, and he inspected half the cars in the garage before he came to the one he wanted, and inspected the rest of them before he came away."

"Good. It's very likely Jones did drive the car, but we can't be certain, and we mustn't put the wind up him."

"It might have been his daughter," Joe Marshall suggested. "It seems obvious that the car was parked somewhere near, waiting for the Captain and Jones to come out."

"It certainly might," Muir agreed. "These fanatical young women are capable of anything——"

The telephone again broke the conversation. Muir looked annoyed as he picked up the receiver, but his expression changed while he listened. He replaced the receiver and sprang to his feet.

"There's been a bomb job at the Staterays power station," he said. "We'll get out there right away. I'll 'phone Sir Justin—— Damn! it's later than I thought, but I expect he'll be at home by now or at his club." He caught up the telephone and told the operator to contact the Assistant Commissioner if he could. "Tell the Special Branch, Joe, and order a car for us. York, have you ever seen that girl Myfanwy Jones?"

"No, sir."

"Right, then ring Mr. Kair's flat. If he's in, ask him to meet us outside Baker Street station in quarter of an hour. Tell him it's urgent, and warn him not to tell his servants where he's going. I'll meet you both downstairs, but I must wait a few minutes in case we get through to the A.C."

The telephone operator intelligently tried Sir Justin's club first, and in a few minutes Muir was telling him what little he knew of the explosion.

Sir Justin said he would remain at the club until Muir telephoned again, and would then return to the Yard and hear the rest of the story.

York and Marshall were waiting in a police car in the forecourt when Muir appeared.

"I got Kair," the former said. "He'll be waiting for us."

"Good. All right, driver. Step on it."

At Baker Street station Kair was standing on the pavement and the car barely halted while he got in.

"What the devil is it all about?" he asked rather shortly, for the quick restart of the car had made him sit down suddenly.

"You know Myfanwy Jones, don't you?" Muir asked.

"Yes, of course. Why?"

"Because you may have to identify her, if there's enough of her left to identify."

"Hell!" Kair muttered in shocked surprise.

CHAPTER XVII

THE Staterays plant, built by the Government after the nationalisation of electrical supplies, was one of the biggest undertakings of its kind in the country. In addition to being the power station which provided current over a large area, it was a factory for the design, improvement and manufacture of the many accessories used in the industry.

There was not much conversation in the Yard car as it sped towards Hendon. Kair ventured a further question, but was curtly told by Muir that all they knew was that there had been an explosion at the works and that a young woman had been killed; the chief superintendent added that discussion of a matter of which they knew practically nothing would obviously be futile. The addendum was actually phrased more tersely, and Kair took the hint.

Presently Muir said to the chief inspector, "Did you notify Finger-prints?"

"Yes, sir," Marshall replied formally.

Good, Muir said to himself; it was like Joe to do it without waiting for the order his superior had forgotten to give. He was thankful to have those solid, reliable fellows like Ash and Marshall with him on a job like this. He had always had confidence in his own ability, but he was not blind to his weaknesses. Even now, a fullblown chief detective-superintendent, young for his rank, but no longer to be excused on the score of youthfulness, he had continually to curb that tendency to rush his fences which he condemned so strongly in his lectures to budding detectives. Outwardly he was cool and competent; only Gloria and Joe Marshall—and, he felt uneasily, that infernally astute Assistant Commissioner, Sir Justin Soames, from whom no man's secrets were hidden— knew his torment of self-reproach when he had fallen below the high standard he had set for himself. Muir was that not too common type, a man who loved his work and believed in its moral as well as material importance. Like the Assistant Commissioner, he could forgive a mistake, but he had no use for the man who scamped his job.

As Marshall had said so bluntly, he was proud that Sir Justin had given him a post which several older men might have claimed with some justice. It was true that officially he was merely *liaison* officer, the link between many experts of various services; but he knew that his chief looked to him for much more than that. He had been given a wider degree of authority than even Marshall knew, and Sir Justin expected him to use it tactfully, but with fearless initiative. Well, he told himself grimly, he would justify the A.C.'s confidence—or throw in his hand and let a better man finish the rubber.

There was no sign of his thoughts on his face when the car stopped at the main gates of Staterays and he got out.

To Kair it seemed as though half the Metropolitan Police force was milling about the place. He saw Chief Inspector Harry Fenn directing a party of print experts and photographers; he recognised at least one man whom he knew belonged to the Special Branch; and other men, uniformed or in plain clothes, flitted about on missions of which he could only guess the nature.

They had been received at the entrance by the district detective-superintendent, the local superintendent, and a few other notables, with whom Muir talked as the party walked along a covered way that led to the central block of buildings. In the main hall there was a brief consultation. Then Muir said something to York, who remained behind when the rest of the party moved off down a long corridor that ran through the left wing of the building.

Kair was about to follow, when York stopped him.

"This is where you come in," the inspector said. "I'm afraid it won't be pleasant, but they've done the best they can."

What this meant became apparent when a sergeant took them to a whitewashed room which was normally used as a laboratory, but had been transformed into a temporary morgue. Powerful lights glared down on a long table covered with a sheet. But it was not the bloodstains on the linen that mattered. . . .

Kair's imagination had drawn the picture he had prepared himself to see, but it was what he did *not* see that made his stomach heave. He looked instinctively for the outline of a body, but it was horribly not there. The twin hummocks raising the sheet at the end nearest him must be feet. Beyond them, the tapering cylinders of limbs, one shorter than the other. Then a ghastly flatness, and after that . . .

He must have turned white, for he felt York's hand grip his arm. Almost angrily he shook it off and said hoarsely:

"Let me see—it."

He walked forward as the sergeant gently turned back the other end of the sheet, and stared down at the torn but still recognisable face of Myfanwy Jones.

Muir spoke only once on the way back. He said to Kair:

"Where shall we drop you? Canton Court?"

Kair said: "I was hoping you'd let me come with you. In case there's anything I can do," he added lamely.

Muir thought for a moment.

"All right," he assented. "Sir Justin might want to see you, though I doubt it."

Big Ben was chiming nine as the car stopped in the Yard forecourt.

Marshall took Kair to Muir's room and then busied himself in the little office that adjoined it. The chief superintendent hurried off to see the Assistant Commissioner, who had arrived shortly before them.

Kair tried to read an evening paper that lay on the chief superintendent's desk, then threw it down and paced up and down. All through the weary time he had spent alone in a waiting-room, while the others were closeted in the room of the Assistant Director of the works, or passed and repassed the door on various errands, he had tried to forget the picture of that bare room with the sheeted table. He had failed, and he failed again now. He longed for a stiff brandy, but was ashamed to ask Marshall if there was any to be had.

It was a relief when Muir came in, looking tired, but not

depressed. Apparently his interview with Sir Justin had been satisfactory.

"Sir Justin asked me to thank you for your help," the chief superintendent said. "It wasn't a nice job, but we wanted to be sure of the identity as quickly as possible."

"Only too glad to be of use."

"Thanks. Sorry to have left you to hang about on your own up at the power plant, but there was rather a lot to do. You must be famishing, so don't let me keep you any longer."

"I should think you could do with a drink and a spot of food yourself."

"Oh, we get used to missing meals. But we're practically finished now, for tonight."

"Are you? Then why not——"

"What?"

"I was going to suggest," Kair explained, "that you should all come and have a meal at my place, but I forgot that you didn't want to be seen with me."

"I can't believe anyone could have suggested you were as disreputable as all that," Muir protested, laughing. "But I know what you mean. Things have changed rather rapidly. The gloves are off now and I think we'll have to drop some of our precautions. If our Red friends don't know already that you're working for us they probably won't be long finding out."

"Then you'll come?"

"Where? Oh, I see. Heavens, my dear fellow, there's no reason why you should feed three healthy policemen, especially at this hour of night!"

"Look, Muir, you and the others have got to eat. If I'm not mistaken, you'll want to put your heads together, now you've got a minute to breathe, and go over things quietly. Mrs. Cradoc's used to scratching up meals at all hours, so you needn't worry about that. After you've eaten I'll leave you three to talk, and only come in for a nightcap before you go. Do let me be that much use."

Muir hesitated. Gloria was away for a few days and he had told their housekeeper that he would be dining out. He had had a gruelling evening and Kair's offer was tempting.

"If you're quite sure——" he began doubtfully.

"Only too delighted! May I use your 'phone?"

Kair got through to Canton Court and said things that caused the Cradocs to become very busy.

When the four men had reached Kair's flat Cradoc had drinks ready, followed by an improvised but excellent meal, for which they drank Mrs. Cradoc's health in a Chambertin worthy of its name.

The meal over, Kair rose.

"Cradoc will bring you coffee in the lounge," he said. "If you'll excuse me, I'm going to get on with a bit of work——"

"You're not," Muir interrupted. "You're staying with us, please. Damn it, Kair, we're not going to eat your bread and salt and then turn you out of your own tent. Seriously, we know we can trust you to keep your mouth shut, and Sir Justin's agreed to my letting you in on things a bit more."

Kair flushed. "Thanks," he said. "It's good of you. I'll try not to get in the way."

"You won't."

When Cradoc had settled them in the lounge, with coffee and some decent brandy, Muir said:

"I think I'd better begin the palaver. When we were at the power station Marshall and York were dashing about a good bit while I was talking to the Assistant Director and doing other things, so I've got to bring them up to date before we hear what they've got to say. I'll begin at the beginning and try to make a connected story.

"It appears," he went on, "that the day staff had gone off duty and the night staff had come on. Most of the workers use a side entrance. Heads of departments and senior officials use the main entrance—the one we used when we arrived. There are gate-keepers, as they call them, at all entrances, and no one is allowed in without being recognised or producing some form of credentials."

He took out a note-book, looked at some notes, and continued:

"The man on duty at the main entrance is named Thomas Waring. He's an ex-sergeant of artillery, has a good record, and has been employed at Staterays ever since he took his discharge from the Army. He's a teetotaller, married, and has never missed a day's work or been late on duty. You can put someone on to check his record, Joe, and find out if he bets or keeps a woman on the quiet.

"Waring says he was reading an evening paper in his office at the main gate when a car stopped outside. It was a blue four-seater. A young woman got out and rang the night bell. She was dressed as a nurse and was carrying a black bag. As we know," Muir interrupted himself, "that the girl was Myfanwy Jones, I'll call her that from now on.

"Myfanwy said the St. Christopher Hospital had received an urgent message from Staterays saying that a man had been badly hurt—too badly to be dealt with by the local first aid squad—and she'd been sent to deal with the case. The St. Christopher isn't a big place, but it's the nearest hospital. Myfanwy explained that the hospital's two ambulances were out, but one was expected at any minute and would be sent after her. As she could drive, she had been told to take the car used by the secretary and other officials for general business.

"Waring was surprised. He hadn't been notified of any accident, but he supposed that someone had forgotten to warn him. He has strict orders not to leave his post. There's a telephone in his office and if anyone arrives at night that he doesn't expect he rings up the Assistant Director's office and someone is sent to meet the visitor and take him wherever he has to go.

"Waring did what I should have done in his place. He thought it would be silly to keep the nurse hanging about there when a man might be dying, so he told her how to go along the covered way and where to find the Assistant Director's office if she didn't find someone waiting for her in the main hall.

"When she'd gone, he telephoned through. The Assistant Director said there hadn't been any accident and they hadn't telephoned to the hospital. Waring didn't wait to hear any more. He seems to be a chap who isn't afraid to use his own judgment and he decided that this wasn't the time to be particular about rules and regulations. He made sure that the main gates were locked, and sprinted up the covered way after Myfanwy.

"All this takes some time in the telling, but Waring says it all happened very quickly, and I believe him.

"He's a lean, fit-looking chap, not at all the fat and wheezy type, and he says he used to do a lot of sprinting in army sports. Anyhow, he says he ran like a hare to the main hall. There was no one in the hall, which was usual enough at night.

He looked down the corridor of the left wing and saw Myfanwy. She seemed to him to be walking fairly quickly but 'sort of carful', as he put it. There are swing doors with glass panels at long intervals along the corridor, partly to stop draughts. Myfanwy was just reaching one of these doors. He shouted and began to run after her. She looked over her shoulder, hesitated, and then pushed the doors open and made a dash for it. Through the glass panel he saw her stumble and fall. There was a hell of a noise and the next thing he knew was that he was lying on a couch in the Assistant Director's room, badly bruised and cut by flying glass, but all in one piece. Myfanwy was holding her bag in front of her. You'd expect the bomb in it to have been for time explosion, but either it was a percussion one and she thought she'd be able to throw it round a corner and get away in time, or—what seems more likely—something went wrong and it went off when she fell. As you know, it blew the middle part of her to bits, smashed the doors, and did a lot of damage to the pretty solid walls of the corridor. The scientific blokes from our laboratory are working with the Staterays people, looking for fragments that may tell them something about the explosives used, and so on.

"Well, that's the main story, as far as we've been able to get it. Any questions or remarks? Joe?"

"Yes, sir. First, about the car the girl used. It's David Jones' car all right. It had false number-plates, but the real ones were under the back seat, ready to be replaced. We're looking for Jones, but he didn't go home when he left work and we haven't found him yet. There's another thing about the car, too. When Hunt saw it at the garage he was only able to give it a once-over, as you didn't want any fuss made. Fenn's men have been busy on it tonight, and they found a tiny shred of material caught in a screw on the front bumper. Fenn sent a man with it to the nursing-home to compare it with the coat Larry Doyle was wearing, and just before we left the Yard Fenn 'phoned me to say that it matches all right."

"Good," said Muir. "Mr. Jones is going to have to answer a few awkward questions when we find him. Anything else?"

"Later, sir, if I may."

"All right, you old fox. York?"

"You said, sir, that when Waring reached the main hall there was no one there. I'd have thought the Assistant

Director would have given some sort of alarm and gone out to look for the girl."

"I put that point to him, and his answers seem reasonable. He said, first, that he didn't want to cause a general rumpus and have everybody rushing about in a flurry until he was sure it wasn't some sort of hoax. Secondly, he waited to telephone to the local police and ask them to send a man round to help him in his inquiries."

"Sounds reasonable, as you say, but I don't quite get what he meant by a hoax."

"I didn't either, especially as he thought it worth while to notify the police. It seems that some fool of a practical joker's been up to his tricks in that neighbourhood. Several doctors were called out of bed to go to addresses that didn't exist, and the fire brigade went twice to Staterays on fake telephone calls saying the place was blazing."

"Was that recently?"

"No; a couple of months ago, but it does show that the Assistant Director wasn't talking through his hat."

"You'll want him looked up, of course?" York suggested.

"No," the superintendent replied, to his surprise. "I happen to know a good bit about him already."

He left it at that, so the others left it at that. Muir would not have refused such a routine suggestion without good reason.

There was a short silence. Then, as no one else seemed to have anything to say, Kair took courage and spoke.

"I don't know if I ought to put my oar in," he said tentatively.

"Shove it in and pull hard," Muir smiled. "At the worst you can only catch a crab."

"I'll risk it, then. Everything you've told me goes to show that these Red so-and-sos are damned clever, but for the life of me I can't see what their game is. I know the general idea is to upset governments and start revolutions, and all that. I can even see that it might cause alarm and despondency, as one used to say, to have the Home Secretary murdered, especially a rather competent chap like the present one. But I can't see the point of tonight's job. I don't know much about explosives, but I imagine the bomb Myfanwy carried could not have blown up the whole works. Even if she'd hit the engines that make the power I suppose new ones could have been put in fairly quickly. A lot of plants and people would have been temporarily deprived of current and there'd have been a good deal of cursing. So what? It seems rather a poor result for a lot of careful planning."

"I was thinking along those lines myself," Marshall remarked.

Muir nodded. Leaning forward, he said in a low voice:

"Forgive me, Kair, but is your man addicted to listening at keyholes?"

Kair was sitting well away from the door. He got up and said loudly:

"I know I put the damn book somewhere—on the window-seat I think. Let me look——"

Tiptoeing round the wall, he flung the door open. There was no one in the corridor outside. He closed the door and went back to his chair.

"Cradoc and his wife have been with my family for thousands of years," he explained. "They treat me like a naughty boy sometimes, but I honestly believe that if I'd committed sixteen crimes, and they knew it, they'd chuck you out of the window if you tried to arrest me."

"All right," Muir said. "I wasn't trying to be theatrical, but what I'm going to say now is a top secret of top secrets. Myfanwy Jones knew exactly what she had to do, and she must have known that she was risking her life—to say nothing of being caught if she didn't die in the explosion. Let me run over the facts. When she got to the main hall, why did she turn to the right? The power plant isn't in the left wing, it's on the other side. When she heard Waring shouting after her, why didn't she bluff it out by pretending she'd lost her way? I'll tell you: it was because her orders were to get into the left wing and she meant to do it at all costs. Why? That's where the secret comes in.

"Frankly, I don't know much about it, and it's only because of this job I've been given that I know anything at all. For several months some of the big scientific people have been working on a device to stop aeroplanes in flight. It's something quite new, I believe; not the old death-ray idea we used to hear about years ago. Anyhow, it's being kept as dark as possible."

"But a place like Staterays is hardly very suitable for

secret experiments of that kind," Kair could not help objecting. "You'd expect that kind of work to be done at the atom bomb place, or somewhere like that, with dozens of armed guards at every door."

"You would," Muir agreed, "and that's where our people have been clever. Staterays was chosen for two reasons. In the first place, it has facilities for making instruments of various kinds, and the staff are always experimenting quite openly with new devices, so any unusual bit of work can be done there without causing comment. Secondly, the most astute foreign agent wouldn't suspect the staff of an ordinary power station of working on a scheme that would make it practically impossible for an enemy to bomb this country, or any country we protected."

"It's a hell of a big thing, sir," York remarked.

"It is. Mind you, they don't know yet whether they'll pull it off, but they've gone all out on it. One point is that no great space and very elaborate plant are required, at least at this stage. The models and drawings and so on are in a couple of connected rooms in the left wing. I said just now that you needn't check up on the Assistant Director. He was given the job because he's one of the men in the secret. He works at night and puts in a certain amount of time doing the ordinary duties of an Assistant Director, but they're not very exacting as each department has its own head. The rest of the time he helps the men in the left wing. I needn't go into the precautions that are taken. They're pretty thorough. There are two Special Branch men working as shorthand typists, for instance. That's really all I know, and now you understand why Myfanwy Jones was so anxious to smash up those rooms in the left wing, and the things and people in them into the bargain."

"I wonder they didn't try to pinch the plans, instead," said Marshall.

"It was almost impossible. The men on the job are all handpicked, of course, and at their own request they're under observation. They don't want to take any risks."

"I suppose there's at least one duplicate set of drawings and models?" Joe suggested.

"Yes, but where it's being kept even I don't know at present."

"But——" Kair began.

"Well?"

"I suppose I'm being dull, but there's still one thing that puzzles me."

"What is it?"

"You've told us how carefully the whole thing's been kept dark," Kair answered, "and that only a few high-ups know about it. Then how the hell can these Reds have heard about it, let alone knowing where the work's being done?"

Muir's face hardened. "If I could tell you that," he replied grimly, "I wouldn't be sitting here now. I told you before, I think, that there's a leak somewhere in the official piping. That leak's got to be found and plugged. In plain words, someone's doing the Judas, but so far's he's been too clever for us."

"You told me once," Kair said thoughtfully, "that Sir Justin Soames sometimes quotes from the old detective story writers—Gaboriau and chaps like that."

"He does. He says some of their ideas were quite sound. But what's that got to do with it?"

"Only that I was thinking of something Conan Doyle made Sherlock Holmes say. I've forgotten the exact words, but it was to the effect that when you have eliminated the impossible whatever remains—however improbable it may sound—must still be possible."

"Thanks for the memory, Watson," Muir retorted acidly. "Of course that's true in a general way, but are you asking me to believe that the Prime Minister or the Home Secretary, or even such notorious crooks as the Assistant Commissioner of the C.I.D. and his merry men, are deliberately trying to sell their country for thirty pieces of silver?"

"I've never met the Prime Minister or the Home Secretary," Kair replied, "and my acquaintance with the notorious crooks you've mentioned hasn't yet made me lock up the spoons when some of them come to see me."

"Sorry," Muir smiled. "I wasn't trying to be rude. But you must admit——"

"I admit that the idea's fantastic," Kair broke in. "If you'd told Judas that men would be able to fly in the air or talk to each other when they were hundreds of miles apart, he'd have said those ideas were equally fantastic. But fantastic things have a way of happening, all the same. I'm not attacking the

P.M., or anybody else. All I'm saying is that someone's been blowing the gaff. Let X equal the number of people who *could* have given it away. Until you know which of them *did* it, you've got to keep an open mind—and from now on," he added, laughing, "you've got to include me in your list of suspects."

"All right," Muir agreed, getting up. "If you'll give Marshall your measurements he'll get a special pair of handcuffs made for you in case we need them. And now we really must go if we're going to get any sleep tonight. Many thanks for——"

But Kair insisted that the obligation was on his side.

Cradoc produced the police driver, whom he had been entertaining, and trying with complete lack of success to pump.

The car went first to Buckingham Gate to drop the chief superintendent at his house.

"The infernally annoying thing," Muir said, "is that Kair's perfectly right! Good night, Joe; good night, York."

"Good morning," Joe said ruefully, and the others laughed.

CHAPTER XVIII

On Chief Superintendent Muir's table lay a collection of objects which Chief Inspector Fenn had brought down after they had been examined in the Finger-print Department.

When Kair, who had been asked to call, came in he said:

"Is it true about David Jones? I saw a few lines in a paper saying he'd fallen in front of an Underground train and been killed."

"It's true enough," Muir answered.

"Suicide?"

"That's as may be."

"What really happened, or mustn't I ask?"

"Of course you may. There was a pretty wide net spread for him. We were going to pull him in for running down Doyle with his car, and get him remanded in custody. One of our men spotted him at Oxford Circus tube station. As soon as he said he was a policeman Jones bolted. I suppose he lost his nerve, or perhaps he thought he could really get away. Anyhow, he ran down an escalator. Our fellow went after him.

Jones got to one of the platforms just as a train was coming in. It's impossible to say whether he couldn't stop himself in time, or whether he jumped deliberately, but he went under the train and——'' He made an expressive gesture, and turned to Fenn.

"Any luck at Jones' flat?" he inquired.

"No, sir," Fenn replied. "The place was well kept and comfortable. Plenty of books, mostly rather solid reading, but no really Red stuff. Karl Marx, of course, but all sorts of people have him on their shelves. Practically no private papers, barring birth and marriage certificates and that sort of thing. There was an account book showing daily expenses, and there was a file of receipted bills from tradesmen. All very neat and tidy."

"Money?"

"I was coming to that, and it's interesting. We found a cash-box with seven pounds, fourteen shillings and eightpence in it. The box wasn't locked; it was kept in a drawer of an old bureau. In the box there were also National Savings certificates to the value of four hundred and fifty pounds. That was all we found at first, but the bureau had a secret drawer of the kind that used to be popular years ago. It was simple enough, really, if you know that kind of furniture. You take out one of the ordinary drawers and press a spring behind it. That releases a panel that looks like part of the woodwork. Behind the panel we found a bank pass-book showing that a certain Derek Johnson had nearly eight thousand pounds to his credit on deposit."

"I went round to the bank," Chief Inspector Marshall put in. "The branch is in Holborn. When I described Jones the manager said he'd no doubt it was the man who'd opened an account there about two years ago in the name of Derek Johnson. He showed me Johnson's signature, and it was plainly the same writing as Jones' name on the fly-leaf of his books; he hadn't bothered to disguise it. We're getting it checked upstairs, of course, but I haven't any doubt about it. The manager said that Jones—I mean Johnson—told him he was an expert in printing machinery and was a traveller for one of the biggest firms in that line, though he didn't mention the name. He said he sometimes put through orders for very large sums, and his firm paid him a small salary but a handsome percentage on sales. He said he was saving up enough money to retire, so he lived on his salary and banked his commissions. That was why he only wanted a deposit account, and not a current one as well. The bank manager told me he had other customers like that and had no reason to doubt the story, especially as Johnson never withdrew any of his money."

"Reasonable enough," Muir agreed.

Kair looked curiously at the desk on which the Welshman's personal possessions lay. There was a wallet containing some Treasury notes, postage stamps, an identity card and another showing his membership of a trade union, his motorist's driving licence, and a small photograph of his daughter. The other things included a handkerchief; a battered silver box containing snuff (a common habit in his trade, Kair reflected); some loose change; a watch of the old-fashioned half-hunter type; a fountain-pen and a pencil; a pocket diary in which the entries seemed to be confined to classes at the various branches of the Teener organization; and a chain with a buttonholed leather tab at one end and a ring with a number of keys at the other. There was also another key, not attached to the ring.

Marshall examined all these objects in turn; then he said: "Will you excuse me, sir? I'll be back in a minute or two."

Muir nodded. He would have been astonished if he had not learned not to be astonished by anything Joe did, but he was puzzled and interested.

"I wonder what's bitten him now," he remarked.

The others had no answer to that purely rhetorical observation.

Meanwhile Joe had made a telephone call, and afterwards hurried to the Receiver's department.

The Receiver of the Metropolitan Police is a sort of Chancellor of the Police Exchequer appointed by Royal Warrant to administer financial affairs, deal with official property, pay court expenses and receipts, and a hundred other things. Among his other functions is that of custodian of private property held by the police until its ownership and destination have been legally established.

He had handed the effects of Joseph Ostrod to the Receiver for safe keeping, and Marshall now asked for the return of a certain article. Having obtained it, he returned to the chief superintendent's office and apologised for having exceeded the minute or two for which he had asked.

"All right," Muir replied. "What's your idea?"

Joe took from the desk the separate key found in Jones' pocket. It was an ordinary piece of metal of the type used for a mortice lock; its solid barrel was about three-sixteenths of an inch in diameter and four inches in length. Its flanges, grooved to engage the wards of the lock, projected some three-eighths of an inch from the side of the barrel, the end of which terminated in a ring. A very ordinary-looking key.

"Had you time to identify the keys on the key-ring?" he asked.

"Yes," Fenn replied. "At least, most of them. One's for the front door of the flat, another for the bureau, and another for the lock-up where he kept his car. Then there's the car ignition key. That one with the initials and number cut on it is the key of Jones' locker at the firm he worked for; they told me the number over the telephone."

"What about this separate one that isn't on the ring?"

"I don't know. It didn't fit any cupboard or box at the flat. It certainly isn't the door key; that's the biggest Yale one on the ring."

"That's what I hoped," Joe said with quiet satisfaction. He took from his pocket the object he had brought from the Receiver's office. It was an almost exactly similar key, but smaller, the barrel being about one-eighth of an inch in diameter and two inches long. Borrowing a pocket ruler from Fenn, he measured both keys and found that his estimates had been almost exactly correct. He laid both keys on the desk, side by side.

"Where did you get the second one from?" Muir asked.

"I found it when I was going over Joseph Ostrod's things."

"What's it for?"

"I don't know. It didn't fit anything in his flat or his office. When I saw Jones' key it sort of rang a bell; at first I couldn't remember what it reminded me of. Then I remembered Ostrod's key."

"It's a coincidence," Muir admitted, "but is it anything more than that? There must be thousands of similar keys about."

"I agree, sir, but there's just one other chance——"

The telephone interrupted, and Muir took the call. "It's for you," he said, passing the receiver to the chief inspector.

Joe listened for a moment, put a question, and replaced the receiver.

"I got through to the man who took the inventory of Lonneker's things," he said, "and asked him to look it up and ring me back. He says Lonneker had a key like the smaller one of these two."

The three others digested this information in silence. Then Muir took a lens from a drawer and examined each of the two keys in turn.

"It looks to me," he said, "as though neither of these keys had been used, or at least not much. What do you think?" he asked Fenn.

The expert took the glass.

"I think you're right, sir," he answered. "I'm afraid we missed that point, as far as Jones' key goes. I'll take them both upstairs and have a proper test made presently, but I can't see any of the marks you'd expect to find if they'd been in even fairly common use."

"Well, Joe, that seems to be one to you. What do you make of it?" Muir asked.

"I don't know, sir," Marshall said thoughtfully. "It may be just a coincidence. If it isn't, the only answer I can think of sounds a bit far-fetched."

"Everything in this blasted case is far-fetched," Muir declared. "Take Myfanwy Jones' death; that business was like something out of a thriller or an old melodrama, but it was real enough all the same. Fetch it as far as you like, we shan't laugh."

"As I see it," Marshall said, thus encouraged, "the Captain's show is very well organised. You couldn't get much out of Lonneker; that may be because there wasn't much he could have told you even if he'd been willing. Suppose one of the Captain's agents was sent to see another man he hadn't met before. There'd have to be some way by which they could recognise each other. Passwords are tricky things, as you know; they couldn't have too ordinary a phrase in case it might be used accidentally by someone not in the know."

"Quite," Muir agreed, "but these keys are ordinary, too. There must be hundreds of people who have them. And another thing: say you go into a pub. You're looking for another man. It would be natural enough to take out a cigarette-case or a pipe, but what reason would you have for producing a key? Wouldn't that look a bit queer?"

"I think it would depend on how you did it," the chief inspector answered in his quietly dogged way. "Naturally you wouldn't wave it about in the air. But, for instance, I'm sure you've often seen a man take loose change out of his pocket and spread it on the bar while he picked out the right coins to pay for his drink. He could take the key out with the money. I'm only guessing, but I think it might depend on the way the key was laid on the bar. For instance, the ring or the other end might be pointing at the man he expected to meet—he'd have his description, of course, and the exact time and place of the meeting would have been arranged. When he'd put his change and the key back in his pocket he'd watch the other man, who'd probably get into conversation and use some word with 'key' in it. When no one else was looking the second man would let the first one have a glimpse of a similar key, partly hidden in his hand. There'd be a dozen other ways of doing it, especially as the second man would be on the lookout. My point is that it would establish a contact which both sides could verify in a few seconds' talk. A badge of sorts might easily attract attention, but no one would be likely to pay any attention to a key like this, just because there *are* so many about."

"That sounds reasonable to me," Fenn said, "but may I put a point? You say Ostrod had that key, but I thought the idea was that he *wasn't* one of the Captain's gang?"

"It was, and that's what we still believe. Now I'm wondering whether he hadn't got hold of this key when he was sniffing round, perhaps have pinched it from Pasquale Vico, and that may have been one of the reasons why the Captain had him croaked."

"Or he might have belonged to the gang and let them down in some way," Fenn suggested.

"He might, but there's nothing to establish it. One thing seems clear: they were in a great hurry to get rid of him, or they'd have cleaned up his flat and tried to get this key back."

"Why?"

"Because they'd give us credit for noticing that it didn't fit anything he had."

"Yes, I see. That's sound."

Joe shifted his acid drop with the noiselessness of long practice.

"The keys," he observed, "are of different sizes."

"Why shouldn't they be?" Fenn inquired.

"Why should they?" Joe answered mildly.

"That's right," said Muir. "Why should they, if they weren't to be used for different locks? Any ideas?"

"I was wondering the same thing myself. Could it mean that the more important people had the bigger keys and the rank and file had the smaller ones?"

"It might, indeed." Muir picked up the larger key and toyed with it absently. "David Jones was certainly a Big Noise in the outfit."

"But what about Lonneker, sir?" Fenn put in. "He as near as dammit shot the Home Secretary. Would you say he was just a ranker?"

"Yes, I think I would. He did the dirty work planned for him by the people who kept in the background."

"Doesn't that go for Myfanwy Jones as well?"

"I don't think so. Lonneker had a comparatively simple job. He was intelligent enough, but it doesn't need much brain to fire a gun at a man coming out of a house. Myfanwy's case was different. She had to do quite a bit of acting, and we must admit she did it well. After all——"

He broke off with a sharp exclamation. Turning the key about in his fingers he had felt that the end of the barrel, beyond the flange, seemed to be loose. He twisted it and the end unscrewed and came away in his hand.

"Well, I'm——" he began.

"Just a minute, sir," Fenn said quickly. "May I have it? You never know——"

Muir handed it over without argument; Harry Fenn had forgotten more about queer weapons and other devices than the three others put together.

Taking Muir's glass he peered at the key, then began to press and twist it. Suddenly there was a click. From the end of the barrel, where the now unscrewed cap had been, sprang a thin but strong steel rod about three and a half inches long. It tapered to a point as sharp as a needle. The key was now a small but deadly stiletto. The blade was released by giving the ring a half turn and sliding the flange a fraction of an inch up the barrel.

"A neat piece of work," Fenn remarked contentedly.

"Too blasted neat," Muir declared. "I've got you to thank that it didn't go through my hand. How did you spot it, Harry?"

"It's an old dodge, in a way, but I haven't seen it used in a key before. This'll be something for our museum. You'll notice that the blade is quite firm as long as the ring at the top is in its present position. Just watch, sir." He turned the ring, and the blade slid back into the barrel. "All you have to do now is to screw the cap on. Jones must have been careless to let it work loose."

"Is the little key the same?" Marshall asked.

Fenn spent some time examining it. "No," he answered; "at least, I don't think so. It doesn't respond to the same pressures. I'll test it later on, but I'm pretty sure I'm right."

"Which suggests that the underdogs weren't allowed to use weapons without permission," Muir commented.

"Or that the chiefs liked to carry a handy means of suicide in case they wanted it in a hurry. That poison pen Lonneker had was a bit crude. I suppose he intended to use it after he'd delivered a powerful oration from the dock."

"This thing suggests something else, too," Joe said. "Remember how Ostrod died, sir?"

"I do indeed! That stab he got was just the wound this knife could have made. But David Jones wasn't the bloke that used it. We happen to have been able to check his movements that night."

"The Captain himself, then?" Fenn suggested.

"No. He didn't move out of Pryse's house all that evening. The Special Branch watch the house at night, though they let up a bit in the daytime, not to scare him . . ."

"Mr. X," Joe observed.

"Yes," Muir answered savagely, "Mr. X, damn and blast his guts! I'd give five years' pay to know who he is. We hold conference after conference and yap our heads off, with the doors locked, and as far as I can see Mr. X knows all about it within half an hour!" He broke off, annoyed at his outburst. The other men looked very hard at nothing in particular.

Inspector York knocked, entered, and said:

"Excuse me, sir, but——"

"All right. I'll be ready in a few minutes. Wait for me downstairs."

"Right, sir."

York went out and Fenn and Marshall followed him.

Kair rose, but Muir said: "Half a minute. I want to talk to you."

He talked for nearly five minutes, after which Kair said:

"All right. I'll do my best, but I'm damned if I can understand what you're up to."

"Good," Muir responded cheerfully. "Good-bye for the present."

Several cars left the Yard soon afterwards and proceeded at a decorous pace to the Islington shop of the popular local chemist, Mr. Evan Jenkin Pryse.

There arrived at that flourishing establishment a select party which included Chief Superintendent Muir, Chief Inspector Fenn, Chief Inspector Marshall, Inspector York, a Special Branch man, an officer from Military Intelligence, and a medico-legal expert on the staff of the police laboratories.

The whole body did not leap from a chariot and invade the premises simultaneously. Their cars parked in adjacent streets and Muir and Marshall entered the shop, while the others waited.

"Good morning," Muir said to the white-coated spectacled man who came from behind a low screen at the end of the counter, where he had been making up prescriptions. "I'm Chief Superintendent Muir, New Scotland Yard, and this is Inspector Marshall. Can we speak to you privately?"

Mr. Pryse kept no qualified assistant; he did all the dispensing work, and a smart lad who was studying for his preliminary examinations sold the non-dangerous drugs and other articles.

"Please come inside," the chemist replied, leading them into a combined office and store-room behind the shop.

"I'll explain," Muir said. "As a chemist, you are familiar with the provisions of the Dangerous Drugs Acts and the Statutory Regulations relating to them?"

"Naturally."

"And you keep the required record of the drugs you obtain and dispense in prescriptions?"

"Of course. Are you suggesting——"

"I'm not suggesting anything, Mr. Pryse. From time to time you've received confidential notices from the police regarding thefts of such drugs or attempts to bring them into this country illegally?"

"Certainly, but I've never been concerned in anything of that kind. Are you accusing me——"

"I'm not accusing you of any such thing and I've made no suggestion that you've had anything to do with that traffic."

"Then I don't understand what you want here. I'm a busy man, Mr. Muir, and I've a lot of prescription work waiting for me. You'll excuse me if I say that I wish you police people would spend more time trying to find criminals and missing people and less in hindering me in my work of relieving the sufferings of the sick."

"We are doing our best in that line," Muir answered, "but we've a good many other things to do as well. We're trying to break up a big drug-running organisation and we're making inquiries among chemists and other people who may be able to help us."

"Quite right. I should be glad to help you if I could, but I'm afraid there's nothing I can do."

"I see. You haven't any drugs here beyond the quantities accounted for in your books?"

"Certainly not! That's an offensive remark, sir."

"I'm sorry. I have my orders and I must carry them out. You don't object to my men coming in and having a look round your premises, I suppose?"

"I object most strongly. I've been in practice here for many years and I've never had such a thing happen before. I shall have to ask my lawyer to deal with you if you persist in this—this most insulting and objectionable conduct."

"Do, by all means, but I must warn you that I hold a search-warrant. Here it is. Perhaps you would like to read it."

The chemist snatched the document, read a few lines, and thrust it back into Muir's hand.

"Very well, sir," he said angrily. "You may bring in your men, but I warn you that you'll hear more of this. I shall ask the Pharmaceutical Society to take up the matter. Busybodies like you need to be taught a lesson.''

He strode into the shop and told his astonished assistant to pull down the blinds. ''You can take the day off,'' he said. ''If anybody asks you why the shop's closed you can tell them they can't get their medicines because it doesn't matter if they die while the police play the fool, looking for a thief that isn't here. Go on, get out, and don't be late tomorrow.''

When the assistant had gone Pryse said sarcastically: ''Do what you like. As I happen to care more for the needs of my customers than I do for your tomfoolery, I'll get on with my prescriptions, if you have no objection.''

''None at all,'' Muir assured him politely.

Pryse went behind the counter and took up a measuring-glass, but he stood where he could see round the corner of the little screen, and the watchful Marshall observed that as more and more men of the police party began to drift into the shop Mr. Pryse's hand began to shake, and presently he put down the glass, seized a pestle and began to pound something in a mortar instead.

Muir and his party went to work with the efficiency of long training and experience. Chief Inspector Fenn set some of the men to work in the shop, and led another party to the living-rooms above. Pryse smiled sourly as he agreed to Muir's suggestion that he should lend his keys so that it would not be necessary to damage locks. He did not smile, however, when some time later Muir asked him for the book in which he kept a record of prescriptions dispensed.

''That is quite unnecessary,'' he declared haughtily. ''In the first place, you're too ignorant to understand the prescriptions; in the second place, I must refuse to disclose confidential information about the health of my customers— it's impossible to say what improper use you might make of it.''

''I'm afraid that argument won't stand up,'' Muir replied with the patient politeness he had shown throughout. ''I'm not a chemist, but this gentleman is Dr. Leeds, one of our experts. He'll understand the prescriptions, and as he's a qualified medical man you needn't have any qualms about letting him see them.''

Pryse's pale face grew livid, but he could think of no further excuse.

"You can see it if you want to, Doctor," he said contemptuously, "though you know as well as I do that it won't be of any use to these people. I keep it here, for handy reference when I need it."

From a drawer beneath the counter, which had not yet been examined, he took a thick volume and handed it to the doctor; but he looked uneasy when Leeds, instead of opening it at once, carried it into the back room. Muir, the Army officer and the Special Branch man followed him, and the door closed behind them.

Joe Marshall, apparently bored by his inactivity, found a chair. Putting his feet on the counter, he half closed his eyes and sucked his acid drop audibly.

Mr. Pryse put down his pestle and wiped his forehead. Then he began stealthily to pour some liquid into a glass.

It seemed an interminable time before the door of the back room opened again and Muir emerged. Taking a paper from his pocket he said:

"Evan Jenkin Pryse, I hold a warrant for your arrest on a charge of being concerned with others in——"

Marshall was out of his chair and across the counter with astonishing agility for a man of his bulk, but Pryse had swallowed part of the contents of the glass before the inspector could snatch it from him.

What followed was unpleasant, and involved the use of a stomach pump.

"He'll do now," said Dr. Leeds at last. "Close thing, though. If Marshall hadn't been so quick I wouldn't have been able to save him. As it is, I suppose he'll live to hang another day?"

"We'll do what we can," Muir promised. "I don't much enjoy helping to send a man for the nine o'clock walk, but I shan't shed any tears if this one swings. Can he be moved?"

"Oh yes."

"Right. Get him away, Joe. Thanks, doctor; we shan't need you any more."

Dr. Leeds would have liked to ask a lot of questions, but he knew better than to do that. It would all come out in the wash, he reflected philosophically as he lit a cigarette and departed to the car which would take him back to the peaceful seclusion of his laboratory. Such little adventures were a

welcome relief from the monotony of test tubes and micro-
scopes; they did not come his way very often, and were all the
more welcome when they did. Lucky chaps, those detectives,
he thought.

In the back room Muir and Army and Special Branch
regarded each other with joy.

"Damn fine bit of work, Muir!" said Army heartily.

"More luck than good management," the chief superintendent returned. "That's why I had to be so careful. The Big
Noises would have backed me up, and it's quite true we've
been after that drug gang for a long time, but Pryse certainly
wasn't mixed up in it. If we hadn't found what we wanted he
could have raised a nasty stink about high-handed policemen,
and all that."

"Well, we *have* got it, sir, praise be," said Special Branch,
who had been born in the fair city of Dublin. " 'Twas a smart
dodge to keep the list of the Captain's people in that prescription book. You've got pretty well all the missing names now,
sir, haven't you?"

"Yes. We'll be able to take them as soon as we're ready,
and the small fry don't matter. We can always pull them in if
they give trouble, but they're not really dangerous, and when
they find their leaders have vanished they won't know what to
do."

"There's still the Captain and one or two more," Army
remarked.

Muir smiled. "There's still the Captain," he agreed, "and
Mr. Curtis Frost and one or two more, but I shouldn't lose a
lot of sleep about them if I were you."

Army grinned as he took out his cigarette-case and passed
it round.

"If you say so, I won't," he promised.

CHAPTER XIX

WHEN Superintendent Ash returned to Treporth after a
rather longer absence than he had anticipated—for Muir had
kept him in London to make certain inquiries in which he had
Kair's assistance—he had a private talk with Colonel Bassenthwaite Lake.

The Chief Constable was inclined to be apologetic.

"I hope," he said, "you don't think I wanted to keep you in the dark. I just couldn't help it. The Home Secretary himself telephoned to me, and sent me a secret and confidential letter in two envelopes, with about a pound of sealing-wax on the outer one."

"That's all right, sir," Ash replied. "I quite understand. We're all in the same boat. It's a case of not letting the right hand know what the left is doing. This isn't a one-man job, you know. There's half the Yard on it, besides a lot of other people. I only know the bits I've been told."

The colonel nodded. "I can take a hint as well as the next man," he said drily.

"I wasn't trying to give you one," Ash assured him. "This thing is so big that the people at the top are trying to keep everything in watertight compartments, and I don't blame them."

"I see your point. One thing seems to be obvious, anyhow, Upwey seems to have got on to something important, or you wouldn't be here now."

"That's what I've got to find out, if I can—though, of course, I'm still officially investigating his murder."

"The question being: was Upwey killed because somebody thought he knew too much?"

"Yes. If Trevone didn't kill him, who did, and why? The jealousy motive was a good one; without it, there seems no reason why Trevone should have done it. By the way, sir, I take it you haven't told Morris or Haydn Hughes about the other angle?"

"No, though it makes me feel a bit disloyal. They're good chaps."

"They're first-class chaps, if I may say so, and I dislike it as much as you do, but my orders are quite definite."

"I know, and I'm not grumbling. After all," the colonel added shrewdly, "it can't be altogether pleasant for you."

"I don't quite get that, sir."

"Look here, Ash, I'm not trying to flatter you, but a man of your rank and reputation usually handles a case on his own and does pretty well what he likes."

"That's true, but we believe in team-work in the Yard. And, as I said, this is much too big a business for me."

"Oh, well, so long as you're satisfied! What are you going to do now?"

"I wish I knew," Ash said frankly. "Potter around and follow up one or two ideas."

"Fersen?"

"Yes, among other people. Just why did you mention him?"

"I've been doing some thinking, too. I know nothing against him, mind, but he's a foreigner and this whole business has a foreign smell to me. I'm not trying to pump you, Ash; I'm just wondering how we can help."

The superintendent thought for a moment.

"You're quite right," he answered. "It *has* a foreign smell, but whether the Fersens—either or both of them—are mixed up in it I can't say. Hughes and I did have an idea that Oscar Fersen might have killed Upwey, but we failed to get any line on that. At the Yard, they think Axel Fersen's just a dreamer who has no time for anything but his inventions, but they're not so sure about Oscar."

"What about that Sweeney woman?" the colonel asked. "She's not exactly a foreigner, but she's pretty thick with the Fersens. They play a lot of bridge together. I rather like her, myself, but it was just an idea that occurred to me."

"Thanks, sir. I'd already decided to improve my acquaintance with Mrs. Sweeney. She struck me as being a clever woman. Do you know her well?"

"Not really. I've played bridge with her. She plays an excellent game and I will say she's a damned good loser."

"That's one point in her favour," Ash agreed.

"Do you play?"

"Not if I can help it. I know one card from another, and that's about all. By the way, I'm having dinner with the Fersens. I met Oscar in the town and he invited me."

"That's interesting. I suppose he won't try to knock you on the head?"

"I don't think so. Mrs. Sweeney and that government chap, Ingrow, are to be there, and Trevone and Miss Dermot Lloyd and her father are going as well."

"Quite a party. What's the occasion?"

"Congratulations to Trevone and the girl, I believe. Fersen told me they're engaged to be married."

"Quick work! Well, I'm not sorry. I like those young people. But——"

He stopped and reddened.

"You're thinking that I don't fit in very well, as the copper who might have got Trevone hanged," Ash said, smiling. "I suggested that, but Fersen said the idea was to show that there's no ill-feeling. They seem to think the police weren't quite so brutal as they might have been. I'm glad to have a chance of getting a look at the Fersen set-up without making an official visit. I told him I hadn't brought any evening clothes, but he said it was to be quite informal and no one was going to dress."

"Well, I hope you'll enjoy it. You'll get good food and drink, anyhow. Tell Hughes what time you want a car."

"Thank you, sir. I'll drive out, not to be too dusty when I arrive, but I'll probably walk back. It looks like being a fine night."

The colonel cocked an eye at him. "A quiet look round after the others have gone, eh?"

"Partly, but it's more an excuse to have a word with Ingrow without making the meeting too obvious."

"Ingrow? How does he come into it?"

"He is quite important, you know, in his job. I want to hear what he thinks of the Fersens, and about the Upwey murder."

"He might be helpful," the colonel agreed. "I can't stand the little man, to be honest with you, but he's certainly no fool. It's just that he's such a ghastly snob. I don't mind a man being a keen fisherman—I do a bit in that line myself—but Ingrow overdoes it. Goes about with trout flies in the band of his hat, carries the butt end of an old rod instead of a walking-stick, and quotes bits out of Izaak Walton in season and out of season." He laughed. "Oh well, I suppose there's no reason why he shouldn't, if it amuses him. And I must admit he plays good bridge."

"Can he really fish, or is it only a pose?"

"He's genuine enough, and I really oughtn't to have said all that about him. I've seen him play a fish like an artist. He comes down whenever he can get away from London; that's why he keeps a cottage on the cliffs. He wouldn't be a bad sort," the colonel concluded handsomely, "if only he wouldn't insist on being so very much the *Compleat Angler*!"

Ash smiled as he got up.

"He ought to take up golf," he remarked.

The colonel chuckled, and it was not until after Ash had gone that he frowned suddenly.

"Golf?" he muttered. "Why the devil did he say that?" Then he grinned unwillingly.

The colonel was the best golfer in the county.

Ash was surprised and a little embarrassed by the warmth of the reception he received when he reached the Crow's Nest, the Fersens' house.

The door was opened by an elderly Swede in the spruce uniform he had worn when he had been Captain Oscar Fersen's steward on many a voyage. The Fersens kept no women servants; their establishment was run by men, and run very efficiently.

Oscar came into the hall, shook Ash's hand, and took him into a big lounge with windows overlooking the sea.

"I think you all know Mr. Ash," he said, "and I'm sure you're as glad as I am that he was able to join us tonight."

There was a chorus of greetings.

Dermot Lloyd and his daughter and Miles Trevone came across to shake hands, and Mrs. Sweeney, sipping sherry in an armchair, waved to him.

"It's certainly nice to see you again," she said. "I've got a pair of socks nearly ready for you. I've guessed your size."

They all laughed as Ash thanked her.

Alfred Ingrow, wearing a tweed plus four suit, anklets and thick shoes, coughed and said in a stately manner:

"Mr. Ash and I have met before, and I am glad to have the pleasure of meeting him again."

It was generally understood that this was tantamount to kissing the superintendent on both cheeks.

The steward offered sherry and other drinks, and when Ash had made his choice Oscar said:

"Nils, go and tell Mr. Axel we're waiting for him."

The steward bowed and went out.

"I'm sorry," Oscar went on apologetically, "but you know what my brother is when he's at work. He'd forget to eat if we didn't drag him to his food by force."

He shrugged and smiled, but there was an affectionate note in his voice that sounded genuine.

The door opened and Ash watched interestedly as Axel Fersen shambled hurriedly in with the air of a man who knew he ought to be there but could not quite remember why.

Axel, about five years older than his brother, was at least three inches over six feet tall, spare and gaunt, with a mass of white hair that needed cutting but somehow did not look unkempt. He was careless but not slovenly in his dress, and his long, sensitive hands were well kept. He smiled and peered at his guests through horn-rimmed spectacles for a moment, then went round the group, making a little bow to each visitor before he shook hands. Ash was rather taken with his manner. He spoke good English, but not quite so easily as Oscar.

"And this," Oscar explained, "is Mr. Andrew Ash."

"Ash?" Axel's eyes gleamed. "The author of *Observations on the Reaction of Atoms to Light*? Sir, a great honour——"

"No, no, Axel," Oscar broke in, laughing. "Not *that* Mr. Ash —although this one often throws light on dark matters, I believe. Mr. Ash is a senior officer of the London detective police. He is down here in connection with the death of Guy Upwey."

"Ah yes. Poor Upwey. A nice young man and a promising player of bridge. It is nonetheless a pleasure to have you with us, Mr. Ash; you are very welcome. But you must all be hungry. Shall we go to eat, Oscar?"

They went into a dining-room and sat at a round table. Axel had Mrs. Sweeney on one side and Alfred Ingrow on the other. Oscar's neighbours were Ash and Kate Dermot Lloyd. Trevone sat beside Kate and Dermot Lloyd beside Ash.

As the Chief Constable had predicted, the food was excellent and there was a claret that Ash, who enjoyed good wine, was unable to name but drank with respect.

Presently there came the sound of popping corks. Nils served champagne.

Oscar coughed and said, "Axel!"

His brother broke off a conversation with Mrs. Sweeney, beamed, and replied, "Yes, my dear Oscar?"

"You really are hopeless, Axel," Oscar declared, laughing. "The toast, man, the toast."

Axel looked bewildered until Mrs. Sweeney whispered in his ear.

H

"Of course, of course!" he exclaimed. "A thousand pardons."

Getting to his feet, he raised his glass.

"My friends," he said, "it is a great honour and a great pleasure that I am permitted to announce formally the engagement of Miss Dermot Lloyd and Mr. Trevone—I am so old that I may be allowed to say: Kate and Miles. I ask you to drink with me to very long happiness and life for them both."

Everybody said, "Kate and Miles" and drank the toast.

Miles, red-faced, uttered the usual few ill-chosen words common to young men in such circumstances, and general joyousness ensued.

They returned to the lounge for coffee and liqueurs.

Ash contrived to exchange a few words with Ingrow under cover of the hum of conversation.

Axel proposed bridge, which in truth was his only interest outside his laboratory, but seemed well content when Mrs. Sweeney declared that it was much too gay an occasion for the solemnity of serious card-playing; what she wanted, she said, was to have Mr. Oscar play the piano and sing to them.

This, to Ash's relief, was carried by acclamation.

While Oscar opened the grand piano Axel slipped happily away to immerse himself in the abstruse calculations in which his soul rejoiced.

Oscar exhibited neither false modesty nor conceit; as he ran his hands up and down the keys his smile frankly invited the little audience to share his pleasure at being able to amuse them and himself.

Ash was no connoisseur, but he had heard enough music played to realise that the Swede was well above the average amateur level. Oscar, wisely avoiding the heavier classics, began with some excerpts from Italian opera.

Then, in a pleasant baritone, he sang three songs: the first (he explained) a Scandinavian sea-shanty; after that a gay little *chanson* with the fragrance of a French summer, and finally the robustious "Rolling Down to Rio", in the chorus of which the whole strength of the company assisted with enthusiasm.

When he stood up everyone clamoured for more, but he declared that he had only performed the overture to the concert, and led Kate Dermot Lloyd to the piano.

Knowing that the people of Wales are born with music in their souls, Ash was not surprised when the girl sang the exquisite "One Fine Day" from *Madame Butterfly* with a purity and sympathy that made up for a lack of power which kept her out of the soprano front rank.

She received an ovation. Even Alfred Ingrow, who had looked disappointed when bridge had been outvoted, rose and made her a ceremonious bow, which she acknowledged with a laughing curtsey. Mr. Ingrow, as Ash observed, had been paying homage to the Swedish punch, a pleasant but potent concoction which Nils had brewed and served with the liqueurs.

Kate and her father sang a duet in Welsh, and Oscar played some Cymric airs, after which conversation became general until Mrs. Sweeney said it was time for an old woman to go to her bed. She had told her chauffeur to call for her, and she suggested that the man should drive her to her house and then take Ash to his hotel, but the superintendent replied that he intended to stretch his legs and walk off the effects of Mr. Oscar's excellent brandy.

Dermot Lloyd had brought his car and Miles Trevone said he would go with them as far as their house and then walk home, an arrangement of which Kate appeared to approve.

When they went into the hall Ash repressed a smile as he saw on a table a hat decorated with flies for trout and other fish, and the butt end of a rod, brass-bound and ornamented with a silver plate on which an inscription had been engraved. Remembering the Chief Constable's prediction, he waited until Ingrow had found his hat; then he handed him the rod and said respectfully:

"Looks like a presentation piece. I've heard a lot about your fame as a fisherman."

"Let us say that I've been lucky," Ingrow answered complacently as he tucked the rod under his arm. "The inscription is a little tribute from an anglers' club. They were really too kind—though, as a matter of fact, it *was* rather a fine fish."

"But nothing to the one that got away!" Oscar Fersen chuckled.

The time-worn jest was not well received. Ingrow gave the Swede a dirty look that seemed to startle that gentleman.

'You said you wanted to stretch your legs, Mr. Ash," he went on. 'I'd like a breath of fresh air myself. May I walk a little way with you?"

Ash said he would be delighted.

There were general farewells, and when the two cars had left Ingrow said stiffly:

"Good night, Oscar. Please thank your brother for a very pleasant evening."

He walked out. Ash, having taken leave of the disconcerted Fersen, followed him.

On the cliff road Ingrow halted.

"It was a good idea to arrange our meeting in this very natural way," he said. "Since you have arranged for a car at the local police station when you want it, I suggest we might stroll as far as my cottage for a whisky-and-soda."

"Thank you very much," Ash replied, "but I'll have to go easy on the drink. The Fersens did us well, and I took my share of that very good claret."

"Yes, they're hospitable people," the other agreed. "That Swedish punch is pleasant, but it's tricky stuff and I'm afraid it excited me a little and made me resent Oscar Fersen's stupid buffoonery."

Whatever the reason, the usually stiff civil servant was undoubtedly letting his hair down, Ash reflected, but he answered admiringly:

"You certainly didn't show it. To tell you the truth, I thought his joke was in rather bad taste."

"I am glad you agree," Ingrow said, swinging the rod he carried. "However, that is a small matter and we have more important things to talk about. I understand you have been told about my activities here. In ordinary circumstances I come down for week-ends, or during longer periods of leave, but lately I have been coming for an odd day or so in mid-week as well. My visits cause no surprise to the local people, of course, but I am afraid," he added with a chuckle, "that my personal staff must think I am beginning to neglect my official duties."

"I can't imagine anyone who knows your reputation thinking anything like that," the superintendent assured him. "You can understand how glad we are to have a trained observer like yourself on the spot, and I'm very glad to have this chance of a private chat with you. Tell me, what do you think of the Fersens?"

Ingrow strode several yards before he replied.

"I expected you to ask that question when we met," he said weightily, "and I have given a good deal of thought to my answer. I began my observation—as, you will agree, one should always begin—with an open mind. I was acquainted with the Fersens, as one naturally becomes acquainted with neighbours of one's own class in a small community, before I heard of Sergeant Upwey's suspicions. After that, it was not difficult for me to get on intimate terms with them, though of course I was careful not to let them suspect I had any ulterior motive."

He paused, and Ash with difficulty restrained a desire to shake him.

"My conclusions," Ingrow proceeded, obviously enjoying his leisurely eloquence, "are these: Axel Fersen is a dreamer with no real interest in anything except his scientific work. He has neither the head nor the heart for intrigues of any kind. Neither the head nor the heart," Ingrow repeated with the satisfaction of one who had achieved a phrase. "His brother, Oscar, I cannot dismiss in such definite terms. Oscar is of the shrewd and active type, and from what he has told me I imagine he led a somewhat wild life in his earlier years. Even now he carries a swordstick, which I must say is rather ridiculous in this peaceful neighbourhood. But we are concerned with his present, not with his past. He has a lot of interests, knows a great many people, and likes to have at least one finger in every social pie. In fact, he's a busybody, and very often a bore. But beyond that I can find nothing wrong about him. He and his brother are rich; they take no part in local or national politics; I can see no motive that should cause them to harm the country which has given them shelter."

Here Mr. Ingrow decapitated with his rod a weed growing by the wayside, and continued:

"Sergeant Upwey was an intelligent and ambitious young man, but I am afraid his imagination was stronger than his judgment. I believe a major cause of his suspicions was the fact that the Fersens often go out at night in their cabin cruiser or one of their other boats. He forgot, or disregarded, the fact that Axel is making experiments connected with light rays—I don't know whether that is the proper technical term —and that Oscar likes to fish, or just to take a short cruise on a fine night. I have accompanied them myself more than once."

They had been walking briskly, and now Ingrow stopped at the gate of a small thatched cottage.

"This is my little place," he said, "but before we go in let me make my final point. When I heard of Upwey's death I was both shocked and puzzled. When I had learned some of the details I was still more puzzled. I could not believe that Trevone was the murderer. I am not a sentimental man and I did not allow myself to be swayed by personal feelings, although I like Trevone, in spite of his difficult temper. But if Trevone was not the murderer, who was? You may be surprised when I say that my thoughts turned to Oscar Fersen. You will ask what possible motive he could have had. I asked myself the same question, and I could not answer it—except to consider whether he might have been in love with Miss Dermot Lloyd and have tried to get rid of two dangerous rivals in a very clever way. That may sound absurd, but you will remember that Oscar knew the movements of both young men, and that he *could*—I only say *could*—have taken the boomerang from Trevone's locker without being noticed.

"Then, Mr. Ash," he went on, chuckling, "I realised what no doubt you are too polite to say: that it is stupid and dangerous for an amateur to jump to conclusions without properly considering the facts. When I *did* consider the facts again, I realised that Oscar Fersen could not possibly have killed Upwey."

"Indeed?" Ash said interestedly. "What made you so certain?"

"A very simple fact—so simple that for the moment I had forgotten it. You see, that week-end I was having some repairs done to my cottage, and the Fersens very kindly put me up at their house. I was out fishing all the morning, came back to lunch, and then took a nap. I had tea with Axel in his laboratory, and then went up to the square tower which you may have noticed at the top of the house. It has big windows on all sides and one gets a fine view. After a time I saw a car come out of the side road into the cliff road and turn towards the house. There was a telescope in the tower and through it I saw that the car was Oscar's and that he was at the wheel. I went downstairs to meet him and we had a drink together before dinner. And that," he concluded, chuckling again, "is why I am sure Oscar Fersen did not murder Upwey. And now you must be tired of hearing my opinions, so come in and have a drink and tell me yours."

CHAPTER XX

THE path that led to the cottage door was fairly plain in the pale moonlight, but the door itself was obscured by the low eave of the thatched roof.

There was a large, old-fashioned keyhole in the door, but above it a modern Yale lock had been fitted.

Ingrow, taking a bunch of keys from his pocket, explained that he had not thought it worth while to have electricity installed in the place, and the woman who did the cleaning had evidently forgotten to light the lantern which hung in the porch when he was staying there.

He fumbled at the lock. Ash produced an automatic lighter, and as they bent down their heads somehow knocked together and Ingrow dropped the keys. Ash picked them up for him, amid polite apologies on both sides and a cheerful allusion to the Swedish punch.

The living-room was small and was furnished for comfort rather than appearance. The walls were adorned with glass cases containing fish of various kinds.

Ingrow lit a lamp, and then an oilstove that sent a cheerful beam through its red glass front.

"I've whisky, gin, rum or beer," he said, unlocking an oaken corner cupboard. "Which would you like?"

"After my debauch at the Fersens'," the superintendent replied, "I think a little cold beer would be advisable."

"I'll join you," Ingrow agreed, filling a couple of glasses. "A cigar?"

"Thanks, but I'll have a pipe, if I may," Ash replied.

He filled and lit up.

"I'm much obliged to you," he said, "for what you've told me. You've given me a lot to think about. May I say that it isn't every day we meet people who can put their ideas so clearly?"

Ingrow expanded his chest and waved a podgy but well kept hand.

"Training, my dear fellow," he replied; "training, and perhaps some small share of natural aptitude and initiative."

Alfred Ingrow, smugly drinking his beer, appeared comfortably satisfied that all was for the best in this best of all possible worlds. His parents had kept a small shop in a mean street, and Alfred had gone first to an elementary and then to a secondary school. He had the examination mind and successive scholarships gained him entry into the Civil Service. To public school colleagues he said vaguely that he had been educated privately. The war years had brought him unforeseen advancement, and he had recently been transferred from the Home Office to the newly-created Directorate of Departmental Intelligence, with the rank of a Principal Assistant Director. He and his widowed sister were determined climbers, and when his increased salary and allowances, and a legacy from a distant relative, enabled them to move into one of the smaller flats in Canton Court, they felt that they were about to take their rightful station in society; but it was not until they had played their way into the Canton Court Bridge Club that they were able at last to claim acquaintanceship with such other residents of the great block of flats as Barnabas Kair.

It was Ash's habit to classify the people he met, and he had to meet a great many. This little man—he was barely five feet and six inches tall in his thickest shoes, and was sensitive about it—was plump, with small hands and feet, a button nose and rosebud mouth. His fair hair, getting thin now, at forty-seven, was brushed sleekly back from a forehead that perspired easily, and he had a habit of wiping his brow, and the spectacles with semi-transparent rims which he wore for reading and playing cards, with a large white handkerchief which he would draw from his pocket with a flourish. The cold, light blue eyes in his pale face gave him rather the appearance of a well-groomed codfish. Not an impressive picture; yet Ash felt that there was an indefinable suggestion of controlled but ruthless strength that went beyond the rigid efficiency of an undoubtedly capable civil servant.

They chatted a little longer, and then Ash rose and said:

"Do you know that you're the most remarkable fisherman I've ever met?"

"Why?" Ingrow demanded in surprise.

"You haven't even mentioned those wonderful specimens you've got on the walls."

The little man beamed.

"Oh, you don't want to be bored by talk about my fish," he protested.

"I don't want to be bored, and I'm quite sure I'm not going to be bored, but I do want you to tell me about your fish, please."

Ash was merely being polite, but he had been perfectly right when he said that he would not be bored. Ingrow the fisherman was a different being from Ingrow the ambitious civil servant. Quite briefly and without conceit he described how he had caught some of his monsters. Ash, who never lost an opportunity of learning something that might be useful, found himself listening with a degree of interest and respect which surprised him.

They parted on excellent terms at the cottage gate.

"I hope we'll meet in London sometime," said Ingrow.

"I hope so too," Ash responded.

And they meant it.

As Ash strode cheerfully along the cliff road he decided that the evening had been both pleasant and instructive.

All the people he had met had been interesting in their several ways, and Alfred Ingrow particularly so. It was apparent that, despite his vanity, the little man was remarkably astute, and it was not surprising that he should have been chosen to create the organisation of the Directorate of Departmental Intelligence and to succeed the amiable veteran who had been made its head as a graceful preliminary to retirement to a life of pensioned ease.

Ingrow's view of Sergeant Upwey's suspicions of the Fersens had been expressed very reasonably, and his point about the impossibility of Oscar having murdered the detective was well taken. As he had declared, Ingrow was obviously not a sentimental person, and Ash felt sure that he had weighed carefully every word he had spoken.

It was not a long distance to the police station, and as the

superintendent's steps sounded on the trimly gravelled path
the door opened and Sergeant Jack Jones greeted him.

Ash declined a respectful invitation to come in and take
something for the road, and the men went round the house
to the garage in which Jones housed the small car allowed him
for perambulation of the fairly extensive area for which he was
responsible.

Jones had got the car out of its lair and Ash was about to
get in when the sergeant stopped the engine and cocked an
attentive ear.

"Just a minute, sir," he said. "My 'phone's ringing. Maybe
Mr. Morris or Mr. Hughes asking about you. Mind waiting
while I see?"

"Of course not. Go ahead."

Ash followed the sergeant, who could move nimbly enough
despite his portliness, into the office.

"Pentref police station," Jones said into the telephone
receiver. "Sergeant Jones speaking . . . Who? Oh yes. 'Evening,
Luke. What's the trouble, boy?"

His voice changed as he listened.

"All right," he said sharply. "You're sure she's not dead?
. . . Right, then stay you by her, and don't you touch nothing,
see? Mr. Ash is with me, and we'll be over there in a couple of
ticks."

He put down the instrument and turned to the superintendent.

"That was Luke Hollis, sir. He's Mrs. Sweeney's chauffeur. He
says a man got into the house and tried to murder her—knocked
her out with a cosh. Luke tried to hold him, but he got away."

"You'd better get a doctor——"

"Luke did that before he 'phoned me, sir."

"Sensible chap." Ash thought for a moment. "Get on to
Treporth, Sergeant. Ask the duty officer to tell Mr. Morris and
Mr. Hughes, and ask them to inform the Chief Constable. Say
I'll be glad if they'll send any reserve men they can spare, as
well as the finger-print and camera chaps. And say I particularly want them to send an ambulance and to engage a
room in a private nursing home—*not* a hospital—for Mrs.
Sweeney. Jump to it, Sergeant; I want to get to the house as
soon as we can make it."

There was a private line to police headquarters. In a very

few minutes Jones had delivered the message and had scribbled on a pad instructions for a constable who would shortly be reporting in from patrol, and he and Ash were speeding in the car to Mrs. Sweeney's house.

There a scared maid in a dressing-gown opened the door and showed them to the drawing-room.

Mrs. Sweeney lay on a couch. An elderly man was bending over her and a second, but older, dressing-gowned woman stood beside them with a basin of water.

Brooding stolidly over the group was a burly man in shirt-sleeves and the breeches and leggings of a chauffeur, who came automatically to attention when Jones said to the superintendent:

"This is Luke Hollis, sir. And that's Dr. Wilson Wynn."

Ash nodded and looked round the room, but waited until the doctor straightened up and looked at him.

"Good evening, Doctor," he said. "I'm Superintendent Ash. How is she?"

"She's had a bad blow on the head and she's severely concussed, but as far as I can see at present there's no very serious injury," Wilson Wynn replied. "She'll have to be kept quiet, of course. I'll put her to bed——"

"I've sent for an ambulance," Ash interrupted. "I'd like to get her into a nursing-home in Treporth, unless you object to her being moved?"

The doctor was evidently a man of few words. He gave Ash a shrewd look and said:

"No, I don't object, provided I go with her."

"Of course not. I'll be grateful if you will."

The doctor turned to the maid and told her to pack some things that would be useful.

Inspector Haydn Hughes must have worked fast, for he and his party and the ambulance arrived soon afterwards.

Mrs. Sweeney was sent off to Treporth, accompanied by Dr. Wilson Wynn, the maid, and a police escort.

Men were sent out to search the neighbourhood, a task in which Sergeant Jack Jones and his local constables participated.

When the finger-print and other experts had finished their work Ash cleared the room of everyone except himself, Haydn Hughes, and Luke Hollis.

"Now, Hollis," he said, "sit down and make yourself comfortable. Smoke if you like. We want you to tell us all you can about this business. By the way, you're an ex-Service man, I imagine?"

"Yes, sir," the chauffeur replied. "Royal Army Service Corps. Clean discharge papers."

"Londoner?"

"Camberwell, sir."

"Married?"

"I was, but the wife got killed in an air raid while I was in the East."

"Sorry about that. Now, what happened after you left Mr. Fersen's house tonight? Take your time and don't leave out anything."

Hollis sat up, squared his shoulders, and spoke as though he had been making a report to an officer.

"I drove madam—Mrs. Sweeney—home," he began. "She told me to put the car away and come to this room. When I'd garaged the car I reported to her here, like she'd said. She was wrapping up a sock in paper. It was one of them socks she was always knitting for people. She gave me the parcel and told me to take it to you at your hotel. I was to be there at nine o'clock next morning—that'd be *this* morning now, sir. I was to ask you to try if it was the right size for you. Then I was to bring it back here."

"Where's the parcel now?" Ash interposed.

"In my room, sir. Shall I fetch it?"

"No. Please finish your story first."

"Right, sir. I told madam the maids had gone to bed, like she'd told them to, and asked if there was anything she wanted. She said no, and said for me to go and get my sleep. Always considerate, madam is. She said she was going to read for a bit, and she sat down and took up a book. She often sat up late, reading, and sometimes she'd go for a walk at night. When we come down here first I asked her to let me go with her if she wanted to be out at night, on account of not knowing what sort of characters she might meet, but she laughed and said she could look after herself. I didn't like it, but I couldn't do nothing about it.

"I left her sitting here and went to the garage. I've got a bed-sitter over it. I took off my coat and messed about for a bit, polishing my buttons for the morning, and that."

"Like a good soldier," Hughes put in.

"Yes, Mr. Hughes," Hollis grinned. "Force of habit, as you might say. After a bit, I remembered that I'd left a packet of fags in the car. Well, you know how it is, gents: when you haven't got nothing to smoke, that's the time you *wants* to smoke. So I goes downstairs into the yard. Just as I'm going to unlock the garage doors I hears madam calling out. I runs like —well, I runs to the kitchen door, that being the quickest way into the house. Sometimes the maids forget to lock it, though I'm always on to them about it, but this time they hadn't. But the window beside was open. I squeezes through and runs to the drawing-room. There's a bloke there with a handkerchief tied round his face; biggish bloke in a light oilskin coat nearly down to his feet, and a hat pulled over his eyes. He's got what looks like a cosh in his hand. Madam pulls a little gun from her bag and lets him have it. He claps his left hand to his ear, like he's been nicked by the bullet, and swipes madam a nasty one. I'm half across the room by this time and I leads for his chin with my left, but he ducks and jabs me in the belly with his cosh. That turns me sick for a bit. He snaffles a couple of things that's lying about, and hops it out through the french window. I gets up and goes after him, but he's got a good start, and I thinks it's more important to see after madam. So I comes back, don't like the look of her, and rings up the doctor and the police. I hope you gents think I did right?"

"You were perfectly right," Ash assured him. "Can you remember what things the man took?"

"Yes, sir. He didn't get a lot for his trouble. There was a gold cigarette lighter; a fountain pen Miss Kate Dermot Lloyd had left here by mistake; and madam's bag; but," Hollis added with a chuckle, "I reckon the swine's kicking himself about that bag now."

"Why?"

" 'Cause he took the wrong one. I'll bet he thought it was the one madam kept her money in, but it was the one she used for her knitting wool!"

Ash smiled thoughtfully.

"Well," he said, "if it hadn't been for you, Mrs. Sweeney might be dead. It was hard luck you couldn't get the chap, but you did your best."

"I'd do a hell of a lot more than that for madam," Hollis answered. He paused, and added, "There was a time when I hadn't a lot of use for Yanks, but madam's the finest lady that ever stepped, and if I get a chance to lay my hands on that perishing——''

He stopped abruptly.

"That's all right, Luke *bach*," said Hughes. "We know how you feel and we'll do our damn best to get *our* hands on him." He looked inquiringly at Ash, who shook his head. "Go you now and have a drink, man, and don't fret about madam. She'll be all right."

"And you might just bring me that parcel she gave you for me," Ash put in.

Hollis got up, stood smartly to attention, and marched out of the room.

"A good type," the superintendent remarked. "Said what he had to say without a lot of blather. Now I'm going to leave you to carry on here, if you don't mind. Is there a car free to run me in to Treporth?"

"Aye, indeed. There's three of them."

"I'll send it back at once," Ash promised.

"As you like about that," Hughes grinned. "Do some of our lads good to have a bit of walking for a change. I'll go and find a driver for you. The colonel's champing on his bit, waiting to hear from you!"

Superintendent Ash, however, did not go immediately to the Chief Constable when he reached Treporth.

He locked himself into Inspector Hughes' room, opened the parcel he had obtained from Luke Hollis, and took out the nearly completed sock it contained.

From his wallet he produced a slip of paper covered with odd-looking symbols and began to compare it with the pattern knitted into the top of the sock.

Presently he rose, opened the door, and called the night-duty sergeant.

"I want a call to the Yard," he said. "Please tell the operator it's priority police business. When you get the Yard, tell the man there I want to speak to Chief Superintendent Muir at his house. When Mr. Muir comes on, put him through to me in Mr. Hughes' office. And see that I'm not disturbed by *anyone* until I tell you."

He returned to the room, relocked the door, and sat down beside the telephone.

CHAPTER XXI

THE railway porter happened to be people's warden at the church of St. Andrew-by-the-Ponds and he prided himself on his knowledge of ecclesiastical hierarchy. Touching his cap as he took the passenger's small bag and light overcoat, he said:

"It'll be platform three, Mr. Archdeacon, sir. If you'll follow me . . ."

The man in the clerical collar, apron and gaiters smiled benevolently and followed his guide across the busy station, leaning on a stout and clumsily rolled umbrella.

The porter's respect for the Established Church was not lessened when, having settled his archdeacon in a corner of a first-class compartment for non-smokers, he received a tip worthy of the clerical gentleman's rank and generosity.

The archdeacon unfolded *The Times*, but his gaze strayed now and then to the platform.

When the train left the station, however, his proceedings would have surprised people familiar with archdiaconal life. Reaching down his bag from the rack, he extracted from it a silver flask from which he gave himself a stiff tot of neat brandy. He put the flask back and looked out into the corridor; there was no one in it; taking a revolver from the bag, he assured himself that it was fully loaded and in working order. He put the weapon into his hip-pocket, closed the bag and restored it to the rack.

Taking off his spectacles, which had black horn rims and side pieces, he held them in his hand, ready to put them on again if anyone appeared in the corridor. They were, in fact, more ornamental than useful, as they were fitted with plain glass.

These matters arranged, he relaxed against the cushions and smiled.

He congratulated himself on the precautions he had taken, using alternately taxi, bus, and tube train and changing into his present garb in a compartment of a big public lavatory which had three exits. He had not wanted to make this journey; he would not have made it if it had not appeared to be absolutely unavoidable; but as it had to be made, he had made sure that, even though he had no reason to think he was suspected, he had done nothing to arouse the suspicion or even attract the attention of the most alert policeman.

He would not have smiled and relaxed so contentedly if he had known that, while he was graciously acknowledging his porter's thanks for the tip, the worried man in riding breeches and leggings who appeared to be a farmer unable to find his train had nipped into a telephone box at the end of the platform and said a few words to no less an official than the general manager, in his office above the station. Nor would it have increased his satisfaction had he known that shortly after the departure of his train a 'special' consisting of a light engine, a coach in which the window-blinds had been drawn down, and a large van, pulled out of a siding and followed, all signal boxes being instructed to give it a clear line and priority over all other traffic.

As, however, he did not know these facts, he sat in arch-diaconal dignity and considered his plan of campaign for the battle that loomed ahead. It was going to be a tough fight, he knew, but he believed that in his armoury he had a weapon which would give him victory—and he was not thinking of the revolver in his pocket.

His train was not an express; it stopped at several stations before reaching its terminus. It had still a number of miles to go when he put on his overcoat and took his bag and umbrella from the rack. A minute later the train stopped and he got out. On the station platform a man in chauffeur's uniform stepped forward and took the archdiaconal bag. It was Hank Peters.

"This way, sir," he said, leading the way to a car in the yard. They got in and Hank started the engine.

When they were clear of the station lights, for it was getting dark, the American dropped his formal manner and laughed.

"Say, you certainly look the goods," he said. "Curtis Frost told me you'd be dressed like a big guy in the Church, but I've forgotten the name he gave it. A bishop, is it?"

"An archdeacon," the other responded shortly.

"Well, Archdeacon," Hank grinned, "I guess you aren't dressed for a voyage, but we'll get you aboard without being spotted."

"You'd better," the archdeacon retorted in a tone that made Hank scowl and attend to his driving.

Meanwhile the 'special' had reached the station. After a brief talk between its occupants and a plain-clothes man of the local police the van doors were opened, a ramp was lowered, and what looked like a commercial delivery car was rolled out with remarkable celerity. On its sides was painted the name of a well-known catering firm. Three men got in and it drove away on the road taken by Hank Peters.

It did not take Hank long to reach a small coastal town. He stopped in a back street and asked his passenger to get out and wait for him while he took the car to a garage near. Five minutes later he returned and the two men made their way to the harbour. A little beyond it there was a patch of shingle; a low wooden landing-stage, now abandoned and half rotted away, ran a few yards into the water. In the shelter of this stage Hank produced an electric torch, pointed it seawards, and flashed it three times, then twice, then once. He sighed with relief when six similar flashes replied, and presently the dark shape of a motor-boat could be seen approaching slowly. She was Frost's cabin cruiser and she was carrying no lights. Her helmsman nosed her in cautiously. Hank threw the bag on her deck, dropped after it, and turned to help the gaitered man who was plainly not accustomed to gymnastics of that kind.

The archdeacon was unceremoniously bundled into the dark cabin, the boat backed a little, then swung round and headed out to sea. Presently the man who had brought her in gave her the usual navigation lights, having turned the helm over to Hank. He went into the cabin and switched on the light.

"So you got here all right," he said, producing a bottle and glasses from a locker. "Weren't followed, I hope, Archdeacon?" and he smiled at the other's appearance.

"No, Fisherman, I was too careful," the archdeacon retorted, surveying in his turn the first man's worn blue jersey, battered cap, serge trousers and rubber boots. "You certainly look the part, Fersen."

"I ought to, Archdeacon, as I really was a sailor once. You look pretty good yourself, though I don't suppose you ever had much to do with the Church. Have a drink?"

He poured rum into the glasses, and the archdeacon gulped his down quickly. The sea was what Fersen would have described as like a millpond, but his companion was not such a hardy mariner, though he was not actually sick.

"We've got to do some talking before we meet Frost," Oscar Fersen went on. "That's why I told Hank Peters to take the wheel."

"Frost's being difficult?"

"Of course he is. He thinks he's only got to crack the whip and we'll jump through the hoop."

"Does he, indeed?" the other commented, with a most unclerical oath. "That young man has got a lot to learn before he's much older."

"Before he's dead, you mean," Fersen said grimly. "Now, this is what I suggest——"

So earnestly did they discuss their plans that they were surprised when a hail from Hank Peters told them that the end of the voyage was near. They joined him on the miniature bridge.

"Oughtn't we to put out the lights?" the archdeacon inquired.

"That wouldn't do at all," Fersen explained. "We picked you up in the dark so as not to attract attention, but it's different at this end. Frost often brings the boat up when he calls on Muldoon, or fetches him for a night cruise. If any longshoreman is about he'll recognise us, but if we went in without navigation lights there'd be the devil to pay."

They were running slowly up a river and Fersen explained that in a few minutes they would moor in front of Con Muldoon's cottage.

As Hank stopped his engines and Fersen sprang ashore with a mooring-line a man stepped out of the shadows. It was Skelton, Curtis Frost's butler and strong-arm man.

"They're waiting for you," he said, and led the way to the cottage. Hank made all fast and followed them.

Inside the cottage Frost and Muldoon were snugly settled on each side of a log fire that took the slight chill out of the night air. Bottles and glasses were hospitably arrayed on a table.

"Come in, fellows," Frost said cheerfully. "Say, that archdeacon rig is a peach. What about giving us a sermon?"

"I'm getting a little tired of that joke," was the acid reply. "If I preached a sermon to you, Frost, *Pride goeth before a fall* would be my text."

The American flushed. "Listen, you," he exclaimed, "if you've only come here to make cracks like that you can get the hell out of it right now! You thought you were the big cheese, didn't you? A fine mess you've made of it. I'm in the chair at this festive gathering, and you'd better not forget it."

"I'm sure neither of us wants to quarrel with you," Fersen put in smoothly. "Personally, I'm grateful for all you've done, and I hope to be able to show my gratitude later on."

"Excuse me if I have to laugh!" Frost said offensively. "You can get it into your thick skull that any rewarding or kicking that has to be done from now on will be done by me, not you. You had it all nicely worked out, hadn't you? You were going to be prime minister, or gauleiter, or commissar, or whatever you like to call it, and boss the treasury as a side line; and our friend in the leggings was going to be minister of the interior and head hangman and chief grafter, and a few other little jobs you didn't want. And David Jones was to . . . Ah, hell!" he interrupted himself. "What's the use? You thought I was a sucker who'd do what he was told and be thankful for what he was given. Fersen says there's no need to quarrel, and how right he is. The boss doesn't quarrel with his men; he gives his orders, and if they're not carried out it's just too bad for the men. Get this straight, friends: You're in this thing for what you make out of it. I'm in it for—well, for reasons guys like you couldn't begin to understand. I'm going to smash the people who're running this country, from the king down. If you want to help, you can, but don't think, Mr. Kremlin Fersen, that I'm going to have a gang of Moscow toughs tramping about in dirty boots. No, sir! The people behind me know what they're doing and they're not reaching the chestnuts out of the fire for Russia to eat."

He paused and drank from the glass beside him.

"Well, I've said my piece," he went on more calmly. "Skelton, take a walk outside and make sure the coast's clear. Hank'll relieve you presently. Now, gentlemen, it's up to you to talk if you want to. Sorry I forgot to ask you to have a drink. Please help yourselves. And by the way, Archdeacon, clergymen don't usually go heeled in this country. You'll be more comfortable without that gun, so Hank'll take it off you to save you trouble."

Grinning, Hank Peters removed the archdiaconal weapon and dropped it into a waste-paper basket.

Fersen mixed a whisky-and-soda and lit a cigarette.

The gaitered man refused with a gesture the drink Muldoon offered to compound for him.

"Quite an eloquent speech, Mr. Frost," he said calmly, "but one feels that it would have been better addressed to a cheering mob of fanatics than to intelligent people like Mr. Fersen and myself. However, one must forgive the enthusiasm of at least comparative youth. You've told us what you propose to do, but you have not explained how you propose to do it."

"That's up to me."

"True, but are you up to it? I'm afraid that, as they say in your country, you've bitten off more than you can chew. For instance, you won't deny that Mr. Fersen and I have dealt firmly with certain, shall we say, difficulties? There was that man Ostrod, for instance. He found that key you very carelessly lost, and he found out a good many other things. I must admit that friend Vico was careless. Those Latins are always so impulsive——"

"What happened to him, by the way?" Frost put in.

"The sort of thing that happens to people who put too high a price on their services. I had a talk with him in his flat last night, and I'm sorry to say he tried to blackmail me. He thought we could not do without him. I hope, my dear Frost, that you will never make such a stupid mistake."

"I'm asking you what happened to Vico," the American persisted grimly.

The other shrugged. "I had foreseen what would happen. Vico was called to the telephone while we were talking. The caller explained that he had dialled the wrong number, and apologised. When Vico returned, he finished his drink. I'm afraid it disagreed with him. The police have probably found him by now, and I hope they'll think it was suicide."

"You mean you poisoned him?"

"Naturally. What else could I do? But we were speaking of Ostrod: I was about to say that fortunately Vico knew where I was that night. I was dining out and he telephoned and warned me about the little Pole. I don't like violence and I intended to talk to Ostrod, but when I found him alone in Canton Court the opportunity was too good to be missed. If it had not been for me, Mr. Frost, you would probably be, as you would put it, chewing your nails in prison."

"Well? So would you both."

"No doubt. I was just reminding you that you owe us quite as much as we owe you, if not more. For instance, you spoke of smashing the throne and the ministers and other people who support it. Easier said than done, and I'm afraid I doubt your ability to do it. I hope you'll be honest enough to admit that if it hadn't been for the inside information I have been able to pick up our organisation would have stood very little chance against the government's really quite efficient police force and secret service."

"I'm not denying it," Frost conceded. "I shall keep you on that job, of course, as long as it's necessary."

"The question is: will I keep on the job, and what are you going to do if I don't?"

Frost deliberately drew out a pistol.

"You'll keep that job," he said, "or you won't go out of here alive."

The other crossed his gaitered legs and smiled.

"This isn't the second act of a melodrama," he sneered. "You can't afford to kill me, and you know it. Put down that pistol, my good fellow, and listen to me. You've played your cards, and played them rather badly. Now it's our turn——"

" 'Scuse me," Hank put in. "Beef Skelton didn't close the door properly when he went out, and I thought I heard something——"

"Go and see if he's all right," Frost said.

"I shouldn't bother," said Chief Superintendent Muir, pushing open the door, gun in hand. "Don't move, any of you," he added sharply as Frost made a motion towards the pistol he had laid on the table. "You are all under arrest." He turned to the man in the clerical collar and said crisply:

"Alfred Ingrow, I arrest you on a charge of murdering Joseph Ostrod on——"

Fersen hurled his glass at Muir and there ensued what Joe Marshall afterwards described as the most enjoyable scrap he'd been in for years.

CHAPTER XXII

THE celebrative dinner-party given by Chief Superintendent and Mrs. Muir was a great success.

The guests were Mrs. Jake Sweeney, Superintendent Andrew Ash, Chief Inspector Larry Doyle, Chief Inspector (for once without acid drop) Joe Marshall and Mr. Barnabas Darley Kair.

Mrs. Sweeney and Larry Doyle were enjoying their first freedom from medical trammels.

Kair was suffering agonies of impatience. He restrained himself until, replete, the mob had disposed itself comfortably in the lounge for the appreciation of coffee and of an old brandy presented to Gloria Muir by an uncle who had devoted most of his life to the consideration and consumption of the finer forms of alcohol.

"And now," Kair said plaintively, "may this poor ignorant civilian ask for a little enlightenment on your dark deeds, or must he perish miserably of curiosity before the whole story is revealed in the criminal courts?"

"The *whole* story will never be revealed in the criminal courts, I hope," Muir replied, mellowed by food and drink; "but you've helped a lot—oh yes, you have—and *this* court feels that you're entitled to a little information under the seal of confidence. What do you want to know?"

"Lots! For instance, what on earth made you suspect that pillar of the Civil Service, Alfred Ingrow? It was very clever of you——"

"It wasn't clever at all," Muir interrupted. "I still kick myself for not having spotted him long before. It ought to have been obvious that in his job at the Directorate of Departmental Information he had the chance of hearing things of the most confidential kind, especially as he took most of the work off the director's shoulders and was going to succeed him very soon. It was the old story of overlooking the obvious thing: he was the obvious man, and I overlooked him."

"But you got him in the end, dear," Gloria said stoutly.

"The loyal wife! But *I* didn't get him; *we* got him, between us. It's all rather complicated because there were so many strings to be pulled, and some of the most important were pulled by Mrs. Sweeney and Andrew Ash." He grinned at Kair's look of astonishment. "Mrs. Sweeney is an old friend of ours. For years she's been a voluntary, unpaid agent of the International Criminal Police Commission, but you'll please keep that fact under your hat. It was while she was doing her splendid work for the Teeners—no, Mrs. Jake, I *won't* be quiet!—that she began to suspect David Jones and his associates."

Muir paused, sipped his brandy, and continued:

"If I tell it this way, we'll be here until tomorrow night. You all know a good bit of the story. Oscar Fersen has turned yellow and talked in the hope of saving his skin, and with what he's said and what we've found out ourselves I can fill in the gaps for you without too many words.

"The International Commission had been forging a chain for a long time, and we at the Yard were able to contribute a few links. Another link was provided by the unfortunate Sergeant Upwey, and he might have provided more if he hadn't been murdered. My beloved wife, who loves to make up names, called that the Boomerang Murder, and it wasn't a bad name. The boomerang wasn't thrown quite cleverly enough and it came back and hit Fersen and his friends in the nasty way boomerangs have."

"Did Fersen kill Upwey, then?" Kair asked.

"No. We're still not sure why he suspected Upwey. Probably the young man had been prowling round the Fersen house too openly. Anyhow, Fersen thought he saw his chance when Upwey quarrelled with Trevone. I must admit it was a clever idea. Fersen swiped the boomerang out of Trevone's locker. He drove away from the club, but stopped at a call-box and telephoned to his house, where Ingrow was staying for the week-end. Ingrow came to meet him. When Upwey came along the cliff road they got him into conversation. Fersen knocked him out with the boomerang and Ingrow killed him with a bullet from an air rifle they'd made out of the butt of a fishing rod Ingrow used to carry about with him. It was Andrew who spotted that gun later on, by the way. He also spotted on Ingrow's bunch of keys a key like the one we found on Lonneker, the supposed Dutch student.

"When they'd killed Upwey and thrown his body over the cliff, where they knew it would be clear of the water, they put the boomerang where they knew it would be found. Altogether, they made things extremely unpleasant for Miles Trevone.

"There's an old saying that murder will out, and it's a true one. A lot of other things outed as well, chiefly because of another old saying: when thieves fall out, honest men come by their own. If Curtis Frost hadn't quarrelled with Ingrow and Fersen we might not have been able to bowl them out so soon. There are a lot of other people in this game, but I'm not allowed to talk about that. The International Commission is looking after them. All I can say is that I don't think you need be afraid of people in jackboots kicking people in this country around for a long time to come. I was going," Muir added with a smile, "to say that between us we've managed to give that foul crowd socks, which reminds me that we have to thank Mrs. Sweeney for a very ingenious idea. It was most important that her connection with the authorities should not be known. Letters can be stolen and telephone lines tapped. So Mrs. Sweeney used to knit code messages into the socks she posted to an accommodation address, where one of our people picked them up. It's surprising how much you can say with a pair of knitting needles!

"That was why Fersen sent Nils, the steward, to stage the fake robbery at Mrs. Sweeney's house and, of course, get hold of her knitting. He admits that he was suspicious of her already, and he must have had the wit to wonder why she told Ash she was making socks for him on so short an acquaintance.

"And, now," Muir concluded, with the air of a courteous host who thinks it time to change the conversation, "what about a game of gin rummy? We're too many for bridge."

Kair stood up.

"One toast first, please," he said, "but only for Mrs. Muir and me." He raised his glass. "God save the King, and God bless the police—and Mrs. Sweeney!"

After which they played gin rummy uproariously and Joe Marshall won all their money.

THE END